THE VOTIVE CROWN

PAULA CONSTANT

FEHU PRESS

For my parents, Frank and Bev, for whom no dinner table was complete without five encyclopaedias and a good debate.

FOREWORD

Please note that appendices of place names and characters can be found at the end of this book. The Votive Crown is a work of fiction set amid real events and characters. Whilst every care has been taken in research, any errors in historical fact are mine alone.

VISIGOTHIC SPANIA AD 687

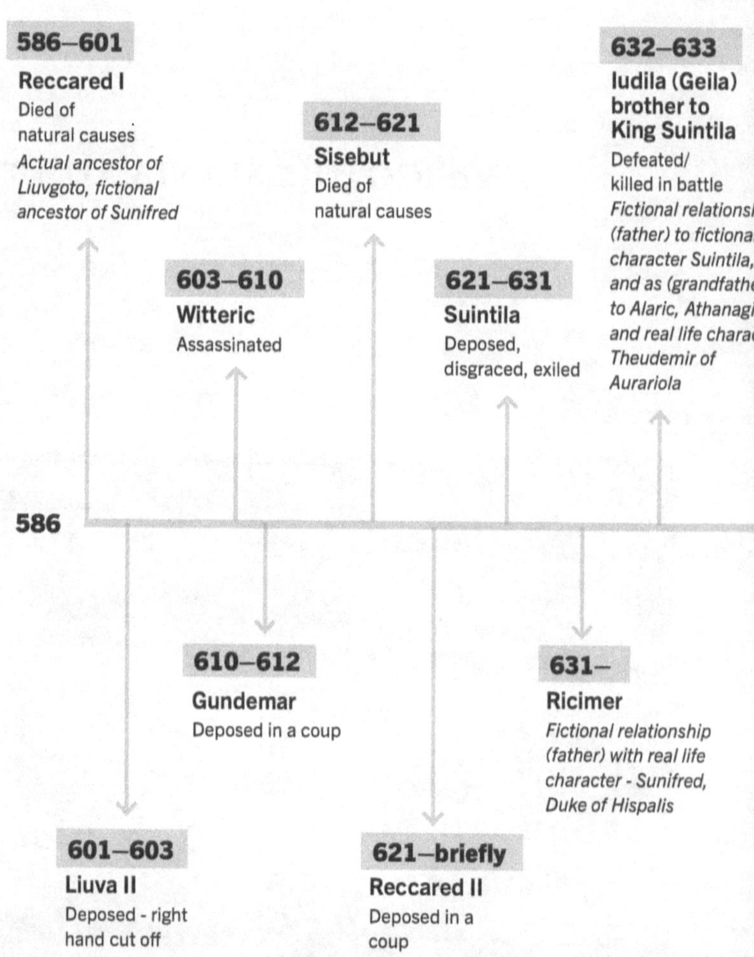

**VISIGOTHIC KINGS OF SPAIN,
AD 586 – AD 687**

672–680

Wamba

possibly poisoned/
forced to relinquish rule

*Uncle to real life
character Egica,
brotherto real life
characters Giscila
and Ariberga,
grandfather to real
life character Oppa*

642–653

Chindasuinth

Co-ruled with his
son Reccesuinth
before death

*Father of
Reccesuinth,
Theodofred (Duke
of Corduba) and
Favila (father of
Pelayo)*

636–639

Chintila

Co-ruled with his
son Tulga before
death

**687—until
his death**

Egica

*Egica is widely
assumed to
have fathered
real life Oppa*

687

631–636

Sisenand

Died of natural
causes

653–672

Reccesuinth

Died of natural
causes

639–642

Tulga

Deposed in a brutal
coup - tonsured and
sent to monastery/exile

*Father to Giscila and
Ariberga, assumed
father of Wamba,
grandfather to Egica*

680–687

Erwig

*Gave up crown to
Egica on deathbed.
Father of Cixilo
(Egica's wife)*

PROLOGUE

ILYAN

September AD 687
Septem, Mauretania, Africa
Ceuta, Morocco, Africa

Dahiya strode through the heavy wooden doors of Septem's palace, brushing the guard aside with barely a glance. "Ilyan," she said. "You sent for me."

Her face was burnished brown, body as lean and hard as the animal she'd ridden in on. As he always did in her presence, Ilyan, Count of Septem, felt keenly the wasted muscles and pale skin of his politician's life. Not by a flicker, however, did his face betray any regret at the compromise.

"Dahiya," he said mildly. "Can I offer you refreshment? Pomegranate juice?"

The sound and scent of men and animals drifted through the open doors and mingled with the sultry afternoon sea breeze. Ilyan raised his eyebrows, nose wrinkling. "Camel milk, perhaps?"

"I have fifty men waiting beyond your gates," said the tall woman brusquely. "You would need a lot of pomegranates. And camels."

"For you, anything," said Ilyan.

The corners of her mouth twitched. "Your tongue could make a she-lion purr, Ilyan."

He put a hand over his heart. "If you would just allow me to prove it to you," he murmured.

"Ah!" she scoffed, smiling nonetheless. "You did not summon me here to flirt, Ilyan."

"A pity." Ilyan sighed and gestured at the cushions opposite. "So much more interesting than politics."

Dahiya stepped out of her sandals and onto the dais, legs folding beneath her in a fluid motion as she sank down on the cushions. A summer breeze carried jasmine and citron through the latticed windows. It mingled with the incense rising from a brazier in the corner, which a slave wafted toward them with a long date palm branch. The dais was surrounded by tall marble columns, and a fountain in the centre of the room trickled weakly after the long, dry summer.

"Will you be staying? Pomegranate juice for fifty may be beyond my means, but wine and a meal I can manage."

"That is generous, Ilyan. I will accept, for my men, too, and with thanks."

"Of course." Ilyan clapped his hands and the slave approached. "See that the Jerawa men are made comfortable," he said. "Their queen will be my guest this evening."

The man poured them both wine and withdrew, unable to resist a surreptitious glance at Dahiya. Her knife was jewelled at the hilt and sheathed in silver and ivory; bronze cuffs encircled her forearms. A single, enormous ruby hung from a webbed chain around her forehead, sitting like a red teardrop between high, arched brows. Her hair was unbound, falling to her waist in a rippling black sea. Her long legs and high buttocks were clearly outlined in a man's flowing trousers, and the slave's eyes lingered. She frowned fiercely, and he scurried out.

"Must you intimidate all of my household staff?" Ilyan said mildly.

Dahiya pulled the long shift of white linen from the jewelled clasp at her waist. Ilyan wondered idly, as he always did, how the desert dwellers managed to keep their robes so white. The skin of her neck was richly dark by contrast, and her eyes above the long, straight nose and angular face were a vivid amber, startling amongst the dark colouring of the tribes. Her black turban, normally worn as a man would, wrapped around her head and with the end tailing over her right shoulder, lay in thick coils about her neck. He could see the end of it resting on the high swell of her breasts and he swallowed, raising his eyes to hers with an effort.

Dahiya smiled slightly. "You flatter me, Ilyan."

"You are magnificent, Dahiya." He shrugged. "As ever. But, as you said, you are not here to flirt."

She threw her head back and roared with laughter. "Oh, Ilyan," she said finally, wiping her eyes. "Your conversation is like summer rain. I have been too long with my men. They lack your subtlety."

"Although one presumes they have other attractions," said Ilyan, smiling at her. "Speaking of which, I had an interesting visitor recently."

"Ah." Dahiya sat back and eyed him speculatively. "Now we get to the point."

"A Goth," said Ilyan.

"Goths are rarely interesting. Generally, they are homeless, bitter, looking for either money or arms, and depressingly pious."

"A succinct, if somewhat harsh, summary," Ilyan said, smiling. "But this one is a little different. I say a Goth – all in Spania call themselves such in these times. Laurentius Severianus, however, is from old Spania. His is a Roman family, of scholars and landowners. He has been these past ten years in Constantinople, ostensibly in the *Karabisianoi*, the imperial naval fleet."

"Ostensibly?"

"His family have always employed Jewish agents for the management of their estates and for trade. Laurentius was sent by his father to Constantinople under the guise of serving in the emperor's forces, but primarily to re-establish ties with Jewish interests there, despite the somewhat draconian measures taken by our Gothic friends and their priests to limit Jewish trade."

"And this brings us to the reason you summoned me here."

Ilyan did not deny it. "Quite so."

Abruptly he stood, thrust his feet into pointed slippers, and paced across the room in five long strides, gathering his robes behind him and letting them fall. He turned and retraced his steps. There were days when he did this so many times that his daughters joked he would wear a trench in the marble floor. Ilyan had a mind that contemplated many things simultaneously. It was how he had managed to maintain his precarious existence on the rocky outcrop at the edge of Africa, a lone outpost of the Greek remains of the Roman Empire, juggling a thousand competing interests with the dexterity of a sorcerer.

Movement, he had found, helped him to open the doors in his mind that connected those interests and find the passageways of diplomacy that turned the labyrinth of self-interest into a free-flowing treasure trove of revenue and information. It had made Septem the intelligence centre that anchored the west in the Circle of Lands, and Ilyan a wealthy and powerful man.

"In recent years, several parties of Jews have set off from Iberia and Francia, travelling the old merchant's route across the seas to Serica, for the purposes of establishing trade beyond the stranglehold of Constantinople. They have all been lost upon the way – and their goods with them."

Dahiya nodded. "The seas are dangerous now. Gothic exiles, Arab slavers, and Greek deserters vie for spoils, and news of riches travels quickly. Few travel the ports with impunity from either imperial forces or pirates."

"Quite so." Ilyan paced again, turned abruptly, and came to a halt in front of Dahiya, who watched him in some amusement. "But none of the merchants have attempted to travel overland."

She raised her eyebrows. "Across the sands?"

He nodded.

She sat back. "Impossible."

"No." Ilyan began pacing again. "You have done it, Dahiya. You do it every day. Your Rider army travels through those wastes leaving barely a trace, able to come upon Arab outposts with lightning stealth or to remain hidden as you choose."

"My army are Imazighen. The desert is their mother. They know her secrets. They are not" – she waved a hand in the air – "Jewish merchants, accustomed to comfort and the feeling of stone beneath their feet. And we travel our own sands. Not the wastes beyond African shores."

"You can teach them." Ilyan stopped and drew himself up, wrapping his robes behind him again. He stood over six feet. Although slender and fine boned, he could command when he needed to – and even Dahiya, leader of the Imazighen Jerawa tribe, listened when he did.

"It is to be a small party, no more than two in fact. A father and son, of the old trading house of Radhan. Their goods are arriving here as we speak, to be exchanged for letters of credit. It has been done in secret, under Laurentius's eye, smuggled across the sea in *dromons* containing the Illiberis horseflesh your men so prize."

Dahiya stilled. "Illiberis?"

"The Jews are from Garnata. They trade in secret, under the protection of their neighbour, Count Paulus of Illiberis." Ilyan cast her a speculative glance. "You met Paulus's wife once," he said. "Long ago."

"I remember." Dahiya's eyes were oddly opaque. "She wore the staff and serpent symbol that marks the horses of Illiberis, and she came in search of vengeance."

Ilyan nodded. "Though she did not find it."

"No," Dahiya said quietly. "She did not."

Ilyan waited. Dahiya turned her wine cup thoughtfully.

"The Arabs, it seems, have a new warlord."

Ilyan raised his eyebrows at this turn of conversation.

"Zuhair bin Qais al Balawi." She said the name with flat finality. "This one is no politician from Damascus, Ilyan. His orders are to rid the north of the Greeks and gain Africa for the Caliphate. The man has proven himself on a hundred battlefields, and he knows that if he succeeds in taking these territories, he can command any position he demands."

Ilyan nodded, his lips pursed. "Have you met him yet?"

"Not directly. But already we feel the heat of his breath."

She frowned, and Ilyan noticed small lines of fatigue about her eyes. He felt slightly shocked by their presence; in all the time he had known Dahiya, she had seemed to him unchanging, her graceful physicality free from the mundane process of ageing faced by mere mortals. He smiled at his own fancy. Perhaps the Arabs were right after all, and she really was Al Kahinat, the Sorceress.

"In the past month alone, we have fought more skirmishes than in the six years previous," she said now. "My men are tired. Most are wounded. These are no raw recruits he is sending out from Kairouan. They are battle-hardened warriors from the mountains and deserts in the east. They know how to fight, and they know how to survive. Zuhair does not fear the desert."

"But you fear him," said Ilyan.

She looked at him sharply. "I fear no man, Ilyan. Nor army. But I would be a poor leader of men if I did not know when I was outmatched. We drove back raids a dozen times over the summer. But he continues to send his spies, and every time he does, they dare further."

"And yet still you hold them back." Ilyan's admiration was sincere. "An army that has defeated the best of the emperor's forces."

Dahiya's eyes burned, and for a moment Ilyan saw the feared sorceress of Arabic legend.

"Ah," she said, her tone deceptively soft. "But the Greeks fight in Africa for gold. We fight for Altava, our own land. We fight because Altava is our mother. It is our heart." She hit her chest hard with her right hand and stared at him. "These Arabs would rape our mother, deny her power and her heart. Their prophet is even worse than the poor nailed bastard your priests chant to."

Ilyan couldn't stifle a grin. "You should be careful of the company in which you express your opinions," he said. "The priests have an increasingly strong hold on politics these days."

"Ha!" Dahiya dismissed him with a wave. "They are weak men, praying to false prophets, as any Jew will tell you. As for us, we have no need of prophets at all. Our gods walk the earth still. Ghurzla, our great god of war, would cut their balls off where they lay and take them like the women they are."

"And here we are," grinned Ilyan. "Back to flirting already."

Dahiya cast her eyes skyward, but her mouth curled in a reluctant smile.

"What of Cæcilius?" asked Ilyan.

Dahiya's eyes narrowed. "Aksil" – she used Cæcilius's Amazigh, rather than Christian, name, placing a slightly sardonic emphasis on it – "believes that Zuhair is no real threat. He still rests on the laurels of his victory over Uqba. Although it is four years past."

The forces of the Arabic leader Uqba bin Nafi had penetrated so far west that they had reached the sea undefeated, and yet Uqba had declared himself still unsatisfied. Had he not been taken in battle by the forces of Aksil, the Imazighen leader, upon his return, Ilyan himself would be speaking Arabic by now. It had been a lesson hard learned – and a victory that had given Aksil himself supremacy over all the Imazighen tribes. He had since styled himself Cæcilius, in the Greek tradition, and affected many of the mannerisms of the foreign forces.

"Are you and Cæcilius – Aksil – a united force?" Ilyan asked the question bluntly. It was a measure of their friendship that Dahiya considered it thoughtfully.

"We are Imazighen," she said at length. "We will fight together as long as our enemy is foreign. And then, we will fight amongst ourselves." She shrugged. "For now, we fight the foreigners. Soon we must face Zuhair in open battle. Aksil and I do not agree on how that should be done, but I must defer to him. For now."

She frowned. "As it happens, I have a desire to know more of the plans of this Zuhair bin Qais and his forces," she said finally. "I had been planning to send some of my own into their midst, to discern what manner of man he is. Your Jews could be part of that plan."

"They cannot be caught," Ilyan warned. "They must carry their letters across the desert to Carthage, and beyond, all the way to Serica, then return safely to Spania, or at least here to Septem. They cannot die slaves of the caliph in Damascus. You will teach them how to survive, that they may cross the unknown sands also."

"And why will I do this, Ilyan?" Dahiya asked, not without amusement.

He moved with the swiftness of a serpent, leaning close so his face was only inches from her own. She smelled of frankincense and desert wilderness. It was intoxicating.

"Cæcilius grows complacent." He leaned on his knee, one foot on the dais, so close he could feel the silk of her hair against his skin. "The tribes whisper that he grows too fond of the Arabic invaders, has come dangerously close to calling them ally rather than enemy. Even defeating Uqba has not completely restored his reputation, nor faith in his command. But you" – one long finger stroked Dahiya's face – "you have conquered all in your path. Men hail you, and not only as a warrior. The Arabs fear you in the way men can only fear what they do not understand. They call you Sorceress." His finger slowed on her face. "They think you know the future."

Dahiya trembled slightly beneath his touch. "Perhaps I do."

His eyes held hers, the current between them a palpable thing. "Yes," he said slowly. "Perhaps you do."

He stepped away, his mind returning to the rational. Above all, Ilyan was a rational man. Superstition and religion were, for him, one and the same. Gods, Ilyan could not control. People, on the other hand, he could, and he did.

"I cannot foretell the future," he said. "But I do all I can to create it. And I know this: Cæcilius is not the man to fight Zuhair's army."

"Your support will make no difference to whether I oust Aksil or not," said Dahiya, her face carefully blank.

"No." Ilyan stood back and his face lightened, the playful smile in place once more. "But there are only a handful of Greek fortresses left in Africa, and none of them act without my agreement. To combat an Arabic army the size you describe, the leader of the Imazighen will need the co-operation of all – and the support of Spania, also."

"And you can give me that?"

"I *will* give you that." Ilyan held up the same long finger that had recently stroked her cheek. He could still feel the tawny smoothness of her skin tingling on his own.

"Spania's king is dying. The man rumoured to succeed him, Egica, is married to the king's daughter, but he does not possess the compliant nature of his predecessor. He is ambitious, and he harbours old resentments. Egica's father, Ariberga, was condemned a traitor and raised his son in exile. Only after Ariberga's death did Egica return to Spania, when his uncle, Wamba, came to the Spanish throne. Egica's road back to power has been long and arduous."

Dahiya looked up sharply at Wamba's name. "I have heard of this king before. Another of his brothers was exiled here, to our shores. He haunts our ports still." Her face twisted in distaste. "He is a man without honour."

"Ah." Ilyan eyed her speculatively. "I did not think you so interested in the affairs of Goths."

Dahiya shrugged, feigning carelessness. "The woman from Illiberis spoke of her country's kings. I was a girl who dreamed of leading men. I listened."

Another man would have been deceived, but Ilyan, noting her fingers tight on the wine cup, stored her reaction for future reference.

"Division in Spania grows with Egica's ascendancy," he went on. "He does not like the independence of the southern lords, nor that they flout the Church's rules by protecting the Jewish merchants in their midst. It is less than a generation since the south drove the Greek imperial forces from their shores and united with the rest of Spania. They maintain their own armies, pay only nominal fealty to the Spanish king, and govern their provinces as they see fit. If Egica succeeds in his bid for the crown, he will likely challenge their sovereignty – and if he does, it will mean rebellion."

"What has this to do with us, Ilyan?"

He leaned forward. "We do not have the resources to protect our borders – and we cannot rely on the imperial fleet to defend us. I have sent a gift of coin to Spania, in Laurentius's care, to fund the restoration of the Spanish fleet. He will present it to the new king, and we will learn if we have a friend or foe upon the throne. Meanwhile, the south will send some of its most honoured sons to train in the Karabisianoi so they will be fit to command Spania's own. Amongst them will be the one chosen by Laurentius to ensure the success of the Jewish mission to the East. You will get the merchants across the sands and meet the fleet at various ports to exchange news. Laurentius's man will remain with the fleet and meet them again in Constantinople, from where he will ensure their safe return to Spania. None can know the fleet protects them, on the outward journey at least, which is why we need you."

"What is this mission I must work so hard to protect, Ilyan?" Dahiya looked at him curiously.

"It would not help if you knew," said Ilyan. "But if it succeeds, it will forge a trade partnership between Illiberis, Septem, and the Radhanite Jewish merchants, bringing coin from all over the Circle of Lands. Coin enough to buy the forces we need to protect our seas if the new Spanish king proves less than a reliable ally." He glanced at her. "The Count of Illiberis understands the importance of such a force, as do the other southern lords, even if the king does not. The north of Spania is concerned with the Frankish border, but Laurentius has seen the Arabic forces at first hand. He knows the dangers we face. The Count of Illiberis has traded with us for as long as there is memory, as have the Jewish merchants he protects. He will listen to Laurentius's warnings, even if the Spanish court in Toletum dismisses them."

"Illiberis risks a great deal in defying the king, does it not?"

"Does it matter?"

She returned his gaze blandly. "Illiberis horseflesh is the best in the Circle of Lands. I would not wish to lose access to it."

"Can it be that you have a concern for something other than your beloved Altava, Dahiya?"

"Ah." She smiled at him, turning the cup slowly. "You have your plans, Ilyan. I have my caves and the visions my ancestors allow me to see there. My personal concerns are my own – as are yours."

"I do not afford myself the luxury of personal concerns. I intend for us to defeat the Arabic armies. But first" – he met her eyes directly – "you will take my Jews across the desert."

"I cannot ensure they will reach Serica." Dahiya stood and stretched. She moved with the easy physicality of a large cat, powerful yet fluid. "But I will do as you ask: get them safely across the desert and teach them how to become invisible. And you, Ilyan, will be held to your promise."

He bowed his head. "You know I always stand by my promises, Dahiya."

"Yes." She looked at him quizzically. "You make them so very infrequently that you must. In general, you speak in such riddles that a person can leave thinking a promise has been extracted only to discover that it was nothing but a mirage in the desert, changing shape as soon as the gates of Septem close. But when you deal, yes, Ilyan, you keep your promises. As do I."

Her lips curved, and in the burnished light of late afternoon, she seemed to glow like the ruby between her eyes. For a moment he glimpsed the woman within, the one of legend: the girl who had been forced to marry her father's murderer only to then put a knife through him on their wedding night and seize leadership of the famed Jerawa Riders; the woman rumoured to have seduced a Greek commander and openly borne him children; the feared warrior who rode into battle wearing the horned mask of Ghurzla. Dahiya, Ilyan knew, was a mystery far greater even than the illusion of Al Kahinat.

And then she was gone, the mocking smile back in place. "Pour me wine and talk to me of the world. Tell me stories of the Circle of Lands, of kings and queens past and present. I know my own histories. My ancestors walk with me still. But when you speak, Ilyan, you bring the past alive and make me dream of glories no Amazigh woman has any right to. So, let us drink," she said, taking the wine jug and pouring for them both. "And tell me stories until I am insensible."

Ilyan bowed his head. "As you wish," he said, and they drank.

1

YOSEF

OCTOBER AD 687

Garnata, Bœtica, Spania
Granada, Andalusia, Spain

"H e is too young."

"No, *ahavi*. If we begin now, he will be at least eighteen when we return. A man already formed. This is his future, our future. He must come, no matter the dangers."

Yosef held his breath, pressing his ear against the wall. He had heard his parents have the same argument in hushed tones for weeks now. Always it was the same: his mother believed Yosef too young to journey the way of the Radhanite merchants, and Arun believed it imperative that his son learn the way of his ancestors, and the family business, as soon as possible.

Nobody had asked Yosef what he thought. If they had, he would have told them that his clothes had been bundled together for weeks, together with his heart, and that both were already travelling the spice ports from Africa to Constantinople.

"We will discuss it after Shemini Atzeret."

"We can discuss it until your hair turns to grey, *ahavi*. But Yosef and I will leave after the Sukkot festival and before the planting of trees in the month of Shebet." His father's voice was quiet but firm.

"My hair is not grey."

"No, but I think that perhaps I see just one or two strands. Let me check…"

Yosef slipped away from the wall, smiling at the sound of his parents' laughter. He left the house quietly. It was just past dawn, and the first chill of autumn was a breath on the morning air. Seasons changed quickly in Garnata. Any day now the rains would come, capping the mountains behind him in snow. But today the last summer figs were dropping from the trees, the two rivers bounding the town were mere trickles of dirty brown water, and the midday heat would still be sufficient to drive all indoors.

The walk from his family's home by the river to the marketplace was barely a mile on a gentle uphill slope. The stalls were bustling when he arrived, and the scent of freshly baked bread mingled with that of *posca*. The posca stall was the first he passed, and Yosef grinned at the men holding out pottery cups to be refilled, already raucous and red faced despite the early hour. Beside the posca stall, a rich scent of garlic and butter rose from an enormous iron pot suspended over a fire, and Yosef stopped to get a bowl of chicken and chickpea *hamin*.

He ate it sitting in the sunshine, dipping his bread into the rich sauce. It was his favourite market-day treat. He wondered, as he ate, how many more times he would be able to taste it before he began the great journey to Serica. Lately he thought of every experience as if it may be his last. He couldn't breathe without thinking of how the air would smell in Africa or drink without wondering if water tasted the same the world over.

A hand flicked his head. Yosef looked up, startled, then relaxed when he saw who it was.

"Lælia," he said, shaking his head. "Only you would think of attacking a man trying to eat his *hamin* in peace."

Dark eyebrows arched high. A hand drew a derisive sketch in the air, then pointed at him, clearly questioning his right to refer to himself as a man.

Leaning from her mount, she whipped the short knife from his belt.

"Hey!"

For a man, you're not very fast, said her hands. She slid from the horse, landing beside him with feline grace. She sat on the stone wall and poured some water over her hands, then turned and helped herself to some of his chicken. The sauce dripped down her chin and Yosef laughed, wiping it off affectionately with his tunic.

I thought you would be with Sarah.

Yosef shook his head, though he couldn't stop the colour rising in his cheeks. Seeing it, her mouth curled, and the yellow eyes flashed mischievously.

Your father still doesn't know, then.

"No," said Yosef. "Sarah's mother has converted, and her father is a Christian. If either of our fathers knew, they'd kill us both." He shook his head, suppressing the familiar resentment with long practice, not willing to talk about it further.

I wish they'd let you marry me. Yosef looked at her in astonishment, and she waved dismissively. *I don't mean like that. Just…*

Her face set in a way that was rather reminiscent, Yosef thought, of her grandfather, Count Paulus of Illiberis.

Then you could be with Sarah whenever you wanted. She threw his knife into the earth with a deft flick of her wrist. *And they would all stop planning my betrothal.*

"Your aunt Riccilo is here," guessed Yosef.

Lælia clicked her tongue softly. *No. But a visitor arrived with a message from her. I heard him speaking with my grandfather last night.*

Yosef grinned. "Fifteen is too old to listen at doors," he said.

Lælia shrugged. She plucked the knife out of the dirt and threw it again with unnecessary force.

"Are you here with your grandfather?" Yosef thought it best to change the subject.

Lælia nodded, gesturing with the hand that wasn't throwing the knife. *He's come to see your father. He made me come too.*

"Why?"

I don't know.

She shrugged again, but this time Yosef saw a faint frown between her brows.

"Yosef!" On cue, the tall figure of Paulus materialised in front of him. "I need to see your father." His face, always stern, seemed even grimmer than usual.

Yosef nodded. "I will take you to him."

"I'm bringing a visitor." Count Paulus drew his horse aside to reveal a second figure, lean and tall, clad in a foreign military tunic.

"This is Laurentius Severianus," said Count Paulus. "His father and I — and yours, Yosef — were friends."

"I remember the name," said Yosef. He gripped the proffered arm, trying not to show his surprise. It was not every day that a stranger was willing to take the arm of a Jew in plain sight. They left together, Yosef walking beside their horses.

Lælia grinned down at him. *Ride behind me?* she offered. Yosef cast a look at Count Paulus, who nodded curtly. Lælia offered her stirrup, and he swung up behind her. The horse danced for a moment, but she held it calmly in check and they rode on.

Lælia was a year his junior. Yosef had known her from the day she was born, and he could barely remember seeing her without a horse. Her family was famous throughout Spania for the horseflesh they bred, but with Lælia horses were more than a family business. She was unlike any other girl he knew, with her deep yellow eyes and wild tangle of dark curls. Some of the boys in Garnata muttered that she was *kashaph* when she rode by with the swarthy horse herders employed by her family running at her side. But Yosef did not think she was a whisperer, although he knew the stories of the horse herders in the mountains and their sorcery. Horses were simply part of who she was, just as cloth and spice and coin were part of who he was.

He suspected the boys wanted to cast her as a sorceress because she could outride and outshoot all of them. Lælia's prowess with horse and bow was a lesson most of the boys in Garnata and Illiberis learned early, and to their own cost.

On the road to the house by the river they passed some of the local youths, who cast Lælia covert looks of mingled envy and curiosity. She ignored their glances with supreme indifference. Yosef sat tall behind her, pretending not to notice the stir they were creating.

Fallen leaves from branches cut to build the booths for Sukkot blew into the gutter by the road. Joining branches of citron, palm, myrtle, and willow was a mitzvah prescribed in the Torah and forbidden under law. Yosef made a mental note to brush them away before they drew unwanted attention. The thought made him frown. He wondered if the Jews of Garnata would ever be free to build their booths without fear. He turned from the thought as he had from those of Sarah, the deep stab of irritation so familiar he barely noticed it.

The entrance to his father's house was low and unassuming. Yosef pushed open a thick wooden door and they entered the cool atrium. Above, the sky showed clear cerulean blue. The marble floor was pockmarked and scarred, but clean. Citron and laurel trees stood in urns against the wall. A shallow rainwater pool in the centre was dry; the rains had yet to come.

Arun ben Radhan was in his private study at the rear of the house. It was a beautiful room, with arched windows cut into the stone and covered by lattice screens and thick chestnut shutters that stood open to allow the breeze through. It was here that he kept the large, leather-bound books in which he tallied cloth, coin, grain, and wine. Dangerous books indeed for any Jew to hold. They were evidence of industry and trade forbidden to them by Spania's own code of law, the *Lex Visigothorum*, and evidence of an alliance with Illiberis, which could cost them all their lives if discovered.

The ledge beneath the window was covered in the tools of Arun's other clandestine trades. Those who sought these services entered not by the front door as Yosef just had, but by the rear, from a lesser-used alleyway that led directly into the small family garden.

A polished mahogany box inlaid with ivory was open and empty on the ledge, its contents spread across the heavy wooden desk in the centre of the room. Arun had been cleaning the metal discs of the astrolabe. Yosef could smell the tamarind paste he used for the task. It mingled with the scent of herbs, parchment, ink, and leather, and Yosef inhaled deeply. He loved his father's study.

Arun was gently working a sheepskin soaked in tamarind around the fine edges of the astrolabe. He put it down as they entered. "An unexpected pleasure," he said, his smile genuine as he gripped Paulus's arm at the elbow.

"I do not bring good news."

Arun's smile faded at the curt manner of Paulus's greeting. Courtesy was as intrinsic as hospitality in the south.

Paulus drew Laurentius forward. "There is nothing to fear." He addressed the unspoken wariness in his clerk's eyes. "At least," he amended, "not today. You remember Severianus's son, Laurentius? He is recently returned from serving in the Karabisianoi and has ridden here from the Toletum court."

Arun smiled politely as he took Laurentius's arm, but his eyes were cautious. "We have been expecting you, of course. I was sorry to hear about your father."

Laurentius accepted Arun's condolences with courtesy, but his expression was grave, and his eyes were on Paulus. Arun packed away the astrolabe as Laurentius and Paulus sat on the other side of the desk. He waved Lælia and Yosef to sit on a *lectus* in the corner.

"King Erwig is dead."

Paulus's words caused the dust motes to swirl, setting them spinning into the air where they gradually fell through the golden sun rays to the stone below.

A hush fell. From beyond the open window came the sound of people returning from the market, their light-hearted chatter incongruous against the backdrop of Paulus's words.

"And who have the council elected as the new king?" Arun's voice rasped like old metal.

Paulus's eyes seemed to sink even further into his gnarled face, dark with something Yosef could not read. "Egica," he said harshly.

The word hung in the air like an indrawn breath, even the dust motes seeming to pause. Beside Yosef, Lælia was as tense as a drawn bow. Arun stood and moved to the window. He unlatched the chestnut shutters and slowly drew them shut. The wooden lock thudded closed with dull finality. The noise of the day disappeared, no sun remaining to light the dust motes in the air. There was only the rank smell of the votive oil lamp lighting his father's face. It seemed uncharacteristically haggard and old as Arun took his seat once more.

"What now?" he said flatly.

Laurentius cleared his throat. "My sources," he said, "tell me he will send Oppa, his bastard son, to collect fealty from the south." Laurentius had a well-modulated voice, lacking the heavy intonation of the Visigothic court.

Arun shook his head. "That is not good news."

"No." Count Paulus's voice was equally grim. "It is not. Oppa is an acolyte serving under Julian, the archbishop of Toletum. He comes not only as representative of the Crown but also of the Church."

Arun paled. "So soon," he whispered, staring at the lamp.

"You know the laws the archbishop has enacted regarding your people." Count Paulus leaned forward. "Whilst we have, for the most part, been able to ignore them here in the south, Egica's reign will change that." He smiled faintly. "Our local priests have enough to occupy them with converting the horse tribes in the mountains without attempting to monitor the Jews of Garnata. And God alone knows, as do those priests, how dependent we all are on the trade and skills your community provides.

"I have done what I can to protect you. And I've paid the Church to look the other way. Egica, however, has long coveted the south's wealth. This visit will mean scrutiny. Of your businesses and of mine. On paper, I own your lands and industry. On paper, you, and the people of this town, are no longer Jewish. You are *anusim*, converted to the one true faith."

He said the last in a tone of faint irony, looking pointedly at the menorah standing on a shelf in the corner above a neatly folded tallit.

"Our goods are stored in your warehouses," said Arun slowly. "Our accounts are kept amongst yours. On paper, I appear as your servant only."

Yosef saw the faint tinge of red on his father's cheeks and suddenly wished he were anywhere but here. He saw Count Paulus's eyes narrow as Arun's glance flickered to his son. Count Paulus nodded at Yosef. "Your family settled this valley, just as Lælia's settled in Illiberis. Together, we will preserve both. But now is a new time, with new laws, and we all must adapt to survive." He smiled faintly. "Even me, and I am not a man who likes change."

Lælia's eyes glowed gold. She looked between Yosef and the men at the desk. One hand touched the bow on her back as if for reassurance.

If anyone wishes to take them from us, they must first pass the tribes – and me. Her fierce movements broke the tension in the room.

"Perhaps I should warn Oppa to protect himself," said Laurentius, smiling. "I have heard talk of those arrows of yours, Lælia."

Count Paulus, Yosef noticed, did not smile. "The women of our family have ever considered themselves exempt from the rules of society that the rest of us are unfortunate enough to have to follow."

He turned stern eyes on his granddaughter. "Listen to me, Lælia. Both of you." He nodded in Yosef's direction. "During this visit, we must all of us tread with exceptional wariness. The king's bastard will seek excuse to ruin us all. He and the king's priests come looking for weakness and the opportunity to bend us to their will. We must be certain to give them none." Count Paulus's mouth tightened into a grim line. "You are supposed to be *anusim*, Arun. Converts. It will no longer be enough to wear the title in name only. Tell the people of Garnata they must do what is necessary to maintain the illusion of conversion, or risk their own death and destruction."

"And what would you have us do, *hachever sheli*? Hang hams in our homes?

Despite his father referring to Count Paulus as his friend, Yosef could see Arun's anger, the high points of colour on his face.

"If that is what it takes!" Paulus's anger was as sudden as it was raw. "We have not spent these last decades carefully managing our affairs to see it all lost because you will not bend your principles."

"My principles are all that are left to me!" Arun pounded the desk with his fist, rising from his chair. Paulus, too, was on his feet, the two men glaring at each other across the table. "Or is it that you are afraid of losing your own wealth?" said Arun softly.

Yosef saw Paulus's fist curl, and for one horrible moment he thought the older man would strike his father. Count Paulus had been a warrior, Yosef knew; songs were still sung about his victories in the service of the great King Chindasuinth. Arun had never wielded anything more dangerous than a quill.

Then the tension went from Paulus's shoulders and he smiled reluctantly, shaking his head. "If I thought it would save you," he said heavily, "I would gladly give up every head of barley, trade our horses, and pour our wine onto the earth."

Arun gripped the hand he proffered. "I know it," he said gruffly.

"It is no longer about coin, Arun." Paulus gestured at Yosef and Lælia. "It is about your life. The lives of our children. It is doubly dangerous for you. You are not only a wealthy merchant but a learned man – an astrologer, a physician. Should any of those things be discovered, you risk condemnation for more than just trade. I cannot lose you, Arun. Your community cannot afford to lose you. This once, do you not think that God may understand?"

Arun's face was gaunt. To Yosef, who already stood as tall as his father and looked to grow even further, Arun seemed oddly insubstantial, animated only by the dark fire of anger in his eyes.

There was a long pause, then Arun spoke. "My son and I leave after the fast of Tebet to take the merchant's route to the East." His eyes flickered to Laurentius. It was the first time Yosef had heard the words said in his own presence.

"I cannot hope for your goodwill to protect us indefinitely, Paulus. My son must learn how to manage in this new world. We can no longer own land or slaves or animals, nor the means of manufacturing. In the church state of the Goths, we are the lowest of servants without even the means to maintain our own houses. Now it is time for us to find a new way." He gave his old friend a twisted smile. "And besides," he added, "the journey will bring profit to your house, also."

"That journey," said Laurentius, "is the reason I am here." He glanced at Paulus, who nodded at him to continue. "Count Ilyan has contributed coin for the restoration of the fleet currently rotting in the river at Hispalis. Coin of such amount that the Crown could not easily refuse when I presented it at court. The fleet is my excuse for returning. Before his death, Erwig gave permission for me to begin work upon it, though it was clear he and the rest of his court – Egica in particular – thought it a mad indulgence."

He leaned forward, clasping his hands between his knees. There was, in his movements, a fine, honed strength that revealed the warrior behind the polished urbanity. "The fleet is not an idle pastime," he went on. "I have spent more than a decade fighting in the service of the Karabisianoi under the direct command of the emperor himself, and I believe Spania is in dire need of such a force if she is to hold her coastline.

"For now, Egica does not object to the restoration. Ilyan's coin, however, has disappeared. It is clear Egica has no intention of honouring the commitment of his predecessor, nor the alliance with Septem. He does not trust the south with his coin, nor foreigners and their motives. Ilyan believes, as I do, that your journey has increased in danger. He has – alternative routes in mind."

"Why would he help us?" Yosef asked, looking between them.

"The Jews who flee Spania cross the sea to Ilyan's city of Septem," Laurentius said, "where they trade freely. Ilyan profits from that trade. He holds Septem by a meagre thread, one that costs coin and relies on safe trading routes. He has a vested interest in seeing trade thrive and Spania's coastline well defended." He pushed a small pool of white silk across the desk. Upon it, wrought with exquisite precision, was a delicate, heart-shaped tree. "We can trust Ilyan. He knows what you seek, and he offers his support."

Lælia leaned closer. *This is the silk tree, is it not?*

It was Count Paulus who answered. "*Ja,*" he said, unconsciously slipping into Gothic as Yosef had seen him often do when he was thinking. "Isidore of Hispalis says in his encyclopaedia that it is the tree from which the cloth is woven."

Lælia met her grandfather's eyes with a derisive expression. *I can read,* said her hands dismissively. *Why do we have it?*

Lælia, thought Yosef dryly, shared her grandfather's brevity. It was Arun who answered her question.

"The last time I travelled the merchant's route, my father and I were bound for Serica. We went to discover the secrets of making silk." He touched the cloth softly, almost caressing it. "We were given the symbol of the tree by a family in Serica who helped us, until the imperial palace discovered they had dared to trade with foreigners. I barely escaped the city of Chang'an with my life. My father was not so lucky." He looked at Yosef. "This time," he said, "we cannot afford to fail."

"I have made arrangements to help you," said Laurentius. "I am sending my own nephew, Theudemir of Aurariola, to train in the Karabisianoi."

Yosef felt Lælia stiffen beside him.

"Theudemir – Theo – will join the fleet when it arrives at the port of Sexi, after midwinter. He is but one of many sons of the south who go to learn the skills they will need to lead our own fleet. He comes from a long line of military service and is his father's second son rather than his heir, so his joining will draw no notice.

"He alone knows of your journey. I could, perhaps, have entrusted others in the fleet with the knowledge, but the Jewish merchants in Constantinople who also rely upon your success would be at risk should even a whisper of it reach the wrong ears. They face oppression from the Church just as the Jews of Spania do. The imperial palace in Constantinople controls all production of silk and has a monopoly that extends throughout the Circle of Lands. Any threat to that monopoly will result in immediate, and savage, retribution."

"You have put our future in the hands of a boy?" Arun looked between Paulus and Laurentius, not attempting to hide his scepticism.

"Theo has good reason to protect your secret." Paulus's eyes rested for a moment on Lælia, and Yosef tensed. "Theo's father and I have agreed a betrothal between Theo and Lælia." Paulus spoke flatly, as if he were announcing nothing more mundane than a horse sale. "Egica does not send his only bastard to Illiberis to have him return without the prize. Refusing a proposal without good reason would be dangerous for us all."

Yosef could not look at Lælia. *This is what she overheard them discussing,* he thought, his heart aching for his friend. *That she is to be traded just as any horse might be.* Despite the sudden attention from all in the room, Lælia stared stonily ahead, her set face betraying nothing of her thoughts.

"Theo knows you rely upon him, for news, and for your return." Laurentius's eyes rested briefly on Lælia, not without sympathy, then returned to Arun. "He will meet you both in Carthage after the first part of your journey over the sands, and perhaps again whilst you travel across Africa – if not, there will be messengers between those who help you and the fleet. After you leave African shores, Theo will remain with the fleet until you find your way back to it. In Constantinople, our Jewish allies await you. They will help you return to the fleet, and find Theo, if you have not already done so.

"From there you will travel under his protection back to Spania. Theo will by then be a seasoned warrior in service to the emperor. Two Jews travelling in the service of a senior member of the Karabisianoi will not be remarked upon, for all know your people's talent with language and parchment. It is the safest way."

Arun frowned. "I do not like trusting an outsider with this."

"Laurentius and I have given this much thought," Paulus interjected. He glanced at Laurentius, who nodded. "As a new recruit, Theo will be insignificant, invisible to any who may be watching. His family and ours are bound by old ties of friendship and blood that are stronger than any coin can buy, but few, if any, are now aware of the connection. And he will not be an outsider." Paulus's tone was flat. "He is betrothed to the heiress of Illiberis."

"Betrothal?" Arun glanced at Lælia, colouring when he saw her set face. His eyes slid away uneasily. "Why not marriage?"

"I cannot risk Illiberis." Paulus was brusque and businesslike. "If Theo is discovered, he and his family will be named traitor. A betrothal will serve to protect Lælia in the immediate future and whilst Theo is abroad. If all goes well, they will marry on his return. If not, the betrothal will be dissolved and Lælia married to someone else who can protect Illiberis." Paulus frowned. "There are few left whom I truly trust. Theo's father, Suinthila, is one such man – as are his sons."

Lælia's hand clenched convulsively on the handle of her knife, the only visible sign of the impotent rage Yosef knew she must feel. Yosef wanted to reach out to her but knew she would hate any sign of pity, so he didn't.

Arun turned to Count Paulus and put out his hand, smiling. "We will be partners again, my old friend, then, will we not?"

Count Paulus accepted the peace offering with a smile of his own. "But you will heed my words?" he said, holding Arun's eyes. "The booths of Sukkot will have barely been dismantled when Oppa arrives. You must be careful."

Arun's smile curved into one of rueful acceptance. "I will tell the people to hang the hams." His eyes rested on Lælia once more. "When does Theudemir of Aurariola arrive?" he asked gently.

"He rides here even now." Paulus stood, and they all followed. "He will be with us in less than a moon's turn."

2

LÆLIA

NOVEMBER AD 687

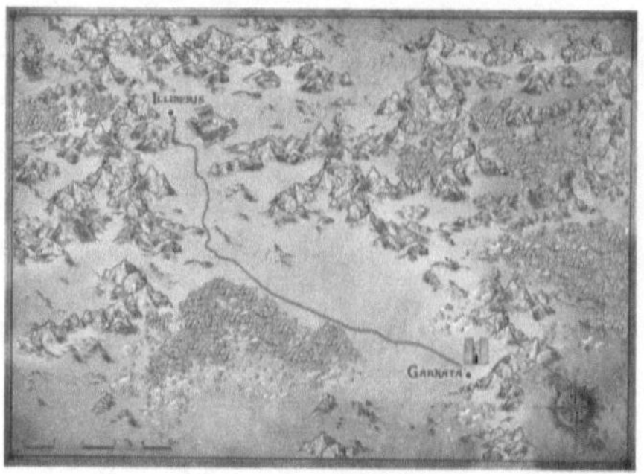

Illiberis, Bætica, Spania
Granada, Andalusia, Spain

Lælia woke from a dream of horses and blood. A cry died in her throat before it found voice in the darkness. Heat pricked her skin, though beyond the open window snow on the mountains glittered beneath a full moon. Lælia swallowed hard on the choking sensation, and her hand went to her neck where a leather cord had twisted tight and caught in the tangled mass of black curls that had come unbound in the night. Lælia touched the symbol it held, her heart still racing. The carved bone felt hot beneath her hand as if it were still part of the horse from which it had long ago been wrought.

Darkness, running. *The wind screams, but nobody says where it lives.*

Lælia trembled. The words whispered through her heart and upward, strangling the place where, in her dreams at least, her voice still lived.

Where did you go? Lælia thought, her fingers tentatively touching her throat. *Where did my words go? Are you there still, lost inside me somewhere, in the same place I hear the voice whispering of wind?*

She closed her eyes, trying to recall the sound of that voice. It was already fading, the memories a confused jumble of images. Running. A horse dancing from a cliff. Blood. So much blood.

And a strange tune, vibrating against her back, the sound of safety, of life…

Flinging back the bedclothes, Lælia strode to the window and took deep gulps of the night air. The faint sound of drums rumbled in the distance. Under this full moon the tribes dug up the horn buried at the start of spring, at the Bull's new moon, when the harvest was planted. Now, as the full moon blazed in the same sign, they celebrated the harvest their efforts had wrought. In round huts high in the mountains, the horse herders would drink fiery liquor and feast until dawn. Her grandmother, Acantha, was probably there amongst them, Lælia thought bitterly.

She glanced at the chestnut bedside table. It was inlaid with a curlicued pattern picked out in ivory. Acantha had brought it back from Septem long ago when Lælia had been an infant, her parents only recently dead from the fever that had taken so many in what people still called the Summer of Blood.

Lying atop it was a torc that had once belonged to her mother. It, too, had lain by her bed as long as she could remember, though Lælia had never worn it, choosing instead the crude bone rendering of the Illiberis horse brand: two snakes entwined about a central staff. The torc, by contrast, was a lone serpent, wrought in a gleaming silver pattern with sapphire eyes staring commandingly at all who beheld the wearer. Lælia could imagine the kind of lady who would wear such a torc: one accustomed to fine gowns, at home at the Toletum court and amongst the Visigothic nobility found in the royal capital.

The only commonality between the sophisticated torc and her own crude bone amulet was the ancient hands that had wrought both, in a time when the women of Illiberis had ruled their lands with bow and horse without the consent of any man. Even now, Illiberis was inherited through the female line – *in theory at least*, thought Lælia grimly, remembering the message her aunt Riccilo had sent with Laurentius Severianus.

Lælia turned away from the serpent's knowing blue stare. It had been many years since women had ruled Illiberis. Their gods had long been replaced by that of the bishop of Illiberis, who took Count Paulus's coin in the grey stone church and pretended not to notice the remnants of the Sukkot booth branches scattered along the road to Garnata.

Acantha, however, was another matter. The same bishop pursed his lips in disapproval when mention was made of the low, stone abbey high in the mountains in which Acantha had dwelled for as long as Lælia could recall. The iron cross outside the abbey had not blinded him to the stone cairns by the stream there or the offerings laid on rocks nearby. Even had he managed to ignore such signs, Acantha's flat refusal to enter the church in Illiberis, and the barely disguised amusement with which she tolerated his conversation, made it plain enough. None but the most casual visitor to the abbey was fooled by that iron cross. The women who lived there were devout enough, but they followed gods long forgotten by those in the town below and long outlawed by the church of Bishop Iohannes. Their church lay in the caves under the dull stone, their prayers in the whisper of water amongst the moss far beneath the earth. These were secrets no man should know, and that only women could hold. Secrets Lælia would inherit, even if she was to marry Theudemir of Aurariola as Riccilo and her grandfather planned.

The unwelcome thought galvanised her into action. Lælia pulled on hide trousers, a linen tunic, and soft leather boots. She swathed herself in a woollen cloak. A gift from the tribes, the cloak smelled of pine fires and horse, familiar scents that had calmed her as long as she could remember.

Moonlight played on the mosaic beneath her feet as she made her way into the courtyard, so it seemed as if the horse and rider depicted there rode into life. Lælia stepped cautiously around it. The night had called to her, the signs unmistakable. She slipped from the villa and across ground white with hoar frost, heading for the stables.

Outside, the rumble of the drums beat an incessant rhythm, which seemed to come from the earth itself. A lynx growled somewhere in the foothills: a low, bloodcurdling yowl that sent a shiver through Lælia. It was not the first time she had heard its cry. It had been coming ever closer; soon she would follow its tracks into the mountains. It was dangerous for such an animal to be so close to their fields when foals were due to be born. The herd was on the lowlands for the winter, and hungry cats were not the only predators that came seeking their flesh.

The stables were made of adobe bricks and chestnut, a dull shadow thrown into relief by the cloud of almond blossom gleaming under the moonlight. The trees had flowered early. They stood around a pomegranate tree in a small, private orchard planted when the Romans had first come to Spania. The tribes of Illiberis had been old even then, when the Romans had named their southern province Bætica. Lælia bore the name Bæticus, an acknowledgement of her family's ancient claim to the earth she now crossed on her way to the stable door. Riccilo had once borne the same name. Her mother was Acantha's sister, gone many years since to a husband far to the north, in Gallaecia. She had sent her daughter south during the repeated border wars of Riccilo's youth, to be raised by Acantha at Illiberis. Riccilo's marriage to Theodofred, Duke of Corduba, youngest son of the great King Chindasuinth and one of Paulus's oldest friends, meant that Riccilo had remained in the south. Lælia called her aunt, though sometimes she wished her relative would take a less active interest in her affairs.

Inside the stable she lit an oil lamp, which threw a flickering pattern across the straw. Hera whickered softly from the corner. Lælia knelt, feeling the mare's swollen belly and the growing forms within it with a practised hand.

Twins.

All knew such births were doomed. There was not the life force in one mare to sustain two foals. Lælia suspected the only reason her grandfather had stayed his axe was because Hera had once belonged to his daughter. All knowledge of Callista, Lælia's mother, was locked behind a door of silence to which only Count Paulus and Acantha held keys and to which they seemed uncharacteristically united in denying Lælia entry. Even Riccilo, who Lælia knew had loved Callista as a sister, rarely spoke of her. Lælia's father, Beremund, lay behind the same door of silence. Lælia had never so much as visited the lands he had once ruled, lands that had been reclaimed by the crown during Erwig's rule and granted to a count named Frogellus.

Hera was Lælia's sole link to the parents she knew only through dreams such as those this night had brought, vague impressions she would clutch at in vain upon waking, only to find herself bereft once more when they dissolved into blackness.

Lælia stared into the mare's brown eyes, which seemed already to hold a presentiment of death. *You will not die,* she vowed fiercely, as she had done ever since the mare had uncharacteristically wandered off. Lælia had tracked her for days, until finally she had discovered Hera caught amidst tumbled rock on a mountain track – and in foal.

You will live. I will make it so.

Beneath her hand the foals stirred, and she felt a bolt of life lick through her veins like fire across the horizon.

For a moment, she allowed herself to think of the parchment she had seen on her grandfather's desk. Lælia had learned her runes beside Yosef at Arun's hand, so she had no difficulty in reading the contract of betrothal that Riccilo's husband had negotiated on her behalf. Beneath the details of the property settlement that safeguarded her right to inherit Illiberis, a name had been signed in a firm, sure hand. Theudemir of Aurariola, it appeared, had not suffered any of her hesitations.

The cry of the lynx cut the night once more. Lælia Bæticus of Illiberis crooned a silent song to the unborn foals, whilst in the mountains the tribes danced beneath the last of the summer moons.

3

THEUDEMIR OF AURARIOLA – THEO

NOVEMBER AD 687

Illiberis, Bætica, Spania
Granada, Andalusia, Spain

The fortress that marked the eastern border of the Illiberis latifundium sat high above the ancient Jewish town of Garnata. It was perched on a ridge so steep that Theo wondered, as he rode down the descent, how men had ever come to build it, let alone how any would dare attack it.

Theo had never seen such country as they had ridden through on their way to Illiberis. It was like voyaging into a secret land,

31

where old legends came to life and mystery lay around every corner. They had crossed the desert wastes beyond Aurariola only to find themselves in a land of caves carved into steep red rock, from which unseen eyes watched them pass. Then had come the fierce mountains, steeper and more labyrinthine than any route Theo had previously travelled. His dreams, always vivid, had become disturbing since they had entered those closed passes. The land gave up its secrets reluctantly, revealed in a series of folds each more magnificent than the last, whilst his dreams seemed to hint at things hidden.

His horse picked its way down the steep track. In the rose dew of dawn, the earth smelled wild and dusty, the scent of dry ground reinvigorated by night moisture. A spiderweb glistened before him and Theo paused, reluctant to ride through its delicate tapestry.

"How beautiful." Athanagild drew to a halt beside him, admiring the pattern. "It is a pity Loni is not here. She would love this."

"She would." Theo suppressed a pang of sadness. His little sister was two, the same age Theo himself had been when his uncle Laurentius had sailed from Spanish shores. Theo had not known him when Laurentius returned. He could not imagine Egilona's face not lighting with joy when he picked her up, being confronted with the blank courtesy of a sister who knew him no more than the sailors who docked in their port.

And what of Athanagild? Theo looked at the tall, thin figure of his brother, riding slightly apart. His deep auburn head gleamed in the growing sunlight as he pulled a leaf from a tree in passing, examining it so closely he was nearly swept from his horse by another branch. Athanagild was so quiet, he sometimes seemed lost in the raucous company of his father and brothers. Theo worried for him, too, entering the monastery at Toletum. And yet Theo felt the pull of distant shores like a siren call.

At night, when he thought of the stories Laurentius told of Constantinople, of battles fought on foreign soil, Theo yearned for the adventure so much that he could already feel the deck of the dromon beneath his feet and smell the sea salt.

Theo spurred his horse onward to catch Shukra. The small Persian man had fought abroad alongside his uncle Laurentius since the two were boys together. Barely a decade older than Theo, he had seen enough of battle to command respect, but retained the youthful demeanour that made him confidant rather than guardian. He was accompanying Theo to Illiberis and then on to the fleet.

"You will miss them, no? Your family." Shukra watched Theo with the uncanny perception to which Theo had become accustomed in the days they had ridden together.

"Yes," he said quietly. "I will."

"It is hard to leave those we love. Many times, you will want to return, *aziz-am*. It is the same for all men."

"I know my duty. I hope to prove worthy of Laurentius's faith in me."

"Ha!" Shukra, Theo had learned, was at times shockingly irreverent. "What duty do you think of?"

"To Spania." Theo met his eyes. "To the fleet. To the mission you and Laurentius have laboured to set in motion." He paused. "And to my wife, of course."

He fell silent, retreating at the mention of his wife-to-be. Theo knew theirs was a betrothal in name only, one designed to protect the heiress of Illiberis from any ambitions Egica, the new king, might have. It was rumoured that Oppa, the king's bastard son, would ride south, and all knew his father coveted the rich latifundia of the southern lords. Particularly the lands of Illiberis, which had held as a single latifundium since the first days of the Romans and was guarded on all sides by formidable mountains as well as the several thousand men Count Paulus commanded in his *thiufae*.

But still: betrothal. Theo had not imagined himself taking a wife at any point in the immediate future. Marriage was a responsibility Theo felt ill equipped to bear. His father lay abed in Aurariola and may never be well enough to rule his latifundia again. Theo's older brother Alaric, who already carried the burden of ruling his father's lands in Emerita Augusta and training the men there, must manage Aurariola too, without Theo at his side. Athanagild would enter the monastery without Theo to visit him. Egilona would grow up and become a lady without her older brother to protect her.

Theo was determined he would rise in the Karabisianoi as his uncle had done. He must, if he was to learn enough to lead men against the Arabic armies Laurentius warned were coming. The Toletum court, Theo knew, had scoffed at Laurentius's warnings. But his uncle was an educated man. Laurentius and Shukra said the Arabic threat was real, and Theo believed them. There was also the matter of the covert trade Laurentius had worked so hard to set in motion, trade that Theo knew might be needed to fund Spania's defences if the Crown did not.

He just could not imagine how, in addition to all these responsibilities, he was also to protect a wife, from far away on the other side of the Circle of Lands. He feared he must prove inadequate in one of these areas, and to Theo the thought of failing in his duties was more terrifying than any Arabic sword he may face in the service of the fleet.

His hands gripped the reins tightly. He did not wish Shukra to think him reluctant to marry Lælia of Illiberis. Such betrayal would be unworthy of him and insulting to the lady he rode to meet. He stared straight ahead and hoped his reticence would be interpreted as respect toward his future wife.

"Duty," mused Shukra, diplomatically pretending not to notice Theo's abrupt silence. "It is a strange thing, duty. Laurentius, too, takes his duty very seriously, I am thinking."

"Do you not also?" Theo looked curiously at Shukra. "Is there anything more important than duty – to country, king, family? What can matter more than this?"

"Oh, *aziz-am*. I am Persian." Shukra shrugged, spreading his hands helplessly as if this explanation covered a multitude of imagined sins. "And besides, I have been fighting for the emperor for many years. Duty now is something I am feeling in my heart, not in my head."

He cast Theo a sideways glance. "My master, Zoroaster," he said, "whose name none in your country know and who died many years before your Jesus Christ walked the earth, spoke of three things: good thoughts, good words, good deeds. This is where I am finding my duty, Theudemir of Aurariola. In the harmony of these things. It is this that all men must find if they are to do their duty from their heart. Duty is nothing but words unless it is coming from the place in a man where he knows his thoughts, his words, and his deeds match."

For a moment, the dark eyes were uncharacteristically solemn as they regarded Theo. "It is wise if you are remembering this," he said quietly. "In marriage, as in any duty."

Theo was saved from replying when his horse stumbled, then came to a trembling halt.

Theo dismounted. His horse held its near foreleg bent at the knee to keep the hoof from the ground. A sharp piece of flint stuck from it, wedged deeply enough that blood fell to the ground in thick, red drops.

"Go ahead," said Theo without looking up. "I will need to get this out before I go any farther."

He crooned softly to the horse to calm it, and Athanagild smiled as he rode by. "You have hummed that same tune," he said over his shoulder, "to every animal we've owned. Some might call you a magician."

"If I were a magician," Theo said, grimacing as he tried to pull the stone, "I would already have this out."

Athanagild grinned. "We will meet you at the villa."

The creaking of leather and clinking of stirrups faded, and a breeze blew across Theo's back. He bent over the hoof, gently trying to work the stone out, his horse flinching at every tug.

It was strangely peaceful to be alone after so many days in company. Alaric had once joked that Theo's face hid his every thought, but the truth was that Theo worked hard to keep any hint of his inner life from showing upon it. He could not imagine anything worse than men seeing beyond that façade. Sometimes he saw his own reflection in a pool of water, and it seemed that his face, clear and trouble free, belonged to someone else. He had never ceased to be secretly amazed that others believed the lie of that perfect face, for Theo knew that beneath it lay a world of uncertainty and doubt. It was only in these quiet, solitary moments, free from the awareness of others, that he could truly relax.

As he probed the horse's hoof, away from watching eyes, he allowed himself the rare treat of imagining life in the fleet. Theo knew the prospect of joining the Karabisianoi went deeper than any sense of obligation, and he nursed his anticipation like a guilty secret. Theo's grandfather, Geila, had been the greatest general Spania had ever known, brother to Suinthila, the king who had finally won the south from Greek control, and for whom Theo's own father was named. War ran through Theo's veins. Theo knew he longed for the chance to rise in the Karabisianoi. He was secretly ashamed of his ambition, for he had been raised to duty, not glory.

He pushed his thoughts aside as the horse shifted uneasily, and he braced himself against a tree. "Steady," he murmured, as the horse made an indignant noise and swung its head to nip his shoulder at a particularly painful movement. "Stand there."

The horse had decided enough was enough, however, and began dancing away from the hand causing it pain. The breeze came again, but this time in a rush of air that made him turn.

A slender girl, not much younger than himself, was frowning at the hoof in his hand. Behind her was a young horse, standing placidly, reins hanging free. *She must be one of the horse herders' children,* Theo thought, looking at her curiously. She certainly looked wild enough.

Large golden eyes stared at him through a tangle of black curls that had escaped from the thick plait that fell over her shoulder. A curved bow hung on her back, and long legs were encased in the hide trousers of the horse herders. She seemed both too tall and too graceful, Theo thought, to belong to the short, dark tribes they had met upon the road, but she wore leather boots rather than the sandals made of *atoche* grass of a village dweller.

She gestured to the hoof in his hand. Pushing him gently aside, she took it, making a chirruping noise in her throat that made his horse cease fidgeting and stand quietly. For a moment, she stared at the stone with narrowed eyes. She made another noise, this time a faint hum, both of warning and reassurance, and the horse braced itself. In one deft movement, she slipped the flint free and pressed her hand to the wound to staunch the bleeding.

Theo made a soft exclamation of surprise. "How did you do that?"

She shrugged but did not answer him. Theo struggled to remember the local dialect of the tribes, but he couldn't recall more than a few words overheard on the way. He tried instead in Gothic. "*Awiliudo þus*," he said. Thank you.

She tilted her head to one side and regarded him with frank curiosity, still silent. Theo noticed a bone amulet about her neck, a pagan symbol of entwined serpents that would have made the priests in Athanagild's monastery purse their lips in disapproval. It was another reminder, after the hostile country they had ridden through, that Illiberis followed rules unlike those that governed the rest of Gothic Spania.

Theo rose, dusting his clothes. The girl looked between him and the horse and frowned.

"I'm not going to ride," said Theo, still in Gothic. He nodded in the direction of the villa, a large, square building set in the distance beyond sloping fields of olive trees. "I am staying there. I will walk the rest of the way and take good care of him." He stroked the horse's shoulder.

She was still staring at him, and Theo felt a strange urge to hold on to the moment. "*Wēnja ei aftra gamōtjaima unsis missō*," he said, and then coloured. I hope I will see you again.

Her eyes narrowed, then flashed with such savage hostility that Theo took a step back and reached for his sword. But the girl had already turned her back. Flowing onto the horse in a smooth movement, she rode silently away without a backward glance, her slender figure lost in moments amongst the trees.

Frowning, Theo watched her go, then led the horse along the empty approach toward the villa of Illiberis.

4

YOSEF

NOVEMBER AD 687

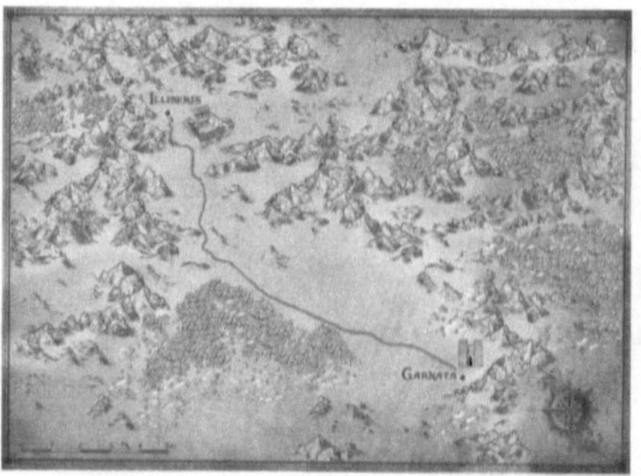

Illiberis, Bætica, Spania
Granada, Andalusia, Spain

Count Paulus's *œca* may not have been the grandest hall in Spania, but it had been built at the height of old Bætica's glory using the finest materials and talent the Empire could supply, and it had been well maintained ever since. The wooden coffered ceiling was decorated with gold leaf. A wide mosaic depicting a hunting scene covered much of the floor, and there was a dais at one end for formal occasions. Yosef found Count

Paulus in the centre of the room, talking to a slight man clad in a military tunic.

"Ah, Yosef! Thank you for coming." He gestured brusquely to his companion. "This is Shukra, Laurentius's friend. He will wish to speak with you later."

It was typical of Count Paulus's grim brevity, Yosef thought, to dispense with the formalities of introduction. By the way Shukra's eyes danced, he, too, found the count's abrupt manners amusing.

Shukra was flanked by two young men. One wore the same tunic as Shukra, the scarlet of the Karabisianoi. He was tall, and already hard muscled from sword training, though he couldn't have been much older than Yosef's own sixteen years. His hair was worn long in the Gothic style, a wild shock of white that gleamed in the late afternoon light. He stood slightly ahead of his companion, as if unconsciously shielding him, and regarded Yosef with piercing green eyes and a half smile. The man behind him was slender and pale skinned, clad in the brown homespun of an acolyte. He had auburn hair and deep-set hazel eyes that seemed to notice everything about him. He regarded Yosef solemnly.

The servants had barely served them cups of wine when there was a faint stir at the end of the œca. Yosef turned to see who had come into the room and almost choked on his wine.

The fact that Lælia had chosen to enter the room on the dais and thus draw every eye was, to Yosef, only superseded in oddity by the fact that she wore a formal gown of scarlet wool embroidered with gold thread. So accustomed was he to seeing Lælia clad in hide trousers and a linen tunic, bow strung on her back, that it took a moment for him to recognise the vision that stood on the dais surveying the room below with icy dignity. In place of her customary plait, her hair was unbound, tumbling to her waist in a wild mass of untamed curls. The serpents wrought in horse bone on her neck gleamed ivory, seeming to dare the room to object to their presence. Lælia's eyes, rich amber in the afternoon light, stared a blatant challenge at the room below.

Following the direction of her gaze to the young man in the military tunic, Yosef's amazement rapidly gave way to fascination.

This, he realised, must be Theudemir, the man to whom Lælia was to be betrothed.

Theudemir looked up. For the briefest moment, recognition flared in his eyes. So rapidly was it quelled that Yosef wondered if he had imagined it; then he saw the faint shadow of a smile before the young man's face settled back into a courteous mask. Satisfaction flashed just as briefly in Lælia's face, vanishing as she stepped imperiously from the dais for the formal introductions.

"Theudemir of Aurariola," said the young man as he stepped toward her, the smile lurking suspiciously at the corners of his mouth.

They have already met, Yosef thought, looking between them.

Theudemir was still waiting for a response. Yosef realised that nobody had told him she could not speak. Lælia returned his stare with blank indifference. It was a trick Yosef had seen her employ before. Much could be deduced about a person, she had once told Yosef, by the manner in which they responded to silence.

If she was expecting a reaction, however, she was disappointed. Theudemir merely inclined his head and regarded her with faint amusement. "It is an honour to be welcomed in your home," he said courteously to Count Paulus. "My brother Athanagild has accompanied me to bear witness to the contract, as you requested of my father."

Count Paulus made a dismissive noise. "I thought it better to keep the matter between us, and the bishop of Illiberis out of our affairs," he said bluntly. "Lælia, fetch the contract from my study." He gave his granddaughter a somewhat caustic glance. "I believe you know exactly where it is to be found."

He turned to Theudemir. "Theo – it is Theo, is it not? I recall you from Toletum several years ago. I do not wish to appear ungracious, but it appears we may at any moment be made to play host to a delegation from our new king's court. I would see our contract agreed before that occurs."

"Of course." Theudemir nodded politely. His eyes, though, followed Lælia as she left the room. He was still watching the place where she had exited when she re-entered. Yosef saw her eyes flash with hostility as she noticed Theudemir's regard. Holding his eyes, she raised her eyebrows haughtily. Yosef had the feeling that she was extremely pleased with herself, though he was unsure why.

"I know you have signed it already," said Paulus. "I wish for the witnesses to be present when I affix my own consent if you have no objection?"

"None." Theudemir, eyes fixed on Lælia, was paying him little attention.

Athanagild and Shukra both moved to the writing table, which had been placed in the œca for the purpose. Carefully, they each took the quill, Shukra handling it with more familiarity than Yosef had expected from one who had come from service in the emperor's fleet. Lælia, he saw, was watching the group with a calculating expression that Yosef knew, from long experience, did not bode well.

"Lælia," said Paulus, as Athanagild finished his careful, elegant signature. "You will also sign." He pointed to the parchment, his tone brooking no argument. Lælia moved forward with every appearance of compliance. As she did, she turned her head and frowned at the open arch behind them as if her attention had been caught by something. So evocative was her expression that the room turned as one to follow her gaze – everyone except Yosef, who knew this trick of old, and to his surprise, Theudemir, who watched Lælia with a slight crease between his brows.

Taking the quill, she leaned over the table with her back to them, blocking the parchment from view. Her arm moved as if she was signing. Beyond the arch came the sound of raised voices; Paulus, making an impatient sound, went to investigate whilst Athanagild addressed a comment to Shukra that made them both smile.

In the moment of inattention, Lælia spilled sand over the parchment and made a pretence of blotting the ink. Turning to face them, she shook it, careful to ensure the side on which the ink was drying faced her. Turning back to the table, she slowly rolled the document and tied it with a leather thread. As her grandfather re-entered the room, she was carefully sealing the tied thread with the wax Count Paulus had left warming by the table.

"*Gut*," said Paulus in satisfaction, as she raised the wooden stamp and smiled at him. "Take it back to my study. I wish to speak to Shukra." Casting Theudemir a cursory glance, he said, "The servants will show you to your chambers. I will enjoy your company at meat." Without further condescension, he left the œca.

Yosef, staring at the parchment leaving the room in Lælia's hand, opened his mouth to speak. Theo put a warning hand on his arm and gave a barely perceptible shake of his head: *Don't.* Yosef frowned. At the archway, Lælia paused. Turning, she looked at Theudemir, eyes blazing with angry triumph. Waiting long enough to ensure he had not missed her disdain, she turned and stalked from the room.

"It would have helped," said Theudemir mildly, to no one in particular, "if someone had told me she does not speak."

"Ah," said Shukra, about to follow in Count Paulus's wake, "but that would have taken all the fun from the game, *aziz-am*, would it not?" Winking at Yosef, the little man left the room, leaving Yosef wondering if it were only Theudemir and himself who realised the contract had been sealed without Lælia's signature.

* * *

YOSEF WAS a frequent visitor at Illiberis. He took advantage of this familiarity by escaping to the stables as soon as he could make an excuse, expecting to find Lælia there. Instead he found Titus, the bay gelding she had been training for the past year, his coat clearly marked from recent riding. Titus snorted softly when Yosef entered, and he nudged his body for treats.

"Where is she?" Yosef murmured, stroking the gelding's neck. "And what did she make of her betrothed, I wonder?"

"The question of the moment, it would seem," said a dry voice behind him.

Yosef swung around.

"Since our host seems unlikely to effect a formal introduction, I am Theo." The young man put his arm out, and Yosef grasped it at the elbow.

"Yosef ben Arun," he said and waited for the inevitable recoil.

Instead, Theo held up a wine jug. "I have only one cup, I'm afraid, but if you will share it, I would be honoured." He held

Yosef's eyes as he spoke. Yosef read nothing in them but steady regard.

He held his hand out and took the cup. "*Awiliudo þus*," he said quietly in Gothic. Thank you.

"*Al-lo-Davar*," responded Theo.

Yosef's eyes widened in surprise. "You speak Hebraic?"

Theo grinned. "I have two phrases only. There is a Jewish merchant in the marketplace at our home in Aurariola. He taught me to say "thank you" and "you're welcome". I'm glad to have the chance to use them."

Yosef drank, regarded Theo over the cup, and handed it back. With neither hesitation nor ostentation, Theo raised the cup and drank from it.

Theudemir of Aurariola, Yosef thought with increasing respect, was not at all the haughty son of a nobleman he had imagined. He was also impossibly handsome. Yosef rarely noticed the appearance of his own sex, but the chiselled planes of Theo's face were so perfect it was almost disconcerting. Lælia, he was surprised to find himself thinking, could do much worse.

"Theo!" An auburn head appeared around the door of the stables, hazel eyes lighting up when they found the pair inside. "There you are!" Seeing Yosef, the acolyte came to an abrupt halt, his earlier exuberance disappearing behind a cool mask.

Looking between them, Yosef realised the mask was something they had in common. Despite his open manner, Theo, too, had a watchful air, as if expecting at any moment to draw sword in his own defence.

"Athanagild is my brother." Theo drew him forward with an arm over his shoulders. "Well, one of them," he went on, grinning. "But by far the less offensive of the two. Alaric will arrive in the next few days. He is with my uncle, Laurentius, in Hispalis. I believe you already know Laurentius?"

Athanagild blushed as they were introduced, his eyes falling away from Yosef's own. He was painfully shy, Yosef realised. There was nonetheless a wiry strength in the slender arm that held his own and no hesitation in his grip despite Yosef enunciating his Jewish name clearly.

"You remind me of Laurentius," said Yosef, smiling at Athanagild.

"I am not related to Laurentius." Athanagild's colour deepened and he looked away. Yosef, a little taken aback, glanced at Theo.

"He means not by blood," Theo explained. "Athanagild and I are brothers by marriage." He gave Yosef a warning look. "But we *are* brothers," he said with quiet emphasis.

Athanagild drew closer to Theo as if drawing strength from his brother's protection. The smile he gave Yosef, though quick, was genuine and held a note of apology. Noticing Theo's gentle manner with him and the clear affection between the two, Yosef found himself liking them.

"You have met Lælia before now, have you not?" Yosef said. "I understand that your families are friends."

Something passed across Theo's face, there and then gone.

"Before today, once perhaps, when we were very young. I do not remember it, or not clearly." Theo frowned, and Yosef suspected he had tried very hard to recall anything of the girl he had been sent to marry. "I remember only horses. Or perhaps the horses are from a dream; I have dreamed strange things on the road here."

His brow cleared, and he shot Yosef a self-conscious smile as if aware he had revealed more of himself than he had intended. "I admit I thought I might find her in the stables, before we sit formally to meat."

"If you wish to find Lælia, the stables are certainly the right place to begin your search." Yosef turned his head to hide his amusement.

"Does she often ride alone?"

"Always." Yosef did not try to hide his smile this time.

Theo frowned. "In such mountains as these, that is dangerous."

Yosef regarded him thoughtfully. "Lælia is not like other girls you may have met." He chose his words carefully. "She is more likely to ride toward danger than away from it."

Theo inclined his head. "In which case," he pointed out, "she has need of someone to ride beside her."

Yosef, imagining Lælia's outraged indignation at any suggestion she may need protection on her adventures, turned his head from the narrowed green eyes, which he was rapidly realising missed very little.

"Why," he said, thinking it timely to change the subject, "did you not tell Count Paulus that Lælia did not sign the contract?"

Theo glanced at Athanagild, who nodded at Yosef, then diplomatically left them alone.

"My father once told me that marriage is based on trust." Theo gave Yosef a crooked smile. "I thought it would not be a very good beginning to start with a betrayal."

"Well thought," said Yosef, meaning it.

"I'm glad you approve." Theo looked evenly at him. "Since I understand we will be working closely together in the coming years, I imagine it would be best if we began our own association on the same basis."

Yosef met his eyes. "My father and I are… grateful for your help." Despite his best efforts, resentment caught the words like a needle snagged in flesh.

"I understand the Radhanite merchants have travelled the route east for many centuries. You are part of a proud tradition." There was something in Theo's grave expression that implied understanding without sympathy.

"Why did Laurentius choose you for the task?" Yosef had not meant to be so blunt, but Theo did not seem to mind.

"He didn't choose me. I volunteered." His half smile was almost guilty, and Yosef had the impression his disclosure was a secret few knew of. "I wanted to go," he admitted.

Yosef put out his arm again. "I am glad it is you we will be meeting in Carthage, and later, in Constantinople," he said, with genuine feeling.

Theo took it, smiling warmly. Then his eyes gleamed. "Carthage." He said the word as if trying it out on his tongue, savouring its flavour as one would a seasoned meat.

"Do you know much of it?" Yosef asked.

Theo shook his head.

"It is the first place we are to cross paths," said Yosef, seeing the same glimmer of wonder in Theo's eyes he himself had felt when he remembered that the foreign names would soon be real to him. He felt again the rush of adventure that lay before them. "Perhaps," he said, "we can walk together for a time and speak of how we are to proceed?"

They left the stables and walked into the mellow afternoon sunlight. The day grew late, and the young men walked the colonnaded walkway that enclosed the interior of the Illiberis courtyard, inhaling the scent of winter jasmine and citron and seeing in the patterned pathways their own footsteps on foreign soil.

Shadows grew across the valley, and neither noticed the slender figure beneath a stone archway who listened for a time, then slipped away as the scent of meat and men grew on the night.

5

LÆLIA

NOVEMBER AD 687

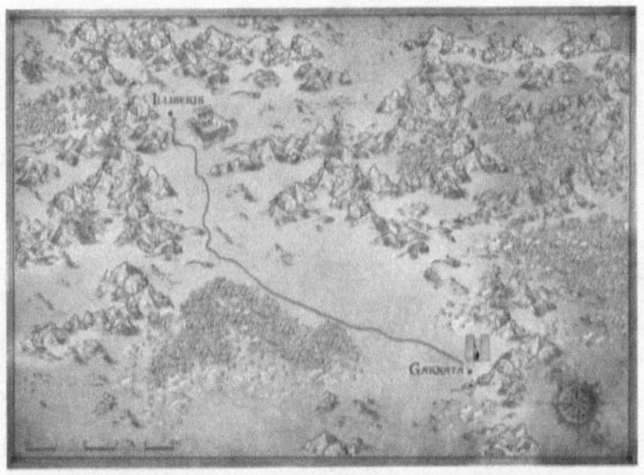

Illiberis, Bætica, Spania
Granada, Andalusia, Spain

I*t would have helped if someone had told me she does not speak.* Theudemir's words echoed in the rhythm of Titus's hooves along the narrow path that led to the abbey above Illiberis.

What does he know of it? Lælia thought furiously. The first stars pricked the sky. She should be dressing to sit at her grandfather's table for meat. *Tyr!* She kicked a passing branch as she mentally invoked the Gothic god of war.

She knew little of her father, who had died the last of his line, but she found the names of the Gothic gods his people had once followed eminently satisfying. Even her own grandfather had been known to invoke the name at times. In the present moment, Lælia felt a god of war would be very helpful. Particularly if he was able to strike down the man who thought she should have someone to "ride at her side".

She knew Theudemir had not intended her to hear his comment about her lack of voice. Nor had he or Yosef known she was in the stables with Hera when they were speaking. It was not her custom to listen at doorways, and had she not caught her gown on a wall sconce in the stable, she never would have heard Theudemir speak. She could have made her presence known, just as she could have refrained from following the pair when they walked together back to the villa. Above all, she could have told Theudemir who she was when they met unexpectedly on the road.

But she did not regret it. Lælia felt again her fierce triumph at Theudemir's shock when he realised that the tribe girl he had met on the road was in fact the heiress he was intended to marry.

Lælia could not have said why, after she realised who he was, she had chosen to continue the pretence other than that something visceral within her could not bear to be served up to her future husband like a richly decorated side of venison, dressed and presented for his future delectation. She knew the duty she owed Illiberis. Understood that a betrothal – or at least the appearance of one – was the only sure safeguard against an ambitious prince, even a bastard one, particularly if he contrived to take her by force. Should a woman be ravaged, her family either negotiated marriage or went to war. Her grandfather had spent the first decades of his life wielding a sword so Spania could know peace. He would not now risk that peace by taking up sword against his king, even if Lælia knew he had no liking for Egica, the man who now sat beneath the votive crown.

Understanding all of that, however, did not make her any more well disposed toward the man who was to play the role of her protector. *Particularly*, she scowled, as Titus's hooves clattered hollowly over the narrow bridge before the abbey, *when that man seems* to think I require his protection not only in name but in all things, whilst he is free to go where he will no matter the dangers that await.

She recalled the barely suppressed excitement in their voices as Theudemir and Yosef had spoken of their shared mission, resentment and envy churning her stomach. The fact that her oldest friend had clearly taken to Theudemir on sight had helped matters not at all. Accustomed to Yosef being her loyal companion since childhood, she did not enjoy the sensation of being on the outside of his adventures. Particularly when the person who had replaced her was Theudemir – whom Yosef had already begun to call 'Theo', an intimacy Lælia found oddly irritating. The fact that Theudemir had chosen not to betray her confidence only served to annoy her more.

I would prefer it, she thought sourly, if he had chastised me publicly. Then, at least, she could have spared herself the vague, unsettling guilt that she felt at her deception in not signing the contract. Worse, she had the sneaking suspicion Theo had found her act of rebellion amusing rather than hostile. Being an object of amusement for her future husband was not something Lælia had ever pictured. In her mind, she would rule Illiberis with an iron hand, her husband a consort of whom the less seen the better. In none of her imaginings did her husband look at her with mocking green eyes that seemed to see straight through the blank silence that usually cowed newcomers into an embarrassed stuttering.

It would have helped if someone had told me she does not speak.

Her inability to speak, she suspected, had not concerned Theudemir of Aurariola at all, and that realisation did nothing to improve her opinion of him.

She nudged Titus hard. The horse grunted his protest but obeyed her urgings, so that when they arrived at the abbey, the horse's flanks were heaving and steaming with sweat. Lælia was unsurprised to find Acantha outside and waiting for her, still and silent beneath the first pinpricks in the indigo sky. Her grandmother reached for Titus without greeting Lælia. Rubbing him down, she led him into a small yard adjacent to the stone building and closed the rail.

Always, gestured Lælia, the horses first. Her hands felt uncharacteristically clumsy, her face hot and angry.

"Was it you who walked those hard miles uphill to come here?" Acantha countered. She clicked her tongue at Titus's heavy breathing and cast her granddaughter a silent glance of reproach. Sensing an ally, the horse rolled his eye at her, nudging her waist. Acantha found an apple core, and velvety lips plucked it from her outstretched palm, bringing a soft smile to her face. She made a low noise in her throat, and the horse turned and drank. When she looked back at Lælia, the smile was gone, her face set into its customary remote lines.

Always a smile for the horses.

Lælia did not gesture her thoughts. There was no need to; Acantha, eyeing her, said, "You did not ride here for my smiles." She held open the wooden door, and Lælia entered.

The abbey was a humble building. Any who came across it would think it a remote outpost, housing a few women at best. It was no more than four rooms with an external chapel. The room they stood in now was low beamed with a clean-swept stone floor and narrow slits for windows. It was dark and cold and smelled of myrrh, sweat, and hollow prayers. At the rear end, there was an alcove in which sat a reliquary. Behind it, a crude tapestry of the Christogram hung on the wall. Acantha pushed the chest and tapestry aside, turning a hidden latch on a low wooden door. She took a lamp from a niche in the wall, lit it, and gestured for Lælia to enter. She closed the door behind them, and there was only the low glow from the lamp to light their way.

Lælia paused, allowing her senses to adjust. She inhaled, smelling the familiar scent of the cypress oil the women of the caves always added to their lamps, mingled with the more familiar frankincense and the curiously soft scent of earth. The warmth of the underground caves swallowed her in womblike stillness, comforting after the cold stone above.

The lamps were of wrought iron and cast strange, curlicued patterns across the earthen walls. Lælia followed Acantha through the familiar passageways deeper into the mountain, the sound of rushing water coming closer. The path divided, and they climbed up a narrow set of stairs cut into the rock, then passed through the small opening and went down to where water poured from the rock into an underground pool.

Overhead, an opening in the cave showed stars above. The water smelled wild and fresh. Offerings had been placed by it. Lælia smiled at the sight, though it was bittersweet. She remembered creating offerings when she was a child, Acantha's strong, rough hands guiding her own. How she had laboured over the arrangements, gathering flowers, seeds, and fruit, placing them in a pottery bowl and creating ever more elaborate confections as she made her silent wishes beneath the moon.

The gods did not tell me the price I would pay for those wishes, Lælia thought bitterly. *I will rule Illiberis in a fashion.* She touched the amulet at her throat. *But not as I dreamed. Not at all as I wished back then.*

"I remember all of the wishes made here," said Acantha, as if Lælia had spoken her thoughts aloud. "And all those who made them."

She looked from the offerings to Lælia. "It is a place full of memories. I do not come here often." She sat on the rock, straight backed and tall despite her years.

Why did you let them betroth me to Theudemir?

Lælia had intended to wait, to ask the question with more dexterity, but the caves stripped her of dissemination, laying her soul as raw as the stone around them. She did not try to hide the surge of pain and anger when she looked at Acantha. It would not have helped if she did. Acantha had the gift of seeing through any subterfuge. It was one of the many things that made her company so difficult to bear: the critical weight of her deep golden gaze.

"You must marry, Lælia." Acantha sat quietly.

Already stirred, Lælia found herself goaded by the older woman's impassivity, wanting to provoke a response other than the carefully trained restraint that she knew too well was Acantha's favourite shield. It had been Acantha who had once taught Lælia to use her hands to speak, and between them lay an ease of communication she did not share with many others. With Acantha, she could express the more complex emotions she must keep hidden from others. She took advantage of that now, her hands flying rapidly in the dim light.

You train me in bow and sword until I bleed and insist I learn to track an ailing mare in the dark of the moon. Yet you will not take me to the deep caves where the women of Illiberis should go at my age, and you order me to marry with the same arrogant expectation as Grandfather, though you do not live as his wife nor by the rules you expect me to follow.

Faced by Acantha's impassivity, Lælia hit the rock with a flat hand, making a dull slap, which reverberated in the earth. *You wish me to be like Riccilo: the wife of a great man, in a fine gown at court in Tole-tum, her only connection to Illiberis a serpent torc, the power of which she does not even understand.*

"Do not judge Riccilo. You would do well to learn from her."

Lælia gripped the ridge of stone beside her so hard it cut into her palms. *I do not want to learn the skills she has. I want to learn how to rule Illiberis — and how to defend it.*

Acantha leaned forward. Her long, dark hair, marked by only one streak of silver despite her years, curtained her face. She trailed her fingers beneath the tumbling water. It glistened in the starlight from above, spraying a fine mist over the offerings on the rock. She met her granddaughter's eyes.

"All learning begins with sacrifice, and women must master the art of sacrifice early. Do not judge another woman for what you have yet to suffer. And do not think you will not suffer, Lælia. Women learn joy at the altar of suffering and sacrifice. You have lived many hours of joy and freedom. Do not be so foolish as to believe that such moments constitute a life. That you think they do shows that you have yet to live the shadow by which their light can be clearly seen."

Lælia's hands flashed defiantly. *You do not live the life Riccilo does at court — not even that of the Countess of Illiberis. You live here, amongst the tribes and on your own terms.*

"Yes, Lælia. I do." Impatience tinged her tone. "But you know nothing of what led me to this life, nor what it means to live as I do. Even should you come to this point, I would not wish the same choice for you."

Acantha stood, moving restlessly and not looking at Lælia. "This is a dying life, a world fading beneath crosses and priests. One better forgotten than taught anew. Riccilo understands that. Callista understood it."

The rare reference to her mother stilled Lælia's hands. She would have asked more, but her grandmother's hard expression forbade further question.

"You want to become a warrior," said Acantha harshly. "You think that tracking animals beneath a dark moon, or seeing a vision in a cave, will teach what you need to win the battles the world will send to your door. You do not see that for women, battlegrounds come disguised as harmless things such as love or a betrothal. It is our job to walk onto every one of those battlefields, Lælia, and learn the skills we must in order to survive."

I choose my own battlefields. Her hands seemed to move without her bidding. *And I do not play games.*

Acantha's mouth twisted. "The games will come to you whether you wish them or not," she said. "Learn to play them, or you will find yourself on battlefields where you cannot win.

"I can teach you many things. Some I already have. Others, you are not yet ready to understand. Perhaps, when you have found the courage to face the challenges life already offers you, we might discuss again the great deeds you think yourself destined to accomplish."

She turned stern eyes on her granddaughter. "But for now, you will sign the contract of betrothal. You will find a way to communicate with Theudemir of Aurariola, and you will give him no reason to worry for you when he must sail from here to face unknown wars. And when your grandfather bids you join Riccilo in Toletum to learn the ways of the women at court, you will don a gown and face the women there with your head held high and a smile on your face. You will show all who look at you that the women of our family fear nothing this world can bring them. Do I make myself clear, Lælia of Illiberis?"

Pinned beneath her grandmother's unrelenting stare, Lælia cut one hand through the air in a reluctant gesture. *Yes.*

"Very well." Acantha walked to the path leading back to up to the church. "If you ride quickly, you can return to meat before your absence is noticed."

6

THEO

DECEMBER AD 687

Illiberis, Bætica, Spania
Granada, Andalusia, Spain

Oppa had sent men ahead of his party to ensure all was in order for their arrival. Fráuja Frogellus, who held lands near to Illiberis, headed the party. Though a count in his own right, he was a coarse Goth with little breeding and even fewer manners. He and his men were trying out horses. Lælia sat on the post-and-rail fence in the morning sun, watching. Theo, a dozen paces away, watched Lælia.

"I like this one." Frogellus stroked the neck of Titus, the large, dark bay horse Theo remembered Lælia riding the day he met her. Titus stood placidly beneath Frogellus's hand, tail swishing away the flies. "But would it stand in a fight?" he added for the benefit of his men. "This animal is so calm I wonder if it will run at the first sign of battle."

His men guffawed. From the corner of his eye, Theo saw Lælia tense.

"*Ja*, let's see, then," said Frogellus. He swung himself up onto the horse. Titus stayed still whilst he mounted, only grunting softly as his bulk landed with a heavy slap in the saddle. Frogellus reined the horse to the far corner of the yard and began putting it through its paces. Like all the Illiberis breed, Titus could turn on a silver coin, obeying the slightest hint of pressure from knee or hand. Theo had never seen horses of the like. He understood now why men came from across the sea to purchase them. Though strong and wide in the haunches and steady on their feet, it wasn't only for their mountain hardiness they were so prized; the horses were also uncannily intuitive. Theo watched now as Titus, anticipating Frogellus's command, sank the left shoulder and pivoted smoothly in a hook turn, springing straight back to the gallop, then stopping abruptly at the slightest shift of body weight.

The watching men clapped admiringly.

But it isn't the rider who deserves the applause, Theo thought. Titus glanced over at the fence, and for a moment Theo could have sworn the horse looked directly at Lælia for approval, just as a child would after performing for its parents.

Riding back to them, Frogellus was frowning and shaking his head. "It obeys orders well enough," he said. "But a man doesn't need an obedient horse on a battlefield. He needs a warrior. I'm not certain this one has the heart for war."

Privately, Theo thought that since Fráuja Frogellus was best known for doing all he could to avoid the battlefield, his concerns seemed unimportant at best. Watching his own father train men, however, had taught Theo that the more a man feared something, the more he wished to appear master of it. The bay had none of the dancing, prancing fire of horses of battle legend, though Theo himself knew that such animals were of little use in the chaos of battle. His father had always told him that the best warhorse was one that could stay its feet all day and stand still when all about it was mayhem.

"Hm. Quiet, isn't it?" Turning his back on Lælia, Frogellus added, "A common thing around here, it seems, being quiet."

His men chuckled. It appeared that despite some time in Lælia's company, they had still to distinguish between an inability to speak and the faculty of hearing.

Theo tensed. He felt the light restraint of Shukra's hand on his arm. "No, *aziz-am*," murmured the little Persian. "Not yet."

He nodded imperceptibly at Lælia, who sat stony faced. Not by a blink did she indicate she had heard the insult. But Theo, who had begun to notice the small signs of emotion others seemed to miss, saw an infinitesimal narrowing of her eyes. He wanted to reach out to her, but there was a certain pride in the tilt of her head that forbade sympathy.

Frogellus was about to dismount when Lælia raised her hand to her mouth and coughed. At least, it seemed like a cough, but Theo, watching her, saw that her eyes didn't close at all, and the sound that came from behind her forearm was more of a growl, a low, menacing sound that carried on the clear morning air like an angry wasp.

Had Theo not been sitting only feet from her, he doubted he would have heard it at all. But the horse certainly did. Dark ears flicked back, flattening against his head. With a fierce squeal of rage, Titus reared high; coming down, his neck snaked out and he streaked across the yard, carrying the hapless Frogellus straight to the far fence where he reared again, hooves striking out at the men who stood watching. As they scrambled through the railings, he turned and galloped back, scattering Frogellus's men into the dirt, teeth bared and gnashing at the seat of their tunics as they leaped for safety. When Titus reared a final time, Frogellus lost his hold and fell into the dust.

A low sound, like water tumbling through rocks, came from Lælia's bowed head. The horse stopped as abruptly as it had begun. Lowering his head, Titus snuffled Frogellus's tunic curiously, as if searching for a treat. Frogellus, lying winded in the dirt, raised a fist and cuffed the horse angrily on the nose. Titus jerked his head up and looked at the man in wounded affront. He rolled an eye at Lælia as if to say, thought Theo, stifling a grin, "What did I do wrong?"

"*Tyr jah Fairguneis!*" Swearing in Gothic, Frogellus clambered inelegantly to his feet and glowered at the now peaceful animal, brushing dirt from his tunic as he did so. His men eyed Titus warily. Theo, glancing at Lælia, tried not to laugh at the serene expression of innocence on her face. Yosef, who had come to stand beside him, ducked his head to hide his smile.

"*Jus auk Satana!*" Frogellus swore again.

"Well, Satan is what is required on the field of battle, is he not?" called Theo. "A worthy animal to carry you onto the field, Fráuja, *ne?*"

Frogellus spat into the dirt and looked balefully at the horse. "And what is the meaning of the mark on its flank?" He gestured angrily at the brand all the Illiberis horses bore. It was a replica of the one on the stone pillars at the entrance to the villa: a straight line overlayed by two entwined serpents making two full circles and half a third, which remained open like a cup with the line bisecting it. "Even the brand has an evil look," he snarled.

Lælia glanced at a small, dark, wiry tribesman standing by the fence, who stepped forward and bowed to Frogellus.

"The brand of Illiberis has remained unchanged for many mothers," he said. His Latin was heavily accented. Theo noticed he looked away from Frogellus as he spoke. His voice was soft and chirruping, like a bird call. The horse stood still when he began speaking, watching the little man with a curiously intelligent eye, as if it understood perfectly what was being said.

"Many mothers?" Frogellus repeated, mocking his accent.

Theo frowned. "He means many years," he said. "Many generations."

"Well, *thank you*, Fráuja," said Frogellus sarcastically, managing to make the Gothic honorific sound like an insult. "But I asked what the brand meant, not its age."

"This" – the little man crouched in the dirt and drew a line – "is staff of shepherd and mark of messenger Hermes, who sees all trades between men. This" – he drew the two serpents – "is earth mother, Nin, the Lady, who is living beneath us and giving us her milk." He pointed at the finished mark. "So Illiberis horse is protected by the gods, traded by men in honest exchange, and is also best, because has Mother Earth milk inside." He looked up at Lælia, who nodded once, briefly, granting the little man a small smile.

Frogellus hawked and spat. His men crossed themselves.

"Bloody heretic tribesmen." Frogellus glared at him, then shifted his eyes to Lælia. Theo tensed as Frogellus's gaze roamed over her body. "I hear," he said, leering unpleasantly, "that horses aren't the only thing the king's bastard comes to buy."

Lælia returned the scrutiny with a blank yellow stare.

"*Baguadae!* Bandits!" called one of the men in warning, looking uneasily across the yard. Some more tribesmen had silently materialised, wearing bows slung over their backs and knives at their hips. Frogellus and his men frowned, reaching for their swords.

"They are not bandits." Theo leaped down from the railing, landing easily on his feet. "The Illiberis latifundium has always worked with the horse herders." He eyed Frogellus coolly. "That brand you disdain is respected from Africa to Greece. You asked for warhorses – you got them. If you have chosen those you wish to take, perhaps it is time for you to pay."

Placing himself between Frogellus and the watching tribesmen, Theo held the eyes of the nobleman steadily. "And if your master is seeking anything else in Illiberis," he said softly, "you may wish to inform him that there is nothing available. Lælia of Illiberis has been formally betrothed to me."

"*Ja?*" One of Frogellus's men, a rough, heavy-set Goth the breadth of a wall, stepped forward. "You seem very sure of yourself, pretty boy." Moving quickly for such a big man, he pulled out his *spatha* and bared his teeth at Theo in a grim smile. "Perhaps we should find out if your balls match your words, *ne?*"

Theo spun beneath his arm, knocking the spatha to the ground as he kicked the man's legs out, sending him sprawling to the ground in an undignified tangle of limbs. He came up to find

Frogellus reaching for his own blade. Before he could draw it, however, a blur of movement shifted the air.

Shukra had flipped neatly from his perch on the railing over the heads of those below and landed on the mounting block behind Frogellus, from whom he had somehow taken not only the blade Frogellus had reached for but his short spatha, too.

Frogellus's head was back. Shukra, crouched like a cat on the top of the mounting block, held a third knife to his throat. It was so sharp that a thin line of crimson was clearly visible beneath the steel edge. Frogellus's eyes, wide with shock, looked frantically around as he searched for his attacker.

"I am thinking that even in this barbarous land," said Shukra conversationally, "it is being bad manners to draw a sword on your host's grounds."

Shukra was speaking in a low tone, but his voice carried, nonetheless, to the furthest corners of the drill ground. The eyes of Frogellus's men shifted uneasily between Shukra and Theo, calculating the odds.

"I wouldn't advise it," said Theo coldly. "Not if you wish to chew your meat tonight."

"Let me go," hissed Frogellus, eyes rolling to either side in an attempt to glimpse his attacker. "You will pay for this."

"I am not certain I will," said Shukra carelessly, his knife caressing Frogellus's throat. "You see, in my country – which, I must inform, would not tolerate one of its citizens to wear such terrible clothing, but no matter – in my country, you would be having at least one hand cutting off for such behaviour." Shukra tilted his head to one side and looked about him, as if assessing Frogellus's men. "But I see that perhaps peoples here are more desperate, and so it is possible the law is different." He turned to Theo and raised one eyebrow in silent query.

"That's enough," said Theo, grinning at Shukra's antics. "Stop showing off."

Twirling the knives between his fingers with lightning speed, Shukra slid them both back into Frogellus's belt, then neatly vaulted from the block, landing with his own knife having somehow disappeared into the folds of his cloak.

Theo turned back to Frogellus. "And you, Fráuja," he said quietly, "should know better than to draw a knife on another man's ground. Consider yourself fortunate Count Paulus did not witness your disrespect to his granddaughter."

For a moment, Frogellus looked as if he might argue, then his eyes shifted to Shukra and he scowled. "You are a foreigner," he said, as if that lone sentence contained all the evidence needed for condemnation.

"Ah." Shukra made an elaborate bow, involving a great deal of flourishing hands and exaggerated depth. "Forgive me. We have not yet, I think, been formally introduced. Shukra Arshad Farzani. Originally of the great state of Ērān, more recently of Constantinople, and even most recently *topotērētēs* to Apsimar, *droungarios* of the Cibyrrhaeot fleet, known now as the Karabisianoi. Which, I am most certain to explain to you, is less of an honour than it sounds."

Frogellus stared at him in dumb confusion. Finally, feigning indifference, he sneered and turned away. "Fetch the man here who takes coin," he called rudely. "I won't hand it to a tribesman."

Once the deal had been completed, Theo turned to find Lælia, but she had already gone. A tribesman in the stables informed him that Lælia had left to ride into the hills. Mounting his horse, he cantered after her.

The sun shone brighter than any he had seen, far more so even than at his family's villa at Aurariola, by the eastern coast. Theo loved Aurariola, loved the rolling fields of barley and the sharp tang of sea salt coming over the cliffs. But there was a wildness to Illiberis, he thought, that cast a spell. The mountains around it were fierce and steep and covered in snow despite the warmth on his face; Theo had heard from the servants that even in high summer fragments of white remained on the peaks. They folded around the small valley like a protective mantle. *Or a rugged fortress,* Theo thought, *as if they repel unwary visitors, and hold Illiberis like a secret land.*

He allowed the horse its head. It was one of the Illiberis breed, a gift from Count Paulus and a delight to ride. It seemed to know the path, and Theo was content to let it climb, enjoying the sun on his face and the peace after the crude company of Frogellus and his men.

Eventually he came out on a plateau. The grass was short and rich here: good grazing. Ibex clung in shadows to the surrounding hillsides, feeding on the brilliant-coloured rock rose that grew there. On the far slope by a stand of scrawny holm oak, he saw Lælia. Dismounting, he drew the horse behind some granite boulders and watched her. She was standing with her hands out. He thought she might have been making some kind of noise, though he could not hear it from this distance.

A herd of horses grazed on a nearby slope. They began to slowly move toward her, drawn by whatever she was doing. One in particular stood still, watching her, head up. It was a tall, midnight-black horse with a long mane and tail. By the large chest and wide head, Theo recognised it as a stallion – the head of the herd.

It approached Lælia cautiously, stepping to the front and whickering a warning at the others to remain behind. It approached with a tossing head and short whinnies, rearing slightly and turning away, then snorting and coming closer to the slender figure who stood very still, hands out, palms flat and pointing to the ground.

It came on until Theo tensed. The stallion was huge, he realised; he had not seen its size until it stood before Lælia. By comparison she seemed very small indeed, vulnerable next to the wild animal. He began to move. Then Lælia lifted her right hand to hip height and made a gesture for quiet, like water rolling over rocks. The stallion tossed its head, then lowered it. She made the gesture again, and the head dropped to the ground, swaying from side to side. One last movement of her hand and, to Theo's astonishment, the stallion dropped first to its knees, then onto its side, lying comfortably on the grass at Lælia's feet.

Coming down to the grass herself, Lælia curled into the horse's belly and laid her head on its shoulder. Reaching over, the stallion nuzzled her once, then began nibbling at the grass contentedly. Horse and girl sat in companionable stillness, Lælia chewing a stem of grass.

Theo watched them for a long time. He knew he should move, should make her aware of his presence, but there was something so peaceful in her lying there with the horse that he felt like an intruder. So he lay on his belly with the sun on his back and watched in silence as the herd of horses grazed around the girl lying on the large stallion in the middle of the pasture.

He had lain for some time when a sudden cry cut through the peaceful stillness. Lælia leaped to her feet, the stallion standing behind her, ears up and alert. A group of boys were coming down the slope toward her. They were roughly clad and looked like Illiberis townsfolk from their shabby appearance and dirty tangles of blond hair. They carried a brace of wild birds tied to a stick, having obviously been hunting.

"Ha! The *heliarun*," Theo heard the leader say, speaking a coarse mixture of Latin and Gothic as they drew close to Lælia. "*Hva waurde þata?*" What is this?

Theo had barely time to register the word *heliarun* before he was on his feet. If they were calling her a witch, the mother of the Huns, nothing good could be meant. Drawing his bow, Theo shot an arrow into the air over Lælia's head. It landed in the earth between Lælia and the boys, who stared at it in surprise. Stepping out from the rocks, Theo walked over to where they stood, drawing his spatha as he came.

They watched him, eyes narrowing as he approached. "*Þu hvas is?*" Who are you?

Their language was coarse and thick, the accent that of the lowliest of his father's men.

"*Ik im Theudemir sunau Suinthila.*"

They looked at him, then at the sword in his hand. He stood in front of Lælia.

"I am a guest of Count Paulus," he said levelly, in Latin.

"*Ja?*" The tallest of the boys nodded, looking between Theo and Lælia. "Well, mind you say your prayers at night. This one mates with horses."

His friends guffawed, waiting for Theo's response. The boy's Latin, like Frogellus's, was heavy with Gothic inflection. *They could be brothers,* Theo thought, looking at him with dislike.

"You should keep moving," he said lightly. "There is more than *heliarun* in these mountains."

The smiles faded, and the boys looked around them with sudden expressions of fear. *That scares them,* Theo realised. The boys sensed magic in these hills too, but where Theo found it thrilling, they clearly feared what might lurk with the mysterious tribes and their gods. Muttering amongst themselves and shooting Theo and Lælia resentful looks, the boys walked away down the hill. Theo turned and trained his bow on them, watching until they had left. He turned back to find Lælia glaring at him.

Why did you do that? her hands asked.

Theo, who had spent quite some time in private with Yosef, learning to read her gestures, found he followed them with little difficulty.

"Because they were going to hurt you," said Theo.

I would have stopped them.

"By ordering the horse, as you did with Frogellus?"

Her eyes widened in surprise. *Maybe.*

He held her gaze. She did not look away from him. In the afternoon light, her eyes glowed like burnished bronze.

Finally, he spoke. "Why," he said gently, "didn't you sign the contract of marriage? It is done for your protection. To protect Illiberis."

She did not seem surprised by his question. Her hands moved rapidly, but Theo had no trouble discerning their meaning.

Illiberis does not need your protection. Neither do I. She glared at him. *I will do my duty if it comes to it. But never think I need your protection.*

She walked away without looking back, leaped onto her horse, and began making her way down the path. Mounting his own horse, Theo cantered to catch her up.

"What horse was that?" he asked as he came to her side. "The stallion?"

She didn't look at him, but her hand drew a line in the air, the same as the one the tribesman had drawn in the dirt earlier.

"Hermes?" he guessed.

She nodded. *Always there is one stallion,* her hands said. *One Hermes. He guards the herd. The foals born of Hermes are our finest horses.* She glanced sideways at Theo. *This year there is only one mare carrying his foals.*

"Only one foal?"

Lælia frowned and shook her head. *One mare. Two foals.*

"That's impossible," said Theo flatly.

Lælia shrugged and looked away. Theo wished he'd said something different.

They rode in silence for a short while. Theo could hear the sound of the river coming closer, smell the fresh tumble of water on the air. He did not realise he was humming under his breath until she turned sharply to face him.

That tune. How do you know it?

Theo coloured. "My brothers tell me I do it often," he admitted. "In truth, I do not even know what it is."

She gave him a searching look, then turned away. Theo had the feeling there was more behind her question, but when her hands moved again, they formed quite a different one: *Is this how people marry?* She gestured with a sudden savagery that took Theo by surprise. Her smile was gone, face closed over again. He wondered if he had misunderstood.

The hands moved quickly again. *A contract? Like* – her hand spiralled in the air – *selling a horse?*

"No," said Theo slowly. "There are – other things."

Other things like what?

Theo cleared his throat. "Well," he said, awkwardly. "Like a... a promise, for example."

What kind of promise? The hand gesture for promise was curiously intimate; Lælia's hand lay over her heart, her shoulders slightly forward. It touched Theo, as if the gesture came from deep inside her.

"It is usually made with a ring," he said. Then, flushing, "And with a kiss."

She turned to him, eyes a burnished challenge. *Well,* said her hands. *It's a good thing I'm not marrying you, then, isn't it?* And, laughing silently at his discomfort, she nudged her horse and sped away into the afternoon light.

7

OPPA

DECEMBER AD 687

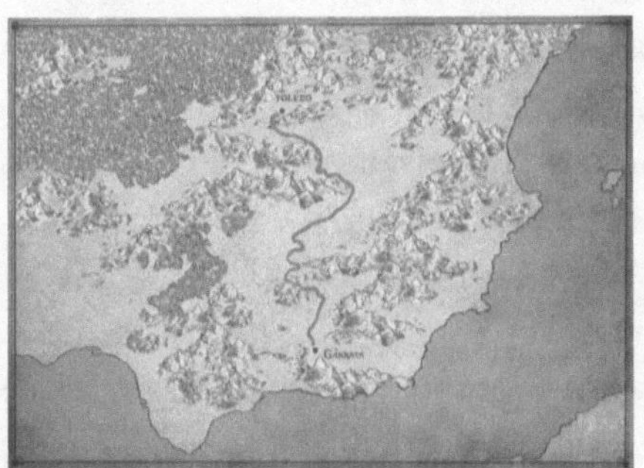

Illiberis, Bætica, Spania
Granada, Andalusia, Spain

They had ridden through nothing but mountains for days now. Oppa failed to see the necessity of visiting such land.

Strange peaks thrust from the ground in red crags, dotted here and there with the low, round mud huts of the tribespeople. Lone birds of prey wheeled high above in a vivid blue sky. Horned ibex grazed on improbable perches on the mountainside.

Occasionally, a flash of yellow revealed a lynx watching from higher ground.

Oppa's father had explained the strategic importance of Illiberis and the power wielded by its count, but travelling through the hostile wilderness that separated Illiberis from civilisation, Oppa was inclined to think Count Paulus best left to the horse breeding he was famous for.

It was not only the slow pace of the clergymen that Oppa resented as he eyed the sombre procession behind him, but the restriction they placed upon his activities. King Egica's bastard was accustomed to playing the part of dutiful priest by day. By night, however, his mother's brothel by the river in Toletum offered the opportunity for a man of Oppa's particular talents to buy both information and secrets. Oppa preferred the latter to the former. Information could be bought by the highest bidder. Secrets, however, forced men to do things they could not imagine themselves capable of. Oppa enjoyed helping people discover the new horizons that fear forced them to reach for. The study of fear was his greatest pleasure, and though he was not yet eighteen, Oppa had learned there was little more delicious than witnessing a soul stretched tremulously between fear and hope.

The two companions who rode beside him at the head of the procession were sons of men from his father's *gardingi*: Nicalo sunau Count Vitulo and Ataulfo sunau Count Gisclamundo. The gardingi were the king's personal guard, his most loyal companions, and their sons were amongst the elite of the Toletum nobility. They, too, had grown tired of such sombre company. Now they spurred their horses to stay at his side as Oppa moved ahead of the procession. Oppa liked to meet the future before others did.

His hair was clean cut to his shoulders and oiled back from his face. Nicalo and Ataulfo both wore theirs long with beaded braids at either side. The straggling beards they had grown on the long ride south made Oppa doubly determined to remain clean shaven. Even after weeks in the saddle, his robes were spotless and fell in neat folds. Oppa despised anything unkempt in his appearance.

Both of Oppa's companions were thickset and heavy, unlike Oppa himself, who was lean and tall with straight, dark hair and flat black eyes that missed little. They were easy to have around, Oppa reflected, glancing at Nicalo and Ataulfo. It was why they remained his servants. They cost no more than the odd coin, and he had long ago fooled them both into thinking it was he who conferred privilege upon them by his friendship. Neither had the brains to recognise the reality: that it was Oppa, the bastard product of a whore and a beggar lord, who needed *their* patronage. Now, though, the beggar lord had become king. And there was nothing – *nothing* – Oppa would not do to keep his father in that position. Oppa was now a prince. And his ambitions did not end at princeling status, even if the fat bitch his father had married in order to gain his throne had recently whelped a legitimate son.

There were, Oppa reflected as they approached Illiberis, many ways for a man to rule. A throne was but one of them. And whilst Oppa craved his father's approval with a fierce, though well-hidden, ache, he craved power even more.

Oppa knew what it was to be born an afterthought, something society could cast off. His had been a childhood of service, of discovering how he could serve his father's cause and making himself indispensable to that end. His reward had been to rise from the gutter and from his mother's fearful, sordid existence to become his father's shadow at court. Now he intended to create his own power base. One that not only bolstered his father's rule, but rather upon which that rule was dependent. Only then, when his father's reign lay entirely in the power of the son whose origins Egica never quite let him forget, would Oppa know himself bastard no more.

Such meditations aroused him in a way no woman could, and he thought with dark pleasure of the township that lay ahead. Oppa rarely took a woman, but tonight, he promised himself, would be one of the times he did. He touched the whip at his side with unconscious longing.

They crossed the bridge at last.

If one could call it a bridge, Oppa thought, sneering slightly at its meagre proportions. He thought of the great expanses over the rivers at the southern cities of Corduba and Hispalis, to which he unfavourably compared the small fortress and arch they rode beneath to cross the narrow rush of water that flowed from the mountains above.

"This bridge was built by old King Chindasuinth himself, or upon his orders, at least." A member of the thiufa his father had sent to accompany his son and the priests on their journey rode up beside him, reaching out to touch the stone arch as they passed beneath it. "It is said that when the local people saw them building it, they believed at last that the Goths were deserving conquerors, for they knew the secrets of stone as the Romans had before them and which the tribespeople do not."

Oppa feigned interest, but privately he thought his forebears would have been better served killing all the native inhabitants. The tribespeople had harassed them the entire way from Hispalis, begging coin from their camp and stealing food under cover of darkness if they didn't receive it. The men of the thiufa called them *baguadae*. Oppa agreed: tribespeople were ignorant criminals with no faith. Their shrines to innumerable gods were littered through the mountains, standing on large rocks, nestled at watering places, and covered in moss at the foot of trees. For once, Oppa thought Archbishop Julian had the right of it – Mater Spania could not truly advance whilst the savages beyond her cities insisted on displeasing God with their pagan practices.

"Does crossing this bridge mean I can finally piss safely in the trees?"

The guard grinned at Oppa's question. They had all grown tired of the lack of privacy, but after one of the thiufa had gone to relieve himself and been found with his throat cut and purse gone, the order had been given to remain close. Oppa had found the restrictions on his activities tiresome. One of the benefits of growing up a bastard was a certain freedom of movement; it was anathema to him to be so closely watched at every moment.

Now he nodded at his companions, and the trio peeled off from the slow procession and rode into the trees by the river, below the walls of the town.

The noise of the river and the procession faded in the forest. Tall trees whispered softly overhead. The light here was dim, and Oppa squinted to rid his eyes of sun blindness.

To his left, there was a sudden movement. He whirled, knife at the ready, but it was only a loose horse. Saddled and bridled, it had clearly wandered off from wherever it had been tethered.

"Aren't you fine," said Oppa as he took its reins, admiring the elegant lines and proud head carriage. "What are you doing all alone, wandering in the forest?"

"Being stolen, looks like." Nicalo pointed at the slender figure who had materialised from behind a rock.

It was a girl, Oppa saw with a sudden stab of interest. Oppa had particular tastes, and none of them could be indulged in the close company of a party of priests. Now here he was, isolated in the woods, and God had seen fit to place in his path one who fit those tastes exactly.

She was young, but slender and quite tall, and clearly a daughter of the local tribes, going by her wild mass of black curls and strange yellow eyes. Her tunic was of better cloth than the usual rags worn by the tribes, but then they were close to the town of Illiberis, and Oppa supposed the pickings to be richer.

She made a brief gesture with her hand, indicating the horse and then herself, as if to claim possession.

"I don't think it likely," murmured Oppa, eyeing her lithe form keenly. "It is a fine animal. Whoever lost it will want it back. One less prize for the tribes today, *dulcissima.*"

The girl's eyes narrowed. She stepped forward, reaching for the horse. Oppa caught her wrist. She jerked in his grasp, golden eyes blazing. Her free hand moved rapidly, fingers flying in the air.

"I see," said Oppa softly. "You can't speak, can you?" Eyeing her with keen interest, he handed the horse's reins to Nicalo. "I should like to discover, though, if you can scream. Do you think you can scream, *dulcissima?*"

Nicalo and Ataulfo sniggered.

"Nicalo," said Oppa mildly, "take the whip from my saddlebag." He caught her free hand in the act of reaching for the bow slung on her back and raised his eyebrows. "You truly are a savage," he said, not without admiration. "What did you hope to do with this, *dulcissima?* One little savage against three men?"

He handed her bow to Nicalo and pulled her closer, examining her face with curiosity. She stared back at him. "You aren't afraid of me, are you?" One long finger stroked her cheek. She flinched, and he smiled. "But you know what it is to fear, then," he said softly. "That is good. A good beginning.

"Ataulfo," he said, not looking away from her. "Tie the savage to a tree. Let's see how long it takes for her to find her voice."

He released her into the brute hands of Ataulfo, who breathed heavily as he tied the knots with more force than was necessary. The girl did not wince as the rope cut into her flesh, Oppa noticed. He unpinned the eagle fibula at his shoulder and slipped it into his pocket for safekeeping, then removed his robes and tunic so he stood bare chested in the glade, weighing the knotted rawhide whip in his palm. It would be a messy business, and Oppa disliked soiling his clothes.

He loved these moments: the lull before the fury began, when defiance remained and the victim had yet to understand the pain they were about to experience. Usually he could see the fear in their eyes as they realised there was no escape from what was to come, but the golden eyes that stared back at him now gave nothing away at all. *They really are most extraordinary,* Oppa thought, looking at her with interest. Like one of the great mountain cats he had passed on the way. Alert, wary, and lethal, as if at any moment she could leap from her bindings and slink into the forest. He felt the first stirrings beneath his trousers. This promised to be a rare treat, one he intended to savour.

The girl pursed her lips and made an odd noise, low in her throat.

Ataulfo had barely time to call a warning before Oppa felt heat and bulk behind him. Horse teeth sank deep into his side, clamping on his flesh hard enough to break the skin, tossing his body from side to side, then releasing him so he was flung into the undergrowth.

A sudden rush disturbed the leaves over his head, accompanied in the same instant by a yelp of pain. Turning, Oppa saw an arrow sticking from Ataulfo's shoulder. Oppa rolled to his feet and retreated, clutching his side, eyeing the horse warily and reaching for his own sword. Nicalo, arrow notched, was aiming his bow nervously at the incline from whence the shot had been fired. A moment later, he was clutching his hand in pain, bow on the ground. He gave a cry as a second stone caught him on the forehead, this time drawing blood.

Oppa crouched, sword in hand, looking about tensely, trying to ignore the agonising pain from the horse's bite.

"Let her go."

A young man stepped out from behind a boulder on the slope ahead of them. He was as tall as Oppa and clad in a scarlet military tunic Oppa vaguely recognised as belonging to an imperial force of some kind.

This was no tribesman.

Oppa's eyes narrowed as he made some quick calculations. Perhaps the girl was a slave?

"I took her as a savage," he said, lowering his sword and smiling easily. "She looked to be stealing a horse. I thought to prevent a crime, my friend." Holding up his hands, he shrugged in an affectation of innocence.

"Untie her." The young man did not lower his bow. He watched Oppa, his green eyes hard and implacable. His hands did not shake at all, and the taut muscles in his shoulder warned that the arrow, if loosed, would fly with deadly accuracy.

"Of course." Oppa nodded at Nicalo. "You heard our new friend, Nicalo. Untie his slave girl."

Nicalo rose from the ground, eyeing the white-haired young man sullenly, his eyes flickering to the horse, which seemed to eye him just as grimly as the man with the bow still trained on Oppa. He fumbled with the knots, blood dripping from his forehead. As the last one fell away, the girl whirled silently from his grasp. Reaching to her hip, she drew a long knife and cut a wicked line of crimson down Nicalo's face, taking her bow from him as she did so.

She glanced at the white-haired youth as if to judge his reaction. Her eyes were both defiant and unsure, questioning. The brief, savage flash of pride and possession on his face must have answered her; for a moment, the hard reserve was gone from her face and replaced by a small, almost shy, smile. She flitted to his side as if drawn by an unseen force.

Oppa felt a curious mixture of pain and desire low in his gut. He thought he had never craved anything as he did the hidden force between them in that moment. He knew not the nature of what he craved, only that until this moment he had not known he lacked it. Their silent exchange was like a previously unknown drink without which, once discovered, one's thirst could never be slaked.

"The bow I found," said Oppa, striving to maintain his light tone. "But the knife I did not. You are eternally surprising, *dulcissima.*"

"Do not call her that." The young man's words were sharp as a whiplash.

"Why not?" Oppa asked softly. "Do you have a special liking for your slave, friend? We could" – he smiled cruelly, goading the youth, craving his ferocity almost as much as he did the girl herself – "enjoy her together."

The green eyes narrowed. They stared at Oppa with a cold contempt that drove the smile from his face and sent an odd shiver through his skin.

The girl had come to stand at his side. Her arrow was trained on Oppa.

"I suggest you leave," said the man, his tone low and deadly. "Whilst you still can." He smiled without humour. "If she looses her arrow, you will die. I assure you, she does not miss."

Nicalo, who had taken shelter behind a boulder, had another arrow notched. Ataulfo, although wincing, had drawn steel. Oppa fingered his whip. "You are alone," he said softly. "And your slave girl will be cut down in seconds. I doubt you are in any position to make such threats, my friend."

He had barely finished speaking when another stone, larger than the one that had hit Nicalo, struck Oppa full on his temple. Blood spurted from the wound. It was by sheer force of will that Oppa remained upright.

"He is not alone."

The second voice came from his right, and when his eyes cleared, Oppa looked up to see a second youth, dark and sloe eyed, staring at him with active dislike. He had another stone drawn in his slingshot and was much of a height with Oppa himself. There was in his appearance something oddly familiar; Oppa, recalling the textile merchants in Toletum, realised what it was.

"You are bold for a Jew, my friend," he said softly. "The king has little liking for your people."

"I am not familiar with your king," said the Jew. "But I have lived my whole life in the province of Count Paulus of Illiberis, and I know well that he has little liking for those who attack young girls."

"Lælia." The white-haired youth stared grimly at Oppa as he spoke. "If you wish to put your arrow through him, Yosef and I will not stop you." He looked briefly at the girl at his side. The sun through the leaves lit her face and, for a moment, showed a warm glow in the golden eyes that made Oppa's stomach twist painfully. A smile tilted the corners of her mouth. She made a brief gesture with her hand: *no*. Then she made a faint noise in the back of her throat, and the horse that had so recently attacked Oppa returned placidly to her side.

"Turn around," said her companion coldly, all trace of levity gone. He had the girl tucked safely behind him now, his body shielding hers from Oppa's eyes. The horse stood beside them, eyeing Oppa with an awareness he found unnerving. "Mount your horses and leave." His bow was trained directly on Oppa's throat, fingers tensed. For a moment, Oppa thought he would let the arrow fly, and he flinched despite himself.

The young man's lips curled in contempt. "Go," he said.

Oppa's eyes hardened. "I think not," he said silkily. Behind him, Ataulfo's hands tensed on his sword. "I have more men not far behind. I can summon them."

"That, *aziz-am*, may not be advisable."

Oppa swung around to find a slight, olive-skinned man standing barely a pace behind him. He wore the same tunic as the white-haired youth, but it was clear from the gold stitching and elaborate embroidery on his cloak that he held the kind of rank not easily dismissed. He spun a blade in his fingers as he watched Oppa. He twirled it with rapid dexterity, the sharp edge gleaming where the light caught it.

"The road to Illiberis is dangerous." The blade flowed over his slender fingers like liquid. Brown eyes did not move from Oppa's face. "The horse herders, you are understanding, *aziz-am*, depend upon the Count of Illiberis for their livelihood. They guard the road carefully to ensure no harm comes to those he considers guests."

For a moment the blade paused. The brown eyes seemed to look in every direction at once, and there was an unsettling, lethal menace in the man's stillness. "They also ensure that none pass who may wish to cause harm. I find myself wondering, Oppa sunau Egica, what the horse herders may make of you, but I am thinking that perhaps it is best if we do not give them an opportunity to consider the question."

His eyes did not move, but his fingers flickered in the air and the blade sang past Oppa's face so close it whispered against his skin, to land, quivering, in the trunk of a tree behind him. Involuntarily Oppa ducked, then swung back, furious to have been taken unaware.

"How do you know my name?"

"I make it my business to know such things; and the horse herders are very observant, I find. I am thinking," said the little man softly, "that it is better if you leave these woods. Better, too, that none should hear a word of this meeting. Perhaps you came across a misunderstanding in the shadows, a trick of the light. Nothing serious, something for laughter, if at all."

He gave Oppa a brief, hard stare. "There are more eyes watching than you have swords, my friend. I advise you remember that – in all you do whilst in Illiberis."

He moved backward, seeming to melt into the shadows of the trees. The white-haired youth stared at Oppa down his drawn arrow; his look was cold and implacable.

"Do not forget the eyes upon you," came the lilting voice from somewhere Oppa could not see. "You may not see them, but they are there."

Humiliation curdled in Oppa's gut like sour milk. For a moment, he considered raising the alarm, but the force amongst the trees was unknown, had the advantage of higher ground, and had been proven to possess deadly shots.

With no small effort, he relaxed his face into its customary easy smile. He had learned long ago the trick of giving men the mask with which they felt most comfortable.

"Nicalo," he called cheerfully, deliberately turning his back on the icy stare. "We have been in this accursed province for less than a day. Already Ataulfo wears an arrow and we have insulted the locals. Come. There must be a tavern serving decent wine somewhere in this wilderness. Perhaps our new friends will join us for a cup, and we can begin again."

He turned back, smiling with the casual confidence of rank and privilege, but it was a wasted effort. The two youths and the girl had gone. The easy smile disappeared from Oppa's face. "Where are they?" he snarled.

Nicalo, recoiling from his fury, pointed over the rise. Oppa pushed past him and took the hill in a dozen long strides. Over the crest, the trees gave way to a plain, and in the distance, he could see the outlying buildings of a large villa.

Three figures rode toward it. Between the two young men who had confronted him rode the girl with the tangled mass of midnight-black curls. Her horse drew closer to the man with white hair, which gleamed like metal beneath the southern sun. The man turned to her and said something that made her toss her head as if to dismiss his words.

But as Oppa watched, a slender hand reached out, and her companion captured it securely in his own so she rode hard up against him. He leaned toward her, then threw his head back, laughing at something she did with her free hand. When she turned toward him, Oppa saw her face glow in a way that made his heart clench with longing. They rode like that toward the villa, and Oppa watched them go, his belly churning sick with jealousy.

8

YOSEF

DECEMBER AD 687

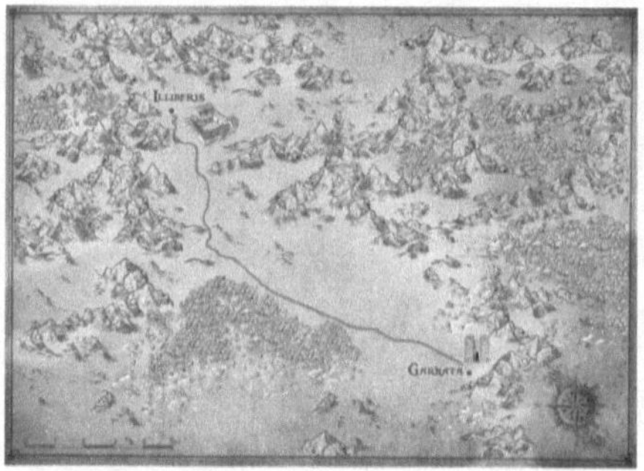

Garnata, Bœtica, Spania
Granada, Andalusia, Spain

Count Paulus's face was as lined and weathered as mountain granite, and at the mention of Oppa's identity, it closed over with the same grim implacability.

"You are certain?" he asked Shukra.

The little man nodded. "The tribesmen are hearing him addressed as such, and the man himself is not correcting me."

Paulus nodded curtly at Yosef.

"I will not risk your life, Yosef, nor will I risk your father's. You will return to Garnata tonight and remain out of sight for the duration of Oppa's visit. The rest of you" – he glared around at Theo, Lælia, and Shukra – "will not speak of this to anyone. You will meet Oppa as if nothing had happened. With luck, he, too, will see discretion as the better part of wisdom."

Neither Lælia nor Theo seemed remotely chastened by Count Paulus's ire. Yosef was aware of a subtle shift in the current between the two. Theo, he thought wryly, had been better served by Oppa's attack than the king's bastard would ever know. Yosef had never seen Lælia look at anyone as she had at Theo that afternoon as he had watched her slice a man's face with no trace of either judgement or censure and then spoken to her as an equal. Yosef suspected that for the first time in her life, Lælia had, in her betrothed, met her match; he felt a kind of relief at the thought. He could not bear to imagine his oldest friend unhappy in her marriage.

The walk back from Illiberis had given Yosef time to collect himself, but he could still feel tension coursing through his body, along with an unsettling war in his heart between gratitude for Count Paulus's protection and resentment that it was needed. Yosef had been raised to the pen, not the sword; like all boys, he knew how to sling a stone or shoot an arrow, but his was a family of scholars and merchants.

At least, he thought darkly, *we were. Before the right to be so was denied us. And what are we now? Even if this journey succeeds, what options are left to us?*

Twilight was falling as Yosef came through the gates of Garnata. A dying sun turned the rammed-earth battlements deep ochre. Two months after the festival of Shemini Atzeret, evidence of their booths remained in the form of rotting branches discarded after Sukkot had finished. The faint scent of citron lingered, betraying the cause of such industry.

Yosef glanced about warily. The Jews of Garnata had long been accustomed to paying the priest at Illiberis to look the other way at certain times of the year, but Yosef kicked the branches into the woods as he walked nonetheless. *Anusim* they may ostensibly be, but conversion in name would not save any from whipping or exile if the Christian priests took it upon themselves to look too closely. Every child born in Garnata understood the dangers of their blood. And after the encounter in the woods with Oppa, Yosef found he had a new appreciation of the danger they were in.

He knew Count Paulus was right and that confrontation with Oppa was madness. And despite his outrage on Lælia's behalf, he knew that not only would she shun his desire to avenge her, but that Theo, now, was the one who would stand by her side.

Yosef knew that his role was to take the journey for which so many had risked so much. And yet knowing that did not remove the sour taste of cowardice from his mouth. For cowardice was what it seemed to be to Yosef: this life his people were forced to live, one of cowering in the shadows, leaving their fights in the hands of others.

Filled with an impotent rage, Yosef lunged at a clump of dried leaves with such ferocity they cracked beneath the blow and scattered into dust. *Like the Jews,* he thought bitterly. *Beaten and scattered to the four winds, exiled, only to be beaten again. Is exile our destiny? Is it mine?*

"Are you troubled?"

He spun at the voice, and coloured when he saw Sarah emerging from the trees. Her long hair was tied back in a heavy roll from which tendrils escaped, framing a heart-shaped face above a body that had long haunted his nights, the lush curves promising delights Yosef knew it was a sin to imagine.

"No," he said, embarrassment making his tone abrupt. "I am not troubled."

"Oh." She walked alongside him for a few moments, whilst he searched for something to say. "You spend much time with Count Paulus's granddaughter," she said finally, in a shy voice. "Are you special friends, then?"

"With Lælia?" He looked at her quizzically. "Why would you ask?"

It was Sarah's turn to colour. "I just thought… You are together often," she finished awkwardly.

"Yes." Yosef, unsure how to answer what he thought she was

asking without betraying Lælia's trust, searched for words. "Lælia is my closest friend. She is like a sister to me." Seeing his words had done little to reassure her, he went on: "She is also betrothed. To someone I consider a friend."

As he said it, he realised with surprise that it was true. He had known Theo only a short time, but there was something in his demeanour, a quiet honour, that Yosef knew was worthy of Lælia – and that he himself felt safe with, despite the challenges they would both undoubtedly face during the mission ahead.

He smiled at Sarah, who blushed and lowered her eyes. Reaching out, Yosef took her hand. The feel of her soft skin against his palm shocked them both into silence, and they walked shyly together up the hill and into the town.

Night had fallen, and taken Sarah with it, when he reached his family's home.

"Yosef!" his father called from the rear of the house. "Come here a moment."

His father was in his private study, packing away bottles of herbs into a mahogany box. The chestnut shutters were closed against the possibility of curious ears.

"Tonight, although it is the Fast of Tebet, you will come with me to fetch some things we will need for the journey ahead. You will not speak to any of this."

Yosef nodded.

His father closed the lid of the mahogany box and stood abruptly. "When a man leaves on such a journey, he can think only of what lies ahead."

He moved to the window and leaned on the ledge, staring at the closed wooden shutters with eyes that searched not for what lay outside, but rather for the distant landscapes that he had once trodden.

"I left after Shemini Atzeret with my own father when I was a young man. Older than you are now, but still a young man, though I thought myself grown." He turned and smiled at his son. "My first child was no bigger than the length of my arm from elbow to finger-tip," he said, "but his mother and I were convinced he was the greatest of all babies born to man, with nothing but glory ahead. It was the hardest day of my life, leaving them both. And no matter how much I wanted the journey ahead, I wanted as much to be with them; my heart felt rent in two pieces, one here, one walking beside my father."

He cast a brief glance at Yosef. "My father knew, I think, how important it was that I had something to pull me back. He made certain I was married and well content before we left. A man may leave forever his country, his parents, and his siblings, but it is only the strongest of men – or perhaps the most broken – who can choose not to return to their wife and child."

He turned back to his desk and leaned against it, arms folded, regarding his son. "You are young, many years younger than I was when I left, and you do not yet have a wife or children to draw you back. But I hope you will come to see that you have as much pulling you home as I ever did. More, perhaps. I hope you will accept the responsibility of both making the journey itself and returning. But I cannot force you to do so. This journey is one a man must choose to take, and it is not a choice to be taken lightly, as you will come to understand."

He took a deep breath.

"My own father died on a lonely roadside, ten miles from the ruins of an abandoned city called Ctesiphon. I buried him with my own hands and said the words over his body, with only strangers at my side to mourn him. When I returned it was to discover my wife and child long dead, buried without me to say the words over them. And yet I thank them, for without their memory, perhaps I never would have returned. I was an old man by the time I met your mother and fathered you. Today I am older than my own father was when I buried him.

"So I must ask you now, Yosef: will you make this journey, knowing that you may have to complete it without me – and will you promise to return?"

His father's eyes held neither judgement nor expectation. Yosef felt the weight of the decision, nonetheless. He nodded quickly. Then, colouring at the stern scrutiny in his father's face, he said, "Yes, Father. I will make the journey. Complete it, and return – with or without you."

"Good." Arun nodded in satisfaction. "Tonight we will begin our preparations. There is much to learn, and only a short time in which to do it. It is a pity we must fast tonight." He smiled wryly. "In the days to come, there will be many times you recall with longing the meals you ate without thought."

9

———

LÆLIA

MIDWINTER AD 687

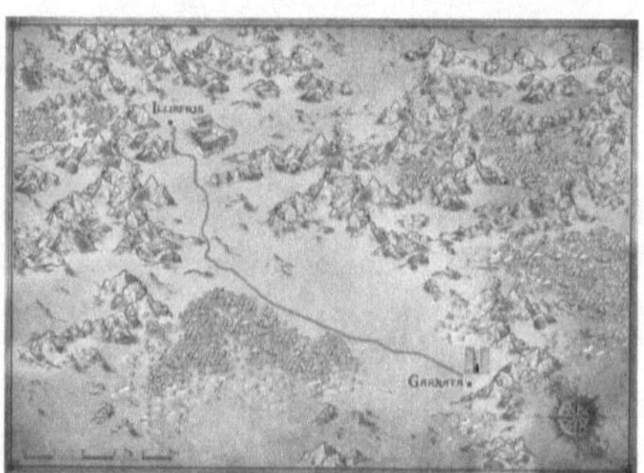

Illiberis, Bætica, Spania
Granada, Andalusia, Spain

L ælia dressed for dinner with particular care.

Her hands were slightly unsteady as she brushed her hair, staring at the polished bronze in which she measured her own distorted reflection. Even in its uneven surface she could see the heightened colour of her face, the sheen of tension in her eyes. The strange excitement she felt low in her stomach seemed visible to any who cared to look. The thought unsettled her.

Her hand faltered for a moment as she remembered Theo's expression when she faced him, after her knife had slid through Nicalo's skin. She had acted with instinct, feeling only pure satisfaction as her blade cut Oppa's companion, but the emotion had been tempered as she turned to Theo, waiting for the shock and revulsion she had met previously when men encountered her deadly skill with either bow or blade.

Instead, she had found Theo staring at her with stark admiration and a raw hunger that made her shiver deep within. In that primitive moment, all artifice had been stripped from them both. Beneath Theo's cool, courteous mask lay a force as hard and savage as her own. She had known, when she saw it in his face, that he was a man who would never shy from the wildness that lived within her. The realisation was both exhilarating and terrifying.

Pushing the memory away with an effort, Lælia frowned as she remembered Yosef's face when her grandfather had bid him leave. Her friend, too, was changed by the events of the day. Lælia feared for Yosef. She could sense the conflict rising within him. Watching his lonely figure walk away down the long drive, she had wondered how long his resentment would stay contained.

Yosef's departure had coincided with the arrival of Theo's elder brother, Alaric, in the company of Laurentius. Grey faced and weary, they had ridden hard from Hispalis, where they had been with Fráuja Sunifred, Duke of Hispalis and ruler of the lands around the Bætis River, lands now contested by the same Fráuja Frogellus who had trialled horses in Illiberis only days before.

Lælia's hand paused as she thought about Alaric. He was burly and good humoured, dark where Theo was fair, and clearly as attached to his two brothers as they were to him. He had greeted Lælia with an easy affection. Only when Theo had tersely recounted the tale of their encounter in the woods had his face darkened and a lethal hardness akin to Theo's own entered his eyes.

"Oppa is a foul creature," he had said. "Sunifred – the Duke of Hispalis," he corrected, but not before Lælia saw Theo's eyes narrow at the familiarity – "says neither Oppa nor his father will rest until they see the south's lands in their own control."

"I thought," Theo said lightly, but with a penetrating stare beneath which his brother looked faintly uneasy, "that Father said the Duke of Hispalis was a man of quick temper and little sense?"

"Perhaps," Alaric said shortly, "men such as Oppa and his father require the sharp edge of a sword more than they do 'sense'."

Alaric, Lælia thought now as she threaded ribbon through her simple braid, had none of Theo's cool detachment. His desire for vengeance had only been quelled after a look from Laurentius, whose own face had appeared far grimmer than Lælia recalled it. Laurentius had left them in the company of Shukra and Athanagild, who Lælia suspected saw a great deal more than his quiet hazel eyes gave away.

The oil lamp caught the sapphire glint of the serpent resting by her bed. Lælia touched the cold metal with one finger, feeling the sinuous curve and fine carvings etched into it. She glanced in the mirror and wondered how she would look if she piled her hair atop her head as Riccilo did and entered the hall with the serpent about her neck. For a moment, it seemed as if she could feel a surge of power in the torc.

A hand went unbidden to her throat, and she felt the place where the serpent would stare out at onlookers. The place from whence her voice should come. She drew her hand back as if it had been burned.

Such power as the serpent holds, she thought bitterly, *belongs to those in possession of the words to voice it.* She looked again at her sage-green wool gown, the girl's braid hanging down her back. *Oppa was right,* she thought. *I am more of the tribes than I am of his world.* She touched the bone amulet that rested on her chest. *My power lies in bow and knife, in the earth of the mountains. Not in fine words said in a feasting hall. Oppa fears my arrows, and Theo admires them. I need no more than that. Words are not my way and never will be.*

She rose abruptly and strode to the door, splashing oil from the lamp in searing drops on her skin. Ignoring the pain, she stepped into the corridor and made her way along the arched colonnades to the œca, from which drifted the sounds and smells of the midwinter feast.

* * *

OPPA, resplendent in ecclesiastical robes, which in their finery more closely resembled royal garb, sat on the dais flanked by Frogellus on one side and Nicalo and Ataulfo on the other. He eyed the crowd below with palpable disdain.

Lælia's entrance drew his gaze. His hand tightened so the knuckles went white around the wine cup. His eyes narrowed. Lælia met them coldly.

I know you come to marry Illiberis, she thought. *Know I do not fear you – and that I will never be yours.*

Deliberately she let her eyes slide to Theo, sitting between his brothers, watching them both with a hard, green stare.

She felt a surge of dark power at the anger that flashed over Oppa's face. Then Nicalo leaned over, pointing to her as he spoke excitedly to Oppa, and she turned away. Her heart thudded with tension, but she felt satisfied, even more so when she looked around her grandfather's oeca.

The presence of such a large cohort of priests had done nothing to lessen the distinctly pagan flavour of the celebrations. Lælia, who had once visited Toletum in Riccilo's company, made herself notice the small details that so distinguished her grandfather's hospitality from that of the more austere north.

On the dais itself, long wooden tables facilitated the straight-backed chairs that were customary in Toletum. But below, the men of Count Paulus's thiufa lounged on low *lecti* arranged around small, round tables. The wild boar and goat killed for the midwinter feast, festooned with bright splashes of citron, winter berries, and white jasmine, were arrayed on a wide table at the rear of the room amidst a flood of candles, instead of along the bench tables she recalled from the capital.

Servants moved hastily between the rear table and the clusters of men and women, serving each group with a central plate of meat and smaller plates of olives, nuts, bread, dates, and oil. The diners ate with a casual informality unheard of in the formal halls of the court, where all sat on benches and ate from a trencher of bread. Here, they shared their plates. Women ate from the same plates as the men, often sharing a *lectus* with them. Even though their bodies did not touch, which would imply a sensuality unheard of in the capital, there was something about the manner in which they lounged together that made the priests of Oppa's party look distinctly uncomfortable as they picked at their meat.

Candlelight illuminated the faded frescoes on the wall. Whilst none were overtly pagan, the scenes they depicted were of the hunt and war. Despite the crimson-and-peacock tapestry hung behind the dais, clearly in honour of the royal party, there was no mistaking the lack of piety in the core decoration. The œca of Illiberis, thought Lælia with a surge of pride, belonged to a Spania that had existed long before the Goths ever walked its shores.

"Fráuja Paulus." Oppa's sneering drawl cut through the thick air. His use of the common term to denote a man of breeding, rather than affording Paulus his correct title, was clearly deliberate. "In my studies under Archbishop Julian, I have spent many hours studying church canon. One of the greatest bodies of doctrine ever written came from a synod held here, in Illiberis, barely four hundred years ago. Your lands have a distinguished place in the history of our church."

The bishop of Illiberis, a fat man with a red face, looked pleased, as if he himself had been responsible for that long-ago distinction. "I recall clearly some of the canons laid down in that synod."

Oppa toyed with his wine glass. His lips, Lælia noticed, were thin and gave his face a cruel cast not aided by the deep red stain of wine. They were, at present, pressed together in an unpleasant smile.

"One of them," Oppa went on, "pertained to the matter of Jews. I believe it specified that no Christian should eat with Jews – amongst other things."

The bishop, clearly wishing to impress, inclined his head. "You are most well informed, *princeps*. In fact, the actual wording…"

"Is clear enough." Oppa's smile had vanished. "And yet those early words of our church fathers seem to have disappeared as completely as the Illiberis church in which they were written, of which no more stands now than a pile of stone on a deserted mountainside." His voice had risen, and the rumbling of conversation faded as men looked to the dais, where candlelight showed the thin angles of Oppa's face as he regarded them with contempt.

"Today," Oppa said coldly, "some of our men visited the Jewish enclave of Garnata."

The name stilled the clatter of cups, eyes swivelling to the speaker. Theo, sitting with his brothers close to the dais, looked at Lælia. She felt heat prickle her skin as his eyes rested on her, and she wished she knew what he was thinking.

"Men from Illiberis stood at the market stalls in the square of Garnata," Oppa went on. "Christian men. Drinking posca from the same cups as Jews. Eating their food. Buying their wares." He turned eyes gleaming with malice to Lælia. "I am told, Fráuja Paulus, that you even allow a Jew to keep company with your grand-daughter."

From the corner of her eye, Lælia saw Theo sit up abruptly, his hand white on his cup. The fleeting look of satisfaction on Oppa's face told her that he, too, had noticed.

"Yosef ben Arun is the son of my clerk." Count Paulus's voice was cold. "He is a converted Jew, as are all of those in Garnata. He is also my granddaughter's oldest friend and an honorary member of this household. He and his father are welcome in my œca and at my table."

"Many in these times pretend to conversion," Oppa said dismissively. "Yet how often, I wonder, do the Jews of Garnata attend your services, Bishop Iohannes?"

Oppa did not wait for the red-faced bishop to stammer his answers, turning instead to stare again at Lælia. "Your grand-daughter should choose better company." He let his eyes roam suggestively over Lælia's form. She felt again the presence of danger and the comforting weight of the knife strapped to her leg. She found herself wondering at what angle she should position herself in order to ensure it struck his heart.

Something of her thoughts must have shown on her face, for Oppa said, "Perhaps it is time she was wed, so that her husband may decide with whom she passes her time."

Through the thick pulse of blood behind her eyes, Lælia saw Theo's involuntary move toward the dais and Alaric's hard grip forcing his brother back into his seat. Oppa's knowing smile said he was clearly aware of Theo's consternation and was content to let the moment linger as long as possible.

It was her grandfather's harsh, gravelly voice that broke the tension. "You will be relieved, then," said Count Paulus, "to know Lælia is betrothed to Theudemir of Aurariola." Count Paulus nodded at Theo, raising his cup in salute.

"As both priest and representative of your father, our king," Count Paulus went on, "you might do us the honour of being the first to drink to their union – and to that of two great southern families, both long allied to the votive crown of Spania."

Count Paulus's voice held a gruff command, the legacy of decades leading men into war. Though courteous, his tone did not brook opposition.

Something savage gleamed in Oppa's dark eyes before the smooth, cold mask slipped back into place. He inclined his head briefly at Count Paulus. His eyes flickered once more over Lælia and then, as he raised his cup in the air, turned pointedly to focus on Theo.

"In the name of my father, King Egica," he drawled in a tone so caustic it bordered on insolence, "and in that of our Heavenly Father, I bless the daughter of Spania I see before me, and" – a sardonic smile twisted his lips – "the man who will take her to wife."

He raised his cup high, dark eyes boring into Theo. "May the marriage serve God, King, and Mater Spania."

"God, King, and Mater Spania," repeated the crowd.

Oppa's eyes never left Theo's face. Wine dripped like blood across the white of his robes as he drank.

Theo, Lælia noticed, did not drink at all.

10

YOSEF

MIDWINTER AD 687

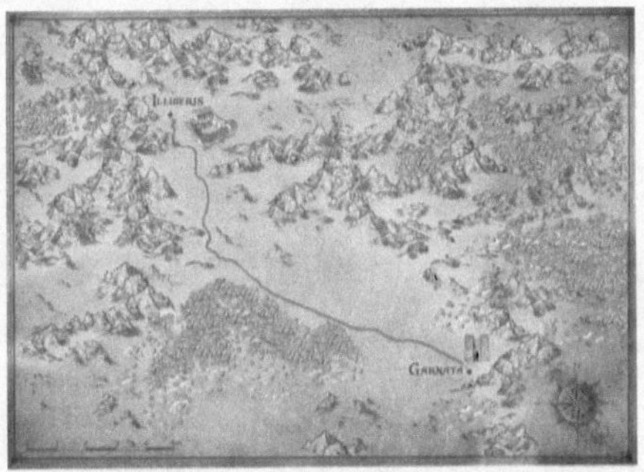

Garnata, Bœtica, Spania
Granada, Andalusia, Spain

Yosef climbed the rocky path behind his father, their way lit by a waxing moon. It shone so brightly that their figures cast shadows across the long *atoche* grass. The air hummed with insects, and creatures scurried in the undergrowth. The strange workings of the earth beneath a powerful moon matched Yosef's mood exactly. He felt an odd thrill running through his body as he followed his father's footsteps. His feet seemed pulled already to foreign shores, part of him wanting to begin now, to simply keep walking, to disappear beneath the light of the moon and wake up across the sea.

The path curved around the mountains to the north of Garnata and they climbed higher, leaving the fortified walls of the town behind. They passed the ribbon of rich grazing that divided the hills and forked to the left where the path narrowed into a rocky trail. At a scattered group of old almond trees, Arun paused and looked behind them. When he was satisfied they had not been followed, he slipped behind the trees, pushed aside a clump of oleander, and disappeared into a narrow fissure in the rock.

Yosef followed cautiously. Beyond the opening was a low, dank hole in the cliff. To the casual onlooker, it might seem that there was little else there, and goat droppings at the entrance suggested that more than one animal had taken refuge on a hot day. Arun moved to a boulder at the rear and gestured to his son to help. As they pushed it aside, another chamber opened, black beyond the reach of the moon's light.

Arun waited until they were both inside the chamber and the boulder was rolled back into place before taking a flint from his pouch and lighting a small bundle of dried *atoche*, from which he lit a candle. Thorn bush branches lay carelessly against the wall. Arun gestured to Yosef to help him remove them.

Behind the branches, the cave wall was lined with carved chests. They were old, made from a wood Yosef did not recognise, the logs riven in two. Crude though the design was, the wood had been fashioned to protect the chests from the damp, carefully finished so the joins sealed tightly. They sat upon wooden boards placed on stones, which held the chests above the earth. Yosef stood beside his father, staring at them.

"Inside these," said Arun, "are the greatest treasures we own. Not the cloth or grain that travels even now to Septem, but something far more precious." He reached over and opened one of the lids. Inside were leather wraps. Carefully, he untied one to reveal the letter within. It was made of a fine material and covered in a strange script Yosef had not seen before.

"This is written in the language of Serica," said Arun. He

handed it carefully to his son, and Yosef touched the material tentatively, tracing the odd strokes of the characters. They looked more like small pictures than letters. "It is not read horizontally," said his father, smiling. "The characters run from the top of the page to the bottom."

"Can you read it?"

"No." Arun shook his head. "I had always meant to learn – but there was never time when I was making the journey, and once home I could find none who knew the language. It is a strange tongue, guttural and complex."

"Do you know what it says?"

"It is a letter of introduction."

Yosef carefully traced the characters. He felt a bodily thrill as he touched them, the intricate strokes creeping through his veins like the most intoxicating wine. His mouth was dry, and the material seemed alive in his fingers.

Yosef looked up at his father. "This letter – it is a form of money?"

Arun was smiling. "In a way, yes." He pointed to the letter Yosef held. "This one introduces the bearer to a merchant house in a very distant city and shows credit for goods of ours sold there. The agent who sold our goods requested this letter in lieu of money. When it is presented, it will enable us to purchase goods to the value written from the merchant family named herein."

Yosef traced the seal on the parchment. It was a curious design, wings spread beside a rising sun, with two lines trailing beneath, making the symbol look something like an eagle taking flight into the sun.

"This is the symbol of the Sogdian merchants who control the mountains passes to the east," said Arun. "They follow a master known as Zoroaster, a religion older even than our own, and they have travelled the dangerous route through mountain and desert for centuries. The way of Zoroaster has faded beneath that of the Arabs who now rule much of the lands through which we must travel. But the Persian and Sogdian merchants guard the mountain passes still, and we will need their favour."

"Must we take all of these?" Looking around the cave, Yosef felt his heart sink. The vision he had of walking unencumbered for endless miles did not match the effort required in shifting such heavy, bulky chests.

"No." His father was arranging scrolls, his back turned. "Only those with the symbol I showed you – and this."

He held up a thin parchment made of a fibre unfamiliar to Yosef, so thin he could almost see through it. The symbol on it was the one Laurentius had shown them in his father's study: a simple depiction of a tree showing a slender, bowed trunk topped by a cloud of heart-shaped leaves. It was unlike any tree he had seen before, and the figure itself was a more delicate drawing than the strong images he had seen used as marks by the great houses of Spania.

"This" – Arun touched the scroll reverentially – "is the mark of the house we seek in Serica, a family whose identity must, under no circumstances, be revealed to anyone. They risked their lives to save me and lost much in so doing. I have sent word that we are embarking on our journey. I do not know if they will receive the word I sent, nor even if they live still. But we must hope, and we must trust."

As he held up the scroll, a small scrap of cloth fell out. Yosef picked it up. "What is this?" he asked, examining the cloth. It was fine silk, but bore thick, childish strokes in a strange hand, drawn crudely with charcoal.

Arun reached out and took the cloth, looking at it with an odd expression. Then he tucked it inside his robes, giving his son a twisted smile. "That," he said, "was a gift from a dear friend. If her gods and ours will it, one day you will meet her. Ah!" He held up another scroll bearing the mark of the silk tree. "I have one."

"The family you speak of," said Yosef. "They know how to produce silk?"

Arun nodded. "The secret of silk making is a carefully guarded one, and the resulting material a strictly governed trade. Outside of Serica, the only centre for production of the cloth is Constantinople itself. It is produced in secret in rooms hidden far beneath the imperial palaces and traded only by consent of the emperor." His mouth tightened. "The emperor – and the Church."

"Isidore of Hispalis says that wool is taken from the trees in Serica and woven," Yosef said.

Arun nodded. "Yet when I came to the East, the men of Serica laughed at my request to take some of the trees with me. It appears that it is not the trees themselves that produce the stuff from which silk is made."

"Then what does?" Yosef asked.

"That," said Arun, smiling at his son, "is what we must discover. I was forced to leave Serica amidst a brutal civil war without learning the secret of silk. But this time, Yosef, we must learn not only how it is produced, but how we can create an industry of our own. For if we are able to do so, if we can become producers of silk, then we will possess a secret none on this side of the Circle of Lands do. And in such secrets, my son, lies the key to wealth."

"And these letters will help us find our way to this secret?"

"Radhanite Jews are not unknown along the ways we will travel. There are those who will look for us and, more often than not, will find us before we do them. Some may recall me from the time I walked with my father. Others we must find ourselves and trust to our own instinct. Each letter will guide us through places others would not dare travel and open doors that would otherwise remain closed. Above all, Yosef, this time, no matter what war we encounter, no matter what obstacles, we must not return without the secret we seek and the means to make production a reality."

He paused, and the eyes he turned to his son were sombre. "The Jews of Spania no longer have the luxury of time," he said quietly. "If we are to survive, we must possess something everybody wants and nobody has access to. Silk is our chance. Nothing, no matter how important, can take priority over us reaching Serica, learning what we need to know, and returning with what we have learned."

He reached over and gripped his son's hand hard. "Returning," he said again, softly this time. "It is often the hardest thing to do. But we must return. We carry with us the hopes and lives not only of the Jews of Garnata, but of all those who share our blood and our faith in this country." His mouth tightened, and his eyes looked over Yosef's shoulder into a distant future. "I do not wish you, my son, to be forced to make potions or cast horoscopes for superstitious fools when you come of age."

The candle guttered in the corner, and Yosef and his father worked silently into the night, the faint smell of distant lands mingling with the dank earth of the caves. Beyond, a lynx called in the darkness, and night animals rustled through the tall grass.

11

LÆLIA

MIDWINTER AD 687

Illiberis, Bætica, Spania
Granada, Andalusia, Spain

I n the early hours of the morning, Lælia woke to the high blaze
of the midwinter moon. She flung back the covers and rose
from her bed. She needed the clarity of open air, the space of
the mountains. The lynx had called again in the night; she determined to hunt it.

Her soft leather boots made no sound as she moved through the
colonnaded walkway surrounding the courtyard. She glanced warily

at the eastern wing where some of Oppa's men were housed. They would leave today, spending some time at the monastery in Illiberis before departing for Frogellus's lands nearby. Oppa himself had dined sparingly and left directly after the feast, saying he wished to pass the night in prayer at the Illiberis monastery. Men of Count Paulus's thiufa had escorted him to the monastery door and watched to ensure he remained there. After the events in the woods, Paulus was taking no chances.

The villa was silent in the predawn, the air thin and sharp. The faintest noise would carry. Lælia trod carefully, intending to be gone before any rose.

She was about to leave the walkway when the creak of a door made her flatten against the stone, heart thudding. A cowled figure stepped out of the shadows, moving hurriedly across the ground toward the stables. Lælia followed, slipping silently through the shadows.

She knew it was most likely one of the priests in Oppa's party who had overindulged, hurrying now to return to the monastery before his absence was noted. The horse he mounted was not one of the Illiberis stable, but it was better quality than those generally afforded to men of the church. Horse and rider did not leave by the main gates, choosing instead to ride across the fields and into the woods by the river. Lælia waited until the trees had swallowed them, then swung onto Titus's back and, on a whim, followed at a distance.

She knew it was unwise. Whatever business the man had at such an hour was unlikely to be anything he wished known. Following him, however, gave Lælia a sense of purpose much needed after the events of the previous day. Never, she thought bitterly as she guided Titus silently between the trees, had she felt so impotent.

It was not only the indignity of enduring Oppa's presence at meat and his thinly veiled threats that she had found so intolerable. The hard set of Theo's jaw and her grandfather's rigid restraint had been evidence enough of their own disgust, and it had ameliorated her own. The difference, Lælia thought, was that whilst the others had clear roles to play in the days ahead, she, once again, was forced to be no more than a passive bystander, a piece to be traded by others in a game over which she had no control.

Recalling the encounter with Oppa in the woods, she remembered the hard, glittering triumph on Theo's face when she drew an arrow on Oppa, the thrill she had felt deep in her stomach when she realised Theo was not angry but proud of her skill. Even now, she burned at the memory of the heat in his gaze.

She knew it had changed something within her, caused her to see him not as an enemy but as an ally, and she had watched him afterward at the feast, too, seen the way his brothers drew unconsciously nearer to him when he spoke, his instinctive move to shield her from Oppa's predatory challenge in the hall.

With every moment that she felt herself soften toward Theo, Lælia also felt her autonomy slipping away. Oppa's toast had been the ultimate confirmation of the role she was destined to fulfil – that of someone's wife. Worse, the manner of his words made it clear that he considered the identity of her husband still to be decided. The thought of being married to Oppa sent a cold finger of revulsion down her spine. She had sensed the barely restrained violence of his touch behind his bland exterior. Even had he not stroked the whip at his side and dug his fingers mercilessly into her flesh, Lælia would still have known that a darkness lived within him. She could feel it as one could the presence of a poisonous serpent in long grass, never knowing when or how it might strike. His wife, she felt, would endure the foul depths of that darkness in ways she could barely contemplate.

Even as she had felt the comforting weight of her knife and weighed how to throw it, an uneasy voice within her had whispered that such an action was impossible. She could no sooner throw a knife across her grandfather's œca than she could stand before the entire court and declare her opposition to the marriage. She could not, Lælia thought with a sour sense of defeat, even speak her own wedding vows aloud, should it come to it. That led to a vision of her and Theo standing before a priest, the feel of his lean form hard against her own; Lælia found she was uncomfortably short of breath.

Forcing the images from her mind with an effort, she focused on her silent pursuit of the figure ahead. To hunt was something uncomplicated, something she understood.

He was indeed returning to the monastery at Illiberis. He did not ride to the monastery door but to the rather more impressive building flanking it, where Oppa and his men were quartered with the bishop himself. He dismounted and went inside.

Studying the building, Lælia noticed the faint glow of lamplight filtering through open shutters on one side of the house and heard the sibilance of hushed conversation. Sliding from her horse, she motioned Titus to remain in the trees and flitted on silent feet through the shadows until she was pressed against the wall beside the shutters. On such a still night, the low conversation within was easily discerned.

"Theudemir will enter the Karabisianoi," said a voice she took to be that of the man she had followed. "I heard him speak of it with Laurentius Severianus. It appears he is not the only one. Several sons of southern houses are going to train in the imperial fleet so that they might return to Spania and command the fleet Laurentius is restoring."

"I know this already, even if his garb had not given it away." Oppa was dismissive. "It is the lie Laurentius gave my father with Ilyan's gift of coin to restore the fleet."

When he spoke again, there was a grim satisfaction in his tone that drove Lælia back against the wall. "Coin my father will never spend on something so pointless as a fleet of dromons in the hands of our enemies. I have much of it in my possession now. Coin is used to buy men and information, not weapons for our opponents to deploy against us." He paused. "Laurentius Severianus has no need to send men abroad to learn the art of war. He and that Persian dog he brought back with him are more than capable of training men to do what they must. Which means there is another purpose for sending Aurariola to train in the Karabisianoi. We need to discover what it is."

"What do you suspect, *princeps*?" It was Nicalo who spoke. Lælia recalled his voice from the woods. His use of the Gothic title given to a legitimate son of the king turned her stomach. To his own companions, it seemed, Oppa had a legitimacy his birth did not confer.

"You saw him in the woods," said Oppa. "Why would the son of a wealthy Christian count keep company with the son of a Jewish merchant? We know Illiberis deals with the Jews here and across the seas. Theudemir of Aurariola is to be married to Count Paulus's whore granddaughter. His role in the Karabisianoi would be the perfect cover for illicit trade. If we can prove it – if it is shown that Count Paulus uses the Garnata Jews to trade with Ilyan and the exiles he harbours in his barbarian port – it will be the end of Count Paulus's rule. He will be executed for treason and his lands forfeited to the Crown."

Lælia shrank at the sharp excitement in his tone.

"We will ride to Garnata whilst we are here," Oppa said, intent making his voice strong. "Discover what we can amongst the Jews there. What else we may need we will find in the fleet if we must."

"Your father expects us to return to Toletum," Nicalo said.

"My father expects me to uncover his enemies." Oppa's voice was cold. "It seems I have a better chance to do that amongst them than by bribing the fools who frequent my mother's brothel."

A short silence fell.

"Nicalo," said Oppa eventually, "leave us."

"*Princeps –*"

"Leave."

Lælia heard the sound of movement, then a door opening and closing.

Oppa waited until the footsteps had receded before he spoke in a low, urgent tone. "Did you find it?"

"Yes, *princeps*."

Lælia heard a movement she could not make out. A short silence was followed by Oppa's satisfied voice. "Well done."

There was the clink of coin and the man stammering his thanks.

"Do not thank me." The man quieted. "Instead," Oppa said, and the chill in his voice froze Lælia where she stood, "remember that your sister resides in the house owned by my mother. For now, she is no more than a cup bearer. But one word from me – one word – and she will be skewered by every soldier from the coast to Toletum, no matter if she is only eight years of age. There are many men who desire such flesh. Do you understand?"

The man gulped. "*Ja.* I understand."

"Good. Make sure you do. Remember that your bed and board at the monastery are paid for by me. Your sister's wages are paid by me. Her flesh belongs to me, until and unless I choose to release it. Mention one word of what I asked of you tonight, and I will ensure you are watching when your sister is deflowered. Now go."

The man left the room. Lælia inched forward, straining to see through the shutters. But as she came close, a soft rush of air snuffed out the lamp, leaving the scent of old oil staining the night.

For a moment Oppa remained where he was, and Lælia had the queerest feeling that he could sense her there, was waiting, as if for the night to bring her to him. Then the long, distant cry of the lynx cut the silence, and she threw herself back as he pulled the shutters closed with a hard bang. She remained there for a moment, feeling her heart thud, the low growl of the lynx in the distance.

Danger was coming. In a matter of days, the moon would obscure the sun. Even though it would happen at night and none would see, all knew evil happened at such times. Arun had the shadows of sun and moon marked clearly, had taught Lælia and his son how to track such movement. The superstition belonged to the tribes, not Arun, but Lælia, who knew both, knew that when the light and warmth of the sun disappeared, evil stalked the earth.

She rode back to Illiberis pondering what she had heard, the low growl of the lynx rumbling through the night.

12

THEO

DECEMBER AD 687

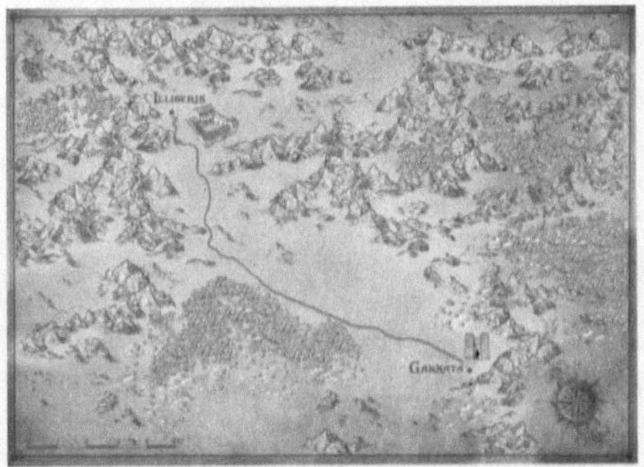

Illiberis, Bætica, Spania
Granada, Andalusia, Spain

"I will send messengers to Garnata immediately," said Count Paulus.

Oppa's presence, Theo thought, was taking an increasingly visible toll on the count. The lines on his face had become trenches. His tall frame was tense with restrained anger. The Count of Illiberis had once been in the gardingi of King Chindasuinth, one of the greatest leaders Spania had known. In those blood-soaked days, Count Paulus had cut down all opposition with sword and spear. His prowess with both was the stuff of legend, the stories young men repeated over their cups as they dreamed of going to war.

Forced inaction, Theo thought now, as he watched Paulus grip the back of the chair so hard the wooden carving left impressions on his hands, did not suit such a man at all.

"I can go." Theo felt the subtle weight of Lælia's eyes and fought not to look at her as he spoke. "It is better if I give Yosef warning. The fewer who know what Lælia heard, the safer we will be."

I will go with you. Lælia's hand created a fluttering shadow in the light of the oil lamp. Theo knew she had returned to the villa in the early morning, but Count Paulus had been gone from the villa all day, and Laurentius and Shukra had taken his brothers hunting. It was only now, at twilight, that they had gathered in the study. Theo, who had become acutely aware of Lælia's presence in the villa, had sensed she was uneasy, but she had not spoken to him during the day and he, increasingly attuned to her moods, had forced himself not to approach her. Now he tried to suppress a surge of excitement that she might want to accompany him. It was quickly dashed by Count Paulus's next words.

"You will go nowhere," he growled, glowering at his grand-daughter. "We are fortunate Oppa did not discover you last night. He is a dangerous man, Lælia. And you are no longer a child. Your place is here. And you" – he turned with an equally grim expression to Theo – "cannot risk such a visit. Oppa already suspects you of allying with Yosef. To ride to Garnata will be confirmation. You will remain here."

He turned to the tall, quiet figure of Laurentius who was standing in the corner, flanked as ever by Shukra. "Laurentius. You and Shukra will go tomorrow morning. You are a scholar, and all know your father's library is one of the greatest in Spania. Only you have a legitimate reason for conversation with Arun ben Radhan."

Laurentius was nodding his agreement when Alaric spoke from behind Theo.

"Is this all we will do?" His voice was belligerent. Theo saw

Athanagild frown at their older brother as Alaric stepped forward. "Will we simply stand aside as Oppa threatens our brother and the entirety of the south? Sunifred is right," he went on bitterly. "We cannot allow this to continue. Oppa and his father will not rest until they have taken all we possess for themselves."

"Alaric." To Theo's surprise, it was Athanagild who spoke. His brother had coloured, but his voice was steady. Theo saw his hazel eyes flicker to Laurentius, as if seeking reassurance. Laurentius gave him an encouraging smile, and Theo felt a familiar wave of gratitude to his uncle. Athanagild continued, "confronting Oppa now will achieve nothing and risk everything. We must remain calm until Theo and Yosef are safely gone. To do anything else is folly."

"Athanagild is right." Laurentius turned not unsympathetic eyes to Alaric. "And I have told you before, Alaric, not to follow Sunifred's path. He wields his blade before his mind. If you wish to succeed your father as Count of Aurariola and retain his lands, you would do well to learn how to wield the mind first." He gave Alaric a half smile. "Even if much of your mind was lost the moment you saw Sunifred's daughter."

His levity lightened the room, though Theo thought as the party broke up that Alaric was only slightly mollified. Athanagild left in Shukra's company. Theo, watching both his brothers walk away, felt an odd twist in his gut. He was not yet gone to the Karabisianoi and already it seemed the solidity of his family unit was shaken, each of his brothers splintering off on different paths. The thought made him lonely and uneasy. In the distance, he saw Lælia's lithe form disappearing into the stables. He hesitated for a moment, then followed her.

The night was mild and clear, the stars high above casting a pale light that caught the dew on the grass. Theo followed Lælia's faint shape as she moved across the ground toward the stables, staying in the shadows. She disappeared inside. He waited until the soft glow of an oil lamp spilled from the doorway before coming closer. He peered around the corner. Lælia was standing by a mare, rubbing a salve into the animal's belly and making soft noises in her throat. She held up a hand and made a brief movement, as if to usher Theo inside, glancing briefly at him.

Her eyes really are the most extraordinary colour, Theo thought, his heart thudding. In the light cast by the oil lamp, they glowed rich gold, flickering with the shifting shadows. Theo could not look away, drawn by an odd feeling of connection.

"Hermes's mare," he guessed.

Lælia nodded. Pointing at the mare's distended belly, she held up a hand with two fingers.

"The twins," Theo said.

Yes.

He shook his head. "I have heard of such a thing, but they do not survive."

These will. There was something fierce in her gesture.

"Why?"

She tilted her head to one side, as if assessing how much to say. *The mare belonged to my mother.*

Theo frowned. "Then she is old to bear foals."

They are the only foals she has ever carried. Lælia gestured slowly, and it seemed there was a question in her eyes with her next movements. It took Theo a moment to understand what her hands were conveying: *I dreamed of them.*

Theo felt something shift inside him. He remembered the day he had met Yosef:

You have met Lælia before now, have you not? I understand that your families are friends.

I remember only horses. Or perhaps the horses are from a dream; I have dreamed strange things on the road here...

The dreams could not be related. Could they? He remembered again the dreams beneath high stars as he rode to Illiberis. Blood and pain. A horse. A strange sense of suffocation, as if he were being silenced.

He drew a shuddering breath.

When he spoke, his voice seemed to come from a distance. "Our mothers were together when they died. Did you know that?"

Her eyes told him she did not.

He nodded. "Before I came here, my father told me. He... never speaks of our mother. Not that I can recall. But when I asked if we had met before as children he told me we had, once, when I was barely walking and you were a babe in arms.

"My parents visited yours, at your father's lands west of here. When my father left for Emerita Augustus, he took Alaric with him, planning to return in two months. I was too young to make the journey by horseback, so I stayed with my mother. She and your own mother were, my father said, as close as sisters, and you were barely a month born. My mother planned to pass the summer there." He held Lælia's eyes. "It was the Summer of Blood. The fever came and took them all. By the time my father knew of it, my mother had already fallen, as had both your parents. Once, when my father had drunk a great deal, he told me that they found you and me together. We survived the fever, the only ones who did."

She watched him, still and silent.

"On the road here" – he swallowed, remembering – "I dreamed of many things. I thought it was the journey that made me dream so. Sometimes it seemed I could recall my own mother, though in my waking moments, I cannot. At other times, there was something else." He met her eyes, feeling oddly exposed beneath her gaze, his voice hard to find in his throat. "Strange pictures," he said hoarsely. "A horse…"

She put a hand to her throat, her eyes fierce on his.

"Yes," he said. "Choking – as if I could not speak."

A knife appeared in her hand and she held it over her arm. For a terrible moment, Theo did not know what she meant, then she drew the blade across her skin and a thin trickle showed ruby bright in the dim light.

She pointed to it.

"Yes." He nodded. "Blood. That is what I saw, in the dream. Blood – and pain."

They stared at each other, then Lælia took his hand. She pressed it gently against the mare's belly, leaving her own atop. Reaching up with the other, she gently brushed Theo's eyelids closed. A hush descended, the world becoming one of the senses. Theo could still feel the trace of her fingers on his skin. Her touch lingered in the air, the faint herbal scent of the salve on her fingers intoxicating.

Beneath his palm, the mare's belly was full and vital. Lælia's hand atop his own moved gently, shifting his touch to follow the outline of the shapes beneath. Her fingers were warm and pliant; her hand became part of his. He could feel the warmth of her body close to his own. His fingers felt the hard curve of a hoof, the smooth roundness of a haunch.

He leaned his shoulder slightly toward Lælia, feeling the soft weight as she rested her cheekbone against it. Her hair smelled sweet, like the wildflowers by the river he had passed on the way to Illiberis. It mingled with the comforting scent of straw and horse. Theo breathed it in. A profound feeling of peace stole over him. He thought he could fall asleep there, standing in the darkness, feeling the new life within the mare creep through their joined hands.

When he spoke, his voice seemed to come from a distance. "I will ride with you to Garnata, if you still wish to go."

He felt her still beneath him. Then she turned in his embrace, and her face was so close to his he could feel her like lightning against his skin.

Why?

He caught the hand that flickered between them, holding it in his own. "You care about him. Yosef. When he goes, you will think of him."

Her eyes narrowed infinitesimally.

He held her hand up, opening her palm. Unable to stop himself, he pressed his lips against it, feeling the slight tremble of her body as he did. It fired him, licking heat through his veins so he was rigid with longing, barely able to keep himself from crushing her to him.

"When I go," he said roughly, "will you think of me?"

Her eyes widened, luminous in her face, and something flickered in them that severed the last ounce of his control. He made a harsh sound and would have pulled her to him but she wheeled at the last moment, spinning out of his grasp so he was left hard and wanting whilst she stood against the wall, only the tight lift of her shoulders betraying her short breath.

His arm reached out and then fell. "I know nothing of your heart," he said hoarsely. "I cannot tell if you even wish for this marriage. I cannot bear to think that you suffer it, that you are forced…"

She moved so swiftly that it was no more than a rush of air, and then he felt the fleeting heat of her lips skim his jaw, every nerve tingling with awareness. She had stepped back before he could reach for her. Slowly, deliberately, she brought her hand up so that it covered her heart.

Promise.

Her lips curled in a small, secret smile, and then she was gone, leaving Theo in the stables, heart pounding, his entire body aflame with the recollection of her touch.

When he left, it was late, and the last light of the full moon hung low on the eastern horizon, its molten gold the same colour as Lælia's eyes.

13

___

OPPA

DECEMBER AD 687

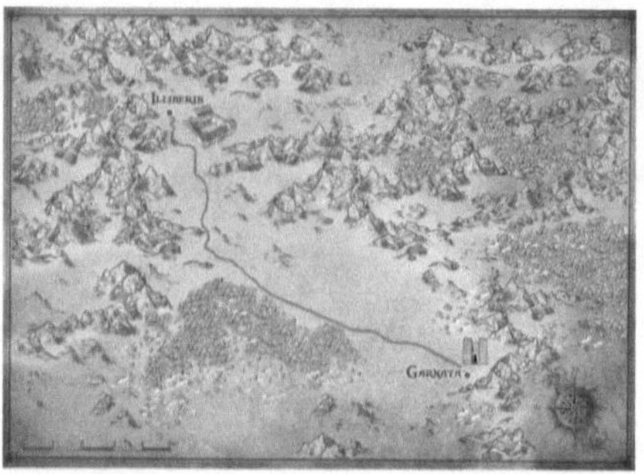

Garnata, Bætica, Spania
Granada, Andalusia, Spain

Oppa's face was set in tight lines as he rode into Garnata the following morning between the tall earthen towers at the base of the hillside. His eyes moved left and right, taking in every possible aspect of the bustling road to the town above. He felt a growing sense of excitement. He was getting close, he knew, to something powerful. Something dark and secret.

The citizenry of Garnata watched the small party warily. *As well they may*, Oppa thought contemptuously. The laws governing Jews were well known but, for Archbishop Julian of Toletum and the priests under his primacy, the conversion of Jews was an obsession that eclipsed all other duties. Under his governance, Spania's Jews had learned a new caution. Born to a learned Jewish family himself, Julian had been adopted by Christians as a child when his parents refused to convert. It was a custom long established but rarely enforced beyond the confines of Toletum. It was whispered that Julian's failure to convert his own parents, right up until their deaths, was a source of deep anguish for him. Oppa sometimes wondered if it would take the forced conversion or subjugation of every Jew in the Gothic kingdom of Spania to compensate the archbishop for his perceived failure. It certainly seemed to be his objective.

Today, at least, Oppa could harness that fervour for a cause in which he actually believed. He pressed his lips together to suppress his happiness. It would not do for men to see he relished the task ahead.

As Julian's priests rode into Garnata, their eyes burning with holy condemnation, women bundled children into their arms and disappeared into houses. Men turned hurriedly into side streets to avoid their party. Even here, hundreds of miles from Toletum, word of Julian's anger at the Jews was known.

"Princeps." Outside the church, which had clearly once served as the Jewish temple, stood a thin, harried-looking priest flanked by two equally poor-looking deacons. They wore robes of the most ragged homespun, and in contrast to the people Oppa had ridden by on the streets, their appearance was mean and dirty. They ushered him inside with pale faces and nervous gestures.

The church itself served as stark contrast to the poor state of the Christians who now claimed it as a house of God. It was large and spacious, from the marble portico to the tall pillars inside. The roof was higher than the relatively humble church in Illiberis, and gold leaf glittered on the cornices. The shape of a menorah carved into the stone wall was still vivid despite having been plastered over. Indeed, the church's origins as a wealthy temple were painfully obvious – as was the serious state of decline that had recently befallen it.

Oppa surveyed the interior with contempt. It was still and silent within, though the practical sounds of people going about their daily business were audible through the open door. Dust motes drifted through the dim light and fell to the simple altar, the cloth covering it of poor quality.

"I would see the people of this town," he said. Turning abruptly, he left the church, his party scrambling after him.

They visited the homes of one local dignitary after another. All greeted Oppa with great courtesy, the generous hospitality typical of old Bætica, and, to a man, with hams hanging openly in their kitchens.

Oppa was contemptuous and abrupt. He had not yet found what he sought. They were following a street within easy sight of the river below when Oppa drew to a halt, frowning at the open doors ahead. The churchman beside him paled.

"Is that a bathhouse?" Oppa's tone was dangerously low.

"Your Grace," began the priest, "we did close it – and we don't patronise it ourselves…"

Clearly, thought Oppa sourly. Since his arrival at the Illiberis monastery, he had more than once had cause to dearly miss the bathhouse in his mother's brothel by the river. He was certain Count Paulus maintained his own private bathhouse, but the Church forbade the practice of bathing, and Oppa could hardly ask his host to provide something his own archbishop had decreed a sin.

"All bathhouses have long been closed to the public by order of the king." Oppa's voice rang clearly through the streets. "Bathing is an affectation of the wealthy and an insult to God and the natural order. Such vanities are the very essence of the sin Christ overcame and the reason for our suffering. Bring out those who believe themselves superior to the form of man God made, and let Him be their judge."

His ringing tones had drawn a small crowd.

The priest stared up at Oppa in horror. "Enter the bathhouse, *princeps*?" he stammered.

A man clad in only a loincloth, moist from the steaming heat within, appeared in the street, his face pale with fear.

"*Princeps*." He addressed Oppa. "I am the bathkeeper. No offence to God is meant here, I assure you. I –"

"Guards." Ignoring him, Oppa nodded at his small party of armed men. "Clothe him. Then go within and bring out all you find there."

"But there are women inside," protested the bathkeeper. "No men enter the left side of the bathhouse. Please allow my daughter to give them proper warning –"

The guards pushed him aside, and he fell to the ground. Half of the guards poured into each of the two doorways, swords drawn; Oppa wondered what resistance they thought they might find. The thought of naked women beneath drawn swords sent a flicker of excitement through his body. From the darkness beyond the street opening came the faint sound of screams and male voices raised in protest.

Oppa dismounted. Glaring at the bystanders, he entered. The fragrant darkness drew him in like an old friend, and he inhaled the familiar scents of rose and almond, of hot female flesh. Passing through the antechamber, he entered the low-roofed bathing area. A group of slaves clad in no more than the briefest scraps of cloth cowered in the corner, hands covering their breasts. In the centre, a group of women of varying ages were surrounded by guards. Most of the guards appeared shamefaced, looking away from the naked forms, or at least casting only furtive glances at the bodies cowering at sword point. Oppa quickly assessed the men's faces. He knew what he was looking for.

"You." He addressed the four most red faced and uncomfortable of the men. "Take these women outside." Moving in a businesslike fashion, he ushered the older and less attractive of the women into the circle of guards, who gratefully took his lead and left as quickly as possible, ignoring the cries of the women calling to those left behind.

Three men were left, Nicalo and Ataulfo amongst them, the latter pale faced and disabled from the arrow wound he had sustained in the woods. Nonetheless, he joined the others in eyeing the remaining small group of women with unabashed greed. They were young girls, all barely at puberty or just beyond.

"It is a sin to bathe," said Oppa, addressing the girls. His voice was low and silky. "But you enjoy it, don't you? You enjoy being naked together. Touching each other." He spoke to the girls, but his eyes watched the men. It was the men's loyalty he sought, and life had taught him that much could be bought by satisfying desire, particularly when that desire came from dark shadows.

The girls huddled close, staring at him with fearful eyes. The watching men breathed heavily. Oppa saw the evidence of their arousal beneath their tunics.

"These men should kill you for your heresy, for your sins against God," he said softly. "They could do it easily. Drive their swords through you, show you how real men deal with whores."

The girls gasped in horror, but Oppa wasn't paying attention to them. He was watching the men. "What do you think?" he murmured to them. "Should we teach them what happens to little whores who displease God?"

One of the men groaned. Fumbling beneath his tunic, he gripped himself. Seeing the horror on the girls' faces, he began to stroke himself with hard, fast movements, eyes glazed.

"Our friend is impatient." Oppa walked behind the guards, moved between them, and spoke close to their ears. The girls huddled together, their fear an aphrodisiac to the watching men. "But we know that punishment is best dealt slowly," Oppa said, his words for his companions. "And in private. Be patient, my friends. I will make certain the lesson is taught properly." The men nodded, as if hypnotised by his words.

"And you, Ilfric," whispered Oppa to the man who stroked himself, his mouth intimate, close to his ear. "You know how it will be when you have them naked and helpless beneath your sword, quivering for you to take them. You know how it will be when you thrust your steel in flesh."

The man gave a brief cry, convulsing where he stood, and Oppa, smiling, slowly withdrew. "Take them outside," he said in a normal voice.

The men all looked into his eyes as they passed, returning his silent nod. They understood one another perfectly.

The girls emerged blinking into the day, whimpering with fear. A crowd had gathered, stony faced and silent at the sight of the naked group in the street.

Oppa faced them. *"Anusim!"* He spat the word in contempt. "Converted Jews, Jews who now profess to be Christian." He raised a remonstrative finger. "God sees!" he said in a ringing voice. "God is not mocked by your lies, and He sees your arrogance! He knows you deny His only Son and practise your godless heresy far from the eyes of the Church. He sees your ambition and your greed." He pointed at the hands covering their genitals protectively. "He sees your desecration of His holy work!"

Every one of the men in the street had been circumcised.

Heady with power, turning back to the men gathered under sword point outside the bathhouse, Oppa felt a jolt of shock as he recognised the sloe-eyed youth, Yosef. His shock turned to pleasure as he saw sick realisation dawn in the Jew's eyes. Oppa saw Yosef's eyes flicker to the girl Ilfric had been looking at in the bathhouse. When Yosef saw her tears, a hard fury entered his face.

Interesting, Oppa thought.

A clatter of hooves broke the tension. The Count of Illiberis appeared over the hill, his face taut with rage, Bishop Iohannes gaunt at his side.

"How dare you!" he snarled, the men of his thiufa riding into Oppa's guard with swords raised, their horses forcing his men back. "You do not rule here, Oppa sunau Egica, king's son or no. You will leave this place immediately – or face my sword."

Oppa felt another rush of lust. He had no need to take any further action; for now, fear was enough. "Fráuja Paulus," he said coldly. "It seems your bishops are sadly derelict in their duty."

Count Paulus's sword was out of its scabbard. His hand rested on its hilt as he spoke.

"It is fortunate that some of your brethren, at least, remain decent men. Bishop Iohannes showed a respect your own party sorely lack when he brought word that you had ridden here today." Count Paulus made no attempt to hide his fury. "It is even more fortunate that I left as soon as he came, for it seems I arrived just in time."

Oppa met his fury with disdain, his face quite unafraid.

"I will ensure Archbishop Julian is made aware of Bishop Iohannes's diligence. There will, I expect, be a new bishop sent to Illiberis." Oppa looked pointedly at Count Paulus's hand on the protruding hilt. "And if you ever draw a sword in my presence again," he said quietly, "I will see to it that you hang."

He turned to his men, smiling for the benefit of the crowd, feeling the exultation of his encounter thrilling his veins. "Come," he ordered them. "Fráuja Frogellus's hospitality is more to my liking – and he does not suffer the company of Jews."

Without a backward glance, he led his men from the town, triumph bubbling inside him.

14

YOSEF

DECEMBER AD 687

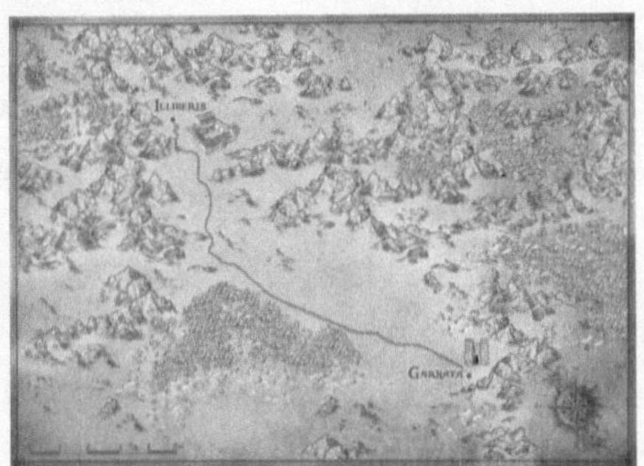

Garnata, Bætica, Spania
Granada, Andalusia, Spain

Rage and humiliation burned Yosef's throat. Unable to look at Count Paulus, he took a cloak from an outstretched arm and wrapped it around Sarah's naked, trembling figure, averting his eyes as he did so. Only when she was being led away by some of the townswomen did he return to the bathhouse to fetch his own clothes. He pulled them on savagely, blood roaring in his ears. He did not notice Theo enter until the man was in front of him.

"Get out of my way."

"Yosef, I'm sorry. Lælia has gone to ensure Sarah is unharmed."

"I don't need your pity."

Theo didn't answer that. Yosef couldn't bear the silent understanding in his eyes. Pushing past him, he stepped into the street.

"Where is your father?" Count Paulus asked grimly.

"Don't pretend," said Yosef harshly, "that you care about my father. The only thing you care about is Illiberis and the fortune you hope to make. This" – his arm jerked angrily to encompass the bathhouse and Garnata as a whole – "is no more than an inconvenience to you."

Count Paulus's mouth set in a hard line. "I will forgive that," he said tightly, "because I understand your anger. But you are no longer a child, Yosef, and there is more at stake here than your own pride. We must ensure your father's safety."

"Why?" Yosef's voice shook with fury. "Because he is a piece in the game you play? Because only *you* are allowed to decide the fate of the Jews under your care? When our blood shall be spilled and for what cause, even when and how our women shall be taken?"

"Yosef!" Theo stepped forward, frowning. "That's enough. We have no time for this. Your father is not at home; we sent men to check. We must find him before Oppa does."

Theo's cool logic did nothing to calm the heat of humiliation. Knowing his friend was right only made the bitterness inside rise in a torrent of bile, which spewed forth before Yosef could prevent it. "You are no different," he sneered, hating himself even as the words came out, but equally unable to stop them. "Entering the fleet because you are told to. Doing whatever is asked with blind obedience – and why? Because you hope for gold at the end of it? Do you have even a thought of your own, Theo, or are you happy to spend your life on the end of a string, dancing to whatever tune wiser men play for you?"

He saw the moment when his taunts hit home. The colour faded from Theo's face, his eyes narrowing to cold green shards of anger. "Do you think," he said icily, "that I would risk my life for a mission

– which is uncertain at best – and agree to a marriage of duty if I did not believe in the cause?"

Theo would have gone on, but a small movement on the periphery of their vision caused him to bite off his words. Unnoticed by them all, Lælia had ridden into earshot. At Theo's words, "a marriage of duty", she spun her horse and cantered up the stone road, Titus's hooves clattering between the tall buildings. As she rounded the corner, Yosef caught sight of her pale, set face, hurt and anger etched in every line.

Horrified awareness dawned on Theo's face. Yosef forgotten, he leaped onto his horse, pushing past Count Paulus's men as he rode after Lælia, calling her name. Yosef stared after them, his anger fading and leaving him shaken and lost before Count Paulus's hard face.

"Where is Arun?" Count Paulus asked again.

"In the mountains, I think." Yosef met his eyes, shame making him colour. "I am not permitted to tell you the location," he muttered. "But I will go to find him."

"Tell him to remain out of sight," said Count Paulus curtly. "We have not seen the last of Oppa today."

Calling a command to his men, he wheeled his horse round and rode toward Illiberis, leaving Yosef standing in the road. Fighting for calm, Yosef turned in the direction of the Garnata caves and walked up the same road Lælia had ridden. He had just left the stone road for the mountain track when he heard someone call his name. He turned to see Sarah hurrying toward him.

"Yosef!" Long strands of rich chestnut had escaped the knot behind her head, falling about her face as she ran toward him, her chest heaving and eyes bright.

"I thought you were in Garnata," said Yosef roughly.

She waved dismissively. "I am not harmed. And there are more important things than hurt pride." Her eyes were hard and brilliant with something that made Yosef catch his breath, and her hand seemed to burn his skin when she put it on his arm. "May I walk with you?"

He had known Sarah since childhood, but now Yosef found himself tongue-tied and awkward in her presence. He nodded.

They walked together along the narrow path that led to the pomegranate trees up on the hill behind Garnata.

He had seen her naked – and she him. Even the most fleeting
recollection brought a rush of colour to Yosef's face and turned his
stomach to water. The thought that she might have looked at him –
seen him – increased his mortification a hundred times over.

Because he had seen her. No matter how full of impotent rage
he had himself been at the shameful spectacle in the street, the
memory of Sarah's naked flesh, shimmering and full like a peach
about to fall from the tree, had seared itself upon his mind, leaving
him with a guilty memory he dared not allow himself to see. That
thought in turn triggered his rage again. He felt a passing branch
catch at him, and he pushed against it, almost hoping it would draw
blood.

"They say the priests will sentence several men to whipping."

"I don't know what is worse," said Yosef. "Being whipped or
living with the fact that it is my fault the whippings are taking
place."

"No. You mustn't think that," said Sarah, turning to him.

"Mustn't I?" Yosef's voice was hard. "I leave with my father in
less than a week, Sarah. On the path of the Radhanites. A journey
that is meant to mark my entry to manhood." He shook his head. "I
am ashamed to walk beside my father." He kicked a stray stone from
the path with unnecessary force. "I am ashamed that I did nothing."

"And what could you do? What could any of us do?" Sarah
caught at a twig and snapped it off. She turned away from the path,
walking deeper into the trees. Yosef followed her. She pulled the
almond blossoms from it as they walked, bruising the petals and
crushing them in her fingers before throwing them to the ground
one by one. She came to a stop in a clearing beside large granite
boulders, facing him.

"You must remain hidden, Yosef, and your father also. If you are
whipped, you will be in no state to leave. Our entire community
relies on the journey that you and your father will make. Our
fortune – perhaps our very future – depends upon it. Do not feel
ashamed for scars you won't have. Your journey will be arduous
enough without them."

"*Our* community?" Yosef stared at her. "Your father is Christian, Sarah. Your mother is converted. You should never have been in that bathhouse. There is no need for you to suffer the disgrace of the Jews."

"Yes, there is." The brittle light was back, her breath coming fast as she met his eyes. "Do you not know, Yosef," she said, holding her head up proudly, "why I follow the ways of our people, of *your* people? Can you not guess?"

Yosef swallowed and looked away. "I wanted to do something to help you," he muttered. "I didn't like… the way they looked at you."

"You did help," said Sarah softly.

Glancing at her, he saw fiery rose enflame her skin. "I focused on your face," she said. "On your eyes. And I pretended it was only you who could see me. Because" – she lowered her voice so it was barely audible – "I didn't feel ashamed when I saw the way you looked at me."

"Sarah." Yosef stopped. Taking her hand, he drew her near. She was trembling, her hand hot in his own. "I have never seen anything more beautiful than you," he said hoarsely.

"Then I don't mind what they did to us," she whispered.

He touched her face, and her hand covered his. "I will come back to you," he said roughly. "No matter how long it takes, I *will* come back."

"I know." She smiled, her eyes so warm and wise that Yosef felt the bitterness in him melt away into them.

Heart thudding, Yosef lowered his head and kissed her.

He had barely tasted her mouth when he felt a knife at his back. The breath hot on his ear smelled of onions and the grip on his arm was like a vice.

"Liked what you saw? Decided to give her some of that mangled cock of yours?"

Sarah was wrenched away from him, a knife held beneath the swell of her breasts. She was trapped hard against her captor, and by the way the man writhed and from the revulsion on Sarah's face, Yosef knew it was not a knife he pressed against her back. He recognised the man from the bathhouse.

"Let her go," Yosef spat, struggling against the man holding him. He was on the ground, arms pinned behind his back. Oppa, sitting on a horse, watched him placidly. The jewelled eagle holding his tunic glinted at his shoulder, the colours vivid in the hard winter sun. A vision crossed Yosef's mind of Oppa in the woods, stroking his whip as he faced Lælia.

"You pretend to be a man of God," he gasped. "You know this is wrong."

Oppa looked back at Yosef, eyes flat and cold. Yosef had never seen such blankness; it was as if nothing stirred behind them.

Oppa shrugged. "You are Jews," he said. "And you were about to sin against God, here, in the open air." He looked about him with an air of innocent regret. "But in all truth, Jew, I don't care what shape your cock is, what sins you commit, or what God you pray to." His mouth twisted into a cruel rictus, black eyes shiny like the back of a beetle. "My men saw your friend naked and now they want her. I intend to let them have her. I like to make people happy. Especially people who can help me." He looked at the guard holding the knife to Sarah. "Does she make you happy, Ilfric?" he said, calmly.

Ilfric grinned in answer, slitting Sarah's gown from neck to waist, baring her breasts to the harsh daylight.

The guard holding Yosef grunted in appreciation. Twisting to look at him, Yosef saw the mark on the guard's head where his own stone had struck days ago in the wood.

"You!" he spat.

"Did you think I'd forget?" Nicalo sneered at him. "You will pay for that stone."

Ilfric was staring at Sarah's breasts in outright lust. He stretched out one meaty hand to a nipple, which jutted forward in the chill air. Feeling it beneath his hand, he grunted and pinched it hard.

Sarah whimpered. Yosef strained toward her, anguish twisting his heart.

"Do you want to reave her?" Oppa asked Ilfric, his voice low.

In answer, Ilfric fumbled with his tunic.

"No!" cried Yosef, struggling futilely against his bonds. "Leave her. Leave her alone!"

"Yosef!" screamed Sarah. "No! Get off me!"

Ilfric pushed her up against a hard granite boulder and raised the linen so the ripe curves of her buttocks were exposed to the air. Shoving his knee between her legs, he pushed them apart. "I saw the way you looked at me in the bathhouse," he panted, licking her face. "You want my cock, don't you?"

"I imagine she has thought of little else, Ilfric," said Oppa dryly. Yosef could hear the derision in his tone, but Ilfric was too focused on Sarah to notice.

"Reave her, Ilfric," urged Ataulfo, holding Yosef's other arm. He was excited, his breath foul on Yosef's skin.

"I will kill you," snarled Yosef, his whole body straining against his captors. "I will kill you all."

"I'm sure you will," said Oppa mildly. "But not before we've reaved your girlfriend bloody. Ilfric," he said, still in the same calm tone, "show me how you split a woman with that sword of yours. Show me what we do with little Jewish whores."

With a hoarse gasp, Ilfric grasped Sarah's hips and shoved himself inside her. Sarah screamed, a sound of such anguish and pain it rent Yosef as if it were he who was speared, and he fought with all he had to escape.

"No," said Oppa, watching his struggles. "But you should watch, my friend. You may learn something. Hold his face so he can see, Nicalo."

A knee in the middle of his back kept Yosef pinned to the ground, and a rough hand held his face so he could not look away. Ilfric thrust himself in and out of Sarah, a sick look of fascination contorting his face as he looked down at his own cock. She was sobbing, crying out with every brutal invasion; the more she cried, the more excited the men holding Yosef became.

"Hurry, Ilfric," Ataulfo panted, and Yosef felt his stomach roil as he heard the meaty slap of hand on flesh as the man readied himself.

"Don't waste it, Ataulfo," said Oppa lazily. "If you carry on like that you will have nothing left for her, *ne?*"

Ilfric roared his release, shuddering inside Sarah, and Yosef tasted fury.

Then the first arrow flew, hitting Ilfric in the shoulder. He yelped in surprise and pain, toppling sideways away from Sarah. Another caught the pale, exposed flesh of his buttock. He stumbled behind a tree, looking about frantically, his flaccid cock still dripping. Sarah sobbed quietly against the rock, her face hidden.

Oppa's horse was dancing, startled by the sudden flurry of movement, and Oppa looked about through narrowed eyes. Ataulfo drew his bow whilst Nicalo held Yosef, releasing one arrow before he himself was caught in the shoulder. He staggered away, grunting in pain as he clutched the length protruding from his body. Nicalo gave a startled cry and he, too, momentarily released his hold on Yosef.

A moment was all it took.

With a snarl of fury, Yosef launched himself at Ilfric. Slamming him against the tree, Yosef drew his knife and, without hesitation, thrust it up beneath the man's ribs with all the strength he possessed.

It was a small knife, an all-purpose tool he used to open packages and splice leather, not intended for attack. But it was sharp and well kept, and it slipped into the man's flesh with smooth efficiency. Ilfric screamed. Yosef pulled out the knife and thrust it again and again. The red fury behind his eyes blinded him to all else but the man before him and the need to wound him badly, to cause him pain and hurt and suffering. He was vaguely conscious of the sound of clashing steel behind him, but he did not turn, intent only on the man beneath his knife.

"Yosef! Yosef, let him go!" He ignored the shouts until a pair of iron arms grasped his own from behind and pulled him away. "Let him go, now. It's enough. I've got you. We're safe."

The voice in his ear was low and calm. Looking about frantically, Yosef saw that Oppa was gone, Nicalo and Ataulfo with him. His vision clearing, he looked down at the man in front of him. Ilfric was lying on earth stained red with blood. He wasn't moving.

Sarah was huddled against the rock, her face turned away. Kneeling beside her, arm protectively about her shoulders, was Lælia. She looked at Yosef with wide, silent eyes, bow on the ground where she had left it alongside one of the blood-soaked arrows with which she had shot his attackers.

"It was you," Yosef said. His voice, cracked and hoarse, sounded alien to his ears.

Lælia gestured behind him. *Us.*

The grip on his arms loosened. Theo stepped into view. "Stand back."

He spoke quietly. It was his low voice Yosef had heard. A short sword covered in blood lay on the ground. Theo bent to pick it up. Wiping it carefully on the grass, he sheathed it. His eyes never left Yosef, and he kept his body deliberately turned away from where Sarah sobbed gently against the rock, hair hanging over her face. He walked over to the body on the ground. "Lælia," he said gently, without looking up, "take Sarah to the stream to wash."

Yosef looked at Sarah, but she kept her head down and didn't meet his eyes. More than anything, Yosef wanted to reach out, to touch Sarah and reassure himself that she was alive and unharmed.

But she is not unharmed, he thought dully, *and she never will be again.*

Lælia caught his eye and shook her head. It was a small but eloquent gesture, warning him against approaching Sarah, and Yosef heeded it.

Theo waited until they had gone from sight and then prodded the man with his foot. He rolled the body over, and Ilfric stared up at the sky with wide, sightless eyes. Blood trickled from his mouth.

"He's dead," said Yosef unnecessarily. He saw his own knife on the ground. It was blood covered from tip to hilt. He held out his hand and drops of blood ran from the end of his index finger down into the earth. He retched, suddenly and violently, turning away from the sight of the body on the ground and wiping his shaking hand on a tree as he convulsed over and over until there was nothing left in his gut.

"Did you kill them? The others?" he asked when he had recovered, glancing at the sword at Theo's side.

Theo shook his head. "No. I wounded Nicalo, and one of Lælia's arrows caught Ataulfo in his injured shoulder – he will suffer. But they got away." His tone was tight, and when Yosef looked up, Theo's deep green eyes were blazing with fury. "That evil bastard. Yosef, I am so sorry. I will see him hang for what he did to Sarah."

Yosef shook his head. "I will kill him," he said. "I'm going nowhere until he is dead."

"No."

They swung around, sword and knife at the ready. Shukra stepped into the clearing. "You are coming with me, Yosef son of Arun."

In a flash, he had taken the knife from Yosef's hand, moving with a rapidity that seemed deceptive, as if he flowed through space. He looked down at the corpse on the ground. "It is being much better if nobody finds this dead person. Bodies tell stories, and the story this body is telling can do no good. I will be making certain it disappears."

"And why would you do that?" Theo was frowning.

"Ah. Now to that, I am having many reasons, and none of them concern you so much, Theudemir Suinthilason." Shukra turned back to Yosef. "You cannot be returning to Garnata, Yosef," he said quietly. "Not for a long time. Are you understanding me?"

The dark eyes held his own for a long moment until Yosef nodded. "Yes," he said softly. To his shame, he felt the hot prick of tears behind his eyes, and he looked away.

"You," said Shukra, turning to Theo. "You and Lælia will return to Illiberis. You will say nothing of this for now. None from the king's party must learn of it."

Theo's brows drew in like thunderclouds over the clear green. "But questions will be asked," he said. "Of Oppa, if he is seen. And of us. Would you have us lie?"

"Let Oppa say what he will," said Shukra. "And yes, you will lie. You will be lying better than ever you have. Oppa will tell no one what happened here. And it matters not what he does tell them. What matters is that you were never here and neither was Lælia. Neither of you saw anything or know anything about what happened here. You argued; you made up. You have been out hunting mountain lynx today. You did not catch anything. Perhaps a rabbit."

Shukra stepped closer to Theo. "If you do not lie well," he said quietly, "Yosef will die. His father will also die, quite possibly Sarah, too. Your brothers. Lælia." Shukra paused for a moment, letting his words sink in, then nodded. "You will lie, Theudemir son of Suinthila, and you will lie well. Too much has been risked for Yosef's journey and the help you have committed to give. It is now that this duty you speak of so often, *aziz-am*, is becoming real." Shukra turned to Yosef. "Are you understanding, Yosef ben Arun?"

Yosef swallowed and nodded. "Yes," he said. And, suddenly, he did.

Yosef turned to Theo. "We must do as he says – all of us. Don't fear for me. I will be safe now." He swallowed hard. "Take care of Sarah," he said, through the catch in his voice. "Tell her… tell her I am sorry. You must look to your own and Lælia's safety, do you understand?"

Theo shook his head. "I am sure there is another way…"

"There isn't." As Yosef said it, he knew it was true. "Do you trust me?"

Theo looked at him. "I do," he said.

Yosef found a twisted smile. "Carthage," he said.

Theo nodded curtly.

"That is where I will see you." Yosef held out his arm.

Theo gripped it hard, holding his eyes. "Carthage," he said. "I will be there, Yosef. I promise."

Yosef nodded. "I know."

It was time for him to leave. His life here, the one he had known, was gone. He could feel it.

"So." Shukra looked between them. "We will be keeping silent about what we are seeing. To speak of it will bring its evil back to life and make only more." He turned to Yosef. "Go to the place your father took you," he said.

Yosef looked at him. "Is my father there?"

Shukra shook his head wordlessly, and Yosef felt his heart sink. Shukra turned to Theo. "Wait here," he said. "I will send Lælia back to you."

Yosef nodded at the body on the ground. "What about – him?" he said, not looking at it.

"I will be taking care of that," said Shukra. Turning, he slipped silently into the trees, and Yosef heard the low murmur as he spoke to Sarah.

He turned to Theo. "If" – he swallowed, hardly able to voice it – "if anything has happened to my father, and something should happen to me, you are the only person who can complete what we set out to do." He gripped Theo's arm. "If I am not in Carthage," he said roughly, "you must find your way to Serica, to a place called Chang'an. Ask Laurentius to give you the piece of silk with the symbol on it. He will know what you mean. Show it to the people there – someone will come to find you."

"Someone will find me?" Theo reared back, staring at him. "Yosef –"

"No." Yosef stopped him curtly. "It is too important, Theo." His grip tightened on Theo's arm. "There is no other I trust," he said. "I go to discover how silk is made. If I cannot make the journey, you must."

He pulled back and searched Theo's set, hard face. "No other can do this," he said again. "It is not a task we can delegate or simply abandon. Too much relies upon it. Do you understand?"

Theo nodded slowly. "I do," he said, and the heaviness of his tone told Yosef that he did, indeed, understand the burden Yosef had just thrust upon him.

Lælia emerged a moment later, her eyes on Theo. *He is taking Sarah somewhere safe.*

She looked pale, Yosef saw, and he felt a stab of remorse, closely followed by a rush of shame. "I am sorry, Lælia," he said. "You should never have had to shoot that man because of me."

She waved her hand in dismissal. Yellow eyes flickered to his face, and she smiled briefly, making a series of quick gestures. *My aim was bad. I meant for my arrow to kill him.*

She stumbled, and Theo was at her side, his hand on her arm. "Are you hurt?" he said, green eyes dark.

No. She smiled at him, but it was a half smile, and something lurked in her eyes that Yosef couldn't read. Her fast hand gesture – *home* – did nothing to clarify it. Theo, though, seemed to understand, for when he turned to Yosef, he was distracted, already elsewhere. "Can you reach the place you are meant to be on your own?" he asked.

Yosef nodded. "Thank you," he said simply.

Theo clasped his elbow. "Go well," he said. He met Yosef's eyes, and they both smiled. He turned to Lælia. "You will ride with me," he said. Reaching down, he picked her up and swung her onto his own horse. Yosef watched in surprise as Lælia submitted to him. He had never known her to ride pillion with anyone. Theo swung up behind her and took her own horse's reins in his hand, holding Lælia safe with the other.

Lælia looked down at him. *Goodbye,* said her eyes.

The clearing was suddenly silent, and Yosef was alone with the body on the ground. He stared at Ilfric's sightless eyes for a long moment and then at the two figures riding away from him.

It was only when they turned the horse that Yosef noticed the blood dripping down Lælia's side.

15

THEO

DECEMBER AD 687

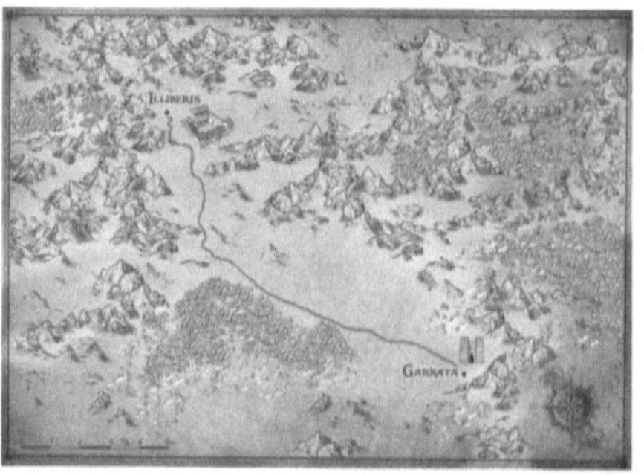

Illiberis, Bætica, Spania
Granada, Andalusia, Spain

Lælia had been silent and withdrawn since they left Yosef standing by Ilfric's corpse. Theo had grown accustomed to her moods, but he had not seen this one, and he did not think it the result of the attack. Something drew her home, an internal force deeper than any outward, physical event. Her hand gesture back in the clearing had conveyed an urgency he had instinctively grasped, responding to the subtle undercurrents he seemed always to feel in her presence.

He had mounted behind her and closed his eyes, inhaling the sweet, wild scent of her hair, wishing for a moment that he could make the ride last forever. Then he felt the wetness beneath his hand and looked down to find it covered in blood.

"You're hurt." He made to lift her from the horse, but she pushed his hand away, her own moving in front of him.

It doesn't matter. We must get back.

"Of course it matters!" Theo would have reined the horse in, but she turned to him with such a fierce look that he was taken aback.

The foals. Her eyes glowed. *Hurry, Theo.*

She touched his face with her hand, and he felt it then, a strange urgency he couldn't explain, like lightning beneath his skin. She nodded, tearing linen from the hem of her tunic as she saw understanding dawn in his eyes.

"But you are hurt," he said again, frowning as he looked down at the blood dripping from her side.

She waved a dismissive hand. *It is a scratch. Nothing bad.*

The stiff set of her shoulders brooked no argument. Theo could feel the strange internal shift, as if invisible clouds were gathering in their souls, pulling them toward Illiberis. It seemed that something had begun, an unstoppable force that held them all, tumbling them into a future that had been unimaginable when he woke that morning.

Lælia's hands moved in front of them, simple but painfully eloquent: *Am I a duty to you?*

Theo did not need her to elaborate. His arms tightened hard about her, careful to avoid the wound at her side, feeling the heat of her slender body like a sweet torture against his own.

"Yes," he said roughly. "You are the only damned duty that seems to matter to me anymore."

She turned her head, her face so close to his that he could take her mouth now, here, and it took everything within Theo to stop himself from doing it. "How am I supposed to leave you?" he muttered, eyes roaming her face hungrily. "And how can I do the duty I am meant to whilst you are here, like this?" His gesture took in her wound, the land around them as they rode, and Oppa's malignant presence somewhere in these mountains.

She stared at him, her eyes hollow and unreadable, and Theo felt a fear in the depths of his body he had never known before, the terrible agony it would be to know love and then to be forced to leave it, and Lælia, alone and without his protection.

It tasted sick and frightening in his mouth. Some of the intensity he felt must have shown in his eyes, for her own flared with a response that he longed to see her hands form but knew, once made, would bind them in a way so deep he was unsure he had the strength to walk away from it.

She turned back to face the road ahead, and Theo's lips moved against her hair. "How can I leave you?" he murmured again, holding her close against him.

She did not answer, just trembled faintly at his words, and they rode into the lengthening shadows.

The stables were set away from the villa, down a gentle slope. The pomegranate trees were bare skeletons, stark against the late afternoon blue. It was too early for the darting swifts of evening. A thrush watched them from one of the trees, iridescent feathers mirroring the sky in the east where the light deepened over the mountains. It called a sweet, haunting cry as they passed, watching through beady black eyes.

Theo reined his horse to a halt at the outer stable yard. He dismounted and turned, lifting Lælia gently to the ground. For a moment, they stood there, so close he could feel the magic between them, then she turned for the stables, gesturing impatiently for him to follow.

Theo quickly unsaddled their horses, pulled the wooden railing fence closed, and followed her inside. The light was dim, the air thick with blood and tension. The smell sat uneasily over the more familiar scent of straw and manure, the comforting sweetness of horse. A soft glow came from an open stall at the end of the building. An oil lamp burned on the wall, the pattern cut into the sconce casting odd shapes on the stone.

The mare was foaling. She lay on her side, flanks shiny with sweat, eyes showing their whites. Acantha, the woman Theo knew to be Lælia's grandmother, looked up as they entered the stall. The mare writhed with birth pains, legs feebly scrabbling the straw as she groaned in low, guttural gasps. Lælia dropped to her knees, her hands flying.

Acantha shook her head. "She has been in foal for too long. The foals are entangled." She held Lælia's eyes. "They will die," she said, with a quiet finality.

No.

Moving to the rear of the mare, Lælia reached for the almond oil in a dish nearby and coated her hands. Lifting the mare's tail, without hesitation she slid her hand inside the animal, her face a mask of concentration. After a moment, she frowned and looked at Theo. With her free hand she gestured to him and the almond oil. He coated his own hand and knelt opposite her. Breathing deeply, watching her eyes, he reached forward and placed his hand on her arm, just outside the mare's opening, and slowly, so their flesh seemed almost as one, he slid it down, gently working it inside until he felt her fingers and the hard bone of a foal beneath them.

The inside of the mare was hot, pulsing so powerfully with life that Theo felt his breath being taken away. It seemed as if in entering the mare's body he had entered an alien realm, a world of unknown life and form that occurred quite outside of his own, a busy city of flesh and blood in which he was a stranger. The mare grunted as he felt inside her, as if protesting this barbarian invasion into the country of her belly.

Theo inched forward. He watched Lælia, the two of them co-ordinating subtle movements so neither tore at the mare, their entwined arms moving as one. Theo felt, with increasing confidence, first the round hooves, then the crumpled folds of the legs. His hand passed over Lælia's as he did so and he realised the two foals were hopelessly entwined. He could not tell what belonged to one animal and what to the other. His hands felt big and clumsy, and the mare shifted uneasily.

"It's facing this way," he said. "But it is all tangled up with yours."

"Close your eyes," said Acantha.

The stable slipped away, and all that was existed in his hands. He felt hard bone and fragile tissue, the rapid fluttering of a new heart. He felt the tired muscles of the mare, the faltering pulse of blood through her veins, and knew that she was using the last of her life to complete this one, all-important task. He understood her sacrifice and the eager thrust of new life. His hands worked in concert with Lælia's as if they were one body, a unique form quite separate from his own.

Finally, he felt the two foals slip apart.

Hold, said Lælia's hand on his.

With his eyes still closed, Theo shook his head. It seemed he was fighting for words, as he had in his dream. "No," he said. "Mine first." He could feel the urgency beneath his hands, knew the foal must come out now or die.

He edged it sideways and pulled; like a snake shedding its skin, a black colt slithered into the world. Theo caught it in his arms and the two stared at each other. The colt's heart raced wildly, its breathing short and fast, and it stared up at Theo with wide, startled, topaz eyes – the same colour as Lælia's. Theo felt a queer thrill run through his body, into the animal, then back again, an odd pulsing that prickled beneath his skin and felt like fire in his veins.

He felt rather than heard the twin come into the world. Lælia held a filly of pure white. It looked up at her with an odd awareness that sent the fire in Theo's veins racing again, every hair on his neck alert. He saw Acantha's gaze flicker between him and the filly, and he knew without asking that the colour of her eyes was an exact match to his own.

Lælia looked at him. He saw in her face the same wonder and thrill that ran through his own body. The colt in his arms stirred, and the filly reached forward. The two heads, one black and the other white, touched delicately. Their nostrils flared as they drank in the life breath and the scent of the other, noses gently touching, frantic breathing gradually slowing as they inhaled the new reality they shared.

The mare heaved a great sigh, and a thick pile of steaming red slipped from her body. Her eyes glazed over, and Theo knew she was gone.

The foals made a low sound, struggling feebly on the newborn hooves still coated with the weird, misshapen covering of birth, nuzzling the fallen body of their mother. Theo felt his heart contract in such pain that it hurt his throat; he thought of his own mother, barely remembered, and the tears he had never shed blocked his chest in a hard lump.

Acantha bent over the mare's head and murmured, a soothing sound that eased the lump in Theo's heart, her hand gently closing the mare's eyes with their long-fringed lashes. Then she reached into the thick pile of bloody matter on the ground. When she raised it, her cupped palm was filled with rich, dark blood.

She held it out to Lælia, saying something in the language of the tribes. Lælia leaned forward and drank from her palm. When she raised her head, her mouth was crimson and her eyes glowed with dark fire. The woman reached out with one forefinger and touched her forehead, leaving a bright thumbprint of red blood between her eyebrows.

Then she turned to Theo, her cupped palm outstretched. He could smell the rich stench of the mare's placenta like a live thing in her hand. She murmured words he did not understand, her dark eyes alert and watchful on his face; without hesitation, he bent and drank from her palm.

The blood hit his throat in a strange, raw burst of life. For a moment, it was as if he were inside the mare's body once more, except now she existed within his own flesh. Theo felt the life of her become part of his own lifeblood, her heartbeat pulsing with his. He opened his eyes, and Acantha, watching him keenly, nodded in satisfaction and clicked her tongue. She leaned forward and marked his face as she had Lælia's.

He stroked the colt's neck gently. It was still struggling to stand, nudging its companion, and Theo watched in delight as the two staggered drunkenly to their feet, looking about at the new place that was their world.

The twilight was gone. He could feel the change in the air, the dead silence of night falling like a heavy veil over the gloaming. Soon the villa would gather for meat, and they would be missed. He looked at Lælia, the dark fall of her hair black gloss against the pure white of the newborn filly.

"We must go," he said.

But the eyes she turned to him were bright and unfocused, the pupils pinpricks in her face. Even in the dim lamplight, Theo could see the high points of colour on her cheeks. She trembled. The faint shiver that ran across her body shook his own with a sudden, terrible foreboding.

"Lælia," he said, scrambling across the straw toward her, arms outstretched. "Lælia! What is it?"

The filly fell from her arms to its side, thin legs scrabbling weakly in the straw, the light in its eyes fading as Acantha bent over it. Lælia tried to stand and swayed, her lithe body stiff as she turned to Theo. His outstretched arms caught her, and she fell into oblivion.

16

THEO

DECEMBER AD 687

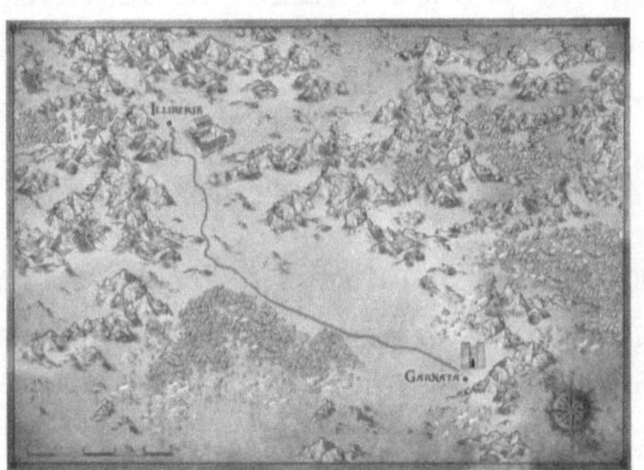

Illiberis, Bætica, Spania
Granada, Andalusia, Spain

Lælia was prostrate beneath the covers, her body wracked with fever. Theo stood just beyond the door in the shadows.

"You can come in now." Acantha spoke without turning. He slipped into the room, closing the door behind him. Lælia's face was flushed. He touched it with one finger and almost leaped back at the heat beneath her skin. As he did so, the lithe body arched, every muscle tight and strained, lifting almost entirely off the bed. Tight fists hit the mattress, curled so hard into themselves the knuckles were white, but Lælia did not make a sound.

"She is burning like fire," he said.

"The arrow was poisoned. I have treated the wound. I may have caught it in time." Acantha looked at him grimly. "Maybe not."

Theo looked up to see Count Paulus at the door. Paulus looked down at the prostrate figure of his granddaughter, his face as closed and forbidding as a mountain storm.

He met his wife's eyes and read his worst fears in them. He turned and, without a word, walked away. Lælia moved again on the bed, sudden and violent.

"Hush," murmured Acantha. "*Ga-waíri, liefs.* Be at peace, love."

Hesitantly, Theo reached forward, capturing one of the fists in his own. It burned like a hot coal from the fire. He cupped his cold hands around it as if the night cool could douse the flames. Lælia's eyes opened, and she looked straight at him, unseeing. Her eyes were the burning russet of the sky at sunset, such a deep bronze they seemed to glow. They searched his face as if to find the answer to a question hidden deep inside her body, in a place nobody could see.

Theo felt, looking into them, as if he were running down dark corridors, through door after door, each opening into deeper chambers, to arrive finally at the place within her where that question blazed, where Lælia fought to find the answer, all alone in the darkness.

He held the fist and felt himself drawn deeper into the bronze fire of her being. He remembered their hands entwining inside the horse's belly, working as if by their own will, knowing instinctively what the other would do.

"Breathe," he heard Acantha murmur over the bed. "Breathe deeply, Theo."

He pulled the cool night air in through his nostrils, feeling it travel down through his chest, into his veins so they tingled, and out through his hands and into hers, into the dark corridors of her being. He saw the air in her body like a fine, cool night mist, the stillness of moisture in the dark hour before predawn, travelling twisted pathways to the burning core where she battled the blaze alone. He breathed in again, and as the cool moisture settled upon the flames in her body, he felt the final door inside her unlock.

Her mouth opened, and for a moment he thought she would speak. But she simply took a long, desperately deep breath, her eyes on his. She kept the air within for a long time, holding his eyes, then she swallowed. Her eyes closed once more, and she settled back onto the bed.

Theo released her hand and stepped back, his heart beating fast. He looked at Acantha. She stroked Lælia's face, but her eyes held his. She smiled faintly and nodded, as if she knew without words where he had just travelled; Theo felt comforted by her tall strength.

"Go, now," she said. "Go to the stables and stay with the foals. They are weak still, and tonight is when they are most vulnerable. I will watch her. I will ensure none enter this chamber who should not. Theo" – she fixed him with a stern eye – "no matter what happens tonight, you keep those foals alive. Do you understand?"

Theo nodded. He took a last look at the bed where Lælia lay, still once more. Was it his imagination or did she seem to breathe more easily? He slipped out of the room into the night.

The stables were dark and deserted. The foals lay in the straw beside the dead mare, alone and weak. The dark colt whickered, but the white filly lay on her side breathing shallowly, eyes distant, fading to dull moss. Theo fell to his knees beside the filly, feeling for a pulse. It was there, but weak and thready, the heartbeat erratic. The untidy hair of birth was slick in whorls and tufts, glistening with sweat in the dim light.

He gave both foals water to drink and then found the dead mare's milk Acantha had taken from her earlier. Twisting a cloth, he dipped it into the milk and held it to the filly's mouth, putting his fingers inside and forcing the cloth in, squeezing the milk onto her tongue. The filly turned her head away but Theo held it, patiently putting the cloth from the basin back into the mouth, stroking her neck and murmuring as he had to Lælia only moments before.

"*Mik haba*," he whispered. It's alright. He spoke in Gothic, hoping the filly understood it as well as the language of the tribes. He felt a terrible, cold loneliness, the weight of a fear he had never known.

He kept his hands on the foals, leaving their side only to stir thyme water on the brazier. Hearing a rustling at the doorway, he looked up. Alaric and Athanagild stood in the lamplight. Theo could see the tension on their faces.

"He dreamed you were in danger," said Alaric. He frowned, taking in the scene of blood and birth, and his brother's face. "We both did; we woke at the same time."

They moved closer, coming down into the straw beside him.

"Lælia," said Theo. His voice cracked. He hung his head, so they wouldn't see the tears blurring his eyes. Of a sudden, the day's events overtook him, unlocked by the comforting presence of his brothers.

"We heard." Alaric put a warm, solid hand on his shoulder, gripping it tight.

"I have to keep the foals alive," Theo said. He wanted to say more, to explain why it was important, but he didn't trust his voice and couldn't have found the words anyway.

"What can we do?"

Theo put salve into Athanagild's hand and a straw rub into Alaric's. He showed them what to do, and they took up position on either side of him, stroking the filly in time with his own movements. Theo rocked back and forth, holding the filly's head close to him. She stared up at him with wide, frightened eyes.

"Don't be afraid," Athanagild spoke up, one long-fingered hand stroking the filly's neck. "We will stay with you." He smiled at Theo, who felt bittersweet emotion clutch at his heart as he looked between Athanagild and Alaric. The feeling travelled through his body so his whole right arm and hand pulsed with a strange mixture of love and longing. He would be gone from them soon, and from Lælia. He remembered the promise he had made to Yosef, felt the weight of it heavy upon his soul, the journey he may have to make stretching unendingly before him. In the dark intimacy of the stables, after the blood and violence of the day, the prospect felt overwhelmingly lonely.

The night grew deep, and surrounded by the silent warmth of his brothers, Theo cradled the filly, willing her to live.

17

LÆLIA
PLACE BEYOND TIME

The fever is like leaping into a waterfall.

I jump, finding myself in the tumble of it, then hit the seething pool of water below and sink into its depths. I fall into a darkness that is like a series of underwater caves, each blacker and hotter than the last. Strange voices cry on a blazing current, searing through my skin and into my veins. I can make out none of the words, but I know they belong to my parents, just as I know I am about to die.

I try to call out to them. I feel the unfamiliar substance of words like bubbles, pushing through the thick stuff of my being. For the first time in my conscious life, I understand the shape and texture of spoken language, and even in the darkness and heat I feel a sadness that it is only now, as life is leaving my body, that I can touch its beauty.

I sink further into the underwater caves, and the air grows hotter and closer still. The sound of my parents' voices come closer, calling me forward into yet another chamber, but I am tired and terrified and want only to let the heat suffocate me, ending the pain.

Still they call me, the voices seeming to become clearer. I can hear my mother saying my name. Her voice is high and clear, and it cuts through the darkness like a shaft of light, my father's presence somewhere behind her, felt but not seen.

"Lælia," she says. "Lælia, come here. Come to me."

I will see them at last, I think. The parents I know only through the inadequate words of others, whom I cannot see in my own mind except in vague impressions when I sleep, in dreams that I clutch at in vain upon waking only to find myself bereft once more when they dissolve into blackness.

Now, when they call, I feel a rush of determination; this time, they will not leave me. This time, I will follow them into the blackness.

I fight the walls as they close in, fight to breathe in the suffocating heat, wading through the dense current toward the thin shaft of light in the distance. Words seem to gather in my throat. I feel them like a corporeal mass in my body, on the verge of being spoken, their shape so close I can taste it. They seem somehow attached to my mother. If I could only reach her, I think, I would find the words. I want their taste more than I have wanted anything in my life.

As I near the sound of her voice, I feel a cool draught touch my skin. I turn my face to it, sucking in air greedily, led by the sweetness into a wider, more open cavern. I am far underground. A clear pool of water glistens at my feet. The dense air is gone, replaced by a cool subterranean stillness that creeps through the heat in my veins, slowly calming me.

I have been here before, in my dreams. I know the paintings on the rock, and I turn to them, tracing the vivid lines with my finger, feeling their strength flow into my body. Finally, I find the one I know best, the one I have seen in a dream, deep within.

The horse flies across the rock in delicate ochre, drawn by hands that understand what it is to be the animal itself. For a moment, it seems I am crouching in long grass, watching the herd race across the valley; they are aware of my presence just as I am of theirs. I know it is a time long past. I am a different being, though still myself somewhere at the core, but here in the grass, the horses are not separate from me as they are in my daily life at Illiberis. Here in the valley, I know what it was to be the horse, and they in turn know my spirit as their own. I run with them, flowing from their body into my own, a soft current that weaves through the air as one indivisible being, and I feel gratitude and wonder at the vivid sensation of life in my veins and in the earth above and below.

The valley fades, and I come back to the cavern. I turn to the pool of water, bending to my own image. It is not a child's face that looks back at me. It is still I, but older. I know myself in the image just as I knew that the spirit in the grass was my own. Behind me, two armies clash upon strange desert sands, the sound of steel ringing out amidst the dust and heat. I feel no fear. My body is sinew and strength, and I feel the weight of the bow at my back. I know those men are mine and that they will follow me to the death.

The armies fade, and I feel a presence beside me. For a moment, I remember my mother and father, and wonder if they have come for me at last. I have felt them in dreams many times before, but this is a new presence, yet as old as the spirit I was in the valley of horses and grass. It is a cool, hard force, like the worked steel of a fine sword. I see the same shaft of light I followed into the cavern. It is a deep cobalt blue, infinite and wise, seeping over my body and into the heat of my soul as untempered iron slips fearlessly into the furnace. It draws closer to my body and I instinctively lean into it, staring into the still water of the pool.

The iron becomes a man with eyes of clear green and a mane that blazes like the dawn sun. He kneels beside me and we stare at each other in the pool. I know his face and yet it is different, riven with savage marks, carved and hard with suffering. The images behind us fade and move, mountains and deserts, strange domes, and cities I have never seen. They don't matter, I realise; they are but shifting ghosts, an ever-changing backdrop to the eternal pres-ence of us.

What matters – the only thing that matters – is the merging of us both, and as we stare into the pool, I feel us join and become something else, a liquid being that dances in the watery depths, magical and alive, amorphous and indestructible. I reach for it, and as I do one of the bubbles in my soul finally finds its way to the surface and explodes, making the cavern and the man disappear.

My eyelids spring open.

I am in my room in Illiberis, the first light of dawn turning the sky to rose. My mouth feels dry, my tongue thick and clumsy.

"Theo," I say.

18

YOSEF

DECEMBER AD 687

Garnata, Bœtica, Spania
Granada, Andalusia, Spain

Yosef sat alone in the darkness of the cave, waiting. It felt as if the night had already gone on forever. Yosef had left the dying yellow moon beyond the cave entrance and with it, his sense of the passage of time. He sat in total darkness and thought it very possible that he might die there.

A part of him knew his father would not come. Had known it from the moment his knife went into Ilfric's flesh. He shuddered at

143

the memory but could not rid himself of it. The knife and Ilfric were part of him now. They felt like a raw wound, one that would not scab over. Yosef knew that if he mended at all, nothing would ever remove the twisted, ugly scar of death. His soul would wear it forever. Men would know it if they looked upon him.

I have killed, he thought dully. *I have taken a life.*

The fact that he could make no sense of it was why he knew his father would not come. It would be too easy if Arun were here. The horrible weight of it would be lifted from him, taken by his father to carry so that he, Yosef, could dwell once more in the peace of child-hood. And he knew, just as he had known he had no choice but to kill Ilfric, that this was a burden none could carry except himself. Knew, even if his father took it, that the peace was gone. His life was now bought at the expense of another, and none could recon-cile that bargain except the one who had made it.

The weight of life settled upon him in the darkness, and Yosef felt his future like a black tunnel he must walk into with no light to guide the way. There was nothing but the shallow sound of his breath and the soft rustle of night animals. His eyes closed in the darkness and the rich beat of his heart slowed. His breathing deep-ened with the night. Somewhere in the blackness an owl called, its haunting cry unbearably lonely.

Yosef fell into a dead, dreamless sleep from which, had he been able to form conscious thought, he would have wished never to wake. The sound of approaching footsteps was the first indication that night was done, pulling him from the abyss of peace back into the cave. He woke alert, heart thudding. The footsteps came closer, and he heard a boy's voice.

"But why do I have to leave? I'm not Yosef."

"I don't care," a woman's voice snapped back, hard with tension and fear. "They say that the king's bastard has not yet left the monastery at Illiberis. This very morning, he stood in the town centre, railing against the sins of the Jews. A girl has been raped, one of the royal party killed, and both crimes are being laid at the door of Yosef ben Arun. A mob is on its way to Garnata – and they carry the blessing of the church fathers with them, God curse their wicked hypocrisy."

"I still think you are panicking," said the boy as they passed directly outside the cave.

"Am I?" The woman's voice was bleak. "The mob from Illiberis will be in no mood to pause to check the identity of whoever they take. You are a Jewish boy of the same age. They will kill you first and ask questions later."

Yosef recognised her voice; she owned a fruit stall in the market. He could see her in his mind's eye, round and cheerful, her bosom straining against the seams of the coarse grey tunic she always wore. Her son was his age and looked uncannily like Yosef; their own mothers had confused them a time or two when they were younger.

"Where should I go?" the boy asked, unable to disguise the faint tremble in his voice.

"Away. Until this dies down or they find someone to burn. If Yosef is smart, he will be far away. They say the bastard's men have already taken his father..."

The voices faded around the hill, and Yosef sat in the dark silence of the cave, his heart thudding slowly.

They say the bastard's men have already taken his father...

His mouth was dry, and he desperately needed to piss. Cautiously, he crawled to the mouth of the cave and looked about. It was well past dawn. Of Shukra, there was no sign. A sense of impotent fury gripped him. He could not sit here, alone in a dark cave, when his father had been taken by the king's men and his friends – who had done nothing wrong – were forced to flee a Christian mob. It was wrong, and he cursed his stupidity in listening to Shukra against his own heart's knowledge.

Yosef could not hide in the shadows whilst his father risked his life. He felt deeply ashamed that he had already wasted so much time. Hastily, he scrambled down the hill, avoiding the paths and ducking behind the large clumps of oleander that grew amongst the tall grasses and boulders. More than one family had clearly decided to take the same path as the woman and her son. Yosef saw several anxious parents escorting their offspring into the mountains. He saw others leaving who had no children but who had obviously decided the danger was too high. He hid from each, careful to remain out of sight.

He could not enter the town from the front, between the red towers, for fear of being seen. Instead, he crossed the valley and climbed the steep hills behind Garnata, coming down carefully until he stood at the thick earthen wall bordering the town on the eastern edge. He knew one section where an old fig tree grew, providing strong branches on which he could climb to reach the top of the wall. None came at Garnata from the east. The mountains were too steep behind him for any to cross, and the fortified wall on this face was poorly kept.

He scaled the wall and dropped silently to the other side. He could hear yelling coming from the square in the distance, and he moved toward it, keeping low and hiding whenever anyone approached.

One alleyway out from the square led to an old house that he knew was deserted and sometimes used as a granary. He entered cautiously, creeping through the musty lower level and jumping when a rat brushed his leg. He climbed the stairs and came out onto the roof. Lying on his belly, he inched across the earthen roof and peered over into the square.

A red-faced man stood on the steps of the church. He had a great belly, which looked unused to hunger, and a bulbous nose squashed onto his face beneath small eyes lost in fat. He raised a fist as he addressed the crowd. "And did not the Holy Father, Archbishop Julian himself, say: *When one heretic is tolerated in your midst, all must bear the consequences?*"

Before him was the rabble from Illiberis, thin and dirty. The houses of Garnata stood closed and silent, their inhabitants behind locked doors.

"He said it!" roared the crowd.

"And is it not true that as our children have died, the Jews of Garnata have thrived, untouched by illness?"

"It is true!"

The man's voice lowered, an ominous hush descending on the crowd. "We have tolerated this heresy in our midst for long enough. Whilst our people starve, the Jews of Garnata grow rich. And now as Oppa, the noble son of our king, just this day has reminded us, they are not only thieves and agents of Satan, but rapists and murderers too."

Raising one arm, the speaker swung abruptly to his right, pointing to the corner of the square where the posca stall normally stood. Atop the fire used to heat the wine, a huge cauldron of boiling oil bubbled, sending noxious fumes into the air. From behind the stall, two men emerged, pulling Yosef's father between them. Feet bleeding, face bruised from repeated blows, Arun stumbled, hanging between their grasp.

Yosef froze, barely able to breathe.

"It was this man's son – the same man who lives like a king whilst good Christian believers starve and their children die – who attacked a poor, defenceless girl, forcing his vile need upon her."

The speaker gestured extravagantly, and the crowd muttered and shook their heads.

"Then, when the king's own son, Oppa" – he waved vaguely toward the edge of the square – "attempted to rescue her, this man's son did foully and in cold blood kill one of his guards and attempt to attack the body of the king's son himself."

The crowd erupted into fury. Fists in the air, they screamed invective, those closest throwing handfuls of dirt and pebbles at Arun's face.

Yosef trembled, clutching the beam on the edge of the roof for support. Through the haze of smoke, he saw, on the distant edge of the square, the tall, lean figure of Oppa, flanked by half a dozen of the king's men. He sat on his horse calmly, eyeing the tumult with mingled disdain and amusement, the jewelled eagle glittering on his shoulder.

Yosef tensed, all restraint gone. He would not lie here whilst his father was tortured on Oppa's lies. He had just gathered his legs beneath him when a firm hand pushed him face down onto the roof.

"You are not to be doing this, *aziz-am*," said a low voice in his ear.

"Get off me," Yosef hissed. "I should never have listened to you."

"If you are going down there, it will not only be your noble father who is burning in oil; it will be you, also."

Shukra's words were calm and clear, and the hand that held him did so lightly, but with a certain fine strength that warned Yosef that it would be no easy task to free himself.

"I cannot do nothing," he gasped and was bitterly ashamed of the sob that caught his words. "You would have me lie here and watch my own father suffer when it is I who should face that crowd, and Oppa who should face justice. Please," he said, as the man's grip showed no sign of loosening. "Let me go."

His only answer was a knee in the base of his spine, holding him mercilessly in place so that he was unable to look away from the square.

"If the boy is innocent," cried a fat, red-faced merchant, "why would he run? Let him come before us and face his crimes."

This raised a righteous cheer of support. Yosef squirmed beneath the whipcord hold.

"We will not be giving them what they want, *aziz-am*," murmured the voice behind him.

"If he will not come out then his father shall answer for him," said the original heckler. "Arun Radhan serves as agent for the Count of Illiberis. We all know it, and we know that Count Paulus pays the Church to look the other way. He pays the wages of sin whilst our children die in poverty."

The crowd roared in approval.

Arun raised his head, facing the crowd of attackers. The deep lines of his face seemed carved by exhaustion like folds in granite; his eyes were dark and hollow in the craggy features. Towering over those who held him, there was a dignity in the great frame that made his captors seem vaguely ridiculous, like children tugging on ropes binding one of the great mammoths of old. It was a measure of his presence that when he spoke, his words cut through the fury of the crowd with the precision of steel, silencing them instantly.

"I do not know the truth of these accusations." Impervious to the ropes tugging at him, Arun spoke calmly, and the crowd listened. "My son disappeared last night. Today, this man" – he nodded at Oppa – "informed me that Yosef had violently assaulted a girl who has been a friend of our family since birth, one who has eaten at my table. A girl whom my son loves and respects and whom I have treated as a daughter."

His words told their own story; he had no need of dramatic flair.

"But not only," Arun went on, "was Yosef accused of attacking this girl in the vilest way any man can violate a woman. When he was interrupted, Fráuja Oppa claims, Yosef killed the man who tried to stop him. Stabbed him. My son, who learned his letters long before his hand ever touched steel, is said to have bested one of the king's own men."

A low murmur rose at this, and heads turned toward Oppa, who met them stony faced.

"Two terrible crimes were committed, and justice must be done," said Arun. "But let justice fall on the head of him who deserves it."

Oppa spurred his horse forward, riding into the square and reining to a halt in front of Arun. For a moment, Yosef thought he would dismount and address the crowd, and his heart surged; none could outdo his father in debate, and the crowd was dithering.

But Oppa did not dismount. He raised one mailed hand and brutally struck Arun with such force that blood flew in a crimson spray onto the stone beneath. Hawking, he spat, full in Arun's face.

"You are a Jew," he said. His tone dripped contempt.

The word "Jew" was both accusation and judgement, and Oppa, Yosef realised, needed nothing more to sentence his father.

"No!"

It was Yosef's mother who screamed. Shukra held him tightly as Yosef saw her push through the crowd and, for the first time, his father's composure crack.

"Stay back!" Arun roared. "Leave!"

Yosef's mother came to his side. She reached out and as she did, Oppa's knife flashed through the air and across her throat. She fell to the ground with a sick gurgle. Arun roared in rage and frustration, straining at his bonds as blood flowed from her body and trickled in a terrible river between the stones on the ground. Yosef's scream died in his throat as Shukra covered his mouth. He watched in silent horror as his mother's body grew limp and then horribly, finally still.

Nodding at the men holding Arun, Oppa gestured at the cauldron of oil. "Burn him."

The steel-capped toe of his boot came out, kicking Arun hard beneath the chin. Yosef shuddered at the blow. His father grunted, knees buckling.

Oppa's contempt had served to remove from Arun any trace of humanity. He was now merely an object of derision, a source of dark entertainment. The crowd, galvanised once more, roared in approbation, and men dragged Arun toward the cauldron.

"Let me go." Yosef struggled, panting, sobs tearing at his throat, but the grip on him was tight and merciless, and now another hand came over the back of his head, pushing his face down so he could not see. A terrible scream rent the air, and the crowd shrieked in delight, a manic sound of glee that turned Yosef's stomach.

"Let me see," he cried into the heat of the roof.

"No, *aziz-am*." The voice was gentle but firm. "Many long nights lie before you. You will not carry these visions into them."

His father screamed again, this time a long, drawn-out cry of such agony that Yosef wanted to close his ears, a cry he knew would haunt him far longer than the visions Shukra wished to protect him from, a cry that seemed to travel through his veins and into his heart until it finally faded into a groan and then, mercifully, stopped.

A terrible stench reached Yosef, burning the back of his throat, so foul an odour that he retched. It smelled as old mutton did when boiled, rank and alive, and he realised with a sick horror that it was the smell of his father's flesh dissolving in oil.

"Stop!" There was something in the hoarse cry that momentarily weakened the grip on his head, and Yosef raised his eyes.

His father hung between the men holding him, but there was no longer a rope tied to his hands, for there were no longer hands to bind. The flesh had melted from his bones, so it hung from his arms to the elbows in strange, tortured tatters, raw and red. But his arms were not the worst of it. His face had touched the oil and been rendered unrecognisable. The once proud features had slithered into an indistinct mass. Where the oil had reached his body the cloth was burned, and holes smoked in his flesh. Arun Radhan was no longer a man, but rather a terrible lump of meat, limp and lifeless.

The shout had come from the Illiberis road. Count Paulus spurred his horse through the crowd until he reached Arun. "Get back!" he roared.

The men of his thiufa rode into the square, pushing their way through the sea of bodies, beating about them with the flat of their swords. Taking hold of the cauldron, they threw it over, townspeople leaping out of the path of the splashing oil, shrieking where it touched them. The oil ran into the cracks of the stone and down the hill away from the pyre, a foul, dangerous river that sent smoke up into the air as it went.

"Take him!" Count Paulus ordered.

A group of Garnata Jews raced forward at Count Paulus's command and gathered about Arun, collecting the horrible mass of limb and flesh in the canvas of the ruined stall and carrying him from the square.

The mob fell back, but they continued to shout, sullen faces eyeing Count Paulus's men resentfully.

"Why do you protect the Jew?" one called. "It is against the law to trade with them, and yet the house of Illiberis continues to do so. It is your fault that this heresy continues. Your fault that we cannot make enough coin to feed our children."

But Count Paulus paid them no heed. "You!" He pointed his sword at Oppa, who had retreated to the edge of the square and begun riding away. "You did this!"

Oppa reined his horse and turned a disdainful eye to Count Paulus.

"You are count of this place," he said coolly. "You should have done this long ago, in accordance with the rule of law."

"Burning in oil? Killing an innocent man with no reason? This is your notion of law?"

"Read your church canons. For Jews, such punishment is the law – or it was. Soon it will be again." Oppa looked out over the crowd. "Perhaps today will serve as a reminder to you of how King Egica wishes to address the foul heresy in our midst." Turning his horse, he nodded briefly at Count Paulus. "Good day, Fráuja," he said with cold courtesy and rode down the hill surrounded by his men. He did not look back.

Yosef saw Count Paulus lunge forward as if to follow. He was held back by two of his own men. The crowd began to disperse, wary of the anger in Count Paulus's face. Yosef felt the grip on his neck slacken.

"I must go to my father," he said hollowly.

"Your father is dead, *aziz-am*."

Maddened, Yosef rounded on Shukra, twisting free of his grasp. "Then I will die with him," he said, his voice cracking. "What other purpose can I now serve?"

"Garnata can still be saved," Shukra said quietly. "As can those you love, Yosef."

Staring down at his mother's limp body, Yosef felt something inside him grow brittle and hard. "Nothing," he said bitterly, "can save the Jews of Garnata."

"Yosef." Shukra gripped his shoulders. "Do you recall the promises you made?"

"What of them?" said Yosef dully. He thought of Theo, carrying a wounded Lælia on the horse before him; Theo loved her, Yosef knew. Now she was likely dead. And Theo – how long would it be before Theo was punished for Ilfric's death, for something he, Yosef, had done?

"None of those promises matter now," said Yosef. "It is all gone. Theo will never sail. Even if he does, I would not have him wander for years for nothing more than a dream. It is over."

"You cannot be knowing that." Reaching beneath his cloak, Shukra drew out the scrolls Yosef and his father had retrieved from the caves. The image of the silk tree sat beside that of Zoroaster. The wings of the eagle seemed poised to take flight. "When we are making promises, *aziz-am*, we must be keeping them, no matter what we do not know of the future."

"I can't do this," whispered Yosef. "I cannot."

"And if you do not," said Shukra, "what then will you do?"

For a moment, Yosef stared at him. Then he looked at the

square, where his mother lay lifeless, and into the mountains, where Sarah's body had been torn and ravaged.

Dead and wounded, he thought, brokenly. *Because of me. I am no use to any here.*

"Come, *aziz-am,*" said Shukra gently. "It is time we are gone."

19

THEO

DECEMBER AD 687

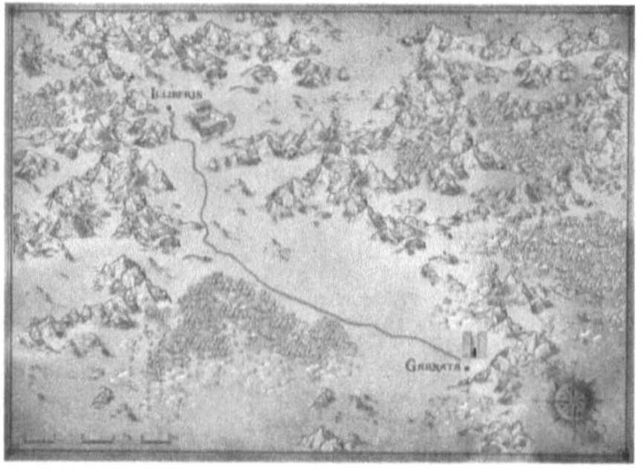

Illiberis, Bœtica, Spania
Granada, Andalusia, Spain

"I cannot leave." Theo stared at Laurentius. "Lælia has barely regained consciousness. The foals…"

"Will be cared for by your brothers." Laurentius's face was unusually grim. "Theo, have you heard a word I have said? Yosef's parents were killed. Oppa has disappeared. Even now, he could be pursuing Yosef to the coast. Worse, he could return to Illiberis and come for you."

"For me?" Theo was taken aback. "Why would he come for me?"

"Because he knows what you saw in the woods."

As Theo began to deny it, Laurentius cut him off curtly. "I have spoken with Shukra." His lips tightened. "We are fortunate he was there, or this could never have been managed. He has taken Yosef to Septem; with luck, they will be gone before Oppa finds them. You and Lælia are in danger. Lælia, at least, will be safe here in Count Paulus's care. But you" – he looked sternly at his nephew – "you have no choice now, Theo, but to go. If you stay here, Oppa will see you hanged or dead on the point of his sword. And Yosef will be alone, with no aid. Too much has been risked for you to be lost now. You will leave tonight, with the horses destined for Septem. The Illiberis goods travel on merchant dromons in the company of a small detachment of the fleet. You will leave Spania in their company and meet Yosef in Carthage as planned."

Theo felt the blood drain from his face as he stared at his uncle. His brothers moved to his side as if to hold him up.

"What if Oppa follows Theo to sea?" Alaric asked, frowning.

"We must hope he does not."

"But he might." Athanagild's face was gaunt with exhaustion. Neither of his brothers had left Theo since he came from Lælia's bedside. They stood beside him now in the deserted œca, the scent of old meat hanging in the air.

"Yes. He might." Laurentius looked at the faces before him. "We cannot prepare for all eventualities," he said. "But you have a job to do, Theo, and you must honour it."

He held out a scroll with the winged sun on it. "When the fleet reaches Septem," he said, "you will give this to Fráuja Ilyan, Count of Septem. He will ensure word reaches Yosef."

Theo's mind whirled. Beyond the œca he could hear the sound of men and movement. He felt his insides clench, a sick tension in his throat.

"What if Oppa comes for Lælia instead of me?" He searched Laurentius's face. "I know what he is capable of. He will not rest until he has had his revenge on Illiberis – and on Lælia. She humiliated him. Not once, Laurentius, but twice. Oppa is not a man to forget that."

He stared down at the scroll Laurentius was proffering and felt a surge of sudden, visceral anger. "How many more people must die or suffer for this plan?" His fists clenched. "Yosef's parents are dead. Lælia is wounded, Sarah violated. A man was killed, Laurentius."

"And more will die if you do not leave, Theo." Laurentius's voice was stern but not unkind. "Duty," he said quietly, "is never easy."

Theo took a deep breath, trying to master his emotions.

"Theo," said Alaric beside him, "I will raise Father's men, should it come to it. I will not allow Oppa to hurt you, or Lælia. We can fight. If you do not wish to go, don't."

His words had the effect Laurentius's had not. Theo remembered, almost as if from a distance, the promise he had made to Yosef. It seemed long ago now, almost unimportant.

If I cannot make the journey, you must.

I cannot go back on it now, he thought grimly, *no matter my own desires.* He gripped Alaric's shoulder. "Should Oppa come for her," he said, holding his brother's eyes, "I will expect you to protect her. Do you understand me?"

He looked between them, Alaric's face dark and solid, Athanagild's slender and hazel eyed. They met his gaze, and he saw their understanding and agreement; they knew he must go.

"She is as our sister," said Athanagild, gripping Theo's arm.

"You have our word," added Alaric, taking the other.

"Good." Theo forced a smile. "Then try not to cause a war before I come back, *ne?* It would be unfair if you kept all the fun for yourselves." He gripped their arms hard enough to leave marks. He turned to Laurentius. "You have a piece of silk," he said. "Yosef told me I should carry it. In case…" He did not finish the sentence, but Laurentius's grave eyes said that he understood. He reached into his tunic and brought out the small pool of white silk.

Wordlessly, without glancing at it, Theo placed the silk inside his own tunic.

"It is not easy, what is asked of you." Laurentius gripped his shoulder. "But I would not have chosen you if I did not think you could meet what lies ahead."

The grey eyes searched Theo's face, seeking answers. Theo withdrew behind it, to the place where he knew himself and allowed no man to see him.

"You did not choose me," he said coolly. "It was I who chose. I will do my duty, Laurentius."

Laurentius winced as if Theo had struck him. He opened his mouth to speak, but Theo had already gone.

Lælia was not in her bedchamber. For a moment, Theo panicked. She had been sleeping when last he saw her, the fever gone, but perhaps she had suffered a decline.

"She is in the stables." Acantha stood in the doorway, her face tired and drawn. "Go to her, Theo," she said quietly. "She will wish to see you before you ride." He began to speak, but she waved him away. "Go," she said, turning her back. Theo had the sense that there was much she wished to say and could not.

He went. The interior of the stables was dim in the predawn light. A movement in the far corner rustled the straw, and Theo spun toward it, eyes adjusting to the gloom.

Were you going to leave without saying goodbye? Lælia stood in the corner, pale faced and drawn but upright and steady on her feet. The foals lay in the straw on either side of her, eyes half closed.

Theo frowned. "You should be resting."

I wanted to make you something.

She gestured for him to approach. Closer, he could smell the rich, sweet scent of the foals, mingled with wild herbs and clear mountain air. Theo closed his eyes and inhaled. He wanted to imprint the scent on his mind, carry it with him where he went, this most vivid recollection of Lælia. She stepped toward him, an offering in her hand. Theo reached out to take it.

Acantha carved it from the bone of the mare.

It was simple and small, but far from crude, a replica of the one she herself wore, the entwined serpents of the Illiberis mark.

Theo traced them with his finger. "I, too, have something for you," he said. Reaching into his tunic, he held up a coin the same as the one he wore.

"It was my mother's," he said. "My father gifted it to her on their betrothal, just as we each were given one when we were born. It is the coin of Geila, my grandfather. It was his brother, Suinthila, for whom my own father is named, who saw the Greeks leave the south and united Spania for the first time. Geila, too, was once crowned king, albeit briefly. Here, in Illiberis, where the coin was minted." He handed it to her. "After my mother died, they tell me, I would not let it go, so my father let me keep it. The coin reminds me of my duty, of the honour all men must find within. If I listen to it, I know what I must do, no matter how hard the path."

Their hands were close together. Lælia opened her palm to show him strands of the foals' manes bundled together in one length. Reaching up with a knife, she gestured at his hair. Theo bowed his head; she cut close to the scalp, taking a clutch of long, blond strands. She handed him the knife, and Theo raised it to hers. Her hair felt glossy in his hands, slipping through his fingers, rich and alive. He cut a length the same as his own.

She laid all three down on the stone partition of the stables – her hair, Theo's, and the foals'.

Together, said her hands.

Theo stood behind her, so close that she trembled. His arms held her; his hands rested on hers. Slowly, they braided the pieces together, weaving the strands in a slow, hypnotic pattern, fingers entwining as they had inside the mare. There was something about the nearness of her death that lent an intensity to their activity, as if threading the braid also wove protection against Oppa and the unknown future. They finished one and began a second. In the growing light, the braids became living things beneath their hands, still soaked with the blood of the anguished mare who had given her life for her children.

When they finished, Theo reached up and took the coin that hung on a leather cord about his neck. He threaded the braid through it and the amulet, then did the same for Lælia's.

"My father made this coin a gift to my mother upon their betrothal." He held her eyes. "Now it is my gift to you."

He tied it behind her neck, his fingers tingling where they

touched her skin. Her eyes were hard and blazing, searing away the last of his resolve.

She gestured, but her hands lacked their customary rapidity, instead moving slowly, almost caressing the air. *Is this how marriage is done, then?*

The corner of Theo's mouth twisted. "This is how our marriage is done," he said.

Cupping her chin, he tilted her face toward his own. He paused, waiting for her to protest, unsure what he would do if she did. He touched his lips to hers.

For a moment, they were still. Then she opened beneath his mouth and he groaned, pulling her against him. His hand tangled in her hair and his body was hard against her, the heat between them rising like fire until there was nothing but the feel of her, and Theo was lost. When he finally pulled away, he was breathing hard, his body aching.

"Lælia," he said hoarsely, holding her face, "I will come back. I will come back for you."

Her hand traced the fine, hard planes of his features, as if imprinting them upon her memory. *Sometimes,* her other hand moved, *I feel like you live behind this, that your real face is something different, something yet to be seen. It seemed I saw it...* She shook her head in frustration, unable to find the gestures she needed.

She took his hand and placed it on her throat where her words should have been. The skin was soft and frail beneath the hard callouses of his bow fingers, his thumb lightly stroking the place beneath her ear. He stared at her swollen mouth and drew a ragged breath.

Her hand flickered between them. *Oppa wants to kill you.*

"He won't."

She made an inarticulate noise, and it vibrated against the place on his palm hardened by the sword. He groaned softly, gathering her to him and taking her mouth again, fierce, hard, and too briefly. "If I start with you," he said roughly, "I won't stop." He caught her hand, crushing it in his own.

I don't want you to stop.

"I wish to Xristus they'd married us," he said harshly.

There is still time.

"No." He stared at her, drinking in the memory of her face. "If they declare me traitor, you cannot be my wife. Like this, the betrothal can be ended, if it must."

Never. Her hands moved fiercely. *Theo…*

"What is it?" He saw her mouth trying to move, her frustration as she tried to speak.

When I was sick, I dreamed. She looked at him. *I spoke, I think.*

He nodded slowly. "I could feel the words. Inside you."

When you go – her face clouded over – *I am afraid the words will go with you. That I will not find them again.*

He held her by the shoulders. "I will come back," he said again, aware of how inadequate it sounded. "And we will find your words, Lælia. Together."

She touched the coin and amulet at his throat, then her own. Her hand moved between them, covering his heart. *Promise?*

He placed his hand over her heart and felt it thudding against his palm, strong and vital, making his own twist painfully. *Promise.*

They stood like that, the pulse of one flowing into the other, the lifeblood of the mare coursing through their veins, as dawn became day.

When the sun rose over the mountains of Illiberis, Theo was gone: to sea, and to war.

20

OPPA

FEBRUARY AD 688

Mare Iberium
Alboran Sea between Spain and Africa

"The Karabisianoi sail these waters in strength. Attack upon the fleet would be folly, nephew."

The man addressing Oppa had a thin, hard face with the same pointed features as his relative. Though Oppa called him "uncle", it was a relationship once removed. Giscila had been brother to King Wamba and to Ariberga, Egica's father. Giscila and Ariberga had been infants when their father, King Tulga, had been brutally deposed by Chindasuinth. Whilst their older brother Wamba had found his path at Chindasuinth's side, rising so high in the old king's esteem to find himself, eventually, upon the throne, his younger brothers had felt the sting of their father's disgrace. Ariberga had rebelled against Chindasuinth until he was executed as a traitor. Egica, his son, was taken to be raised by relatives at the court of Francia until the disgrace was far enough past for him to return. Giscila had lived an uneasy existence in Wamba's shadow until, Egica had once told Oppa, he committed crimes too dark for even his elder brother to overlook and had been banished from Spania's shores.

What exactly those crimes had been Oppa still did not know. They were one of the few mysteries his considerable efforts had been unsuccessful in discovering. What he did know was that Giscila's survival in exile had been made possible only through Egica's own generosity.

Nonetheless, Oppa thought, the years spent in exile had not been kind to Giscila. Though slightly taller than Oppa, his stooped frame gave the impression of someone long beaten by the circumstances in which he found himself. His dark eyes lacked Oppa's hawkish gleam. He spoke now with apprehension clear in every nervous movement.

"If Ilyan should learn that the imperial fleet was attacked in his own waters, he will show no mercy. He is not a man to cross."

"I am not asking for your opinion." Oppa's words cut like whipcord, and Giscila capitulated immediately, taking a small step backward and bowing his head. There was, Oppa thought, something utterly pathetic in his uncle's subservience.

He raised his arm to shelter his eyes and gazed across the slick, still water. The air felt heavy. Giscila said it was always this way before a storm came. There were faint shadows in the distance, which Giscila had told him were the fleet's dromons carrying the new recruits from Spania. The small force would spend the next weeks training off the coast of Spania and collecting more recruits, reuniting with the bulk of the Karabisianoi at Carthage.

"The dromons, you say, are full of new recruits." Oppa frowned as he tried to make out the individual shapes on the horizon. "Which means there are few seasoned fighters aboard."

"*Ja*, that is correct, but –"

"And you say there are goods from Illiberis travelling in the company of the recruits."

"My sources say there are two flat-bottomed merchant dromons carrying horses and other goods, but nothing of the size you seek."

"I determine what I seek." Oppa turned hard eyes to his uncle. "The fortune I follow is not one you would understand. It comes in the form of information, and those who carry it." He nodded at the dromons in the distance. "Somewhere amongst the fleet a Jewish boy hides, and a Spaniard protects him. If I find them, they will lead me to a treasure far greater than horseflesh or gold, though those, too, will be mine. I believe both are sailing now with the Karabisianoi. Once they reach Carthage, they will be lost to me." He turned back to regard the shapes across the water, gripping the hard edge of the dromon, his eyes narrowing. "I must take them here," he said, to himself rather than anyone else.

A breeze rustled the lateen sail above, and Oppa swayed with the motion of the oars below. Giscila's dromon was the largest in his private force of ten and much larger than those of the Karabisianoi. It was a bireme dromon with two banks of oars, each numbering fifty, and bore its own copper and siphon for Greek fire. One of the exiles who sailed with Giscila had once made the fire in the service of the Karabisianoi and knew the formula's secrets. He flatly refused to share the information, even under torture, which made him the most valuable crew member aboard. War fire could destroy dromons at sea with a devastation no sword could match. It took several experienced men to maintain the fire, heat the formula correctly, and operate the pump and siphon. Aboard the training dromons, Oppa surmised, such men would be in short supply, if present at all. West of Ilyan's busy port of Septem, the sea was infrequently travelled and rarely suffered attacks. It was unlikely the fleet was carefully guarded.

Oppa fingered the coin in his tunic. More lay beneath the deck. The bulk of the coin sent by Ilyan to rebuild Spania's fleet had gone south with Oppa and travelled with him still. He had promised his father he would discover the secrets of the south's wealth, and gain the information needed to destroy those who currently controlled it. He knew he should have returned to Toletum by now. But a lifetime of living in the shadows had taught Oppa to have faith in his own intuition; his gut told him that the secrets he needed would be found with Theudemir of Aurariola and Yosef ben Arun. Oppa would lay all the coin he had on both men being found in the company of the fleet.

He turned cold eyes to Giscila, who visibly shrank before them, then nodded curtly at Nicalo, the only one of his companions he had chosen to accompany him on this journey. Oppa had thought it better to travel with few witnesses. "Nicalo, please ensure we are not overheard."

Nicalo nodded and removed himself from earshot, taking the few nearby crew members with him toward the stern.

"You were exiled from Spania when I was a child, so we do not know much of each other. I believe that you were, however, close to my father," began Oppa.

Giscila bowed his head. "If it were not for Egica," he said in a stifled tone, "I would not be here."

"Indeed." Oppa stroked the whip coiled at his side. "In fact, had my father not taken it upon himself, many years ago, to aid you, your exile would have been faced alone, is it not true?"

"*Ja.*" Giscila spoke dully, not looking at Oppa. "It is true."

"And you have always known, have you not, that this kindness my father showed you was a debt that would, one day, require repayment?"

Giscila inclined his head. His mouth worked convulsively as if he had much he would like to say, but he did not answer.

"And now," said Oppa softly, moving closer to the cowering figure, "when your family comes to seek that repayment, you hesitate. You prevaricate. You make excuses."

"*Ne!*" Giscila protested. "I do not! I merely suggest –"

"You *suggest*," Oppa sneered. "You, who would have died in rags were it not for my father's generosity, been no more than another impoverished exile haunting the docks had it not been for his coin. You would dare to make suggestions – to me?"

The contempt in his final words made Oppa's opinion of Giscila so devastatingly clear that Giscila's face folded in upon itself. When finally he lifted his eyes to meet Oppa's, there was no trace of the doubt he had shown earlier.

"You are right," he said dully. "Mine is a debt that will be repaid in any form you see fit. Should it cost my life or the force I have built up on these seas, so be it." His mouth firmed into a line that resembled Oppa's in form, if not resolution. He gestured to the dromons arrayed behind him. "My resources," he said, "are yours to command."

"Good." Oppa's hand touched the whip once more, a caress that did not go unnoticed by Giscila. "You said the weather will soon turn, did you not?"

Giscila nodded.

"Then this is what we are going to do."

21

THEO

FEBRUARY AD 688

Mare Iberium
Alboran Sea between Spain and Africa

The attack came during a storm, when wind tore at the dromon and the waves were a dull grey. The recruits were training and did not at first recognise the danger.

"Stroke!" cried the *prōtokarabos* at the stern, watching the rowers with an eagle eye, standing beside the *kentarchos*, a Goth named Ulric. "Stroke!"

Theo winced as the smooth wood slipped through his hand across raw skin. He tried to shift the weight of it, take the drag of the water on another part of his palm, but the oar juddered and caught, thrusting him backward and opening fresh wounds. He quickly lifted it, gritted his teeth against the pain, and found his rhythm again, relieved his slip had escaped the notice of the man with the drum.

Sea spray came in through the oar hole, stinging the blisters on his palm, and despite the sweat of his labours and two bodies on either side of him, he shivered. They were in peaceful seas and had stowed their leather and tunics in oilskin for the duration of the training voyage. He was clad in only a loincloth, and when the wind whipped through the dromon, it stung like steel knives on his skin. The boy next to him moaned, leaned forward, and retched.

"You think this is hard?" The *prōtokarabos* strode forward, cuffing the boy on his shoulder. "Accustomed to slaves bringing you watered wine when you are ill, and your mother there to soothe your fevered brow? The Arabs won't care if you are retching, boy. When the dromons are spitting flame and a hundred sword-waving Saracens are feeling its breath, it is your oar arm that will save your skinny arse. Spew on the spur if you must. But don't lose your stroke. Stroke!"

The grey waves spilled into the dromon, and the water slopped about their ankles. It was freezing. Amidst the wind and roiling sea, Ulric raised his arm. "Attack!" he roared.

Theo groaned inwardly even as he obeyed the order to drop the oar and reach for his sword, strapped neatly to the side of the dromon. They had performed such drills at regular intervals every day, no matter how far they had rowed or how foully the sea tossed. Theo suspected the loincloths and regular drills to be an initiation of sorts. If so, it had proven effective. Several recruits had given up before they left Spanish shores.

"You think it won't be like this when you fight?" Ulric shouted. Theo joined the others as they staggered to their feet from their rowing benches. "You think the Arabs will give you time to rest before they attack you? You come up from those benches with sword raised and spear ready, using the power of your legs so your arms are free. I don't care if you have rowed a week straight before – you come out of this dromon ready to fight."

Ulric raised his sword to demonstrate, and Theo braced for his blow. But Ulric had frozen. Looking over the spur at the bow, he held up his hand to indicate a halt to practice. He stared at the heaving sea for a moment, frowning. Then, "Back to your oars! Stroke!"

Theo obeyed the order immediately, as did the others, and he felt the vessel surge beneath their combined strength. Only after the first stroke did he look out of the oarlock to see what had galvanised Ulric.

There were two merchant dromons barely two hundred feet away, one laden with packing crates and the other with horses. They travelled at the rear of the fleet, picking up goods each day when they made camp. Theo had spied them in the distance more than once but taken little notice. One of the horses screamed into the wind, and Theo squinted in astonishment. It was Titus. *The shipment from Illiberis,* he thought, *intended for Septem and Ilyan.*

A wide, heavy vessel was ploughing through the sea toward the two merchant dromons. The strange vessel was twice the size of theirs, had two banks of oars to their one, and did not carry the labarum of the Greek fleet: the red standard bearing the chi-rho beneath which white flags were used as signalling and identification. It flew no standard at all, and Theo saw that it did not return the signalling sequence made by Ulric's *prōtokarabos.*

"Tunic and armour!"

The boys scrambled to don their leather and steel, first the front and then the rear. The vessel bore down on the merchant dromons, and now Theo could see the men on the fighting platforms notching their arrows, their intent increasingly clear even as the sea grew higher and the first rain began to fall. The two merchant vessels were to Theo's left. Three dromons of the fleet rushed to surround them. Watching them as he rowed, however, Theo felt his heart sinking. All three dromons carried new recruits. They pitched and tossed uneasily on the water, filled with panicked boys scrambling to prepare for a real attack for which none of them were ready. He could see the recruits aboard the fire dromon fumbling with the copper pipe, blowing frantically to ignite the deadly Greek fire, their kentarchos bellowing orders in exasperation.

The sky above was black with cloud, so thick that the mountains of the African coastline were hidden from view, and rain fell now in hard, driving sheets.

The new vessel was close enough for Theo to see the men within it. They were hard and big: grown men with full armour. Theo felt a chill go through his body. They were intent upon the merchant vessels, the men of which were screaming orders and coming to defensive positions. But the defenders were precious few, and the attackers were fierce and intent upon their prize.

"Oars in! In, damn you!" Ulric roared as the sea picked up their dromon and tossed it like a plaything across a deep trough. The sky opened and lightning flashed into the water as the sea became so steep that Theo lost sight of the other vessels. And then they were all holding fast as the dromon slid down a wall of water so great it took the breath from his body and men cried out in fear.

"The sea is not your enemy – the sea can only ever be your friend! Ride it! Ride it and prepare to fight!"

Ulric roared at them over the wind, and Theo clutched his spear and shield, his short sword unstrapped and ready to be drawn. His hands were numb with cold, and salt water ran into his eyes and mouth. He could barely see in front of him, and the thought of attempting to fight anyone in such conditions seemed impossible.

Their dromon climbed a cliff of water. As it crested, Theo felt his heart catch. Coming directly for them, ramming spurs out at the ready, was not only a second, but a third, fourth, and fifth attack vessel – and they were set on a headlong course, straight for the dromons of new recruits. Theo saw the fire siphons belch flame from the bow of one, settling across the water in an evil spray of fume and heat. From behind, more shapes loomed, a force of untold size.

Theo looked up at their commander, and if he had hoped to find reassurance there, he was mistaken. Ulric's face was stricken; he had not seen the additional attackers either. Theo knew, with sickening certainty, that it was too late to alter course.

The two vessels collided with a crash of timber and the dreadful sound of splintering wood as the attackers' iron-tipped spurs ripped through the hull. Bowmen on the fighting deck shot arrows with deadly accuracy, taking men one after another.

At the rear of one of the dromons men struggled with a pump, and war fire spurted from the siphon connected to the copper pot. It was not doused by the heavy sea but rather sat on the surface, flames licking across the water. As Theo watched, a volley of flaming arrows hit the pot and it exploded, taking the dromon with it in a ball of heat and death.

His own was a mass of burning water and splintered timbers, boys screaming in pain and others already fallen into the sea and lost. Theo realised, in a kind of dumb stupor, that his oar was gone. Then he realised the bench he had been sitting on had collapsed. As he did, a man leaped from the bowsprit toward him, sword outstretched, face contorted with a killing fury. Theo made to rise and meet him, but his feet met only water, his hand found air, and then in a rush of freezing cold, he was in the sea.

The dromon was gone, and Theo felt the sea take him.

22

LÆLIA

FEBRUARY AD 688

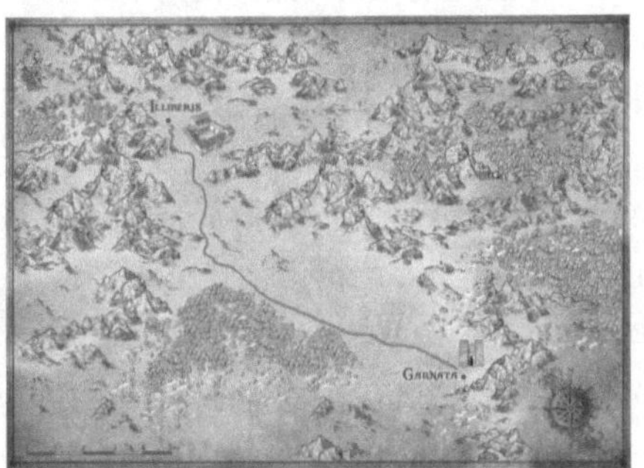

Illiberis, Bætica, Spania
Granada, Andalusia, Spain

Lælia woke abruptly. The room was stifling, the air thick and still. An unseasonal, sickly heat had come with Theo's departure – and so had the dreams. She sat up in bed, every sense alert, trying to grasp at the threads of the dream: Cold water at her feet. Purple sky. The cries of men. Fire all around. Freezing water overhead…

The woven cord was tight and hot about her throat. She lurched from the bed and ran to the window. Throwing the wooden shutters open, she swallowed great gulps of the winter night air, drinking it deep into her lungs. Despite the heat inside the room, a deathly sensation of cold that had nothing to do with the winter air ran through her veins like an icy poison stealing the life from her blood. She felt as if she could not get enough air inside her; even when her head began to spin, still she breathed deeply. The cold seared her throat.

Lælia pulled the mane cord away, and it pulsed angrily in her hands as if with a life of its own. Above, the stars were brilliant in a dark sky, the new moon yet to show its face.

Theo. She mouthed his name silently, leaning against the stone wall, its solidity reassuring.

She felt a pull at her chest, as if a great hand had reached inside her body and was squeezing her lungs, pushing the air from them. She pulled boots on beneath her shift and silently slipped from the villa, heading for the stables.

Just leaving her bedchamber for the clear night made her feel better. She had always preferred the open sky to a roof; she could not think when she was inside. Only outside could she see clearly, feel the truth inside herself and others.

The foals were in the stable yard. She heard them before she saw them. The white filly, recovered as Lælia herself was after her illness, stood in the corner, nostrils flaring. She was watching the black colt race frenetically about the yard, squealing in rage and terror. The filly looked up as Lælia approached. Tossing her head, she danced to Lælia, nudged her, and then danced away again, always focused on the colt.

Lælia held her hand out and made a rumbling sound in the back of her throat. The colt calmed slightly and trotted around the perimeter fence, head tossing, making low, agitated whinnies. Lælia glanced about in case the lynx was nearby, but she knew the problem was no wild animal. Her blood still raced after what she had seen in the dream. The colt wasn't scared of anything in Illiberis. He could feel Theo, just as she had when she woke up. Her throat seized up with what that might mean.

Come, she gestured, this time with more authority.

Snorting and raising his hoofs, the colt sidled over to her, head shaking from side to side, eyes rolling. He stood in front of her, but his eyes were fixed on something far distant. Lælia stroked his neck, murmuring softly, closing her eyes so there was only the colt and her hand. She felt the filly come to stand beside her brother, her silky muzzle joining his, and the three of them stood with their heads together, breathing the same air.

Warmth. I need warmth, she thought. Just as she had upon waking, Lælia felt a deathly cold quite at odds with the still, warm Illiberis night. This was freezing suffocation; she found herself gulping air again. The foals trembled beside her. The black colt made a horrible deep barking sound, as if he were wind-sucking on a wooden post. She pressed closer to him, willing him to breathe, feeling the frantic pattern of his heart as he struggled to find air. His knees trembled. She felt his body begin to buckle.

No, she thought. *No!*

The colt was falling, thrashing wildly in her grasp, the light beginning to die from his eyes. She held him tightly, forcing him upright as he began to sway, her mouth opened in a silent scream of desperation. His movements weakened. Cupping his muzzle in her hands she blew, with all her might, into the open nostrils.

At first her breath escaped to the side, the colt's nostrils blocked and seemingly unable to take anything in. Then he shivered, his legs went rigid, and he inhaled, head rearing into the air so hard he almost knocked her over as he gasped for breath. He swayed, legs splayed wide, head down, breathing long, rattling breaths and taking the air in huge swallows as Lælia had done earlier at the window. The white filly walked to his side, and they stood nose to tail, body against body, with the colt still shaking and covered in sweat.

What is it? Lælia stroked the heaving black shoulder. *What is it that is troubling you so?*

She stayed until the dawn grew pink on the horizon, the colt in her arms, her heart thudding slowly in her chest.

23

THEO

FEBRUARY AD 688

Mare Iberium
Alboran Sea between Spain and Africa

It was cold.

The water closed over Theo. He gulped, swallowed, and burst to the surface, gasping for air. He found no relief. The world was filled with foul smoke, flames licking the tossing waves.

Theo saw a boy's face disintegrate, skin melting away from the bone. The boy slid beneath the waves and was gone.

Theo took a burning breath of heat and smoke. He dived beneath the surface. The sea was grey and ugly with the stench of fire. Sick waves crashed overhead. The flames lived far longer than natural fire could. Every time Theo surfaced, he put his face to the sky, gulped air, and sank beneath the water once more, his legs powering him onward, though he knew not where.

The day grew darker, the sea colder. The sound of men and fighting seemed not to disperse as rapidly as it should have. He heard the squeal of terrified horses, and his heart twisted in pain and longing. He began to tire. His legs gradually became numb. His teeth were chattering, his whole body shaking with cold. A drowsiness stole through his bones. It was a delicious warmth, seductive. Theo felt he could simply slip beneath the waves, cease to fight in the wind and tumult above, and sink into the blackness below.

His face surfaced for breath and water lapped over his mouth. He tried to move his arms, but they were heavy and it seemed impossible. Above him, the sky was thick blackness; night had fallen. The horses were still close by. It seemed to Theo that it was Titus he could hear, the pride of Count Paulus's stable, whinnying in fear and indignation. The sound carried across the night sea, reaching through the darkness. It came to him again. A sharp whinny, more urgent.

Theo was vaguely aware of the sea washing over his face, into his mouth. He choked, spitting and struggling feebly in the freezing water. The terrible lethargy slipped away, carried on Titus's sharp cries of warning. If he did not act now, he would soon be dead.

He forced his legs beneath him to move as if he were running. The effort was so great he nearly wept. Every muscle ached and protested, his body atrophying, no longer wanting to try. He willed it to move. He sent his mind down into each part of his legs, as if he could push the blood through the veins with his own force of will. *You cannot cease struggling,* he told himself fiercely. *If you stop, you will die.* He saw Lælia laughing beneath the pomegranate tree, the image clear in his mind. *I will come back to you,* he thought. *I promised.*

With a surge of strength, he broke the surface and forced his head above the waves. They had died down somewhat, and he was able to see a small distance in the moonlight. He could make out the dark shapes of the dromons ahead. Good. He must keep them in sight, but himself invisible. They would be headed for land. He would follow.

He looked about for debris and found what he was looking for: a section of boat timbers still joined. He pushed through the sea toward it. Grasping hold, he hauled himself onto it and lay there, panting.

It was colder out of the sea, but Theo knew it was his only chance. Shivering in the darkness, he began to rub his legs and arms, gingerly moving the joints. He realised how close he had come to the deathly numbness. He could not afford to allow that slow death to creep up on him again unnoticed. He must remain alert, and conscious, until the dromons reached shore. He could creep ashore at night, he thought, once they had arrived. He would find someone to help him. If it was Africa he landed upon, he would find his way to Count Ilyan of Septem. If it were Spania, he would be home, and safe. Either way he would survive. And he would return to Lælia. Safe in this thought, he felt a surge of strength. Putting his arms into the sea, he began to paddle.

* * *

Sometime in the night, someone else had joined him.

He jerked from a strange half slumber to dreadful terror. *You cannot fall asleep! To sleep is to die!*

He forced breath into his chest and moved sharply, eliciting a grunt from the man whose head he had kicked with his movement. The man looked up at Theo with bloodshot eyes; he had a terrible gash down the side of his head. "Careful," he rasped.

Theo didn't recognise him. He was not one of their own crew, and even in that one word, Theo recognised an unfamiliar accent. "I'm sorry," said Theo. His own voice sounded rough to his ears. It was an effort to speak.

The grey dawn showed a clear sky; the storm was gone.

The man shook his head weakly and lay back down on the timbers. He did not answer.

"You must try to move," said Theo. He reached over and shook the man; he made a small moan of protest but didn't stir.

"You must move!" Theo shook him harder. It seemed very important, now he had found someone else, that the man did not die. Reaching over, Theo grasped him beneath the armpits. He was strong, broad across the shoulders, and made of solid muscle, with scars across his body that showed he was no stranger to a sword fight. Panting and struggling to stay atop the narrow timber raft, Theo hauled the inert body up and onto the timbers. As the man came heavily on board, the raft sank beneath their combined weight. Theo slid his own body off the side, clutching the man for support.

"No," rasped his companion. "You."

He tried feebly to pull Theo back on board but was so obviously exhausted that Theo easily resisted. "No," he said. "I am rested. We can take it in turns. Sleep; I will hold you."

The man barely raised his head. Turning it to one side, he collapsed into unconsciousness.

By midday, they had collected two more. One was a giant of a man, pitch black with a head shiny and bald as a nut. He had gathered several barrels and lashed them together. Wordlessly, he and Theo tied the timber raft to the barrels. The young boy with him was unconscious, his arm hanging at an awkward angle. The big black man was holding him above the water when they floated into view. Theo wondered what kind of strength it would take to have held the boy's weight for nearly an entire day and night.

"Does he live still?" The black man spoke in a deep voice seemingly untroubled by the salt thirst that rendered Theo's own throat raw. He nodded at the man on the raft, who had not moved since Theo had slipped off to allow him room to rest.

Theo, reluctant to lose his only companion, had been unwilling to look. Now he cautiously reached over and slipped his hand under the man's chin. For a moment, the head rested in his hand, a heavy weight, and with a sinking heart Theo thought him gone. Then a wave washed over the timber and the man coughed and lunged up so he nearly upset the raft, glaring about with bloodshot eyes. He mumbled indistinctly in his own language, words Theo was quite sure would not have been acceptable in a mannered hall.

"I believe he lives, then." The black man turned to Theo and grinned. It was so unexpected, the flash of bright white teeth, that for a moment Theo reared back, unsure if the smile was threat or genuine. There was something savage in the combination of teeth, bright white eyeball, and ebony black skin. Theo noticed the man also bore three scars on both cheeks, long precise cuts that ran diagonally down his face toward his mouth. They were unsettling and wild, and Theo thought he would not like to face such a man on the end of a sword. But after a moment, he realised the smile was genuine, and he returned it.

"You." The man Theo had rescued glared at the black man. "Pirate."

The scarred face grinned again. "No, *wenkai*." He held up his hand, showing the crude Christogram stigma of the Greek navy inked onto his skin. The other man's eyes narrowed. With an effort, he raised his own hand, which bore the same mark. They turned to look at Theo.

"*Gota*," said Theo, using the term by which the Goths were known to outsiders. "From Spania. I was a new recruit."

They nodded, and the black man gestured at the boy lying unconscious by his side. "He, also, was one of yours."

Theo looked at the face; it was unfamiliar to him. "I do not know him," he said.

There seemed nothing more to say, and speaking took effort, so they ceased trying. The day grew late, and still no land was in sight. The sea was cold, and as night fell the wind blew up again, whipping the waves into an ugly frenzy. A hard rain began to fall.

Theo's original companion moved off the raft, and together they manoeuvred the unconscious boy on. None said what they all thought, but in the darkness of the night, when the boy's head rolled back and his eyes stared up at the sky, glassy and unseeing, they silently released him, and he slipped into the waves, accompanied by the low murmur of the black man, speaking in a tongue Theo did not recognise but which he found soothing nonetheless.

The storm grew fiercer. Theo could not tell if the deep shadows he occasionally caught a glimpse of were the cliffs of Africa or simply bigger mountains of waves. He had no time to ponder. Every moment became filled with crashing seawater and the effort of maintaining a grip on the fragile raft. The three survivors clutched the timber and each other, the big black man anchoring their tenuous hold with the sheer strength of his own. Once, he reached out when Theo felt his own hold slipping and simply plucked him from the sucking sea, pulling him back into their small circle. He grinned, the white teeth shining in the darkness, and Theo instinctively moved closer to him.

The other man waved a fist into the air. "Now she calls for me, the bitch!" His accent was guttural and thick, and when he swore in his own language, it sounded not dissimilar to Theo's own Gothic. "But you will not have me, you western whore! I will see my homeland again – and you will take me there! I have ridden you this far; I will ride you still!"

"We do not ride," said the black man in his deep voice. "She carries us."

"Perhaps you will be carried, like woman! Me, I am Slavic, and Slavs can ride anything! I will ride her, and the bitch knows I can. Come on!" He slapped the sea, as if urging on a horse. Theo smiled despite himself, and the big man laughed deep in his throat, a rumble that gave Theo more comfort than the raft itself.

They rode the storm through the long night, the Slav haranguing it in foul language, the black man laughing at it, and Theo clutching the wood between the two, thinking of nothing but Lælia and the foals. More than once he went under; each time a hand reached out and pulled him up.

The silk Laurentius had given him was drenched and shrunk but tied still to the woven hair cord where he had placed it on the first day he sailed from Spania. The amulet and coin hung from the same cord. The feel of them at his throat was a warm comfort against the cold tentacles of death reaching from beneath the waves, trying to draw him downward. Theo held the wooden raft and the twin amulets held him, the coin of his past, the magic of his future, and the ties of duty holding him afloat when the storm would have taken him.

It was deep in the darkest hours of night when a thick shape distorted the shadows and the Slav called out hoarsely: "Dromon!"

That one word was sufficient to rouse them all to action, and they steered their fragile vessel as best they could through the walls of sea toward the dark shape that bobbed in and out of view then gradually became more distinct. It was coming toward them. Theo tried to call out, but his voice was drowned by water.

"It is not a dromon of the fleet!" the black man called over the wind, a cautionary note in his voice.

"So? Maybe there we die at their hands. Here, definitely we die," replied the Slav. "I prefer there."

There seemed nothing more to say to that. They kicked the water and bore closer, calling against the wind.

"Ho!" An answering cry from the bowsprit made them increase their efforts, and gradually their cries were heard. Figures appeared at the side and lowered rope for them to grasp; strong hands reached down to pull them aboard.

"Climb!" the black man called to Theo, gesturing for him to mount the rope. "I will come behind you! Climb in!"

Theo tightened his grasp around the rope and climbed, then nearly lost his grip when he realised with a shock how weak he was. Hands reached out and hauled him in, spluttering and choking. He fell face down into the dromon. Weakly, he struggled to stand and motioned behind him, but two men were already leaning over, hauling in the figures from the raft.

Two heads appeared simultaneously over the side of the dromon. Theo slumped in weak relief when he saw the flash of white teeth in the great black skull and the solid face of the Slav. Then his eyes slipped to the right, taking in their rescuers, and all trace of tiredness fled. "You," he croaked.

"Is this the one?" The man spoke to his companion in coarse Gothic. But Theo was not looking at him. His eyes were locked on to the figure next to him – a lean figure clad in rich robes, a wicked whip coiled at his side.

"Yes, Uncle," said Oppa softly, staring at Theo. "This is the one."

Theo balled his fists, fury rising in his gut, but he was weak, and the men who moved quickly to hold him were tall and well fed.

"Do you want us to kill him, *princeps*?" A second figure moved to Oppa's side. With a shudder of revulsion, Theo recognised Nicalo. "We can throw him back over the side as we have the others. None will know of it."

Nicalo moved to replace Theo's captor, pulling Theo's arms hard behind his back. Theo bared his teeth, making a guttural sound of frustration and rage.

"That would ruin my fun, Nicalo," said Oppa coldly, black eyes staring at Theo.

Nicalo chuckled in Theo's ear. "We will see how you enjoy the stroke of the whip, pretty boy," he said. He touched the old mark on his face where Yosef's stone had caught him. "There are scars I bear that you will pay for – and more besides."

Behind him, Theo heard the sound of a struggle as the black man and the Slav fought against their own rescuers turned captors. The dull sound of wood connecting with flesh, combined with soft grunts of pain, told him the struggles were short lived.

"I don't wish you to kill him," said Oppa, folding his arms and staring at Theo. "Or his friends. Giscila." He addressed the first Goth. "We lost men in the fight. Do you need oarsmen?"

"*Ja*," said the Goth, chewing his lips and eyeing Theo and his two companions. "They look strong enough. But then, so did the other twenty you threw back into the sea."

"Ah." Oppa smiled coldly. "But they did not have the information I seek. This one does." He tapped his whip. "I do, however, have one condition."

Giscila's eyes narrowed as he looked at Oppa. "It's your gold, now, isn't it?" he said. "Your gold. Your conditions."

"I'm glad we understand one another, my dear uncle. And it is a simple enough request." Oppa had not taken his eyes from Theo's face. "All I ask," he said softly, "is that you allow me to wield the whip."

Theo lunged forward, his exhaustion forgotten, then something hit the back of his head, and blackness took him.

* * *

"I think the bitch won," Leofric grunted as he pulled the oar.

"This is because you must insist on seeing it as a competition," said Silas, his white teeth flashing in the predawn. "For me, I believe we are simply riding another wave."

"That is because you are savage. If you understood ways of Christian men, you would know, my friend, that we are reaved wide."

Silas laughed. The low, rich sound never failed to raise a smile on Theo's face, even here.

"Do not speak to me of reaving, my good Christian Slavic friend. The whip is one thing. Tormenting a man with thoughts of what he may not enjoy for some time is quite another."

Leofric snorted. "The only time we will see naked body of woman again is vision with last breath."

Silas hissed, a low sound of warning that travelled beneath the slap of the waves and the creak of the oars. Looking up, Leofric swore softly and leaned sideways, stretching his foot across the width of the dromon. "Theo," he whispered urgently, kicking him in the leg. "Theo! *Schnecke!* Wake up! He is coming."

Theo wanted to protest that he was not asleep, that he had heard every word of their conversation, but even as he opened his mouth, he became aware of his physical body and gave an involuntary moan as the agony of it hit him anew.

Forcing his hands to grasp the oar, he rocked forward with the movement of the others, following the rhythm of Silas's broad back in front of him, trying to ignore the white-hot pain shooting through his body with every movement. His arms felt so weak, he was surprised he could manage even the pretence of rowing.

"And yet again, I find you hiding behind the better man."

Oppa's tone was low and sneering. He stood beside Silas, one hand caressing the black man's bald head, as one would an obedient dog. Silas rowed without pause in steady, methodical movements, but Theo could see the rigid tension in his shoulders. New welts crossed old on his back. When whipping Theo had not elicited the information he sought, Oppa had turned his attentions to his companions. On realising the black man had been savagely whipped in a previous life, Oppa had taken it as a personal challenge to better the job done by his predecessor, and barely a day went by without the salt-encrusted tails of his whip laying fresh red stripes on the ebony skin.

But it was not to Silas that he spoke now. Through eyes reduced to slits by the swelling of new bruises over old, Theo saw the dark gaze rest on him. Oppa drew the tails of the whip lovingly through his hands, caressing them just as he had Silas's head.

Despite himself, Theo felt dread deep in his belly at the sight of the whip. He had become intimately acquainted with its every touch these past weeks.

"Yes," said Oppa softly, and a strange smile twisted his mouth. "You are learning to fear the whip, are you not, Aurariola? Do I still call you by that name? It seems unnecessarily cruel, since you will never see those lands again. And yet, still you hope. I can see it in your eyes." He laughed unpleasantly. "What is left of them."

He stepped forward and squatted down, easily riding the movement of the dromon. Its rhythm had become their own now. In his more lucid moments, Theo wondered if he would ever stand easily on shore again.

"My father once told me," Oppa said, his face inches from Theo's, "that hope is the greatest torture of them all. *When hope is gone*, he said, *there is no pleasure left in the giving of pain*. And so, this is the challenge we face: how to cause you the greatest pain, whilst still keeping alive the delicious torture of hope, the faint promise that perhaps – just perhaps – there is a way out."

He smiled. Placing the handle of the whip beneath Theo's face, he tilted it up so their eyes were very close. "There is, you know. Tell me the whereabouts of the Jew, and what Paulus plans with him, and I may yet let you live. No?" He drew Theo's face even closer. "Do you still believe in the possibility of escape? Do you still dare hope, deep down, that you will find a way to leave my grasp and live to seek your revenge?"

Theo felt a surge of mindless fury that cut through pain and exhaustion and seized hold of him. For a moment, it burned so hot that he felt he could break the iron manacles that held his wrists and the chain that tied him to the other damned souls on their oars and simply take Oppa here and now, burst free and kill the bastard with his bare hands.

He felt the rage touch his face and forced it blank again, but too late to prevent something of it showing in his eyes.

"Ah," said Oppa, his smile widening. "The mask begins to fall with the skin from your face, and the hope still lives. That is good." He stood up and caressed the tails of the whip. "That is very good."

Theo inhaled as Oppa moved past him. He closed his eyes briefly, felt the weight of the coin and amulet on his chest. Felt Oppa take up the familiar stance behind him at the very rear of the boat. Heard Leofric suck in his breath, saw the round dome of Silas's head shake in impotent condemnation just as he felt the faint rush of air as Oppa raised his arm.

And then the whip came down, and another day began.

24

LÆLIA

MARCH AD 688

Illiberis, Bœtica, Spania
Granada, Andalusia, Spain

The lynx was high on the cliff, but Lælia was higher still. She had been tracking the cat for hours, since first she had heard the plaintive cry of a curlew in the night.

She woke easily now. Sometimes she wondered if she ever truly slept at all. What sleep she did have was disturbed by dreams, strange glimpses of fear and pain that made her nights long and restless. She had taken to hunting in the small hours of the morning, when the dreams were worst.

The lynx had come closer to the villa than was normal. Mountain cats were drawn by the scent of horseflesh, but usually the dogs Count Paulus kept were enough to keep them at bay. This one, however, had prowled the perimeter for weeks now, possibly from thirst. The winter had abruptly fallen away to a blazing spring, though snow glistened still across the tallest mountain peaks.

Lælia moved soundlessly through the rocks. The lynx was crouched against the cliff face opposite. Her tail curled behind her, quivering faintly as she sniffed the air. She knew she was being tracked. The great head moved low, nostrils twitching, topaz eyes wild and alert.

Lælia had come to treasure the long hours and delicate dance of the hunt. She doubted she would kill the lynx even if it came to it. Despite using all her skills in tracking, Lælia had still not discovered her lair.

The herders, in their round earthen huts high in the mountains, cursed the lynx as an evil spirit and laid invocations on their stones to ward her away, for she had taken more than one goat from the tribes. But still she survived, her tawny body slipping into the rocks like a trick of the light until suddenly, she would be gone, and the shape Lælia thought hers would prove no more than a shadow.

Even Alaric and Athanagild, who had stayed long past the time they were meant to have left, knew nothing of Lælia's private hunt. By unspoken agreement, they remained, as if by staying in Illiberis they could hold on to their brother, just as Lælia longed to. She was grateful for their presence; it served as a shield between her and the unbearable loneliness of Illiberis without either Theo or Yosef.

Their presence, and hunting the lynx, served to distract her from the agonising screams of the colt, who had hovered on the brink of death for weeks now. His fragility was, Lælia knew, another reason the brothers remained. They, as she, sensed what it meant, though none expressed it directly.

Lælia pushed the colt from her mind with a sickened shudder. She could not bear to think of what his illness meant. *Would* not think of it. She focused on the shape on the cliff. Perhaps this was why she liked tracking the cat so much: the complete focus on instinct and corresponding absence of thought. Nothing mattered but the cat and her, joined by an invisible thread, which one moment of inattention would break.

The lynx slunk now along a narrow path, cutting just beside the first rays of the sun, a favourite trick with which she had lost Lælia on previous days. But Lælia was prepared this time, positioned above for a better view. The tawny shadow slipped around a ridge, and Lælia ran silently across the clifftop to the next ravine. The cat was lying on a flat rock beneath the rising sun, and Lælia breathed out softly, aware of the energy that her breath sent on the air.

She felt a moment of triumph. It had been no easy feat gaining the high ground. She could take the lynx, if she chose. The cat was no more than a stade away, and Lælia's arrows were sharp. But she could not find the will to do it. Instead, she lay on her belly, and they watched the dawn together.

The sun grew high. Finally, the cat stood, and then with a last wary glance, she disappeared. Lælia frowned. Her eyes searched every pebble, every sparse bush, but the cat was gone, vanishing as she had done every day. Lælia thought of scrambling down the cliff to the rock, but she did not wish to leave her scent upon it. Finally, giving up, she eased back from the cliff edge and began the long walk home.

Her heart grew heavier with every step as she drew close to Illiberis. Her stomach began the now familiar sick churning, and her feet moved more slowly, dreading what she would find. Her feeling of unease grew as she neared the stable. The foals were not in the yard; they were nowhere to be seen. A strange horse stood with its head down in the feed trough. Its sides were lathered from hard riding, and it trembled with exhaustion. The mark on its flank was from the port of Sexi, on the coast.

Lælia heard the agonised squeal of the colt from within the stables at the same time as she saw the figures of Alaric and Athanagild emerge, a dust-covered messenger whey faced and sorrowful behind them. They opened their mouths to speak, but she did not hear them through the roaring in her ears. She passed them as if they did not exist and entered the dark shadows of the stables where the black colt thrashed in agony in the straw. She reached out, her hands falling into the whorls of mane and clutching them as if they would lift her out of the pain and horror, all the while knowing that they could not and that nothing, ever, could be the same again.

The brothers stood opposite, faces ravaged with grief.

Lælia did not need to listen to know what message the rider had brought. She had known it long ago, had known it the moment she had woken in the night gasping for breath.

Theo, their lips said, the words falling about her like pieces of ash. *Theo is dead.*

25

YOSEF

MARCH AD 688

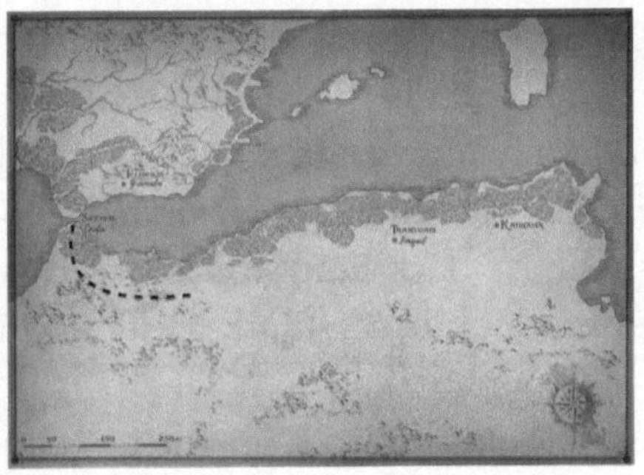

Mauretania, Africa
North Western Sahara, Africa

They had left Septem weeks ago, when Yosef was still dazed and numb from the horrors he had seen. Of the ride from Garnata to the port of Sexi, he recalled nothing. During the sea crossing, he had watched the coastline of Spania fade into a dull blur and wished, as the dromon tossed amongst sullen grey waves, that he could slip into their depths and never return.

They had arrived before dawn, Shukra hurrying him from the

docks into Septem's back alleys where Jewish artisans worked silver and cloth. There he had hidden, lifeless and uncaring, whilst Shukra went to the palace to notify Count Ilyan of their arrival. Days had passed before they were sent for, days during which Yosef had remained prone on the thin mattress, unable to think or eat. He had been vaguely aware of worried whispers, food that came and was eventually removed untouched, but he could not rouse himself to care for any of it. He feared that the sickening events leading up to his departure were so indelibly seared on his mind that they had become all he would ever know life to be again, no matter how long he lived or where he travelled.

When the summons to the palace had finally come, Shukra had forced him to the bathhouse. Yosef had come to a dead halt at the entrance, assailed by memories evoked by the scent of almond and jasmine carried on steam. Shukra, however, had forced him to enter. Inside, he had sat prone whilst the other man gently scrubbed the grime from his skin as if he were a child.

When Yosef emerged, he was led from the bustling Jewish quarter to the gentle murmuring of fountains and the sensual arches of Ilyan's palace. The mercurial governor had looked at him from beneath a wild shock of dark hair streaked with silver and said to Shukra, "He does not look fit to stand, let alone travel amongst the Riders."

That day, Yosef had taken broth for the first time.

Some days later, when Shukra had sewn the scrolls inside his cloak and whispered instructions Yosef had barely heard, the first words passed his lips, as if some force inside him had decided to live despite his own determination to die.

"You must be hearing me, *aziz-am*," Shukra had said, staring worriedly at him. "Your fear cannot be listening now."

"I am not afraid." The words in Yosef's throat were hoarse and as unused as a rusted key grating in the lock. "I will never be afraid again." Though he heard his own words as if from a distance, Yosef knew them to be true. All he could have ever feared had already taken place. He had lost his parents. Sarah was gone to him, for although she had physically survived the dreadful attack on her body, Yosef knew she could never again look at him with the aching sweetness she once had. Lælia was wounded. And Theo – despite the promise he had made, Yosef doubted Theo would ever leave Lælia's side if he feared for her. If Theo had been able to leave Spania at all.

Yosef felt nausea rise when he thought of Oppa forcing Theo to account for the crime that he, Yosef, had committed. They had received no word of what had occurred in Spania after their departure. It was, Shukra had said, too dangerous for him to send messengers to the fleet. None could know there was any connection between the broken refugee lying in a Jewish room in the back alleys of Septem and the fleet, which even now rowed along Spania's shores.

There was nothing remarkable in yet another Jewish refugee being taken from Spania by a foreign smuggler. The Jews of Septem knew how to care for their own. Their arrival had gone unmarked by any; Shukra had ensured that. Then, later, when Dahiya, Queen of the Jerawa, rode through the gates of Septem, she had done so with her two sons, Bagay and Khanchla, and a party of turbaned men. When she left, one of the turbaned men was wearing the clothes of a merchant and would exit the port some days hence. In his place, wreathed in the same anonymous cloth the Jerawa Riders used to shield their faces from spirits, Yosef, mounted on a camel with his father's scrolls sewn inside his cloak, had watched the gates of Septem close behind him.

In the weeks since, his life had changed so profoundly that he barely recognised it, and it seemed his only moments of solitude were to be found beneath the camel blankets whilst other men slept. He sat now on those same blankets, cross legged beneath an open sky, eating skewered goat's meat that had been cooked over coals. They had visited a village earlier that day and traded for a goat, which Bagay had carried on the front of his saddle as they left the low mud dwellings behind and rode into the deep desert, far from settlement and oasis, to a small stand of acacia where they had made camp.

"Eat," Bagay urged, his brown eyes smiling merrily at Yosef. "You will miss meat such as this once we are further into the sands."

"It is true," Khanchla, his older brother, agreed. "We will take camels to our mountains near Carthage where our horses are. We ride hard across the sands, and meat is scarce. It will not always be as it is here, amongst the easy land of the villagers."

"Your mountains?" Yosef queried. The scent of roasting flesh still turned his gut. He had to force himself to nibble at the meat, just as he forced himself to converse, ride, and wake up every day. In the weeks since he had ridden with the Jerawa, Yosef had come to realise that this was how life was done now for him: wake up, ride, eat, sleep.

He lived.

He tried to focus on Khanchla, who was nodding. "We are Jerawa. Our villages are scattered through the mountains south of Carthage." He grinned at Yosef. "Our mountain walls are higher and harder to cross than those of Carthage itself."

"We will meet Aksil there," said Bagay. He glanced at his brother. "And hope he listens to our mother," he added quietly. They both looked toward Dahiya, who was several feet away and in deep conversation with two of her men.

They were unmistakably Dahiya's sons, Yosef thought, following their gaze. They had their mother's tall, rangy frame, slanted cheek-bones, and wide-set eyes. Neither knew their age, and though Yosef guessed it to be about his own, they seemed older, their bodies hard from long hours in the saddle.

It had taken Yosef a day or two of watching them move amongst the men of Dahiya's camp to understand the marked maturity in their manner. Amongst the Jerawa, he had realised, there was no division between adult and child. Accustomed to the hierarchy of age, it had come as a pleasant – and yet strangely unsettling – realisation to Yosef that here, years seemed to count for little. Bagay and Khanchla were old enough to wield a sword and ride with the men. Thus, they spoke at table and during training with the same easy familiarity to a man twenty years their senior as they would to each other. More surprisingly, the men responded in kind.

There was an odd egalitarianism in their company that Yosef had yet to become truly at ease with. And, besides, he was not yet included in it, for he was sadly lacking in the basic skills every

Jerawa seemed born with: the ability to ride a camel, read the desert, and wield both bow and sword – often all at the same time.

"Is Aksil your ruler?" he asked.

"Our mother leads the Jerawa. Aksil leads the Awraba. They are equals, allies. We are all Imazighen."

But there was a faint defiance in Khanchla's voice that hinted at conflict, and Yosef's interest was piqued. "We will ride to meet this Aksil – and then on to Carthage?" he asked.

"We ride to Aksil – and then, probably, to war," Khanchla answered. His eyes gleamed in the flickering light of the oil lamp.

"To war?" Yosef looked between them. "War with whom?"

They looked at him in astonishment. Then, realising his question was genuine, Bagay answered. "The bastard Arabs." He spat contemptuously to one side. "Even now they ride from Kairouan toward our homeland."

"For what purpose?" Yosef asked. "What do they want?"

Bagay and Khanchla looked at each other, then at him. Khanchla shrugged. "They are Arabs," he said, as if that should have some meaning to Yosef. "They want everything."

* * *

THE CAMP BROKE QUICKLY the following day. Men ate dates washed down with camel's milk as they fixed their sparse belongings on to their saddles, leather-covered *guerbas* tied to the high cross points at the front so they could drink as they rode. The dew was heavy that morning, and Yosef's blankets were damp as he folded them to make a saddle pad. The saddle itself was in the Tamzak style, which Yosef had learned the Imazighen here loved and spent hours stitching with intricate designs. It had a high cross at the pommel and a tall, pointed back. The men rode with their feet in short leather loops at the camel's shoulder, and some of them had thick goat's wool padding atop the saddle. Belongings were tied to the pommel or behind the saddle from the high back and were perfectly balanced. Many men had a spare camel that they loaded with woven baskets filled with water and stores. They carried no feed for the camels, which grazed on the rich grasses and trees where they camped. They had been riding for two turns of the moon, and Yosef had yet to see the camels take a drink.

"During the cold months," Bagay had told him, "when the plants are rich with moisture, they have no need for the wells. In the heat of summer, the camels will drink ten times that of a man, and they must do so every few days. For now, and perhaps one more turn of the moon, they travel with no more than the dew of the plants to sustain them."

They had moved into strange, rocky land, made even stranger to Yosef by the swaying gait of his mount, to which he had yet to become accustomed. For the most part, they travelled in silent single file, each man swathed in his turban against the ever-present roar of the wind, a sound both haunting and overwhelming. Yosef felt curiously isolated within the material about his face.

Most nights, they made camp beneath the open sky. Occasionally, as they had yesterday, they came close to the low mountain settlements of the Imazighen, if the people there were allied to Dahiya. On those nights, they ate fresh goat or camel meat, watched by women with faces tattooed with strange designs they called *siyala*. The low, flat-roofed mud dwellings were warm and welcoming and smelled of fresh bread and the spiced goat's milk served to guests. The men, however, covered their faces with turbans when they entered the villages and stayed at a respectful distance from the women. To Yosef's initial surprise, the Riders seemed to dread the nights they spent in the villages. After another half turn of the moon, he had begun to understand why. The dark mud dwellings felt stifling and small after the wide desert sky. Whilst they all enjoyed the fresh meat and bread, there was something about the wild isolation of the desert that had rapidly become as much a part of Yosef's soul as the mountains of Illiberis. In only a matter of weeks, it seemed as if the desert had consumed him, made him part of its wild expanse, holding both his grief and his fear in its lonely winds so they became something lesser, something easier to inhabit.

Today, though, the air was still and the ground flat and wide, hard beneath the silent pad of the camels. Yosef, riding between Bagay and Khanchla, was conscious of the lightness in mood wrought by the absence of wind as men began to chatter and laugh amongst themselves. Turbans were unbound and rewound in deft, vigorous movements; lithe figures darted off over a hill here and there and returned with a bird they had shot, to be plucked as they rode, or with firewood, which they bound to their saddles.

"How many men does your mother lead?" Yosef asked.

He watched Dahiya's tall, straight-backed figure as he spoke. She rode at the front of the men, smiling at their antics, exchanging conversation with a few, but always with that quiet authority that said unmistakably: *I lead you.* Yosef found her fascinating.

Bagay shrugged. "There are a thousand in the camp waiting for us, and another five thousand able to be commanded in camps and settlements between Septem and Barca."

"But that is an army," said Yosef, astonished. It was more men than Count Paulus commanded – and he was the most important noble between Corduba and the coast.

"If we do not defend our land," said Bagay, "then who will?"

"But surely the Greeks hold the sea ports?"

Raised to believe in the concept of the Empire even though he had not been born within its reach, prior to sailing with Shukra, Yosef had had only the vaguest notion of what lay beyond Spania's shores. His vague assumption had been that the land he now rode across remained in the capable hands of the emperor's legions. The opulence of Ilyan's court – whilst mildly shocking after the Christian austerity promulgated in Spania – had done little to change his impression. Whilst he had been surprised to find that Ilyan kept his own small military force and that Septem served only as a stopping port for the Greek fleet rather than a permanent post, he had assumed this to be Ilyan's choice. Now he turned to Bagay to ask further but found instead that Dahiya had reined her mount beside him.

"What do you know about our land, Yosef?" she asked him. She seemed genuinely curious, so Yosef answered her honestly.

"Very little," he said. "I thought – I was taught – that the Greeks hold the sea ports along the coast. I know the last Greek port in Spania, in the south, was taken by our king more than fifty years ago, when we became one nation." He paused, and then smiled ruefully at her. "In actual fact, I know little other than that," he admitted.

She smiled. "Knowing what you do not know is the beginning of all knowledge. I, also, know little about your homeland. So, you will teach me, and I will teach you. You are Jewish, are you not?"

Yosef nodded.

"You need not fear," Dahiya assured him, seeing the wariness in his eyes. "Many of my people are Jewish also. Some are Christian, too. But first, we are Imazighen." She brought a clenched fist across her chest in an automatic gesture of salute. She wore beaten bronze cuffs on both forearms. They were engraved with serpents and inlaid with precious stones. They reminded Yosef of the torc he had once seen Acantha wear.

In fact, he thought, Dahiya herself reminded him of both Acantha and Lælia; she had the same unsettling amber eyes, gleaming with fierce independence. He felt a pang of pain and wondered if everything, in this new life, would remind him of Illiberis or Garnata.

"And your people were here first?" he asked, grasping at anything that would distract his mind from the horror of his recent past.

Dahiya smiled. "What is 'first'?" she said, shrugging. "Yes, as far back as memory and story goes, the Imazighen were in the mountains and deserts of Africa. It was our ancestors who painted on the rock walls deep in the mountains and who knew the ways of waterhole and wind. We have endured on our land no matter who has held it, and our ways are those of the desert, older than the gods that other men bring or the laws they impose. When war comes, we fight; when prosperity comes, we trade. But always we live on the wind, part of the land."

"And your people are the Jerawa?"

Dahiya nodded. "We are all Imazighen, but my clan, my *kel,* is the Jerawa. My father was *amgar* of Kel Jerawa until his death. Now I lead them, but our people are divided." Her face darkened. "And there are those who do not like to be led by a woman."

"Who is the king?"

"The king?" Dahiya looked at him, frowning. "What do you mean?"

"Of Africa," Yosef said, looking around at the steep mountains and rocky ravines of the coastal mountains. "Who rules over the land? Is it the Greek emperor in Constantinople?"

Dahiya stared at him for a moment, and then she burst out laughing. She laughed so hard that she leaned forward over her camel's shoulder, slapping the saddle with one hand, so that eventually even Yosef began to laugh, despite not knowing what he laughed at.

"The emperor!" she said between gasps, and went off in peals of laughter again. Bagay and Khanchla beside her were equally amused, busily relaying his comments to the whole band of men so that soon they were all hooting with laughter, looking at him through dark, almond-shaped eyes and wrinkled faces.

"Oh," she said eventually, wiping her eyes and looking at him. "I see we must begin at the very start, my young Jewish friend, no?"

Yosef found himself curiously untroubled by being the object of hilarity. In his short time amongst the Jerawa, he had found their love of humour one of their more endearing traits – and, in his current mood, a welcome one. Accustomed to the solemn resignation of the Garnata Jews, who lived in a constant state of fear, tension, and defensiveness, there was something liberating about the open hilarity of the Jerawa. Nothing seemed to bother them for long, he had noticed. Even when matters of gravity were discussed, it was done with a light hand and much humour. Yosef could not remember the last time he had heard so much open, unrestrained laughter.

"The Greeks are no more than a presence on our shores," Dahiya explained as they rode. "The emperor's eye is turned east, to the protection of Constantinople and his own frontiers. In my own lifetime, I have seen the Greek presence here fade to no more than a handful of isolated coastal ports, the greatest of which is Carthage, to which we ride now.

"Ilyan allows Greek trade and the forces to utilise his port – for a price. But he does not pay taxes to the Empire, nor does he consider himself a part of it."

Yosef looked out over the vast valley through which they rode. It was land unlike any he had seen: rocky gulches lined with tall stands of *atoche* grass, which the Riders called *sabay*, amidst stony mountains covered in scree. Acacia trees – he had never seen one before they began riding – were dotted in forlorn isolation across the barren ground. Occasionally there was a small forest of them, and Dahiya's Riders made camp in these places. The tall clumps of grass offered good feed, as did the trees themselves, and the wood was used for their fires.

The trees themselves were strange to Yosef. They appeared like a cloudy haze, seemingly soft and welcoming yet covered in deadly sharp thorns that could pierce a foot as keenly as any sword. In the time they had been riding, Yosef had found more things to sting, pierce, and wound him than he had come across in an entire life in Garnata.

"Then to whom do your people pay tribute?" he asked Dahiya now. "If none in this land owe allegiance to a king or emperor, who unites you?"

Dahiya met his eyes, and Yosef was struck again by the sheer force of her presence. He felt a slight jolt whenever she looked at him, as if the vivid amber of her gaze could pierce his soul as deeply as the acacia thorn could pierce his skin.

"Our enemies," she said softly. "Our enemies unite us. And when we defeat them, we return to fighting one another, as we always have."

Yosef frowned. "Who is your enemy now? The Arabs?"

Dahiya nodded. "Yes. It is the Arabs we fight now." She sighed, looking around the valley. Closing her eyes, she tilted her head back and inhaled deeply. When she opened them, she turned to Yosef. "Are you a student of history, Yosef?"

"I… My father was." Yosef, feeling his throat close over, turned away.

"Mine also." Dahiya did not comment on his emotion, but there was something in her voice that made Yosef aware that she had seen it and understood. "He taught me that if a man does not rule himself, he becomes the slave of another. My people are proud. They are good fighters, and they love their country. But for centuries – many centuries – they have been slaves. They have been slaves so long they forget that they are able to rule themselves, not only out here in the desert, but in the cities and towns they have built with their own hands. The Imazighen are a proud and free people. We live according to our own laws."

She looked at Yosef. "In this, our peoples are similar," she said. "The Jews, also, live according to their own customs, their own ways, even amongst the nations of other men."

Yosef nodded.

"And yet, they have no country to call their own," she said. "Just as the Imazighen – even though we live on our own land – do not have a country. Do not have a nation."

Dahiya gave him a twisted smile. "But I intend to alter that. And you, Yosef of Garnata, have a part to play in my plans."

"Me?"

"You." Dahiya nodded. "A nation needs produce. Goods that cannot easily be acquired elsewhere." The amber eyes pinned him once more. "It is my understanding, Yosef, that your journey will bring such produce to our shores."

"It is to Spania I will return," said Yosef.

"Perhaps." Dahiya said the word with a light dismissal that disturbed him. "You may return, for all journeys must end. But I think Spania will no longer be home to you. And by the time you return to it, the Spania you know will no longer exist."

Yosef frowned. "What do you mean?"

"If the Arabs conquer Africa, they will move on to Spania. And if the Arabs do not conquer Africa" – she looked at Yosef – "then they will look elsewhere for territory. Either way, Spania is unprepared to repel them. Your king is weak. Your Gothic lords fight amongst themselves. Spania is a nation of priests and politicians. It will not survive."

She tilted her head to one side. "But this is why your people come to Africa. Jews, you are smart. You have seen this happen before. Perhaps you will make Africa your home. And it will welcome you."

Yosef realised they had separated from the others and that

Dahiya was edging them toward a crest. When they gained the top, he drew in his breath and stared in wonder.

Across a broad, flat plain, tall sand dunes reared into the sky, golden in the late afternoon sun. They rippled into the distance, an impenetrable sea Yosef could imagine no man entering.

"Once," said Dahiya softly, "my people ruled a great kingdom on this land. Its capital was called Altava. Men from far across the seas knew of it, feared it. But now Altava is lost to us. My people know the secrets of the sands. We know how to disappear into them, reappearing when an enemy least expects it. We know how to lead an entire army into a storm and see them lost forever beneath the swirling dunes.

"But after we have buried our enemies, we don't know how to build a nation from what remains. How to take the people of the sands and turn them into a government that can rule, into a nation that pays tribute to itself."

She turned to Yosef, and her eyes glowed in the late afternoon sun, the golden sand turning them tawny. "But this is what I intend to do, Yosef," she said quietly. "I intend to unite my people again and defeat the Arabs. And when I am done letting Arabic blood, I intend to rebuild the nation of Altava on the ground where they died."

She smiled at him, amber eyes like jewels in the morning sun. "Do you know what the word 'Imazighen' means, Yosef?"

He shook his head.

"It means 'free men'," she said quietly.

Free men.

Yosef looked out over the sand dune sea. He felt the wild expanse of it fill his soul, and for the first time since he had left Spania, he felt something beckon him onward.

26

LÆLIA

APRIL AD 688

Illiberis, Bætica, Spania
Granada, Andalusia, Spain

heo. Lælia had barely slept in days. She could feel him. In her dreams. In her chest. In the coin tangled in her hair. She could feel Theo in the very essence of the night.

She heard the plaintive cry of a curlew, and then the low, dangerous yowling of the lynx. She knew she would not sleep again. The pattern of her nights had become all too familiar; she had begun sleeping in her tunic so she could more easily cross to the stables without disturbing the night. Now she donned cloak and boots, following the cry of the lynx.

Since the messenger had come, Lælia had welcomed any opportunity to escape the guilt she felt within the villa walls. Her betrothal to Theo had been the only way in which she could help her grandfather keep Illiberis safe. If Theo was gone, any value she had was gone with him. In the immediate aftermath of Arun's death, it had been grief that kept Count Paulus locked away in his reading room. Now, Lælia feared, it was despair. Every silent day reaffirmed her inability to help in any way, and she felt the failure as a dull sense of impotent rage and frustration. Most of all, she felt deeply conflicted, for Lælia did not believe Theo was dead.

The ongoing presence of Athanagild and Alaric was a source of both comfort and pain. Comfort because she sensed that, despite the oppressive cloak of death beneath which they all moved uneasily, the brothers, too, had doubts that kept them in Illiberis. Pain because she knew that, even should those doubts be voiced, they could not change her fate or that of her home.

It was a waning moon. According to the charts she had learned alongside Yosef in Arun's study, it was the last of the scorpion's moon, one of deep magic and power. Each moon had two lives: one when the moon was new in a sign, and that born under it given life; then the time when it came full in that same sign, half a year later. The tribes in the mountains called the new moon in the sign of the scorpion the moon of the dead, and believed that when it returned, full, it brought the dead with it. Their new warriors used its power to make their first kill. The sound of drums had travelled faintly down the valley during the nights when it shone white over the mountains. Now the disc glowed a warning yellow, and the night felt dangerous as she slipped into it.

The lynx called again, a low, blood-curdling growl that chilled her blood. It was coming from beyond the foals' yard. Lælia increased her pace and ran low across the ground, leaving silent footprints on the dewy grass. She came to the stables and saw the foals standing together, facing the mountains. They were terribly still. Something about their tense stance increased her feeling of dread.

Beyond the light cast by the moon, the shadow of the lynx slipped through the dips and mounds in the ground.

Something was wrong.

The lynx had never come so close to the villa. And though the foals might make tasty prey, the female cat could not hope to drag one back to her lair; she had never tried to take something so large on low ground.

The lynx had not come for the foals. She had come for Lælia.

Lælia came into the yellow light on the grass, and the shadow paused. The cat's eyes glowed in the night, the same colour as the moon overhead. The black colt made a low noise of warning. The lynx moved away, then paused and looked back. Lælia realised the cat was limping, favouring one side, and as she drew closer she saw the dark stain of blood on the ground and the haft of an arrow sticking from her ribs. The cat growled as Lælia approached. She was a wild thing and had not come for help. She moved again, looking back.

She wanted Lælia to follow her.

Beneath the cold moon, they left the valley and climbed into the hills, the lynx ahead, Lælia behind, keeping a distance. The lynx walked just far enough in front so Lælia could see her, but she always maintained a cautious distance. More than once, Lælia felt the presence of another predator nearby. They always hunted by the light of the waning moon. It was a dangerous time for shepherds and foals, and Lælia was uneasy.

She could feel the unsettled tension from the horse tribes in the earth still. This was the moon beneath which new warriors saw visions and then hunted an animal sent by their ancestors. The young men of the tribes were often disorientated from the strong potion they drank to deepen their vision. Lælia suspected one of them may have been responsible for the arrow in the cat's side. If so, they would be heavily punished by their own people. No hunter should leave their prey in such pain.

The cat was moving slowly, dragging her shoulder, and now that the moon sat high, Lælia could see the heavy trail of blood glistening on the scree. She was dying, and Lælia did not like watching.

The cat moved around the ridge to the same rock where Lælia

had seen her lie the last time she had tracked her. Lælia crept closer. When she rounded the ridge, the rock was empty save for a rich smear of dark blood across it.

Lælia heard a faint mewling cry and swung around, knife in hand. The lynx stood behind her. She held a kitten in her mouth. Sweat glistened on the lynx's coat, and Lælia could hear her laboured breathing. Slowly, she lowered her head and laid the kitten on the blood-stained rock, her eyes never leaving Lælia's. The kitten struggled to stand, then nudged its mother, buffeting her belly, searching for milk, for food, but the lynx, exhausted, sank to the ground, legs buckling beneath her.

Lælia approached slowly. The kitten's cries grew loud with fear as she caught the new scent, and she crouched by her mother, searching for the comfort of the rough tongue on her back. Lælia wondered where the other kittens were. She could hear no cries.

The stench of death reached her before she got to the lynx. It was fresh, like the blood on the rock, and Lælia felt horror and fear in the air as well as an alien human presence, which hung about the narrow fissure in the stone from which the lynx had come. The fissure led to the cat's lair, explaining why she had seemed to disappear every day. She stepped around the figure of the lynx and peered inside, but the lair was black, and she could see nothing.

The lynx gave a low moan. Lælia did not need to enter to know what she would find. Outside, she could see the place where footsteps had made an imprint in the dirt at the entrance. Someone had already been here. Someone had come and killed the lynx's babies. Lælia could feel the shock and grief of it, see it in the cat's body, which trembled in pain and exhaustion.

The lynx's head sank on the rock, eyes dull, kitten tucked beneath her neck. She nudged it toward Lælia with her head, even as the kitten tried to crawl back beneath her tired body. Lælia reached tentatively for it and the kitten yowled a protest, but it was small and she plucked it easily from its mother.

She took off her shift and wrapped the tiny body so it couldn't move, then tucked it safely beneath her tunic. She did not want it to witness the last. Slowly, Lælia approached the lynx, eye to eye, her hand on her knife. Her heart beat a steady pulse. The lynx put out a long, pink tongue, as if to taste her. Lælia gestured to the kitten: *I will care for her.*

The cat gave a low, anguished moan of understanding, her body twitching as she eyed the knife. For a moment, the survivor in her warred with the pain. Then the steel was in her heart, warm blood spilling pain, loss, and anger over Lælia's hands, as the last of the animal's life drained into the dirt. The body became limp in Lælia's grasp, and the cat was no more.

All was silent for a time. The night felt heavy and still. The moon was tired, hanging low over the mountains. Its yellow cast was sickly now the passion of it was over. Lælia could not shake the terrible sense of foreboding that had awoken her. The braided cord at her neck was dull and lifeless now, and she felt a terrible, deathly fear.

Theo.

The kitten in her arms mewled, and a slight noise made her whirl, knife in hand. A figure appeared by the ridge. She recognised it as Acantha and relaxed. Her grandmother paused to touch and sniff the kitten. Acantha always breathed in animals. She said she could not hear them unless she smelled them first. The kitten quieted, and Acantha came close to Lælia and squatted down, looking at the lynx.

The other kittens are dead.

Acantha nodded.

Lælia touched the distinctive pattern on the broken arrow protruding from the cat's side. *This belongs to the tribes.*

"The boy who shot it was not worthy of the life he sought to take." Acantha glanced toward the dark opening of the cliff and wrinkled her nose in distaste. "Come," she said. "We will take her from this place."

They skinned the cat by the black water, working in silence during the still hours. The carcass was left exposed; it would be gone by midday. The birds of prey in the mountains were fierce creatures, hungry for meat.

Dawn tinged the sky dull red as they rode back through the gates at Illiberis. The kitten was curled inside Lælia's tunic, comforted by the scent of her mother on Lælia's skin. Acantha carried the pelt. Her horse had objected at the start but now carried it quietly, though its ears flickered back and forth uneasily. Horses did not like the scent of wild cats, even dead ones.

Alaric met them at the gate, Athanagild silent and pale at his side.

"We could not sleep." He frowned. "Athanagild has dreams." He stopped, colour mounting on his face.

I know. Lælia gestured impatiently, her attention already elsewhere.

"What is it?" Athanagild was at her side. "Is it the foals?"

She nodded, already walking toward the stables. She heard the colt's laboured breathing before its prone body came into view. Her grandfather was there, his face grim and drawn. Lælia knew that look. It was the one that preceded the cut of his axe. Count Paulus did not take the life of any horse lightly – but when it must be done, it was he who would do it.

The black colt lay on his side, covered in sweat. His eyes were listless and dull, unseeing, and the hooves twitched weakly, pawing at an invisible foe. As Lælia approached, the colt made a low, guttural moan of pain, and his body convulsed, becoming rigid as if to withstand a blow only he could feel. After a long moment, the colt grunted and went slack again, panting as if he had run a course.

The white filly watched in helpless misery from a short distance. She snorted softly as Lælia approached, the pleading in her eyes piercing Lælia's heart with brutal accusation. Lælia found it hard to let the filly close now. She could not bear to meet the imploring green eyes, knowing that every day the colt suffered, she was failing them both.

"This cannot continue." Her grandfather gave Lælia a grim look. His axe swung at his side. She could not take her eyes from it. He never wore the axe to the stable, not unless he planned to use it. He did not acknowledge Alaric or Athanagild, who stood slightly behind Lælia, reluctant to interfere in an argument they all knew had been coming.

"I have respected the wishes of both you and Acantha in regard to that colt until now." He nodded coldly at his wife, who stood quietly to one side. "But the truth is, every day it grows weaker and suffers more. Whilst the white filly thrives, the colt dies – as is always the way with twin foals, as long as I have known it. One should have died long ago. There is never enough life force from the mare to sustain two."

He frowned at the inert body on the ground. "You have kept this poor beast alive through nothing more than sheer bloody will. I cannot allow it anymore – and I will not, Lælia, no matter your pain in losing Theudemir."

It was the first time he had spoken Theo's name aloud since the night the messenger had brought the news. Lælia met his eyes and he nodded once, sharply.

"You are no longer a child. Death is part of life. You cannot pretend it otherwise. I will not allow your grandmother's mane magic and fantasies to come at the cost of an animal's suffering." He fingered the wooden haft of his axe, the lines in his face set and deep. "You will stay and comfort it in death," he said, gesturing at the colt. "It is your doing this has gone on so long."

He fixed Lælia with a grim, uncompromising eye. "Theo is dead," he said harshly. "Your betrothal to him was all that kept you, and Illiberis, safe. Now we must make other plans. I will soon travel to Toletum to sit at the King's Council. To leave you alone here will expose both you and Illiberis to attack, and I will not allow it. You will come to court with me." His tone brooked no opposition.

Lælia felt her heart slow to a dull thud. Noise rushed in her ears, and the world beyond the colt and the axe faded away. She sank to her knees, hands on either side of the colt's muzzle.

Theo.

She bent her head down so her cheek lay against the colt's, her eye close to his, so close she could feel the fringe of his lashes against her skin. She felt the slow, heavy throb of blood through his veins. In her mind, she could see the rivers of veins branching off, racing beneath the surface, carrying life through the body. She felt her own life move with it, and she knew – knew absolutely – that Theo lived.

You have to live. She felt the cord at his neck pulse weakly with life. *You must get up. Do you hear me? You must, Theo. You must live!* She clutched the colt's mane so hard that the coarse hair cut bloody streaks across her palms, and deep in the colt's topaz eyes, something flickered. He gave a rude squeal, somewhere between pain and rage, and his head reared up, rising from the ground with his body lurching after it until he stood clumsily, swaying back and forth on shaking legs, head lolling low and breathing heavily.

But alive. Alive.

He is a messenger. She stroked the colt's face, her hands rising to flutter the gestures then falling back. She did not look at them. *They both are — but this one most of all because we are here and Theo is not. If Theo dies, so will the colt — you will have no need of the axe. But as long as one lives, so does the other, and if you take the colt's life, you take also the means by which I can help Theo, wherever he is.*

She had never tried to convey such complex messages with her hands. The movements were jerky, lacking grace, but in the roaring silence behind her, she knew they had been understood.

The colt gulped hoarsely, then pawed the ground angrily, shaking and grunting.

"Do you believe, then," said Alaric slowly, his voice uncharacteristically rough, "that Theo lives?"

His question hung in the air. From the corner of her eye, Lælia saw Athanagild slowly make the form of the cross over his body, his hazel eyes sober. Above all, Lælia knew, Athanagild was a priest. Pagan magic was heresy. The fact that he nonetheless remained at her side touched her deeply.

She gestured to the colt. *Look at the light in his eye.*

She turned to find her grandfather staring at the colt and frowning. It took a moment until she recognised the expression in his eyes as uncertainty.

Theo is trying to survive. Accustomed to silence, Lælia had not, before now, tried to communicate what she knew, in some internal part of herself, to be true. Theo and the colt were so entwined in her mind that she had simply reacted emotionally to the colt's illness without trying to explain what she had, all along, known that it meant. Now, as she allowed that internal part to find expression in gesture, Lælia's hands flew with an intensity that surprised even her.

I think he was in water. He nearly died, but he was rescued at the last. But something has been wrong ever since; he is in pain, terrible pain, and terrified. It feels like – torture.

She stopped and swallowed; there were some things she knew only from dream fragments. Things she could not allow herself to come close to.

The colt watched her as she spoke, and Count Paulus watched the colt. He had been a horseman all his life. Lælia knew he could see the awareness in the animal's eyes as well as she could. Nobody who worked so closely with animals could doubt there were things they knew that defied human logic. Men not of the tribes feared such knowing, calling it mane magic, but such men named as magic all things they did not understand.

The colt nudged her ribs, searching for a treat. She reached into her tunic for a carrot and he took it, nibbling gently, then crunching down eagerly. She stroked his muzzle and looked at Count Paulus.

You can't kill him. I won't let you.

"Paulus." It was Acantha who spoke. Just one word, and no more than that.

Her grandfather looked between his wife and the animal. He stepped back. "It is time they were named," he said. He gave Lælia a hard look. "I meant what I said regarding Toletum."

Turning, he walked from the stable without looking back.

* * *

It was late in the day when Alaric sought her out. Lælia was sitting with her back to the wall, staring at the listless figure of the colt, her head in one hand, the kitten held close to her in the other.

"Shukra arrived this afternoon."

Lælia nodded. She had heard him come, had avoided his eyes. The little Persian man saw more than she was prepared to share.

"He will take Athanagild to Toletum when he goes." Alaric slid down the wall to sit next to her, staring at the colt with his arms loosely hanging over his knees.

"Nobody," he said heavily, "will speak of Theo's death. Not to me, or to Athanagild. Today is the first time I have so much as heard his name, and I will not hear it from your grandfather again, I know." He took a piece of straw from the ground and began fraying it into long, thin strips.

The kitten stretched against Lælia's skin, tensing then curling into her again, eyeing Alaric with wide, unblinking eyes.

"I cannot stay here." Alaric tore the piece of straw apart with a sudden, vicious movement and tossed the pieces into the stable. He plucked another and began fraying it. "It was the same when my mother died," he said quietly.

The kitten stiffened, and Lælia turned to look at him. The shadows of twilight showed his face gaunt with grief.

"My father," he said, "never spoke of her. Not then, not since. I know nothing of how she died, except that it was the fever that took her. I do not even know where her body lies."

Lælia's hand flickered uncertainly before her: *Nor I. None speak of my parents. They never have.*

He looked at her then. "You, too?"

She nodded.

He threw the straw away from him, frowning. "Silence is no way to grieve."

No. She put her hands out. *But it is the only way some know.*

He made an impatient noise. "I do not believe the attack on the fleet was an accident, as the messenger said."

I never did.

He met her eyes. "Oppa," he said softly.

The kitten growled. Lælia nodded, stroking it absently. *Even if others believe us, suspicion is not fact.*

"Oppa left Spania," said Alaric harshly. "That is undisputed. He has not returned; Shukra has had the ports watched."

"And it proves nothing."

They turned to find Athanagild's slender figure silhouetted in the doorway.

"Oppa," he went on wearily, "left word that he has taken a shipment of horses to Ilyan of Septem in return for the gift of coin Ilyan made his father. After visiting Septem, it is said, he planned to visit the church fathers in Rome, representing Archbishop Julian himself. We cannot prove he had anything to do with the attack on the fleet. None would believe it if we tried."

"Sunifred would." Alaric stood restlessly, and Lælia watched him, worry twisting her stomach. His face was dangerous with tension.

"Laurentius," said Athanagild, "says the Duke of Hispalis has a hot temper. It is dangerous to trust such a man…"

"The Duke of Hispalis," said Alaric coldly, "is the only man to stand against King Egica and the corruption of his court. He is the only one who sees that Egica will not rest until he displaces the lords of the south and puts sycophants of his own choosing in their place. He envies our lands and our trade – and fears our thiufae."

He faced his brother, his eyes flashing anger. "Spania's years of peace died with Reccesuinth, the eldest of Chindasuinth's sons and the last of his line to rule. Since then, we have become slaves to the Church's dictates and shunned by our own king. I tire of Laurentius's diplomacy. Tomorrow I will ride to Hispalis – to the duke's household."

He looked at Athanagild as if daring his brother to speak, but Athanagild put up his hands in mute surrender. "You must do what you believe is right," he said quietly. "We all must." He turned to Lælia. "Do you truly believe," he said, a catch in his throat, "that our brother lives?"

His words cut Alaric's rage as effectively as a sword. Both brothers turned to Lælia. The kitten sat up, staring intently at Athanagild, and Lælia stood so she faced them both.

Yes, she gestured. *I know it.* She put a hand on her heart. *I know it, here.*

Athanagild nodded. He and Alaric looked at each other.

"Then we believe you," said Alaric.

The three of them stood in the silent stables over the prone body of the colt.

"When you need us," Alaric said, "we will be here, Lælia. Always. You are our sister."

Lælia felt unwelcome tears and turned away, pressing the kitten close to her body. *I know,* she gestured.

Night fell and took the brothers with it, and still Lælia remained in the stable.

In the pale grey of dawn, she slipped into her grandfather's study and opened the drawer in his desk. She prepared the quill and untied the leather containing the vellum. Theo might be lost, but they were still bound, and during her conversation with the brothers, the recollection of the blank space where her name should have been had risen like a spectre from the grave, taunting her with a bittersweet tug at her heart. She would sign it now, in the early hours of the morning, alone, holding Theo close inside. She unravelled the leather and felt her heart stop.

It was empty.

A scrap of memory came to her – Oppa's conversation with the unknown monk, overheard that night in Illiberis:

Did you find it?

Yes, princeps…

Lælia clutched the edge of the desk, the pale dawn whirling about her. The only proof of her betrothal was in Oppa's hands – and Oppa was somewhere out there, on the same sea as Theo.

27

THEO

APRIL AD 688

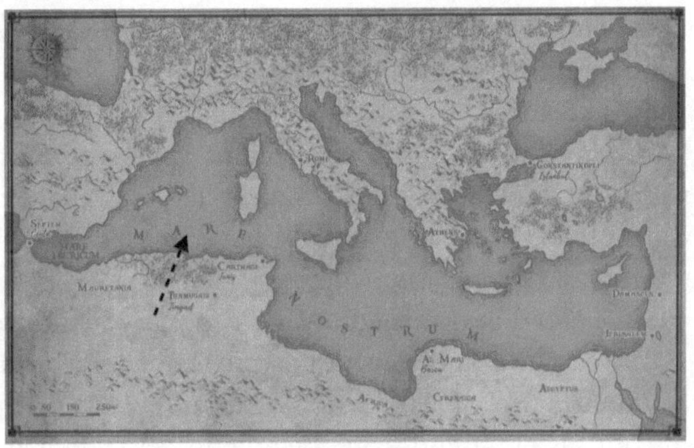

Mare Nostrum
Mediterranean Sea

"This he cannot survive. Not for long."

Theo heard Leofric's voice through a red mist of pain.

"He will survive as long as he chooses to." Silas leaned back, balancing his oar on his knees and nudging Theo with his head. "The water is coming, my friend. You must wake and drink. Do you hear me?"

"He hears nothing." Leofric's voice was bitter with anger. "That bastard Oppa whips ears and face today. After he rips back open again. No man can survive this, savage. Not day after day." He glanced longingly over the oarlock to where an Arabic *fulk* bobbed lazily on the waves in the distance.

"It is third Arabic vessel I see. We must be close to Carthage. The fleet recruits from market there."

"Carthage," rasped Theo. "The fleet is there."

"Forget Carthage," muttered Silas. "First, *wenkai*, you must live."

"Perhaps you should try to escape." Another voice came from the bench ahead of them, and one of the other oarsmen, a squat, rough-featured Goth, glared back at them. "Your friend is causing us more trouble than he is worth, *ja?* We none of us had been whipped before now – no more than a light cut, at worst. Now we face that mad bastard's whip every day. Better your friend decides to die, and soon – or one of us will find a way to speed it up."

"I would like to see you try," said Leofric scornfully. "And I promise this, ugly son of poxed whore: first man who touch Theo will die with guts stretched across dromon like seaweed. And don't think I will not do, because I already have, by God, and to men uglier and more dangerous than you."

The man sneered and turned away. "Strong words from a man chained to an oar," he said, raising his own, unchained hands and making a rude gesture. "I would think carefully what you promise, Slav. Even your savage friend won't be able to help you if we decide it is time you die." He glanced at Silas. "Isn't that right, you mad black bastard? You know better than to raise a hand to any of us, don't you?"

Looking up, Silas smiled. His eyeballs rolled in his head and his mouth was slack. The impression was so convincingly that of a madman that the man shook his head and turned away.

"They think you just mad enough to be dangerous." Theo's mouth stretched in a rictus grin.

The white teeth flashed. "Then they are not entirely stupid," murmured Silas.

Oppa moved toward them, water dipper in hand. It was a menial task he nonetheless performed himself, taking apparent delight in any means by which he might wield the power of life and death.

"The Arabic fulks," rasped Theo, speaking with his head down. "They sail for Carthage?"

"They are likely slavers," muttered Silas curtly. "You want no part of them, *wenkai*. Now stop talking, and drink. Do not upset your friend and his lash, not today."

Silas and Leofric drank from the dipper. Oppa came to stand beside Theo.

Forcing his head up, Theo shakily moved it toward the dipper. His lips had barely touched it when Oppa jerked the water from his reach.

"Tell me where to find the Jew."

Theo turned his head the other way and remained silent.

"You are going to die," said Oppa, in a matter-of-fact tone. "If you tell me what I wish to know, I will ensure it is quick."

Theo coughed weakly and winced as the movement caused a warm rush of fresh blood from the wounds on his face and back. The stain spread easily through the tattered remains of his tunic, brightening material already a dull red from the constant infusion of fresh blood, and metallic rivulets ran into his mouth.

"I will ask again," said Oppa. He leaned hard against Theo's face as he held the dipper just out of reach of his mouth, deliberately pressing against the open wounds. "Think carefully on your answer." He stroked the whip at his side.

Seeing the look in Theo's eyes, he shrugged. "It's your face," he said. Pulling the dipper away, he turned, the bright rubies on the eagle at his shoulder seeming to weep as they dripped with blood.

Theo closed his eyes, rocking with the movement of the oar. The amulet and cord beat against him, seeming to pulse with life, and he felt the softness of Lælia's hair, mingled with his own and the foals', against his skin.

I will come back, he thought fiercely. *I promised you I would come back, and I will.*

"Who was it you gave this promise to?"

Theo opened his eyes to find the sun lowering in the sky; he had slept.

"You say the same words, over and over," Silas said. "That you promised to come back. To whom did you make such a promise?"

"To a girl." Theo's voice rasped with disuse. "Her name is Lælia. She is to be my wife."

"Your wife!" Leofric snorted. "Then she is fool who does not know you as we do. And besides – she does not see our friend's handiwork upon your face. Perhaps her desire is less when she does. If she does. Which, I might add, seems unlikely, given our current circumstances."

"Lælia knows my face," said Theo softly. He raised his head and stared down the centre of the dromon, to where Oppa stood at the stern. As if disturbed by the weight of Theo's gaze, Oppa's head came up. Smiling slightly, he grasped the whip at his side.

Leofric groaned.

"This Lælia," said Silas quietly. "She is the one Oppa called witch?"

"Lælia is no witch. Oppa, also, wants to marry her." Theo's face hardened. "But he never will."

Feeling an odd surge of strength, Theo sat up taller in the dromon. Oppa moved toward him, and Theo held the other's eyes as he spoke. "Lælia is mine. She will always be mine. And there is nothing Oppa can do about it."

"Except kill you," said Leofric drily.

"That amulet you wear," said Silas in his deep voice. "Did she give you that?"

"Yes."

Oppa was halfway down the dromon, his eyes intent on Theo, the whip moving through his hands.

"Then she loves you," said Silas.

"Yes."

Oppa drew even and looked between Theo and Silas. "Yes to what, my friend?" he asked. "If you have the energy to speak, I am not wielding my whip effectively."

Theo could not have said what made him do it, only that he knew to do nothing would be a victory to Oppa and a betrayal of

Lælia – and of the two, he wasn't certain which incensed him more. So, he spoke.

"Yes, I am betrothed," said Theo. He smiled up at Oppa, the savage slices across his face stinging as they broke open. "Her name is Lælia. And, yes, she loves me."

"Xristus," Leofric muttered from across the dromon, shaking his head. The rest of the men tensed in expectation.

Oppa's face darkened, a slow, ugly stain spreading across his skin. "Even now, you dare taunt me," he said softly. "Even as I hold the thin rope of your life in my hands."

Theo's mouth curled. Fear disappeared, and in a rush of warmth he felt Lælia's hair against him, the rich bronze of her eyes warming his soul.

"You can take my life," he said, and his voice no longer rasped from the salt. "It matters not at all. Lælia will never have you. She is mine. She will always be mine."

"Yours!" Eyes blazing, Oppa held the whip high over his head. "You are a mad fool, Aurariola. And a dead one." His whip sliced cruelly across Theo's face. "Your use to me is over. I have gold enough to uncover the Jewish trade routes myself. When I return to Spania I will hold both: the secrets of your treason and the coin you hide." The whip mauled Theo's other cheek, blood dripping into his mouth. "But first, I will kill you. Then I will go to Septem and discover your little Jewish friend's whereabouts. I will bring Count Paulus to his knees before my father – and have his granddaughter on her knees before me."

Reaching into his tunic, he pulled out a roll of leather. Holding Theo's eyes, he unravelled it slowly until the parchment within was revealed.

Theo saw his own signature and felt his heart clench with a pain that threatened to push the air from his body; had he not been chained, he might have fallen to his knees.

Oppa bent down so his face was barely inches from Theo's. "I will have your whore – even if she fights to the death. Go to your grave knowing that. Know that you will die on this dromon – and that all you once had is now mine."

He shook the contract of betrothal in front of Theo's face.

"Did you know?" he hissed, triumph lighting his eyes. "Did you know she never affixed her mark to this parchment? No free woman shall be married without her consent; it is our law, my friend. Law written in the *Lex Visigothorum*, validated by a council of bishops many times over. Without her mark, this contract is meaningless. And this is the only copy. I had Nicalo check."

His whip came down, laying across the raw flesh of Theo's face in a lightning bolt of pain so intense Theo was nearly torn apart in the effort it took to silence his own scream.

"You thought it would keep her safe."

The whip descended again.

"You thought that even if you were lost, that contract would save your whore from me, would protect her from marriage. But it will not. You will come to learn, Aurariola, that I get everything I desire in the end. Everything. One way or another."

The whip cut Theo's back.

"I could give this to you…"

Across his face.

"I could hand it to you, here and now, and all of *this*" – across the other side of his face – "will cease. No more pain. The contract of betrothal safe in your hands. The means to save your whore. You can go to her, marry her if you like. I don't care."

His throat.

"All you need do," said Oppa softly, "is tell me what deal Count Paulus has made with the Jews. Tell me where the Garnata Jew has gone, and what he has gone to do. Tell me who plots against my father's reign and what they plan. Tell me this, Theudemir of Aurariola, and all of the pain, all of the suffering, will cease."

Theo tasted dull blood through his very pores. His head hung, and his eyes watched the roll of leather in Oppa's hand. *I must find a way to take it,* he thought through the haze of pain. *I cannot escape him without it.* Until that moment, he had not realised he had been thinking of escape, but now, even as the lash came toward him, he realised he had been thinking of it all along.

"Cry out!" Oppa's whip descended again. "Tell me how much it hurts you. It is your last chance to speak! Tell me!"

His whip fell again, and again. "Tell me! Tell me!"

But Theo did not tell him anything. He was watching the Arabic fulk he had seen earlier. It was bearing down on them, fighting spars out.

"Oppa!" Giscila's cry of warning cut the air.

Oppa turned around, the murderous intent clearing from his face as he assimilated the new threat.

"It is too late to run!" Giscila called. "We will need to fight!" His eyes cut to Theo; when they rested upon him, Theo felt an odd shock of something, almost like a shadow crossing the sun, there and gone. Then Oppa swung to face Theo and his companions, fury and anger warring on his face, and Giscila was forgotten.

"You will fight," Oppa hissed, leaning down to unpin their chains. "And you will fight like your life depends upon it − for it does, Aurariola. Do not forget who holds your future." He tapped the parchment in his tunic, but Theo was not listening. He felt his hands come free and, with a surge of exhilaration, measured the distance between himself and Oppa; he could, he thought, take the other man.

But even as he tensed to leap from the bench, he felt his wasted body give way beneath him and Oppa's own sneer as he saw Theo collapse in the effort.

"I said you would die," he said coldly, turning to face the fulk, now only feet away. "It seems now is the time."

Perhaps, thought Theo. *But if it is, I will take you, and that contract, with me.* Gathering himself for one last, mighty effort, he willed his body to move and felt Silas's strong arm close over his neck as Leofric's grasped his body.

"No, *wenkai*," said Silas's voice in his ear. "First, we live."

Theo made a strangled sound, but in his pain he was no match for the strength of the others. He felt the rough scratch of the dromon on his back, the moment when the world tilted, and then, as the first sounds of battle came from above, they were toppling backward, the cold water closing over his head once more.

28

LAURENTIUS

11 MAY AD 688

**The Fifteenth Council of Toletum
Toledo, Spain**

Laurentius looked at the twenty-seven bishops elevated on the dais in the Basilica of Saints Peter and Paul, and his fists clenched.

"King Egica," he muttered to Shukra next to him, "has stacked his church as tidily as he has the nobility."

"You expected it, *aziz-am.*"

"One may still wish," murmured Laurentius drily, "to be surprised."

Had Spania slept, he wondered, as the Fifteenth Council approached?

The ashlar blocks and horseshoe arches of the basilica had seen blood spilled in treachery and victors crowned in glory, but as Laurentius noted the clenched jaws of the nobility present, he wondered if any previous gatherings there had held such heavy implications for the future of the country he loved.

Gold votive crowns were suspended from the ceiling over the heads of the bishops. They were ornate affairs, inlaid with jewels, elaborate chains dripping yet more over the heads arrayed below. Nobility past and present had vied for the privilege to sponsor each one. At the centre, Archbishop Julian's chair was still empty. The council would not open until he entered. Laurentius suspected Egica of holding them in suspense for dramatic effect. It was a sad reflection on the farce the Crown had become, he thought, that such a thought should even cross his mind.

"I wonder, sometimes, why the nobles seek to pay so richly for crowns to sit on the heads of those whose sole ambition is to lessen their power," Laurentius murmured to Shukra, who smiled.

"It is ever the way, *aziz-am*."

"Do none of them heed the lesson of their predecessors?" Laurentius said darkly, as he watched the dais. "Queen Liuvgoto is not present, though Egica is married to her daughter. I fear that Egica does not wish her presence to upset his plans. He intends to dispossess the old queen and her family." His mouth tensed. "And when he does, Spania will revolt."

He glanced at where Sunifred, Duke of Hispalis and cousin to Queen Liuvgoto, stood with arms folded, glaring at the dais with barely disguised contempt. Ranged in a loose confederation behind him were many of the southern counts, though Count Paulus, Laurentius noted, stood to one side. Theudemir's father, Suinthila, was not present. It was rumoured the news of Theo's disappearance had taken the last of the man's will to live.

Laurentius, looking at the place by Count Paulus's side where

Suinthila should have stood, felt again the savage guilt that had dogged him since the news had come of the attack on the fleet.

"Tell me again," said Shukra, as the crowd whispered amongst themselves, "about this debate on dispossession."

"On his deathbed," Laurentius replied, "King Erwig made Egica promise that when he took the crown, he would protect Erwig's family and all their possessions. Egica had already married Cixilo, Liuvgoto and Erwig's daughter. The promise was intended as guarantee that Liuvgoto, and all the lands and titles granted to her and her relatives, would be safe after Erwig died. Egica, however, gained an exception to this promise at the time of Erwig's death. He asked what he should do if his promise to protect Erwig's family came into conflict with his promise to serve the people of Spania."

He glanced sideways at Shukra. "Of course, Erwig replied that he should serve Spania. Now, Egica invokes this exception by claiming that a situation has arisen that puts the two promises into conflict: Fráuja Frogellus has laid historic claim to the land and title of Hispalis, saying it was wrongfully taken from his family during Wamba's rule, despite all here knowing it was taken after Frogellus's father rebelled, and despite King Erwig already granting Frogellus other lands in lieu. Frogellus, though, is Egica's ally, and Egica hears the claim under the pretence that he wishes to restore justice." His smile was tight and cynical. "Of course, the fact that the claim is made against Sunifred, Liuvgoto's cousin, is convenient. If the council decides in favour of Frogellus, the door will be opened to claims against all those who were allied to Erwig and Liuvgoto."

He looked at Shukra. "Since it was Liuvgoto's own father who liberated the south from Greek dominance," he said dryly, "it means the entirety of the south is vulnerable."

"And to decide the claim," Shukra murmured, "Egica calls his priests to determine what his God wills and which promise he should honour?"

Laurentius nodded at the votive crowns, which cast jewelled rainbows across the wall.

"He asks," said Laurentius, his mouth twisting bitterly, "and he pays."

A movement on the dais made the crowd stir, and the archbishop entered. Julian was a lean, austere-featured man who, Laurentius knew from personal acquaintance, was as spartan in his habits as he was convinced of his own right. Despite the clear ravages of age, he stared now at the assembled nobility with an intensity bordering on the hostile. He gave the benediction with a harsh lack of ceremony, then nodded to the guards who stood at the great entrance.

King Egica entered the basilica, robed in purple edged with gold, and strode to the dais. His hair was slicked back from his face. A long nose and high cheekbones were accented in the light that filtered through the high windows, giving him the same look of lean hunger Laurentius recognised from his bastard son. Hooded eyes narrowed as he approached Julian.

"In the name of our Lord Jesus Christ," intoned Julian as the king mounted the dais.

Egica prostrated himself at the feet of the bishops, bowing his head to the ground. It was his predecessor, Erwig, who had instigated the practice of bowing to the bishops. It was whispered that obeisance had been Julian's price for bestowing the crown upon Erwig: a deal between the archbishop and Queen Liuvgoto that established Church and Crown as equal rulers of the young nation. But now Julian was old, and it was rumoured he was sick. Laurentius, seeing the sneering disdain on Egica's face, suspected that pact may not outlive its architect.

Egica rose. He took the throne, sitting in front of the crowned bishops, but still below them. Holding a scroll of parchment in his hand, he began to speak.

"I give the bishops of God, for examination, the words of their majesty, written down. Behold, blessed fathers, that to avoid an onerous and complex speech, that which cannot be expressed in ordinary words, I have summarised in brief clauses and assembled in clear written indications.

"Here I am, most eminent fathers and pontificates, whom I must honour by heavenly right. I stand before the illustrious assembly of your order exalted by a mighty joy, for I do not doubt that amongst you is our Lord Jesus Christ giving His blessing, for I believe His words in which He expresses, 'Wherever they may be gathered in

My name, there I may be found amongst them.'" Egica's tone was respectful and sombre. "And the force of this expression is so great, we know that anything that determines your opinion cannot proceed otherwise than by the dictation of Jesus Christ."

The bishops accepted his accolades with solemn countenances, as was no more than their due. *Get on with it,* Laurentius thought, unconsciously clenching his fists. *Show us your face.*

"I will not be ashamed, then, to open to you the most intimate reaches of my heart and allow to flow from it the reasons why our serenity is afflicted, and on what grounds such pain and distress was caused."

This was no more than the usual obsequiousness, but from Egica's mouth it reeked of hypocrisy and deceit. Laurentius wondered that any present could hear it and believe.

"The most important thing for me to show you is that when our father, and father-in-law, of happy memory gave me to succeed on the throne, I found myself bound by a double oath, to the point that if I keep one, I incur the crime of perjury by reason of the other."

And now we have it, thought Laurentius. *Now it begins.* It seemed that a hush had fallen over the room with Egica's words, that Laurentius was not alone in perceiving the gravity of the betrayal they were about to witness. *I had heard of it,* he thought, *as we all had. But I did not truly believe. Not until this moment.*

"For King Erwig, divine father-in-law of ours, to which I swore myself with an incautious and unavoidable oath when he gave me as wife his glorious daughter, committed me to the unequivocal clause in relation to any business of his family: to ensure that their interests are always victorious.

"Having promised this to the king under oath, at the time of death, he imposed another obligation on me, although I urged him to act otherwise: that he would not relinquish the throne before having forced me, with the stern ties of oath, not to deny justice to the peoples entrusted to me. I did so and was confirmed as king with these special obligatory clauses."

Laurentius closed his eyes, remembering Egica's words, said whilst kneeling at Erwig's bedside, amidst candles guttering in the wall sconces and the stench of death:

And about my relatives, and your children whom you have had of your glorious wife Liuvgoto, I promise to show myself and be a friend of them, with sincere love of heart and without hidden doubt … I promise to live with them in sweetness and charity all the days of my life, so that I will not disturb them or their goods, at any time, by any title or reason … nor will I plot or war against them, now or at any moment … I will harbour no displeasure or no evil in my heart or in my spirit…

That day was etched on his memory, as was the hard, predatory expression he had seen on Egica's face as he recited the promise.

"Egica did not urge the king to act otherwise," murmured one of the courtiers behind Laurentius. "He held Erwig's hand and the oaths dripped from his tongue like honey off a cake."

"I have decided," Egica went on, "to submit to your consultation this double series of obligatory clauses contrary to each other: those who demand of me the protection of their children; and those who decided to impose upon me to be elected king; and request that, confirmed by your blessings, I continue on the throne, and instructed of the rule of your authority, find the way by which, having avoided the alley of perjury, I may walk."

A murmur rose from the floor, the nobles stirring amongst themselves, unable to control their reaction to his words.

"What does it mean?" Shukra muttered to Laurentius.

"It means," said Laurentius grimly, "that Egica asks the Church to do his filthy work. That the terrible betrayal he proposes be sanctioned by God, rather than seen for what it truly is – base deceit."

"*Aziz-am!*" Shukra cast a wary glance around them. "Remember where we are."

Laurentius stood as still as the stone column nearby, gritting his teeth. *Who,* he thought, *will take those interests of your wife's family – the lands, the estates, the entirety of the south – if you will not "protect" them? Who will you reward with the fruits of your treachery?*

From the corner of his eye, he saw the nobles around Sunifred stir restlessly. *They know,* he thought. *They know this decision will enable Egica to take their lands and dispense of them as he sees fit, under the pretext of "justice". Every ally of his who was ever dispossessed will benefit, and he will find a way to take even those latifundia that, like Illiberis, have an ancient claim.*

This will send Sunifred over the edge into rebellion — and quite probably the entire south with him.

"For I cannot" — Egica raised his hand and began again, his voice rising above the babble on the floor — "for I cannot escape the note of perjury if I defend the offspring of Erwig against justice, do not proceed with truth for the people or, from my love of the truth and concern for the interests of the people, do not fulfil my promises to the king's family.

"For it is necessary to add that the cruelty of Erwig's oppressions; the judgements against many whom I unduly deprived of property and honour, and were reduced to the king's servants from the state of nobles; and those whom he oppressed, also with violent judgements — that even more, the people of his kingdom are compelled to swear to the safety of his children, and thus the door closes to everyone who would complain."

The stir turned into a rising tide of chatter, drowning out the king's words. This was beyond what any could have imagined.

"What does it mean?" whispered a young acolyte behind them, riveted by the excited babbling of the wealthy men of the realm gathered in the church. "Why are they so stirred?"

"It means that none of Spania's estates are safe," said Laurentius quietly. "It means that no man's property or wealth is safe from the hands of the king, no matter how many centuries it has been held."

He turned to Shukra. "It means war," he said.

* * *

HOURS LATER, they sat in the garden of Laurentius's family villa. Despite the villa's position in the most elite part of Toletum, less than half a mile from the palace walls, it was set in generous grounds, and in the spring twilight they were peaceful with the sound of birdcall. Citron trees vied with white jasmine against the walls, beyond which the Toletum streets throbbed with excited chatter.

The king's speech would be repeated in every tavern until the early hours of the morning. Even the lowliest wine wench understood the implications of the council: Egica meant to dispossess his own wife's family and all those who had once been allied to King Erwig. He meant to dispossess Sunifred and grant Count Frogellus's claim to the lands and title of Hispalis, one of Spania's greatest southern holdings, though he pretended the matter was still before his council and yet to be decided.

"What will happen to Alaric now?" Shukra asked. "He is betrothed to the Duke of Hispalis's daughter."

"Alaric's father, Suinthila, has already sent word to his son to discontinue the betrothal." Laurentius moved restlessly about the garden. He stood with his hands on his hips, legs spread, and when he spoke it was with his back to Shukra and in a weary, grey voice.

"Suinthila and Count Paulus have made a new agreement," he said. "A betrothal between Alaric and Lælia."

Shukra stared at his back, shocked temporarily into silence.

"*Aziz-am*," he said finally, "I am as acquainted with the tempers of young men as you yourself. We have trained them in war from one side of the Circle of Lands to the other. Are you truly believing that Alaric will be agreeing to such a thing? And Lælia? Perhaps, yes, she is a young girl. But she loved Theo —"

"I know." Laurentius cut him off harshly. "I did not say I agreed. But we none of us have choices in such times, Shukra. Not Alaric, not Lælia. Not…" He turned away, staring out over the garden walls. "I went to see Athanagild yesterday," he went on, striving to maintain an even tone. "At the monastery here in Toletum." He turned back to Shukra. "I have never seen a man grieve more deeply than him. And I could do nothing — say nothing — to help."

He shook his head wearily. "I had no right even to be there," he said, feeling his voice catch. "It was I, Shukra, who sent them — Theo and Yosef — to their deaths." He shook his head, unable to continue. Shukra did not offer any words of reassurance, for which Laurentius was grateful. They had faced too many battles together to cling to false hopes like children.

"We know that Yosef made it to Septem," Shukra said instead. "He is somewhere in the sands now, riding amongst the fiercest fighters ever to wield iron. We must believe him alive, *aziz-am*."

"To what purpose," said Laurentius wearily, "if Theo will not be there to assist him?"

"I told you I had a contact, Athanais, who will find Theo if he lives." Shukra looked reassuringly at his friend. "And if not, she will find Yosef and aid his path."

Laurentius nodded. "What do you know from her thus far?"

"I have had no word, but nor did I expect one. Athanais lives on the edges, *aziz-am*. We were children in the temple together, before the last of our magi were killed by the Arabs, and we were both taken slave. I came to the emperor's forces, where I met you. Athanais – she became what she had to in order to survive. But survive she has, and although we have travelled far from the temple, we both follow the way of Ahura Mazda still. Athanais said she would find Yosef in Carthage, and Theo also if he is there." He shrugged. "She will do so, *aziz-am*."

"What have your sources discovered about the attack on the fleet?"

"That it was no random occurrence."

"I never thought it was."

"Oppa sailed from Spania's shores." Shukra came to stand beside him, his face grim. "This, it is certain. Those I know in Septem tell me he joined forces with one who has been exiled from Spania for many years, a mercenary. The name is unfamiliar to me, though perhaps you know it – Giscila."

Laurentius frowned. "It is a common enough name. I do not recall it, but many were exiled after a rebellion against King Wamba of which I know little – I was abroad, fighting in the Karabisianoi. My father wrote little to me of what took place during those years, even the death of my own sister. He said later he did not wish to distress me." He shook his head wearily. "There are times now I wish he had been more forthcoming. Sometimes Spania seems a stranger's land to me."

"The coin sent by Ilyan to King Egica," said Shukra, "it is Oppa who commands this coin. Enough to pay as many mercenaries as he may require – this Giscila amongst them."

They were silent for a moment.

"Theo is dead, isn't he," said Laurentius heavily.

"I think," said Shukra slowly, "that we must believe it so."

"If Yosef's mission is to have any meaning," said Laurentius grimly, "Count Paulus is right – Alaric and Lælia must marry. It is the only way to keep Aurariola out of the rebellion Sunifred is planning and keep Illiberis out of Oppa's hands. There is no point in a mission to save the southern alliance if there remains no south to save."

Shukra was silent.

"I do not like it any more than you do," said Laurentius harshly.

"I know, *aziz-am*." Shukra's voice was unusually weary. "And I do not condemn you. But my heart does not like this. People are not pieces in a game, to be moved at will. I wonder what Ahura Mazda will make of these games we play, *aziz-am*. I wonder if the One, also, believes we have no choice."

"There are times," said Laurentius, staring into the gloaming, "when I wonder if all our choices are only illusion."

"Ah." Laurentius felt rather than saw Shukra smile. "And now you are sounding like a Persian, *aziz-am*."

They were silent for a time.

"The woman," Laurentius said eventually. "Athanais. You trust her?"

"I do."

Laurentius shook his head. "Is there such a thing to be had, now," he said, almost to himself, "as trust?"

Shukra spread his hands wide. "In such a world, *aziz-am*, what else is there but trust?"

29

YOSEF

JUNE AD 688

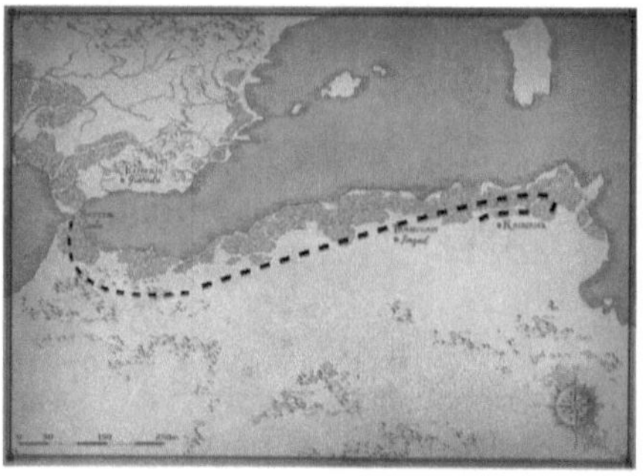

Montibus Awras, Mauretania
Aures Mountains, Algeria

The Jerawa had harried the Arabic lines for nights on end. Yosef had never known men to ride as Dahiya's did. They had circled around and below Carthage and ridden toward Kairouan, from where Zuhair bin Qais marched his men west, through the country where grazing was to be found and water was plentiful, away from the treacherous sands. Dahiya and her men melted into the landscape during the day, making camp in steep ravines and hidden folds of rock. At night, they burst upon the fringes of the Arabic camp in a devastating chaos of camels and arrows.

Whilst not as agile as horses, the camels were significantly faster and became snarling, dangerous beasts when they launched an attack, baring their teeth and sinking them into any who dared approach. Yosef had witnessed a handful of camel-mounted Riders enter a sleeping camp in a silent, deadly circle of rapid arrow fire that took all opposition, even before the first man had so much as called a warning. They stole supplies and horses, spiriting them away to the waiting men in camps and villages nearby.

The Arabs did not dare follow their tormentors. Any stragglers who fell behind met with certain death. Zuhair's forces began to fear the unknown sands and the demons they believed lived amongst them.

Yosef, who remained in camp during these raids, found himself increasingly fascinated by the Riders' technique. It was nothing like the battles of which his father had taught him. The Riders, he thought, were more like the horse-herding tribes around Illiberis – part of the earth itself, impossible to either find or face.

Yosef welcomed the waft of a cool breeze over his face. This far into the Aures Mountains, the nights were still cool after the sun dropped, although the days were hard heat. The stars glittered above, and the smell of meat and men about the fire called a welcome.

Yosef, however, did not feel welcome.

"Daya! Come, eat."

The firelight played on Aksil's face, showing a wide smile that didn't quite reach his eyes and a face beginning to slide into fat. He had been a hard warrior, and a good one, and men still followed him. But, Dahiya's sons told Yosef, it had been a long time since their amgar had fought a real enemy, and the years of lassitude had reduced him to a portly man clad in ornate armour, the iron core of the warrior transformed into gold gleaming from every surface.

His eyes, though, were still wary, and they narrowed as Dahiya approached with her men behind her. Aksil may have no longer walked with the honed strength of a fighter, but something in his face told Yosef his mind was as wily as it had ever been. He felt Aksil did not like Dahiya's presence in his camp.

They washed their hands beyond the circle of men and sat cross legged on the blankets amongst them. Yosef sat with Bagay and Khanchla behind the immediate circle. Those men who jostled companionably at Aksil's side were his closest companions, eating from the plate of meat at the centre. Dahiya's sat behind her, eating from other plates, unmistakably set apart. Yosef was aware of their eyes flicking to their leader as she ate, taking their signals from her. Dahiya, he noticed, ate sparingly, though it had been weeks since any of her band had eaten good meat.

"Aksil," Dahiya said when they finished. "I have news. Can we talk?"

Yosef shivered as Aksil's eyes passed over him. There was a cold assessment in them he did not like. The men drew closer to the fire, blankets over their shoulders to protect them from the cold. Aksil nodded his permission.

"Zuhair is drawing close," said Dahiya. "I believe we should attack him now, whilst he is in the sands and vulnerable."

The men sucked their teeth, glancing at Aksil and shifting uneasily.

"You rode to Septem." Aksil regarded her across the fire. Plump fingers stroked his beard.

"Yes, I rode to Septem. Ilyan is our ally, and he requested the meeting. He has as much to lose if Zuhair continues to ride as we do."

"Ilyan is a tool of the Greeks and not to be trusted."

"Ilyan," said Dahiya coldly, "is nobody's tool. And caution in choosing his allies – and battlegrounds – does not make him untrustworthy. It makes him intelligent."

A low murmur rose from the men, and Aksil glared at her. "I might advise you to choose your words more carefully, Dahiya. It would be easy for you to be… misunderstood."

The flames lit Dahiya's eyes, turning them a dangerous amber as she met those of each man in turn. "These mountains are our home," she said, gesturing at the tall shadows behind her, speaking to them all rather than to Aksil. "In them we feel safe; we have held them from time immemorial and, gods willing, we will hold them evermore."

There was a rumble of assent from the men.

"But Zuhair will not come and fight us in the mountains. He is too experienced a commander for that. I know – I have been watching him for months now. Ilyan, also, agrees."

"Our forces have cut off his retreat to Kairouan. Zuhair moves west to water his animals, but his goal is Carthage – and he cannot reach it without defeating us."

The man who spoke sat close to Aksil. He was young, with a lean, hawkish face and narrow eyes, which watched Dahiya now with barely disguised hostility. "We will do as we have always done. We will lure the battle further and further into our country until he has no choice but to follow us. When he does..." He shrugged, making a vanishing gesture with one hand.

"I do not know you," said Dahiya bluntly.

"This is Tariq." Aksil gave the boy an admiring glance that made Yosef vaguely uncomfortable. "Tariq was once a slave to the Arabs. He speaks their language, knows their ways. I consider his opinion of rather more value than that of the sly bastard sitting in Septem of whom you seem so fond."

"A slave of the Arabs?" Dahiya raised her eyebrows. "But you are Amazigh," she said. It was a statement rather than a question. Dahiya knew the features of one of her own.

Tariq returned her stare coldly. "My village was destroyed in Uqba's time," he said. "My people were killed, and those who lived were taken prisoner. I learned to fight in the Arabic forces."

"And now you are suddenly returned." Dahiya shifted her gaze to Aksil. "Just as we are about to engage Zuhair. Convenient, is it not?"

Aksil frowned. "Tariq was forced for many years to fight for the Arabs on their own soil. As soon as he found himself in familiar territory, he deserted the Arabic army – and nearly died in his efforts to return home. We found him near death in the sands, and he has told us much. Thanks to him, we have knowledge of Zuhair's forces. We know what to expect when we bring battle to them."

Aksil sat back, toying with his wine as he looked at Dahiya

through narrow eyes. "Whilst you busy yourself in schemes for power with Ilyan of Septem," he said, "and raid for glory, I plan for battle for our people. Do not think to return here and lecture me on warfare, Dahiya. Your ambitions are plain for all to see. At such a time we must unite." He gestured expansively at the mountains behind him. "Our people, and our land, are at stake."

Yosef felt his stomach churn uneasily. The contemptuous expressions around the fire indicated that Aksil had successfully claimed the moral high ground. Dahiya must have felt it too, for she bowed her head in acknowledgment and spoke respectfully. "You are the brother of my father," she said, placing her right hand over her heart. "Bound not by blood, but by blood shed on the land we both call mother. We are Imazighen, and you are our ruler. I am proud to offer you my men and my allegiance – and I will ride beside you, until death if I must."

Yosef saw annoyance war with surprise on Aksil's face.

He did not anticipate capitulation, Yosef thought, and he felt a familiar admiration for the manner in which Dahiya seemed to read the men around her, to know exactly what must be said in any moment to turn the tide in her favour.

"I value your sword," said Aksil. "As I do your counsel. You are a true warrior, Dahiya." He smiled reluctantly. "Though, by all the gods, I do not wonder why you have no husband!"

The men laughed openly, grinning at Dahiya, the atmosphere softening. Yosef wondered if any of them saw the wariness in the back of her eyes as she returned their smiles. *She plays your game,* he thought, *but she does not believe it.* Seeing the intensity of Tariq's eyes as they rested upon her, he suspected he was not the only one who saw behind the mask Dahiya showed.

Then the dark eyes shifted, and Tariq was focused on Yosef himself.

"Yosef," Dahiya said, noticing the shift. "Come. Let me introduce you."

The men ceased their talking and looked at him curiously. Yosef had become accustomed to such scrutiny over the past weeks. Well travelled as they were, and accustomed to the diverse populations of Carthage and Septem, still it was an oddity for that world to reach the Imazighen here in their desert wastes. And no matter how similar Yosef's dress might be to their own, still there clung to him the subtle sense of "otherness" that proclaimed him stranger.

"Yosef is a Jewish exile," Dahiya said without preamble. "He rides with me to learn the ways of the sands. From here, though, he will join the Arabs. He carries with him important letters, which must pass through Arabic hands." She looked at Tariq. "It seems meeting you is fortunate indeed," she said, smiling openly. "Perhaps you are the person who can help us on the next phase of our journey."

Tariq did not return her smile. He was still staring at Yosef. "The Arabs welcome Jews," he said curtly. "In the court in Damascus, it is said many of the highest positions of counsel are held by Jews. They are considered 'people of the book' by Arabs, and as such are not enslaved."

Yosef frowned. "People of the book?" he asked. "What do you mean?"

Tariq looked around the circle at the faces staring at him. "Jews and Christians both take their God from a book, no? We have all seen this."

The men nodded, Dahiya too. They were all familiar with the scrolls of the Jews and the book of the Christians.

"The Arabs also worship this same God from the book," said Tariq.

There was a stir of muttering at this.

Dahiya frowned. "I had heard the Arabs had a prophet of their own," she said. "That it was from him they took their God."

Tariq nodded. "He lived. It is true. His name was Mohammed." He looked around the circle. "But the Christians also believe their prophet lived, no? Iesu. And the Jews" – he glanced at Yosef – "you also believe that your prophet lived. Moses."

Yosef nodded.

"The Arabs believe that Mohammed heard the voice of the same God known to Moses and to Iesu. But Mohammed walked the earth in the time of men still living," said Tariq. "He died only fifty years ago, a little more. And his words were recorded in his lifetime – words the Arabs believe were God's words, spoken through

Mohammed. The book in which they were recorded is called the Qur'an. So, the Arabs have their own book of this God, the One True God, as they call him, the same God of the Jew and Christian."

Yosef heard the bitterness in his voice.

"They respect others who also have books from which they worship the same One True God." Tariq looked around the fire. "But," he said softly, "that respect does not extend to peoples such as the Imazighen, who worship many gods and see them in the line of the sands or the whisper of the desert winds. That is why they enslave us, treat us as animals. Unless we surrender to their One True God – they call this surrender Islam – then we are less than men to them and not worthy of respect."

"But people of the book" – he turned dark eyes back to Yosef – "*you*, they meet as equals and will share their meat with."

A short silence followed his words. Yosef felt intense discomfort.

"Surrender," said Aksil, breaking the silence. "The only surrender that will occur on our lands is that of the Arabs with my sword at their throats."

A stirring of excitement rippled through the men.

Yosef felt rather than saw Dahiya's irritation. "If we allow them to cross the sands to water," she said quietly, "they will control the rich land between Kairouan and Thamugadi and be able to reinforce their supplies and wait for more men to arrive."

Aksil's smile was one of condescension, and when he answered, it was with confidence and authority. "They will never get that far."

Men shifted and raised their cups, exclaiming under their breath, eyes shining.

"We will lure the Arabs close to the mountains," Aksil said. "Our mountains."

He gestured around them at the landscape beyond the fire.

"We will draw them to our old city, to the heart of Altava, the fortress at Thamugadi. We will ambush them as soon as they dare ride into our territory. The Arabs know nothing. When they come, we will let them come. Again and again. And we will defeat them – again and again."

They were fighting words, and the men, even Dahiya's men,

murmured agreement. Yosef, who had come to share their moods, could feel the blood coursing through his own veins, Ghurzla's song calling them to victory. He felt it himself, felt his own heart begin to beat with the rhythm of the war drum.

The men raised their cups, shrieking defiance into the night sky. Aksil watched Dahiya, his eyes bright with triumph.

Tariq watched them all, his face dark and impassive.

30

YOSEF

JULY AD 688

Thamugadi, Mauretania
Timgad, Algeria

The library in Thamugadi had once been impressive. A curved colonnaded portico surrounded three sides of the open court. The rectangular reading rooms off the sides were silent now, unused. Yosef stood in the large vaulted hall, staring blankly at walls lined with wooden shelves, only a few rotten shreds of parchment remaining of the great library that had once been there.

The library reminded him of his father's study in Garnata and Count Paulus's in Illiberis. Reminded him of the scrolls sewn into the hem of his cloak and the journey to the East that had begun to seem so very far away.

With every day that he rode, it was the world of the Imazighen that became his own, their struggles that seemed immediate, whilst the purpose that had driven him here seemed to become less important.

It was quiet and still. For a moment, he could forget the chaos and terror that awaited beyond the walls of the old Roman town. The sound of men preparing for battle filtered through the courtyard, but here silence seemed to permeate the stone, and he could enjoy the illusion of peace. Yosef closed his eyes briefly and drew a deep breath.

He felt the faint shift of air as someone entered the room.

"We are caught like rats in a trap," Dahiya said bluntly. She gave Yosef a twisted smile. "I tried to argue," she said. "In truth, I have done little but argue every step of the way here. It is one thing to attack from the foothills of the mountains, quite another to take refuge behind the inadequate walls of a town and attempt to engage the Arabs in siege warfare."

"You do not think we can win," Yosef said.

Dahiya stood beside him, looking out at the dusty plains below.

"I know we can't."

"What will you do?"

"Fight."

She turned and moved restlessly along the shelves, her fingers tracing the places where books had once stood. What had happened to them? Yosef wondered. Did they rest now in a library somewhere in Greece, or had they been burned by Dahiya's people, who saw the written word as a betrayal of their own gods and beliefs? Would order ever come to the Imazighen, or would they descend into warfare once more, fighting one another whilst a new order came to rule them with a new language, written in books of its own?

"We will provide the first diversion," she said, not looking at Yosef. "Aksil has ordered it thus. If – when – the Arabs break our defences, we are to attack them from the west and lead them into the mountains. Where Aksil's forces, I am told, will destroy them in mighty battle," she finished, unable to keep the note of bitterness from her voice.

"You do not believe he will prevail."

"He cannot prevail." Dahiya spoke harshly. "Zuhair has had a week to rest and water his men, whilst our horses and camels have lived on meagre grass and our men have camped in the mountains. Had we attacked their force as they marched from Kairouan – as Zuhair surely worried we would – we might have had a chance. But now? After the Arabs have had good grazing, a week's rest, and trees with which to build siege ladders? No, Yosef. We do not have a chance."

She strode impatiently across the hall and stood staring out at the courtyard. Dusk was falling. The central fountain was a crumbling, cracked stone, long dry.

"After we create the diversion," she said softly, "when the Arabs come, you must ride with my sons, Yosef. Do you understand me? You must reach Carthage. I could not take you there before the fleet arrived, for fear you would be discovered. But it is summer now. The Greek fleet will be in the port. With them will be those who can help you on your way."

"But you?" Yosef paled. "What will you do?"

"I will fight," said Dahiya dully. "As I am sworn to do – and my men, also."

"Then I, too, will fight," said Yosef. "You cannot order me away. And your sons will never leave you."

"Yes, I can. And my sons will do as I order them." Dahiya looked at him with hard eyes. "I will fight as long as there is any chance we may prevail. But you, Yosef, you have a destiny beyond this desert, and my sons are the last blood of my father's line. In them, the hopes of our tribe rest."

Yosef swallowed hard. "You don't understand," he said, his voice choked. "In Spania, very few believe the Arabic threat to be real."

He thought of Frogellus's arrogant pomposity, the incessant squabbling over land and titles.

"The men who rule would consider any talk of an Arabic

conquest no more than a tale told to frighten children. Even the discussion of a fleet to defend Spania's shores is seen as frivolity, the scaremongering of weak men. The Gothic nobility of Spania believe our nation to be invincible. Until I came here, I knew no different." He searched for the right words. "But now that I know of it," he said, "nothing else seems important. What does it matter if I reach the East and fulfil my father's journey if the Arabs have already crossed Africa? If your army falls, Dahiya, if *you* fall, then Spania is already lost."

When she reached out and took his shoulder, the look in her eyes was one of understanding, but her voice was uncompromising. "Even when defeat seems inevitable," she said quietly, "we must hold to the tasks that are ours, the promises we have made. You are to ride to the East. This is your promise, made to your God and your people. Mine is to stand, and fall if I must, in the defence of Altava. You will do as I order. When I signal, ride for Carthage. Do you understand me?"

Yosef swallowed. Reluctantly, he nodded. "Yes. I understand."

"Good." Dahiya turned back to the courtyard and clasped her hands tightly behind her back, holding her body rigid and straight.

"We had best go and hear Aksil's speech," she said grimly. "It may be the last time we ever do."

* * *

"We have defeated them before!" Aksil screamed, striding along the wall. His men, armoured and waiting, roared in response. "Did we not chase Uqba's men to the death through the sands?"

"Yes!" cried his men, brandishing their swords in the air.

"Did we not scourge them with fire and rain them with arrows?"

"Yes!"

"And did not Ghurzla strike them where they rode, killing them in their thousands?"

"Our gods are strong!"

"Our gods are strong!" called Aksil, holding his cup high. "They are not dead ghosts in a book. They ride amongst us, and they belong to the land we hold. We will prevail, as we always have. Altava!"

"Altava!" screamed his men in response, calling their kingdom by name, the kingdom of the Awraba and Jerawa, the mountains and stark sands they had roamed for a thousand years and more. "Altava! Ghurzla!"

The drums beat and the sound of steel rang through the night as men sharpened their weapons and waited, sweating despite the cold. Yosef listened and raised his cup with them. Then he turned and followed Dahiya into the mountains to wait.

* * *

The Arabs came at dawn.

Yosef sat on his horse amongst cliffs turned ochre by the rising sun, breathing in the rich scent of the desert mountains at daybreak, and listened to men scream as they died.

At first, the screams were in Arabic. They could fight, Zuhair's men, and they were brave. Again and again, they threw themselves at the walls of the town, walls that had never been built to hold back an army. Aksil knew this; he did not intend to hold the town, just to exhaust Zuhair's men upon its walls.

"But it is a good strategy, is it not?"

It was one of Dahiya's men who spoke.

Dahiya shook her head. "No," she said softly. "It is not."

As they watched, the sun came up over the walled town, a red ball behind the cloud of battle dust that hung in the air. The Arabs charged beneath the arrows flying from above, hooves pounding across the earth, curved swords raised, their screams chilling even to men who had seen much of war.

The man frowned. "Why do you believe it doomed?"

"Because Aksil fights a method he does not understand against an enemy who has mastered it." Dahiya and the man beside her swung their heads in surprise when Yosef answered.

"And what do you know of warfare, boy?" asked another Jerawa man beside Dahiya.

242

"My father was a scholar," said Yosef quietly. "Warfare was a passion of his. He liked to tell me of it."

"Ha!" The man spat in the dirt. "Stories. Stories are not war. War is that." He nodded at the ground below them. "It is dirt and blood and chaos." He gave Yosef a scathing look. "What do stories know of that?"

"They know that beyond the dirt and blood and chaos is a plan," said Yosef, staring at the battleground. "And that whoever has the best plan wins." He turned to Dahiya. "If what you say is true, Zuhair has besieged towns a hundred times the size of this one – and won them."

She nodded, her eyes not leaving the men below. "Yes," she said. "He has. And if the stories are true, each victory has been won with a plan his enemies knew nothing of."

She touched the folds of her quiver, stroking the strong length of war arrows within. A man shrieked below, a blood-curdling cry of attack.

Yosef saw it then, the battle savagery, reaching for her like a lover. Her fingers travelled over the smooth curves of the bow. Men whispered that the ends of it were carved from her own father's bones, a bow that had sent men to death on a thousand battlefields.

"Yosef," she said abruptly. "Go with Khanchla. Now."

Dahiya's men stirred with edgy excitement. She turned her horse to face them, Yosef already forgotten. Dropping the reins, she placed both hands on the helmet resting on her saddle.

"It is time," she said.

They watched, silent, as she raised the horned mask of Ghurzla high over her head. For a long moment, she stared at the men and they at her. They met her eyes and saw the face of Dahiya their leader, the person with whom they laughed and sat to meat, the woman they rode beside every day. Then she lowered the great god to her head, covering her face to the chin, cloaking herself in the scent of her ancestors and the memory of her father. The horns arced up into the sky as if connecting her to some primal, invisible power, and the woman was gone.

Yosef saw through the narrow eyes of the mask the moment she became Al Kahinat, the Sorceress. The horse tensed beneath her, muscles bunching, beginning to plunge with battle rage, and she raised her bow to her men, who stared at her in reverent awe.

Entranced as they were, Yosef wondered if it was truly Dahiya they saw, or Ghurzla, the god of war, whose mask she wore. For when the mask descended, it seemed to Yosef that a part of her fled, the part that was Dahiya, woman and Rider and daughter and mother. In its place came all those who had been before her, a power that was far greater than any one person or the iron helmet she wore, for the mask itself had become powerful only by the energy that had flowed through it on a thousand battlefields just like this one, into the line of warriors who had worn it and known themselves temporarily taken.

"Altava!"

She screamed the name of their land, an otherworldly cry that galvanised her men and carried across the rocky plain in a chilling, long-drawn-out shriek. She leaped forward and Riders burst from the rocks around her, bearing down upon the Arabs in a sea of raised arrows, led by Al Kahinat, a great horned sorceress on a raging black warhorse.

Yosef watched in mingled horror and awe as the Riders fell into formation, pouring across the plain in a pattern of two intersecting circles spread wide on the horizontal. The forward line charged through the centre and broke to the sides, men with both hands to their bows raising them as they twisted their bodies and released five arrows at every hand, each finding its target with unerring accuracy. Then the Riders were gone before a spear or sword could approach them, veering off and circling around to rejoin the tide that flowed closer and closer to the packed ranks of Arabs. Al Kahinat's bow belonged now to Ghurzla, and the men whose bow strings played left and right beside her rode the same awesome tide of power, a tide only blood could create.

On they came, an inexorable force of flying arrows released with devastating speed and number, and the Arabs retreated from the savage onslaught in a mixture of fear and confusion.

Yosef exulted in their skill, as if he himself were one of Dahiya's famed Riders. Only the Jerawa knew the secrets of such riding, could train their animals to carry them into frenetic mayhem and maintain their precise, collective order. Not one man held the reins. They shot in motion, bodies fluid and graceful, movements they could have made blindfolded and indeed had, many times, in training. In these moments, it seemed to Yosef that Ghurzla and Al Kahinat rode in partnership, the blind savagery of one blending alchemically with the almost occult discipline of the other.

In a deadly swirl of arrows and dust, they closed in upon the Arabic army, which turned from the walls and rallied to meet the charge. The attack had thinned the Arab numbers, and they were pinned, the walls of the town forgotten, facing the merciless charge of deadly arrow fire backed by spear and sword.

"Altava!" screamed the men, and an answering roar came from the Awraba on the walls, saluting the skill of their Jerawa kinsmen. Today they were Imazighen together, and for Altava, their lost kingdom, they fought. For the land they dreamed of ruling once more.

"Altava!"

As they struck, Al Kahinat slung the bow onto her back and drew Ahar, the great sword of her father. To Yosef, it seemed as if the sword, wielded only in battle, were itself alive, gleaming beneath the dull sky with visceral power. The hooves of Al Kahinat's warhorse pounded into flesh, and she screamed in savage delight as a man cried in terror and fell beneath its weight, struck by a death-wielding horned sorceress.

They charged through the Arabic ranks in a hammer thrust of men and horse, and at first it seemed the battle would end there. Yosef felt the dangerous intoxication of victory as the enemy fled before the twin powers of arrow and sword, scattering in every direction.

Al Kahinat swung her horse to counter a blow and shrieked her savage triumph as men began to run. And then Yosef saw them.

Barely a stade from where he stood, appearing like smoke from a narrow fissure in the mountains, came a horde of Arabs on horseback, wielding steel and screaming for death. They came behind a tall man in a pointed helmet, wearing red robes the colour of blood and carrying a brilliant standard of green and gold. A man with a narrow, lean face and dark eyes, which had very recently watched Yosef across a fire.

Tariq had betrayed them.

The men on the walls saw the Arabs coming. They yelled a warning and, on the plain, Al Kahinat's Riders turned to face the new threat. But it was too late to down sword and reach again for bow, to reassemble the deadly circular torrent of fire that could have cut them down. Already the newcomers were almost upon them, Tariq directing his forces so that they flowed into a river of attack on either side of the Riders, cutting off their escape.

Zuhair's army, which had only pretended to flee, returned now in earnest to the walls, and the shrieks of triumph from the Imazighen turned to screams of pain as the Arabs swarmed over the crumbling walls of the old town, a town built for scholars and merchants and never meant to be held by an armed force. Yosef looked up at the wall in time to see the sleek curve of Tariq's Arabic blade thrust through the centre of Aksil's body.

In an instant, Ghurzla was gone, and Dahiya the mother screamed aloud her rage and agony at the loss of her men and at the danger to her children. Raising her sword once more, she shrieked a battle cry, willing Ghurzla back into her veins; but hearing the grief of despair in her cry, Yosef knew that in the torn pieces of her heart, the battle was already lost.

* * *

THE SUN WAS an ugly orange disc. The miasma of fear and war reminded Yosef of burning oil in Garnata and the stench of his father dying. He drew his cloak tightly around him and felt the soft weight of the scrolls he carried sewn into the hem. Their weight had often seemed a burden, an uncomfortable reminder of his unknown future. But amidst the chaos of battle they seemed instead a comfort, a reminder that there was some strange order beyond the storm of ferocity he watched. When all about him seemed so terrifyingly alien, they reminded him that there was a purpose, no matter how tenuous it seemed, to his movement, that he was not merely a leaf on the wind as he had so often felt since leaving Spania.

"We cannot wait any longer." Bagay addressed his brother, and

Khanchla grunted in reluctant response, his eyes narrowed as he stared out over the rocky cliffs of their shelter to the plain below.

"It is lost," said Bagay softly.

The words were meant for Khanchla only, but Yosef felt them strike his own heart nonetheless, and he wondered why he cared.

Perhaps, he thought, looking down at the carnage of battle far below, *it is because they remind me so of my own people, though we fight in different ways.* Dominated first by the Romans, then the Greeks, the Imazighen finally had the chance to rule themselves – and along came another conqueror.

But even as he felt a tide of righteous anger rise in his heart, another thought struck him: *You are about to travel into the very heart of the enemy you see here today. This is not your fight; the Arabs are not your enemy.* He felt a curious sickness at the thought, as if he were a man without principle. *To whom do I owe allegiance?* He felt his stomach turn uneasily. *Am I simply as a leech from the river mud, sucking what I must from all I pass, caring not for the blood I take but only for my own survival? Where is the honour in that?*

"Khanchla," said Bagay, this time with more urgency. "If we wait much longer, they will begin to comb the mountains for survivors. You know what our mother told us."

None of them heard the horse approach from behind.

"Why are you still here?"

They swung around, startled, Khanchla and Bagay already with swords drawn, and Yosef, sucking in his breath, reaching instinctively for his knife.

Astride a sweating black horse streaked with blood, the great horned god of Ghurzla rising from her head, Al Kahinat held a sword still dripping with gore.

Dropping the reins, she pulled away the mask, and even as the god fell away with the horns, to Yosef, Dahiya seemed no less fearsome, her face blazing with battle lust and something else, something tired and angry.

"Come," she said abruptly, and the fury faded as the warrior stared at her sons. "Follow."

They did, without a word, riding behind Dahiya and a small band of her Riders, many of whom carried savage wounds. They rode deep into the mountain crevices, along paths so narrow and steep Yosef wondered how any but goats could have found them; at times, they even had to dismount to bring their animals through the passes.

They rode in dejected silence. More than once, a man had to be pulled from his horse and placed behind another as he fell into exhausted unconsciousness. But none were left behind, and the horses carried them gamely, grunting with pain and effort as they went deeper into the mountains that lay between the desert sands and the coast.

When they finally drew rein, it was deep into the night, and Yosef was so exhausted he could barely dismount.

"No fire," said Dahiya abruptly, as Khanchla drew flint and stone from his pocket. "Tariq is no stranger to this country. We do not know how far Zuhair sent scouts."

They sat beneath the cold, crystal stars and chewed dried meat and dates, but few of the men had an appetite. They tended to one another's wounds and rolled over in their blankets, falling into welcome blackness, none wishing to speak of the day's events.

It was, Yosef thought, watching them, nothing like he had imagined the aftermath of battle to be. In all the poems and ballads, there was feasting and pillaging, a sense of death narrowly averted. Not this dull defeat, the blank eyes and exhaustion. The men turned their backs to each other and curled into silence. A palpable sense of grief hung over the dark lumps on the ground, lit only by the cold stars above and without even a fire to warm them.

"Aksil is dead." Dahiya spoke softly to her sons, and Yosef stayed still, listening. "The fool never stood a chance. Tariq was Zuhair's all along. He must have been reporting on us for months, since Kairouan. The Arabs knew the weaknesses along the wall and they knew exactly from where we were coming. It was over before we ever rode onto the plains."

Bagay spat into the earth and muttered something Yosef could not understand, making a sign in the air that sent a tremor of superstitious awe through Yosef's body. No wonder, he thought, the men were so morose; they had been defeated not by a greater force, but by something much worse – betrayal.

"How did you escape?" Khanchla asked quietly.

"We fought until Aksil fell and the walls were breached. When the slaughter began and our only choice was escape or slavery, we cut a path through their weakest point." She shook her head. "It was Ghurzla alone who saved us," she said softly.

"Ghurzla – and Al Kahinat."

It was one of her Riders who spoke, a muffled figure from the shadows crouched beneath a thorny acacia. "The Arabs fear her yet, and when she screamed curses from behind the war mask, her sword laying waste in every direction, they ran."

He spoke with a faint note of awe at the memory. Around them men stirred, and Yosef realised they were listening despite their appearance of sleep.

"I failed," said Dahiya dully. "I knew what we faced; I knew Tariq for what he was. But I did not insist, and it was our Riders who paid for my weakness. Our people who lost."

"You did not fail." The shadow beneath the tree rose and moved closer, squatting down on his heels before Dahiya, letting his blanket fall away. Yosef recognised one of the men who had sat beside Aksil at every fire, one of his closest Riders.

"Every man here," he said quietly, "owes his life to your bravery – to you and no one else. You fought us to freedom when most men would have thrown down their sword and knelt in fear. You found a way through the Arabic wall and drove us past them. And had Aksil listened to you – had we all listened to you – we would never have been defeated in such a way."

Drawing a long, curved blade from beneath his blanket, he laid it carefully on the ground in front of her.

"I have followed the Leopard since I was a boy," he said. "He was a brave man, and I honour him. But even at the height of his reign, never have I seen the power and bravery you showed today."

A soft murmur of assent rose from the men in their blankets, and gradually they stirred, moving themselves closer to the small group lit only by starlight.

"You are amgar," said the man. He touched the horns of Ghurzla reverently, then raised his wine skin and drank a deep draught. "I will follow you, fight beside you – and die, if I must."

"I am not worthy of this," said Dahiya, and Yosef heard a slight crack in her voice.

"There is no other more worthy," said the man simply, "and no other we will follow. Will you lead us?"

Dahiya turned her head to encompass the men who had moved closer in a group around her. "Is this truly your wish?" she asked.

A rumble of assent passed through the men, and Yosef felt something indefinable shift, the heavy lassitude of defeat giving way to an edgy resolve, to hope; it ran through the small camp like life, and another man stood.

"I, also," he said, coming forward and laying his sword in front of her. "I am a man of the Awraba – but the Jerawa are my brothers, and I take you as amgar, here, before all others." Touching the horns tentatively, he rose as if invigorated and sat tall in his cloak beside her where before he had hunched over.

One by one they came, murmuring their allegiance, laying their swords to the ground before her, and with every man who did so, Yosef felt the pain and grief of defeat slip away in the new brotherhood they were creating and saw them touch the horns of Ghurzla in awe and step away, reinvigorated. The camp altered, and the men who only moments before had been a defeated force were united once more, with Dahiya, Al Kahinat, amgar of the Jerawa and Awraba clans.

When they were done, the man beside Dahiya drank from his flask and rested his hands on his knees. "Where do we ride to from here?" he asked.

"To Carthage," said Dahiya, without hesitation.

"Carthage?" The man frowned. "What lies in Carthage that can help us?"

"An old friend," said Dahiya softly, and Yosef saw the faint glimmer of a smile on her face. "An old friend with a force capable of defeating Zuhair – and the motivation to try."

31

THEO

JULY AD 688

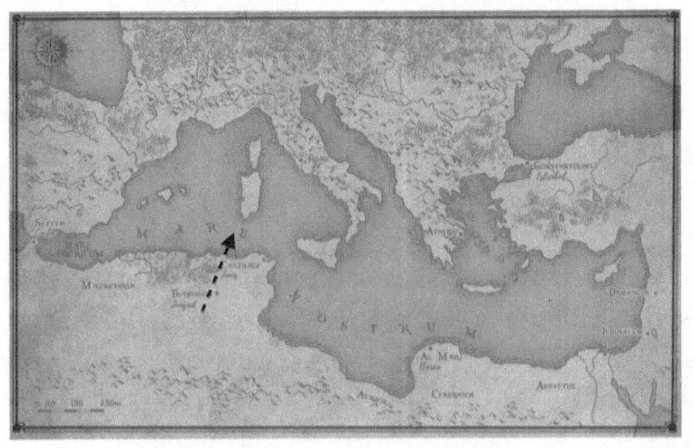

Mare Nostrum
Mediterranean Sea

"Next time we escape, I will choose rescuers." Leofric winced as sea spray came through the oarlock, splashing on his bare torso. "So far Theo's choices all lead to rowing bench and chains."

Silas's deep laugh sounded behind Theo. "And what would you have said, *wenkai*? 'Oh, no, thank you for offering to take us from certain death. We will wait for the next vessel.' As I recall it, you were as pitiful as the rest of us."

"I still blame the *schnecke*." Leofric grunted with the strain as a wave caught his oar.

"Always, you must find someone to blame. Why is it so with you?" Silas's tone was rich and full of laughter.

"Because his slices on face and back lead to these bloody chains." Leofric scowled at the man standing in the stern of the boat, hands behind his back and turban wrapped about his head, watching them row. "One look and he take us for trouble, no matter story we tell him."

"One look at your ugly face and he would have drawn the same conclusion, *wenkai*."

"I am not your brother," said Leofric, but without malice. "At least this one" – he nodded at the slave master – "doesn't love whip so much." He shot Theo a wry smile, intended, no doubt, to take the sting from his previous comment.

No matter how light-hearted their banter, Theo could not deny the truth of Leofric's statement – nor cease feeling utterly responsible for the plight they found themselves in.

Again.

The fulk crested a wave and jerked the oar forward, making him wince as the movement parted the wounds on his back. At least those on his face had healed. Now they were raw open cuts, the pink flesh scoured anew by salt water at every dip of the oar. There had been no chance for scabs to form in the weeks – now turned to months – they had rowed. The wounds were healing as open ravines in his flesh. They would leave ugly scars.

"But they are clean," Silas would assure him daily. "This is good, *wenkai kor*. Sea water is good."

Good it may be, but Theo would give a great deal, he thought, to stand upright for a time. The dromon was a merchant ship and had drawn to shore many times to trade. At first, when Theo was still badly sick, he was certain they had stopped on the coast of Spania itself. For a mad moment, he had clawed at the side of the fulk, calling in a hoarse voice, but Silas had clapped a large hand over his mouth and forced him to silence.

"None will help a slave," the big man had murmured in his ear. "You have got us this far. You are barely alive. Do not give him reason to throw you over the side – there is no guarantee you will find a better reception ashore."

And he had realised, with a jolt of horror, that Silas was right. He himself had seen the slaves on the merchant vessels pulled up on the shore at Cartago Nova when he had come to the market with his father. Had seen the poor wretches working in chains, some for sale themselves, fortunate if their buyer broke their chains before taking them home. He realised, with a sudden burst of shame, that he had never really looked at the men being sold. They were simply slaves. He had always accepted that they must have committed some kind of crime that led them to such a fate. He had never stopped to wonder why it was that some men lived in chains whilst he, Theo, rode a horse as a free man.

But since their enslavement in the Arabic fulk, Theo had thought of little else. All he had assumed his life would be, all he had taken for granted, had been cast into a different light by the long months of captivity. Carthage, and his meeting with Yosef, seemed a distant and almost forgotten dream, one he must force himself to recall. Chained to an oar, living in near-naked squalor through freezing storms and now increasingly oppressive heat, with only the barest amount of bread and water to sustain him through endless days of rowing, had brought a strange detachment and reflection.

As the oar drew him backward, Theo raised his right hand and touched the amulet and coin at his chest, skimming the tatters of silk that clung to the cord, then returning to clasp the oar in one smooth movement. He did it every time he thought of his life before, the points of reference reminding him of who he had been, linking him to what he would one day return to.

For Theo knew he would return. It was a certainty in the pit of his belly he could not describe and had long since ceased trying to. Silas and Leofric joked, and that was their way of surviving;

humour served to sustain many in the fulk who might otherwise have long since relinquished life.

After their recapture, Theo had succumbed to the fever that had gripped him as a result of the infected wounds on his back and face, too weak for many days to notice anything other than the caw of sea birds above and the pale wash of sky he saw when he opened his eyes. That, or the rough, sodden wood he lay on. He had been kept alive, he knew, only by virtue of Leofric and Silas's combined strength. But for their protection he would have been thrown overboard long since. He owed them both his life.

But the only way he could imagine having a life was to see it, in his mind, as he would have it. And in the long months of rowing, Theo had begun to construct it very clearly. With each pull of the oar, he would bring into focus another part of the life he intended to create, and every time he touched the amulet at his chest, he made a promise to himself that he would see it come to pass.

"Tell us," said Silas, as they pulled together, "where are you today?"

"Yes," said Leofric. "Go on, *schnecke.*"

"No," said Theo, smiling. "Surely you are tired of hearing it by now."

"What, with all the entertainment offered?" said Leofric dryly.

"And stop calling me 'snail'," said Theo, though he was smiling.

"That I cannot do," said Leofric. "Anyway, it is compliment. Snails, they live anywhere. Sometimes they die for years then come back to life. Is true. I have seen it. And you, you should have been dead many times before now, and still you live. *Schnecke*, you are. Now tell your stories."

Silas chuckled. "Your word pictures make the hours pass," he said in his deep tones. "Speak, *wamaath kor.*" Speak, little brother.

The clouds parted, and a warm sun shone on their backs, drying the salt in Theo's wounds and sparking the fierce itch that drove him wild. It forced him to speak – anything to take his mind off the agonising prickling in his back.

"It is early morning," said Theo, "and I am high in the mountains above Illiberis." Closing his eyes he could see it, the tall, sharp peaks and narrow cypress trees, a lonely eagle cawing in the dawn.

"Tell us about the horses," said Leofric, a strange yearning in his tone. Leofric, Theo had learned, had a love for horses not dissimilar to that of the Illiberis folk; he spoke of them with the same kind of reverence.

"The black colt is nearly a yearling, now. He is growing big and strong, wide in the haunches as the Illiberis breed is, solid in the chest but with a delicate head and long neck. He is wide footed and sure. He and the white filly are free in the mountains. They run with the horse herd, as they will until they are of an age to come to rein. For now, they graze the sweet grasses of the high peaks and drink the snowmelt.

"I am standing with Lælia beside a large holm oak. The sun is shining with the soft warmth of spring, and we are watching the horses. We are talking about how to bring them to rein. Lælia wants to do it the old way, as the tribespeople have taught her, but I favour leather and saddle. I doubt the black colt will submit to her. We are arguing about it, but we are laughing too."

"What are you eating?" It was one of the other men, a slave who had been aboard long before they came. His tone was rich with longing.

"Lælia brought a basket from the villa," said Theo. "There is the sharp mountain cheese made by the herders. Figs from the trees, dried from last summer; the new ones are yet green buds on the branches. Almonds, from the recent harvest."

"Meat," said the man longingly. "Is there meat?"

"And wine," called Boric, who had been captive the longest of them all. "What wine is there, Theo?"

"Last night we ate lamb," said Theo. A soft groan went up from the men. "Today there is a haunch in the basket, pink inside and seasoned with mountain herbs. Lælia brought a flagon of her grandfather's finest wine; it is a deep ruby red, rich on the tongue, and we eat the lamb inside bread whilst we drink it."

The heavy thud of the slave master's step silenced him. The man stood over him, an unpleasant smile on his face, and addressed his companion in Arabic. Theo strained to listen.

"They are laughing at me," he murmured to Silas. "Saying we will be lucky if we do not starve to death."

Silas shook his head. "I don't know how it is you understand their tongue," he said quietly.

"I can't explain it." Theo hauled the oar. "It was a mass of sound, nothing more, but then one day I began to hear words."

"I have been amongst Arabs often in my life," Silas said, grinning, "and yet I still know less than even the simplest greeting. It is a gift you have, *wenkai*."

"As much use as his word pictures," grumbled Leofric. "No use understand the tongue if only to know when we will die."

But Silas was frowning, staring overboard. He nodded his head, and Theo turned to look.

A faint blue haze in the distance sharpened as they rowed. "Carthage," he said, as an excited murmur broke out amongst the men.

Theo felt the wasted muscles in his body tense at the name of the city and the memories it conjured. It had been so long since he had allowed himself to think of Yosef, of the mission that had been the reason for him joining the fleet so long ago. Throughout the long months, all recollection of his promise to Yosef had faded, so that all he thought of was Lælia and how to return to her.

And besides, he thought, *even if Yosef survived his escape to Septem, he would have passed through Carthage long ago.* He felt a familiar wave of anger and despair, the impotence wrought by captivity; at the same time, he knew himself to secretly hope Yosef had gone, and with him, the promise Theo had made to complete his journey if he did not. He ducked his head and flushed with shame. *I may be a slave,* he told himself, *but I will not lose my honour. I will not wish to be free of my promises. I will not be that man.*

"The emperor's forces garrison the fortress at Carthage." Leofric's voice was a welcome respite from his own thoughts. The Slav spoke under cover of the men's chatter.

Silas leaned forward, his head down, so the three of them could have what passed for a private conversation aboard the slaver. "If we can find a way to be noticed by a member of the fleet at the slave market, that bastard will be forced to let us go," said Silas quietly.

"Why?" asked Theo.

Leofric grinned. "That is best thing about Greek fleet, my young friend. Is tighter with coin than even slaving ship. There is nothing Constantinople coin counters hate more than losing fighter they pay to train. Once you are recruit, Karabisianoi does not like to see you go."

"But," said Silas, frowning as the fulk turned away from the shore, "we are not sailing for Carthage. The men aboard are new. This is a merchant dromon, sailing west to buy goods. We are not the cargo on this voyage."

Theo cleared his throat. "Perhaps," he said quietly, "I can change their minds."

Leofric frowned. "Be careful, *schnecke*," he said. "Men do not like to know they have been overheard."

"If we get to Carthage," Theo said, "you think the fleet will save us?"

"If we can make them notice us in the market," said Silas, "then yes, *wenkai*. The fleet will have their men back."

"And the rest of the men here?" Theo nodded at the thin, wasted bodies of the men who held oars around them, many half dead with exhaustion.

Silas shook his head, frowning. "The fleet will not pay for slaves, *wenkai*, only take back those already theirs."

Theo frowned, but the slave master was moving, and if he meant to speak, he must do it now. He focused all his thought upon the words he knew only from sound and in his head. Trying the unfamiliar sounds on his tongue, he called out to the slave master: "*Khadhna 'ülaa Carthage.*" Take us to Carthage.

The man stared at him in astonishment. "*Limadha a?*"

Theo searched for the words he had not even realised he knew. "*Sayudfae alrijal aleamala,*" he said, hesitantly. Because men will pay coin.

The man, clearly taken aback, frowned at him.

"*Lak?*" For you?

Theo gestured at all the men in the dromon. "*Kul lana.*" For all.

Seeing that he had the attention of the entire crew, Theo reached out and held Silas's and Leofric's hands up, indicating the place where the stigmas had been inked into their hands. "*Kul lana,*"

he said again, gesturing to all the men who were chained to oars.
"*Kul lana.*"

The slave master stared at him, then began a low, urgent conversation with his crew, during which the words "coin" and "Carthage" were the only ones Theo heard.

"What did you tell them?" hissed Leofric.

Then, as the slave master gave Theo a sharp look and shouted an order to his crew, the fulk began to turn for shore, and a murmur of excitement ran through the men.

"I told them," said Theo, "that men would pay good coin for us." He glanced around him. "For all of us."

Boric held up his own, unmarked palm. "But we are not all men of the fleet."

"He is right, *schnecke*," said Leofric.

Theo shrugged. "The slave master will not care if the fleet pays coin for you. And if we are smart, the fleet will pay."

Leofric snorted. "You do not know the fleet so well, I think."

Theo smiled, heaving on the oar. "First we find the fleet. Then we worry about how to get them to buy us."

Leofric stared at him, a grudging smile on his face. "Ah, yes, and this, it will be so easy, *schnecke*, no? Do you want to make promise on this?"

Theo touched the amulet. "I already promised," he muttered.

32

LÆLIA

JULY AD 688

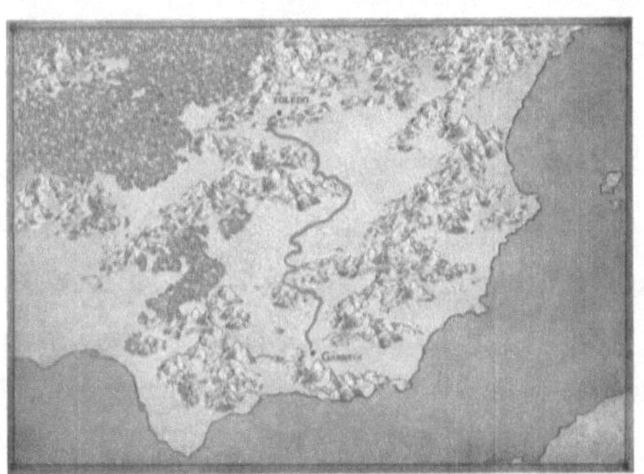

Toletum, Spania
Toledo, Spain

When Lælia had left Illiberis, summer scorched the earth, and men took refuge during the midday hours to escape the heat. In Toletum, summer was late. Clouds scudded across a pale blue wash of sky, chased by restless gusts of wind. From the terrace of her uncle Theodofred's Toletum home, the rolling hills beyond the city seemed barren and colourless.

Despite the mild day she drew her woollen cloak about her and shivered. *Perhaps it is the wind,* she thought, *that makes it seem so cold.*

The palace, high in the centre of the city, glinted palely in the late afternoon sunlight. Although it was by far the most imposing building Lælia had ever seen, she found herself completely unmoved by its grandeur – and by Toletum itself.

"An impressive sight, is it not?" Riccilo came out onto the terrace, nodding at the palace. Her smile faded when Lælia shivered. "You are a true child of the south," she said, a tart edge to her voice. "You will adjust in time. We all do."

Although many said they looked alike, Lælia saw only their differences. Riccilo wore her mass of black hair in smooth coils about her head. A dress of fine wool followed the curves of her body, still slim and lithe after the birth of Roderic a year earlier. Her almond eyes narrowed as she watched Lælia, who was reluctant to follow her indoors and submit to the coming ordeals.

At least here, looking out over the vast fields of olives surrounding the city, Lælia could imagine freedom. Once inside, the illusion vanished. She had arrived in Toletum only yesterday, but already it felt like a year.

Theodofred, Riccilo's husband, was a close friend of Lælia's grandfather. He was also one of Spania's most important men. The now infamous events of the Fifteenth Council had been momentous enough for Theodofred to extend his stay in the narrow townhouse inherited from his father, the great King Chindasuinth, to whom Count Paulus had once been gardingi. Upon their arrival yesterday, Count Paulus had deposited Lælia with Riccilo and promptly disappeared with Theodofred to the palace and court. It had taken less than a day for Lælia to remember all the reasons she disliked the capital.

Jadis growled, butting Lælia's leg with a wide, soft head. She stood higher than the knee now – a kitten perhaps, but lethal nonetheless. A visiting merchant from a place far away in the Circle of Lands had paled with fear when he saw her and whispered a name in his own language, making the sign of the devil whenever she came close. Lælia had liked the sound of it – Count Paulus had said dryly that she liked the fear in his face more – and so "Jadis" the cat became.

Lælia reached down and scratched the cat behind the ears. *You don't like it either, do you?*

"You have barely seen Toletum, and you were a child the last time you were here." There was a note of impatience in Riccilo's voice. Lælia had forgotten how easily Riccilo read her expressions. "Tonight we will dine at the palace, and you will meet girls your own age. I suspect you will feel differently about it after that."

She cast Jadis a disapproving look; the cat's presence had been Lælia's sole victory in her grandfather's plan for her to accompany him to the capital. Riccilo was still wary of the animal and clearly unimpressed to be housing it. "Your beast will need to remain here," she said, frowning. "No matter how attached you may be, bringing a mountain cat to dine at court would cause more trouble than even you might wish."

Lælia heard the veiled barb but chose to ignore it. Riccilo, she knew, wished only to help her navigate the strange world of Spania's nobility. It was not Riccilo's fault if Lælia had no desire to explore that world at all.

* * *

SHE FELT AN OLD, familiar sense of dread and irritation that evening as the maidservant brushed her hair. *As if I were a virgin going to the sacrifice,* she thought, as the maid held up her gown, then pursed her lips at Lælia's clumsy attempts to step into it. The gown had an embroidered panel stitched into the neckline, a clever pattern of dyed cotton swirls, and it scratched her neck as if she were being choked. *Which,* Lælia thought, *is how Toletum in general makes me feel and why I can muster no enthusiasm for the upcoming feast.*

It was strange that whilst she could track a lynx along a mountain path with unerring dexterity, the simple act of dressing for court made her feel inept and graceless. Her fingers, calloused from arrow and bowstring, fumbled on her buttons. As she thought with dread of the ordeal facing her, she turned abruptly and knocked a cup to the floor, earning an exasperated sound from the maid, which in turn made her flush with embarrassment.

"Your mother would be very proud." Riccilo smiled, but a sadness lingered behind her eyes. "I remember the first time Callista dressed her hair the way yours is now – unbound so it fell down her back, ribbons threaded through the plaits at her crown. She was so proud – even more so when Beremund caught sight of her."

Lælia became very still. So unaccustomed was she to having her mother casually mentioned that she did not know how to respond; her hands remained frozen in the challenge to express emotion. Riccilo's smile faded, and Lælia realised, too late, that her stillness had been interpreted as a lack of feeling.

She felt a familiar wave of helpless frustration at the wall of silence that divided her from others, and which had always seemed far more impassable away from the comfort of Illiberis. If even Riccilo, who read her gestures with ease, could misinterpret her silence, then how would the women of court meet her? She felt an unaccustomed tremor of fear, closely followed by a sense of shame and self-loathing. She fought both to keep her face remote and impassive. The only thing worse than her lack of voice was the thought of others knowing the pain it caused her.

"It isn't Callista you resemble," Riccilo said, clearly hurt by Lælia's lack of response. "Though you carry her look on the surface, at least. No – it is Acantha whom you are like."

Her tone was not intentionally cruel, but Lælia heard the thrust nonetheless. Riccilo, she knew, did not approve of Acantha. The comparison was not meant as a compliment.

I do not care for her judgement, she told herself fiercely. *My life is Illiberis, and Theo. It will not depend upon how prettily I smile at the Toletum court.*

As if to mock her, she heard Acantha's long-ago words echo in her mind: *Perhaps, when you have found the courage to face the challenges life already offers you, we might discuss again the great deeds you think yourself destined to accomplish.*

Lælia shrank further into herself, feeling her face flatten into the detached inscrutability she had always used to deflect conversations from herself.

"Well," said Riccilo. "It is no bad thing for you to take Acantha's strength with you to the palace. God alone knows that there of all places you will need it." Her eyes travelled over Lælia, lingering on those places where flesh swelled beneath the cloth. "It is a pity Alaric is not here," she said, frowning.

Why? Her gestures were harsh and still tinged with the emotion of a moment ago.

Riccilo looked at her thoughtfully. "Paulus has not told you," she said. It was a statement rather than a question.

Told me what?

The look Riccilo gave her was not without sympathy. "He did not bring you here only for your safety," she said. "He wants the court to see that the alliance between Aurariola and Illiberis remains strong." She met Lælia's eyes steadily. "He and Suinthila have agreed to betroth you and Alaric."

Lælia stared at her, the words spinning in her head. Jadis twined between her legs, growling softly.

Alaric? Lælia gestured as if she were underwater, slowly and clumsily. *I am to be betrothed to Alaric?*

Riccilo made an impatient sound. "You are not a child, Lælia. What did you think would happen? After the decisions of the Fifteenth Council, Duke Sunifred of Hispalis may be dispossessed at any day, possibly even named traitor. It is not safe for Alaric to marry the duke's daughter as their fathers planned – he would risk Aurariola itself. A betrothal between the two of you is the sensible course."

I am betrothed to Theo.

"Lælia." Riccilo's face was gentle, but her voice was remorseless. "Theo is lost to us. None have heard so much as a rumour that he lives since the attack on the fleet. It has been almost a year. Whether you believe it or not, in the eyes of the Toletum court, he is gone, and you – and Illiberis – are vulnerable. You would do well to remember that."

Lælia's gestures were sure and slow: *Alaric will never agree.*

Riccilo frowned. "Alaric will do as his father orders."

No. Remembering the way Alaric's face had shone when he

spoke of Sunifred's daughter, Lælia shook her head slowly. *Alaric loves Rekiberga.*

"Love has no place in such matters." Riccilo's tone was firm. "Remember, Lælia, you are a prize many will wish to take. Tonight and the coming weeks in Toletum are our opportunity to make it clear that, whilst loyal to the Crown, Illiberis makes its own decisions, as do all in the south. Your appearance at court holds as much significance as Paulus's attendance at the King's Council."

She gave Lælia a warning glance. "Do not dismiss court, and those you meet there, as a frivolity to be barely tolerated. It is a battlefield as bloody as any your grandfather once fought on. In the wake of the council, tensions are high. Egica and his allies watch for weakness, and their spies are everywhere. You must walk onto that battlefield with only one goal in mind: to hold Illiberis by showing a united front to those who would seek to divide the south."

Seeing Lælia's mutinous expression, she clicked her tongue impatiently. "This is no time for childish rebellion, Lælia. For now, the story is all that matters: you are betrothed to Alaric; it is settled between your families, who remain loyal to Egica and show themselves here in amity."

She placed her hands on Lælia's shoulders, looking at her intently. "You will foster friends amongst the women of court, Lælia, and do not show me your silence as an excuse why you cannot, for I know you can communicate perfectly well when you choose. You will move amongst them with no hint of discomfort and show them that the daughter of Illiberis has every right to stand tall at court. You are heiress to one of Spania's greatest fortunes and the granddaughter of a man who fought beside kings. That is the woman you must be tonight and in the weeks ahead if we are to avoid Egica's hands reaching for Illiberis."

Lælia knew there was no use in further argument. For once, she was grateful for her ability to mask her emotions. Her aunt's words had left her with a cold, dread fear and a longing for the sunlit days of Illiberis. Drawing her cloak to her against the cold, she stood and turned to face Riccilo.

I am ready.

* * *

THE GREAT HALL in the palace was filled with people, animals, and food. Long tables with bench seats ran in lines from the dais on which sat King Egica, Queen Cixilo, and a group of nobles amongst whom the only familiar face was that of Frogellus, the man who had once tried horses on the Illiberis drill ground.

Queen Cixilo, Lælia thought as she studied her, was both plain and clearly cowed by her surroundings, not at all what one might expect a queen to be. She seemed pale and listless beneath the jewels blazing in her hair and about her neck, and none on the dais addressed their comments to her. Cixilo, Lælia knew, was herself the daughter of the old king, Erwig. Her mother, Liuvgoto, had a fearsome reputation; Lælia had heard her grandfather say it was Liuvgoto who had won the crown for Egica and ruled as if she wore it herself. It seemed to Lælia that Cixilo had inherited none of her mother's fire and all of her father's reputed weakness. The woman looked terrified.

Lælia was sitting between two girls whose fathers sat on the dais with Egica. One, Amalfrida, was extraordinarily beautiful, with long, straight, blonde hair and clear blue eyes. She was the daughter of a wealthy count from Narbonensis and a little older than Lælia. Gisa, the other, had a sweet, heart-shaped face and brown hair and plainly idolised Amalfrida. She leaned across Lælia often to giggle with the other girl. Gisa's father was Vitulo, Count of Braga and one of Egica's closest allies. He was also, Lælia had discerned from listening to Gisa's chatter, the father of Nicalo, the man who had once held Yosef captive whilst his friend raped Sarah.

That connection was not one Lælia thought politic to mention at meat.

"It is unfortunate that Theudemir was lost at sea," Amalfrida was saying now in a rather strident tone, which seemed to carry across the entire hall. "But I should try to find a better proposition than his brother, if I were you. My father says" – she lowered her voice and leaned in as if imparting a great secret – "that the Duke of Hispalis is likely to lose everything when the King's Council convenes again after midwinter. And yet it is said that Alaric, heir to

265

Aurariola, remains still in his household!" She shook her head, pursing her lips disapprovingly. She nodded at Lælia. "You would do well to think twice of making an alliance with such a man, no matter how well he might swing a sword."

She and Gisa tittered delightedly, their eyes gleaming in a fashion that reminded Lælia of a cook discussing a particularly fine side of venison.

"And I did hear," Amalfrida went on, not waiting for Lælia to respond, "that last year Oppa himself rode to Illiberis with the intention of making you an offer."

Her eyes were the palest blue, like the dawn sky in winter when the rain clears and the sun is yet to fully rise. They watched Lælia with limpid detachment, as if Amalfrida were watching a pail of water fill and assessing when to pull it away from the flow.

"I cannot imagine," she said, with all the sly cunning of a hunter stalking prey, "what your grandfather was thinking in betrothing you to Theudemir in the first instance. Why choose a provincial second son for you over the king's own blood?"

Lælia's hands felt thick and clumsy on her knife, her skin hot and prickling. She was back in the woods, Oppa's hand caressing the whip at his side, his voice like a serpent coiling on her skin – *I should like to discover, though, if you can scream. Do you think you can scream, dulcissima?* – and Theo's face, blazing and beautiful when she drew arrow against her attacker.

For once her expression must have betrayed her, for a stab of interest showed in Amalfrida's eyes. "But perhaps there is more to the story," she said, watching Lælia closely. "Could it be that you do not like our king's son?"

"Oppa *is* a bastard," said Gisa tentatively.

Amalfrida gave her a sharp glance. "And all know his father favours his bastard above all others, even his own infant son. Oppa stands to be the most powerful man in Spania." Her eyes on Lælia were now narrowed in suspicion. "One must wonder," she said pointedly, "the motives of those who would choose betrothal with any other over the king's own favourite."

"Although," said Gisa, her mouth pouting prettily, "given how well the sons of Aurariola appear upon a horse – and, if what I hear from the servants of Alaric's exploits in the local taverns is true, *off* their horses – perhaps her preference is understandable!"

The two girls gave way to a fit of suggestive giggles, but their eyes were as hard as the marble pillars behind them. Lælia's heart raced unsteadily. She clenched her hands beneath the table.

"But we are sorry," said Amalfrida, seeing that she was not sharing their mirth. She placed her hand on Lælia's arm, who had to force herself not to wrench it away. "Theudemir's death must have been very upsetting for you."

Her honeyed sympathy made Lælia want to retch.

"I am glad you are in Toletum," Amalfrida went on, "where we can perhaps distract you from such sad news." She leaned in, drawing Gisa with her so they huddled uncomfortably close to Lælia's face. "After all, it is not too late for you to accept Oppa's proposal, and if he does not return to our shores whilst you are here, no doubt we can help you find a better match than Alaric. It will not do, you know, for you to accept a man who chooses the *gards* of a traitor over that of his own king."

She was so close that Lælia could smell the wine rotting her breath and see the dark shadow where it had stained her teeth.

"It is better that you should seek a match here, amongst those of your own kind, than far away in the wilds of the south. Why, my servant told me there are tribes living in the mountains there who are little better than savages!"

Instead of conjuring a clever response, Lælia's mind saw the tribes, who tonight were honouring the new moon of the lion with fire and meat. Too late, Lælia realised the effect of her inattention on her companions.

"Perhaps you have no need of our help." Amalfrida arched a perfectly curved eyebrow and pouted prettily at Gisa, who tittered obligingly. "Perhaps you have already decided your course."

Her smile became tight and cruel when she saw Lælia's face and realised her arrows had hit home. "It must have been a privilege to host such guests as the royal bastard's party."

Lælia made a non-committal gesture, accidentally brushing a cup as she did so. It clattered loudly from the table, splattering her with wine as it fell to the floor.

Amalfrida's mouth twisted scornfully. "Oppa was our childhood playmate," she said, pointedly wiping the wine from her hand with a cloth. "We miss him sorely at court."

Goaded beyond restraint, Lælia shrugged contemptuously, her eyes flashing. She felt the old invisible veil of silence fall about her like a fine mist – and the moment when Amalfrida recognised it. The pale blue eyes became frigid as ice. Amalfrida pointedly shifted her gaze, as if Lælia were simply no longer present, and gave Gisa a smile of cloying sweetness.

"Is your father bringing you to the king's games, Gisa?"

Gisa threw Lælia a brief, triumphant glance, as if Amalfrida's affections were a trophy she had won after a long battle. Lælia, feeling her face flush a dull red, stared at the wine dripping from the table to the floor.

She endured the banquet until the dancing started, then made her escape, slipping quietly through the crowd toward an arched exit at the far end of the room. It led out to a small courtyard surrounded by citron trees where the air was fresh and cool after the stifling closeness of the palace. Lælia gulped a deep breath, shame and anger curdling her stomach.

Why could I not find the answers to silence them?

She thought of Riccilo's warnings, bitterly aware she had failed spectacularly to meet her aunt's expectations. *But it is unfair to expect me to ingratiate myself with such hypocrisy, to play such ridiculous games. It goes against every instinct.*

Acantha's words taunted her, causing her to shift uneasily: *The games will come to you whether you wish them or not… Learn to play them, or you will find yourself on battlefields where you cannot win.*

Lælia pulled at the tight neck of her gown. *This is no way to fight my war,* she thought resentfully. *I know Theo is not dead, but I cannot prove it, just as I cannot prove it was Oppa who attacked him. What if Oppa returns?* Her hands gripped the balustrade in a wash of cold fear. *What if he insists on marrying me, this time with his father's thiufae at his back?*

She was so absorbed in her thoughts she did not hear Athanagild's tall figure approach, starting in surprise when he spoke from behind her.

"I would offer a coin for your thoughts, but priests, sadly, have none to spare."

His face was as pale and fine as ever, but there was a hardness in it she did not recall from their previous meetings, and he seemed restless, as if a fire burned behind the hazel eyes.

Theo's disappearance, she thought, had affected them all.

"Shukra told me of the plan to betroth you and Alaric." His direct speech was a relief after Amalfrida's convolutions.

Lælia made a contemptuous gesture.

"I think it is a wise idea." Athanagild came to stand beside her, staring out into the inky darkness. "Perhaps," he said, more to himself than her, "for Alaric, more so than you. Alaric should remove himself from Sunifred's side, though I doubt he will listen to me."

Glancing sideways and seeing the consternation in her face, Athanagild gave a strangled laugh. "I make little sense, I know." He turned to face her. "You have always seemed to know what was right for you," he said, a strange urgency in his tone.

If she had not been so taken aback, Lælia would have laughed aloud at the incongruity of his words. *Why,* she thought despairingly, *do people always assume my silence means certainty?*

She thought of Theo's uncanny understanding and missed him with a deep, painful ache.

"Tell me, then." Athanagild's bitter voice drew her back. "How do I choose between two callings? The claim of family and the claim of God? I never imagined the two could be in dispute. But now I find they are, and I am forced to ask myself: to whom do I owe allegiance?"

Staring into the abyss of pain and turmoil in his face, Lælia wondered what it was that had created the dispute he spoke of.

"I cannot tell you," he said roughly, reading her unspoken question. "I wish I could."

Lælia nodded; she understood how it felt to have secrets she could not tell. She wished she had words to soothe his temper. In their absence, she stood back and moved her hands in simple gestures, pointing ahead, then to her heart. When she knew he had understood, she clasped his hands, his trembling heat matching her own, and she wondered to whom she was gesturing – him or herself.

"You are right," said Athanagild, after a time. "To follow my heart – it is good advice. And it seems simple, Lælia. As if nothing could be easier." He glanced at her, his mouth working. "But in truth," he said softly, "I find it the hardest thing in the world to know what my heart wants and to trust its direction."

Lælia felt uncharacteristic tears pricking behind her eyes. She stared resolutely ahead.

"They are both out there, somewhere," said Athanagild quietly. "Theo and Oppa."

Lælia's hand dashed away the tears that threatened to fall.

Do you truly believe, then, that Theo lives?

Athanagild's hands came over hers, he now the comforter. "You said it was so," he said, with a crooked smile. "If you believe it in your heart, Lælia, then so do I."

They stood together, looking out into the Toletum night. Above them, the moon of the lion blazed. Somewhere beneath it, Lælia knew, Theo watched the same moon – and so did Oppa.

33

OPPA

JULY AD 688

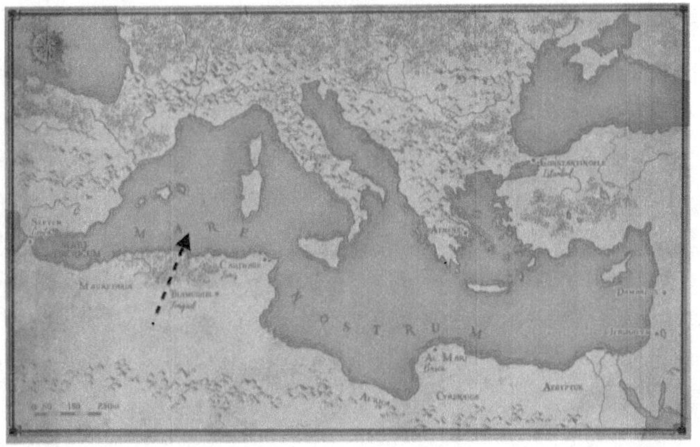

Mare Nostrum
Mediterranean Sea

The whip sang through the air, sending a thrill through Oppa's body. Giscila screamed as it cut across his back. He slumped to his knees, blood running into the wood beneath him. His crew watched in silence. Giscila may once have been their commander, but months of Oppa's presence in their midst had made it clear who now decided their fate.

The whip landed again, ripping the flesh from shoulder to shoulder. Oppa's face was contorted in rage. His whip arm moved with a reckless savagery made more terrifying by its contrast to his characteristic control. Oppa had been goaded beyond fury, and his anger had fallen on the one man he could hold accountable for the failure of his objective.

"You assured me," he hissed, "that we would find them." Two rapid cuts broke the skin on Giscila's rib cage. "First, you allowed Aurariola to escape, then you promised me you knew where to find him." He struck again. "The Jew, you said, must travel by sea. None, you said, travel the seas from Septem without your knowledge. Yet here we are, still afloat, having docked at every port and questioned every worthless whore and tavern wench from Septem to Carthage, and still not the barest hint of their presence have we found. Do you know what this means?"

He paused in his exertions for a moment and stood back, feet spread and whip dripping blood at his side. The water was calm, and the men were bare chested beneath a still, metallic sky. Nicalo stood at the stern. The men had come to fear him almost as much as Oppa; he had much of his master's penchant for pain and none of his subtlety. He watched Giscila's suffering now with an unpleasant smile of satisfaction on his face.

"Perhaps," mumbled Giscila through the blood in his mouth, "it means they are both dead."

"No!" Oppa's voice rose with fury. "It means it is possible that one or both of them are even now in Spania, speaking of things they should not. Things that could damage our family in ways we cannot undo." When his arm came down this time, it was with such force that Giscila toppled sideways, curling himself into a protective ball on the bottom of the dromon.

"I will not allow all we have worked for to be jeopardised by a traitor and a Jew." Oppa pulled the whip angrily through his hands, flicking flesh and blood onto the wood beside the pathetic figure. "At the next port, we will part ways. Nicalo and I will return to Spania whilst you, Uncle, will continue searching for what we have lost."

He leaned close to Giscila, who cowered from him. Oppa's mouth curled in disgust.

"This is why you have rotted in exile," he sneered. "You have none of my father's pride. None of the dignity that placed him, or your brother Wamba, on the throne. You think only of petty victories, of taking what you want by force. Your plans have no elegance, no sophistication. Had you half of my father's sense we would not be rotting aboard a stinking dromon in the middle of a dead sea, still looking for traitors whom I should have already been allowed to kill."

Kicking the prone body, Oppa stepped back, surveying the silent, blank-faced crew. "You will sail to Carthage once more," he ordered them. "Your commander will be well again. You" – he pointed to one of the more able hands – "will tend him until he recovers. In Carthage, you will search for any trace of the Spaniard we lost, and for a Jewish boy named Yosef ben Radhan." His face was set in calculating lines. "I tell you this because you all know who controls the gold you have been paid thus far."

The men sat up a little straighter at this. Oppa, they had learned, might be a cruel master, but he was also a generous one. They had all been enriched by his presence aboard the dromon, and every coin had loosened their allegiance to Giscila, who had, in any instance, paid to secure it in the first place.

"Should any man bring me reliable news of the whereabouts of those I seek," said Oppa, "I shall ensure he is amply rewarded." He glanced coldly at the figure by his feet. "And should my uncle," he said flatly, "not do as I command, I shall likewise pay good coin to the man who tells me of his treachery – but only if he still lives. I give none of you leave to kill him. If I find you have disobeyed me in this, you will feel the sting of my retribution."

He put his mouth close to Giscila's ear. "Do not think I spare your life from kindness or family obligation," he hissed. "I have spent coin, and I expect results. You are the only man aboard this dromon who has incentive other than coin to carry out my wishes." He forced the cringing Giscila to his knees so the man could meet his eyes. "Do you still wish to return to Spania?"

Despite his pain and exhaustion, a light of hope flickered in Giscila's eyes.

"Of course you do," murmured Oppa. "Even now, you dream of standing beside my father, taking your rightful place amongst his gardingi. Is it not so?"

Giscila swallowed. He nodded, his eyes not leaving Oppa's face.

"Then, if you wish to have any chance of seeing that dream fulfilled, you will find what I seek." Oppa pulled Giscila to his feet. The man swayed where he stood, head down, silent and cowed.

"Sail to Carthage," said Oppa. "If you find Theudemir or the Jew, send word, and I will instruct you where to take them. If you discover they have returned to Spania, send word and I will find them myself. My father will have orders for us both. I will send word to you in Carthage of what those orders are."

"What of the treasure you sought?" Giscila said thickly.

"If you can make the Jew talk, do. But Aurariola did not break under my whip. I doubt there is much you can do that I did not." Oppa's face narrowed in a dark, unpleasant expression that made Giscila take a wary step backward. "There is only one thing I can use to force him to talk," Oppa said softly. "She is in Spania, in a place called Illiberis." Turning dark eyes to Giscila, he gave him a thin-lipped smile. "A place I intend to make my own."

Something flashed in the back of Giscila's eyes.

"What will you do there?" he said roughly.

Oppa's smile hardened. "I will claim what I should have at the beginning of all this," he said coldly. "I will force the Illiberis bitch to marry me and make her whoreson of a lover come running."

34

YOSEF

AUGUST AD 688

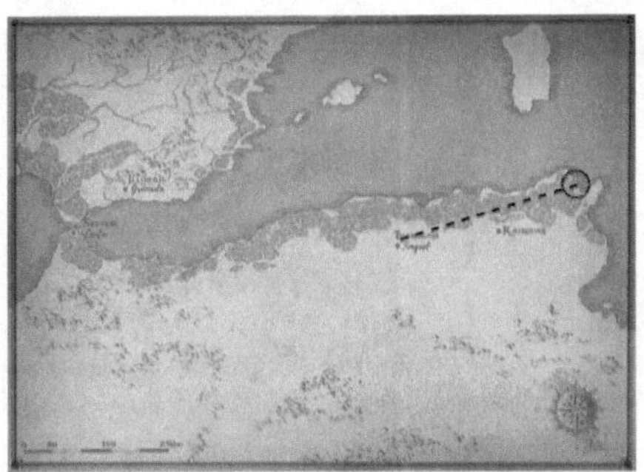

Carthage, Mauretania
Tunis, Tunisia

Yosef had thought Septem the most diverse and exotic place he had ever been. But that was before he saw Carthage.

They had ridden into the city at dawn, after camping on the putrid flats by the lake close by. It was an ugly swamp, infested with mosquitoes and stinking of refuse, but it enabled them to water the horses and wash before they entered Carthage proper.

Yosef had been hardly able to focus. All he had thought of

during every long mile to Carthage was Theo. The fleet, Dahiya said, was at Carthage. If Theo had left Spania, soon Yosef would see his old friend again. He felt an odd intermingling of excitement and trepidation. After his time with the Jerawa, Yosef could not imagine anything more important than defeating Zuhair's army. Travelling thousands of miles beyond the known world of the Circle of Lands seemed like a childish fantasy, a remnant from a time before he had watched his father burn on the orders of Spania's king. The prospect of meeting Theo again was inextricably tied to leaving the Jerawa behind. Yosef was not at all sure he was ready, or even able, to do that; without the comfort and security of his new companions, the road ahead felt unbearably lonely.

They entered through a gate set into a solid stone block wall five feet thick and standing high enough that the men atop it were barely visible. Inside the gate was another earthen defence, backed by a second wall, thicker and higher again. Yosef had never seen a city so well fortified. The walls ran the landward length of the city, joining the sea wall at either end.

Inside, the city heaved with life, and humanity drawn from across the Circle of Lands, clad in a wide array of foreign dress. Imperial soldiers walked through streets lined with merchants vying for their coin. Wiry men pushed wagons laden with wares before them, calling to announce their passage. More than once Yosef leaped out of the way of donkeys pulling carts that were piled high with fresh produce. Tall, dark skinned men with tight curls and pointed shoes walked slowly through the crowds, their gold jewellery and rich robes causing merchants to bow in respect as they passed. Children darted amid the crowd, sly hands slipping coin from unwary pockets. Yosef spied a man hung with copper cups and a series of gourds covered in brightly woven cloth. The man himself was dressed in the most garish colours Yosef had yet seen, small bells hanging from his wide hat. At their sound men tossed him a coin in exchange for a cup of water.

The piazza was a small city of its own. From the central temple and offices ran a busy grid of streets along which pedestrians of all kinds skirted the old circus on their way to the twin ports. It was in the circular port that the Greek fleet kept its dromons. The seaward port was the domain of merchants, and where Yosef hoped to find his next travelling companions.

The warehouses lining the seaward port were huge, vaulted buildings housing craftsmen of every type and producing cloth of such quality that men came from all over the Circle of Lands to buy it. The textile trader in Yosef was excited by the work he saw on display as they rode toward the circular port, and he vowed to spend some time looking at what the artisans produced whilst he was there.

It was the scent of the city that gave away its secrets, he thought, as they rode to the stables by the port and dismounted, handing over a few coins for the care of their horses. The stench was rich and pungent: herbs, sea water, cooking meat, human and animal waste, frankincense from the churches, and another, wilder, scent, which came from some of the older temples – temples which, Yosef noted, still seemed dedicated to pagan gods. Altogether, Carthage smelled of ancient days long forgotten and the relentless ambition of trade. It was exciting and wild, and Yosef could not stop looking about him.

In contrast, the great circular harbour was ordered and purposeful. Men in uniform dominated the wharf, which hummed with activity. Some dromons were pulled out of the water to be washed down and repaired. Others were treated where they lay. All had men coming and going from them carrying supplies, coiling rope, and generally busying themselves with the work of a fleet.

One man stood on a platform at the end of the pier closest to land, yelling orders. He wore the plumed helmet of a commander, and despite the heat of the midday sun he was clad in full lamellar armour over leather, beneath which were the customary tunic and sandals. He stood bare armed but for steel vambraces that glinted in the sun. With his arms crossed, bellowing orders in a multitude of languages, he was an imposing figure.

The bulk of Dahiya's men had dispersed into the city, gone to find entertainment of their own. Only a small group accompanied them to the circular pier, but their arrival was still significant enough to draw the attention of the guards. Two men stepped forward in full armour, spears held in front of them.

"By whose authority do you come?" one of them asked. He was a young sailor, little older than Khanchla and Bagay, both of whom bristled at the peremptory tone.

Dahiya, untroubled, smiled at the lad. "Tell Apsimar the witch is come to see him," she said agreeably.

But as it happened, there was no need for the guards to say anything. As she spoke, Yosef saw the commander look in their direction, as if drawn by Dahiya's presence. For a moment he froze, red cloak fluttering behind him in the sea breeze, then he was striding across the dock, leaping any obstacle in his path and scattering men before him like leaves on the wind. His eyes did not move from his target until he stood in front of her, golden hair blowing in the wind, skin bronzed from long days at sea.

"Dahiya," he said, his face stretched into such an open smile of delight that it was impossible not to feel drawn to it.

"My lord Apsimar," she responded, and despite the regal dignity with which she carried herself, Yosef saw the tell-tale flush on her cheeks as she returned the greeting, the brief moment of unguarded pleasure she allowed herself.

"Your sons." She stepped aside, and Bagay and Khanchla stepped forward. Yosef swallowed hard on his shock.

"Father," the boys greeted him, one after another. Apsimar embraced them both with hard and urgent affection, holding them at arm's length and examining them closely.

"You are men," he said, eyeing them with pride and gripping them both at the shoulder one after the other. "Such men! I am proud to father such sons."

Bagay and Khanchla returned his greeting with open smiles and murmurs of pleasure, completely untroubled by the public stage of their reunion, the curious eyes upon them.

"And your family? Your wife and children? How do they fare?" Dahiya asked.

Yosef looked between her and Apsimar in amazement. He could not detect a note of malice in her tone or any of shame in Apsimar's as he responded.

"They are well! Well, indeed, and thriving. My eldest is not much older than Khanchla, here, and fighting already. And my daughters" – he threw his head back and laughed with unabashed joy – "they are such beauties, Daya, I fear for my sanity as they grow."

"All men should be enamoured of their daughters," replied Dahiya, her eyes shining as she watched him and her sons. "It is a requirement of all fathers to believe no man worthy of his daughter."

"And you?" His eyes narrowed slightly, and he examined her face with a curious hunger that made Yosef slightly uncomfortable. "Have you taken another husband?"

Dahiya gave a low laugh. "I am amgar of many clans now, Apsimar. I find ruling leaves little time for other pleasures."

"Amgar," he repeated, nodding as he watched her.

Yosef had the impression that he was interested less in her rank than in the fact that she had not married again; by the smirks on the faces of Dahiya's men, they, too, were enjoying seeing their leader appraised as a woman.

For the first time since their arrival, Apsimar seemed to become aware that they were the focus of all eyes on the docks.

"Perhaps you could join me for refreshment," he said, loudly enough for all to hear. "I have had no word of military matters in the interior for weeks, and I would value your counsel."

"There is much to tell," Dahiya answered, in an equally ringing tone. She turned to her sons and the men. "The matters we discuss are of state," she said, every ounce the leader of men. "You may find me here again at sundown" – she glanced at Yosef – "when I will bring news of your friend."

They turned as one and strode together from the docks, watched by every man there, the golden head bent close to the dark one, the figures seeming almost mirror images of each other.

They disappeared into a side street of tall, elegant houses built for the city's ruling elite, and Yosef saw through the crowd a flicker of Apsimar's red cloak beneath the portico of one closest to the wharf.

He suspected neither would re-emerge for the rest of the day – and that conversation would be the least pressing matter on their agenda. Turning to Khanchla and Bagay, he was surprised to find them grinning at each other.

"You are not offended by your mother's relationship with him?" Yosef asked, curiously.

"Offended? Why would we be?" Khanchla looked at him in surprise. "Our mother chose him, and he her. He understands that my mother is a warrior, just as he is himself." He glanced at his brother. "And it seems," he said, grinning, "the years have done little to dim the fire, no?"

They both chuckled, and Yosef shook his head. "Sometimes," he said, more to himself than anyone else, "I feel like a stranger here in ways that have little to do with being a Jew from Spania."

Khanchla clapped him on the shoulder. "Well, you cannot help having lived a sheltered life, Jew, can you? Why don't you come with us so we can introduce you to some of Carthage's more worldly pleasures?"

Rolling his eyes, Yosef could not help smiling as he followed them from the circular harbour. He felt a sneaking sense of relief that his meeting with Theo, and his own moment of reckoning, would be delayed, even for a short time.

They wound their way through the streets, back toward the bustle of the seafront. It was here that the taverns lay, bordering the slave market. A small girl ran up to Khanchla and whispered something in his ear; grinning, he tossed her a coin and turned to his friends.

"Now is the right time for us to visit the taverns," Khanchla said, following the girl's small figure as she flitted in and out of the crowd along the docks. "The trade in slaves begins at sundown, after men have done their other business and relaxed with wine in the sun. That way they pay more and look less closely, and the slavers can be gone before sunup."

"Then why would we go to the tavern now?" Yosef asked, as they drew closer to a small building set back from the main plaza.

Bagay grinned. "Because, stupid," he said, punching Yosef's arm, "the girls are cheaper when there are none waiting for their favours."

"Oh," said Yosef, swallowing hard. He paused outside the tavern. The brothers stopped and looked back at him curiously.

"If it is a matter of coin," said Khanchla, "we have enough for you, also."

Yosef tried to force a smile, but he felt the strain. In his mind, all he could see was Sarah's face, her soft passion turned to fear and pain under the attack from Ilfric and Oppa. He felt a sickness in his belly, and the wharf swam before his eyes.

"I…" he began, but he could not find the words to go on.

Khanchla frowned. "What is it?" he asked, and his tone was not unkind. "Is it against your faith?"

"No – yes, I suppose it is, but that isn't the reason." Yosef forced himself to meet their eyes. "I have… I had someone," he said. He stumbled over words that felt thick in his mouth. "In Spania. We – she – was attacked. And she was…" Despite his determination to explain himself, Yosef's throat closed over in sickness and misery at the memory.

Bagay and Khanchla exchanged a glance. Stepping forward, Khanchla put a hand on his shoulder.

"Much has been done by the Arab attackers to the people of our villages," he said gently. "We know what you have seen."

"And we know how to fix it," said Bagay, his tone light.

Yosef cast a look at the tavern door. "I don't think I can. I don't want to…"

"No," said Bagay, taking his other shoulder, "I should imagine you wouldn't. But wine, Yosef my friend, wine can fix anything."

He gestured to a stall with a hessian covering in the square. It was no more than a collection of rough wooden stools about a cauldron of cheap posca, but nothing had ever smelled so good to Yosef.

"Come," said Bagay kindly. "Let's get drunk, shall we?"

He led them to the stall, and they settled down with wine. Within minutes, the boys had become immersed in conversation with their fellow drinkers, and Yosef was left blissfully alone to recover his composure, asked only to laugh at appropriate moments and insert a comment here and there. Settling into the background, he allowed his eyes to roam the plaza, distracting himself from his own thoughts.

The slaves were penned in between the enclosures holding sheep, goats, and pigs. Yosef had seen slave markets before, but never on this scale – or quite so open. In Spania, most slaves had been either freed or placed into service. Whilst the practice still existed, and certainly was not unknown along the coast, where merchants plied trade away from the Church's eyes, in the cities it was in a lesser form; the slaves were more like servants or bondsmen. When they were traded it was done in private transactions and often with the individual's own consent. It was considered a crime against the Church to keep a man against his will. Jews had long been prohibited from owning slaves, just as they had been from conducting any form of trade. Count Paulus of Illiberis did not hold with the practice anyway.

Even if Yosef had been accustomed to the sight, the scale of the Carthage slave market was like nothing he could have ever imagined. There were hundreds of men in varying states of health and fitness. All were chained. Some were washed and dressed in armour, standing proudly in their pens, obviously prime candidates for sale to the men who looked to build their own forces. Others were at least well kept, perhaps meant for the Greek fleet; Yosef knew it was here that many new recruits were found. Given the choice between the oar in chains and the oar for pay, almost all would take the latter, even if it meant fighting on foreign shores.

And then there were those who were simply beaten.

They formed the bulk of the men in chains that Yosef could see. Poor, cowed creatures, backs laced by the whip, little more than skin and bone. They looked down at the ground or listlessly into the distance, their pride and independence long forgotten. For a moment, Yosef felt himself passionately grateful for the turn his own path had taken. As he did, he realised it was the first time he had felt gratitude for his present condition since he had left Spania. Drinking deeply of his cup, he allowed himself for a moment to truly see his surroundings. He felt an odd surge of exhilaration.

After all, he thought, *I am here, no matter how it was that I came to be so.* He was sitting in a foreign land, amongst a thousand languages not his own, drinking wine with men beside whom he had seen war and ridden across mountains and deserts. There was coin in his pocket and none to command his choices. *In this moment,* Yosef thought, *I am free.*

He thought of Sarah, the wine buffering his emotions, recalling her face as she had been led, sobbing, from the clearing where she had been violated.

She will never forgive me, he thought with cold detachment. *Not ever.* And nor should she. Sarah, and all she represented – a home, a family, the life of a normal man – all of it, Yosef felt, was lost the day he failed her. He would never again be the boy whose hand she held, with whom she could perhaps have made a life. Even should Yosef survive, should somehow succeed in this chaotic journey and return, still he would know myself unworthy of her, or of any woman who sought a normal life. *I am forever altered,* he thought, *tarnished, destined never truly to come home.* He thought of Garnata with the same detachment, his mind roaming the streets that had once been as comforting and familiar as posca in a cup.

Even if I fulfil my promise, he realised, *Dahiya was right. Spania will never truly be home to me again.* He was not as his father had once been, with a wife and child awaiting his return. Instead, Yosef had left behind a girl broken forever because she had dared to care for him, and the corpses of parents who had died to protect him. *Never again,* Yosef thought resolutely, *will I allow another to suffer for me as they did.*

"You have dark thoughts for so sunlit a day." Bagay nudged him roughly but there was concern in the eyes he turned to Yosef.

Yosef twisted his cup thoughtfully in his hands. Somewhere between the first cup and now, he had crossed an invisible line in his own soul. When he turned to Bagay, something of his altered state must have shown in his eyes, for Bagay, frowning, said, "I respect your right to sit here and drink all day, should you choose. But I will say I've never seen a man look more in need of a woman than you do now."

Yosef consciously banished the darkness to a place within where it could be contained, never to touch another again.

He gripped Bagay's shoulder. "You know," he said, hearing the new freedom in his voice, "you were right. I believe the wine does fix everything, after all."

Bagay belched loudly and clapped him on the back, grinning.

"Does this mean you are ready to go inside, my Spanish friend?" He nudged his brother.

"Yes," said Yosef, feeling a detached recklessness. "I believe it does."

Amidst the laughter and catcalls of their new companions, he stood with Dahiya's sons and walked past the penned slaves and into the whorehouse.

* * *

It was late afternoon when they reconvened, in the dark back room of the tavern, all three of them laughing in the disjointed way of drunkenness.

"Yours was the best," said Khanchla, pushing Yosef affectionately. "She had the biggest tits." He made mounds on his chest, and Yosef pushed him so he toppled back on his stool, laughing.

Yosef's time in the hot, darkened room had seemed a severance from his past, an acknowledgement that he lived apart now from the rules of other men, that the world he inhabited matched the darkness he knew to be his own secret truth. Yosef knew he could live all the days of his life a good man and yet never expunge that darkness from within. His women, now, would all be bought with coin. Love was for men who had a heart whole and untarnished, and Yosef knew, finally, that his was not and never could be. There was a certain liberation in that.

"She was a goddess," he said, grinning. "Speak nicely about her tits."

"A goddess!" Bagay laughed aloud. "After two jugs of wine, any whore looks like a goddess."

"Don't ruin it for him," said Khanchla. "All men should recall their first with reverence."

"Yosef ben Arun."

All three froze, hands reaching instinctively for the swords that Yosef realised belatedly were at the door and out of reach.

"Do not turn," hissed Bagay.

"You will not be fearing me." The woman who moved into the room was extraordinarily beautiful, so much so that none of the

284

boys found themselves able to adequately return the greeting she gave. She spoke in a lilting, musical accent, which Yosef found strangely reminiscent of someone, though for a moment who it was, exactly, escaped him. She had the longest eyelashes he had ever seen, framing liquid brown eyes rich against the ivory of her skin. She wore a gown made of fine wool dyed a deep indigo and trimmed with an intricate pattern of silver thread. The embroidery matched a delicate chain about her neck, which dripped down into the deep cleft between lush, creamy breasts. Yosef, realising he was staring, coloured and raised his eyes to find her staring back at him with open curiosity.

"The tavern owner," breathed Khanchla, relaxing.

"That does not explain why she knows his name." Bagay folded his arms and glared at her. "Who are you, woman?"

She shrugged, a small smile playing about her lips. "I am being called Athanais," she said. "Athanais the whore keeper."

Bagay and Khanchla coloured.

Athanais shrugged again. "It is a name," she said carelessly. "Nothing more." Her eyes remained on Yosef, who had gone deathly still; she lifted the silver chain to reveal the amulet that had previously been hidden from sight.

The room seemed to swirl about him, darkening so that there was only her face. He heard Shukra's voice echo in his mind long months ago in the back alley of Septem as he sewed the scrolls into Yosef's cloak, scrolls that bore the same symbol as the amulet the woman showed him now: *A woman will find you. Her name is Athanais. She will know what next you must do and with whom. You must be hearing me, aziz-am. Your fear cannot be listening now.*

"Shukra," Yosef croaked, staring at her. Athanais bowed, a gesture so mercurial and elegant it was as if Shukra himself had made it.

"You know this woman?" Bagay looked between them.

"You sent the girl to lure us here on purpose," said Khanchla, frowning.

"Of course I did." Athanais threw the brothers a remonstrative glance. "And the sons of Dahiya and Apsimar, I am thinking, should know better than to be blindly following strangers into back alleys, especially when they guard one of such importance, no?"

Colouring uncomfortably, the brothers looked at their feet.

"Yosef." Athanais sat down on a stool next to him and took his hand in hers. Her skin was cool and smooth. "The man you seek is not amongst those of the fleet."

"Theo never sailed, then." Yosef's voice was flat. He did not know how he felt.

"He did sail."

Yosef felt a cold dread take hold of him. Not Theo. Not another person, dead because of him. "He is dead," he said dully, lowering his eyes.

"No. He lives." She waited until he met her eyes. "He has survived," she said quietly. "But he needs your help, *aziz-am.*" She looked at Bagay and Khanchla. "He will need the help of you all. He has been enslaved. We will ensure he rejoins the fleet, but it must be done in such a way that none suspect who he is."

Enslaved. Yosef thought of Theo, blond and tall and strong; he tried to imagine him chained to an oar and could not.

Khanchla frowned. "But that is easy," he said. "Apsimar will buy him for the fleet."

Athanais shook her head slowly. "*Aziz-am,*" she said, "in the state he is in, none would buy your friend. And certainly not for the fleet."

35

THEO

AUGUST AD 688

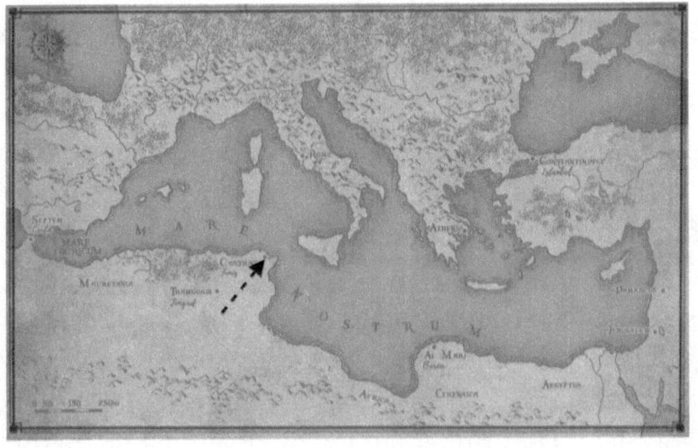

Carthage, Mauretania
Tunis, Tunisia

Theo had never seen such a riotous place in all his life. Carthage was almost enough to make him forget the chains that bound him to Leofric on one side and Silas on the other. They sat close together in a pen placed amongst those containing animals.

"When you spoke of lamb, I think of eating the meat, not sharing their home," muttered Leofric, scowling at the pen next to them. "I'd forgotten how their shit stinks."

"Who are they?" Ignoring Leofric's inevitable pessimism, Theo nodded his head at a group of men in white robes and turbans walking through the market, gold thread stitched through the cloth.

"Ah," said Silas, nodding. "They would call themselves Nabateans, although most here would class them as Arabs. Traders from Damascus – see the slippers they wear, with the pointed toes? And the curved blades at their waist."

He touched his own waist instinctively, and his face darkened.

"I carried the same blades," he said softly. "Before I was captured. The best steel in the world."

"Arabs," said Theo wonderingly, looking at the deep-set eyes and hawk-like features. "I thought that Arabs were the enemy of the Greeks?"

"The enemy!" Silas laughed. "In the market, there is only coin or no coin. There are no friends and no enemies. The Nabateans are here to trade, like the Arabs and everyone else. Perhaps they also trade information – perhaps not."

He shrugged.

"The Nabateans have traded along this coast for as long as Carthage has stood. Their ships are the lightest and fastest in the Circle of Lands – and they bring rare and precious goods like frank-incense and silk." He grinned at Theo. "Even if they had the desire to do so, no merchants could take the port of Carthage."

He nodded along the wharf toward the great opening of the circular port and the walls that rose from it to enclose the city. Men and wagons flowed in an endless stream to and from the dual ports. A hundred vessels at least were moored in the harbour, of types Theo had never seen before leaving Spania: the double-ended Arabic fulk, rigged with rope made of coconut fibre, planks lashed together rather than riven; square-ended merchant ships with sails in an odd, nearly triangular shape; and many lean, fast dromons of the Karabisianoi, with their long bow spurs and fighting decks. The bulk of the fleet, he had learned, was in the circular harbour. The Greeks were here, then, but how to rejoin them?

The owner of the dromon had disappeared shortly after they landed, leaving his heavy-handed slave master in charge. He was a dull-witted, stolid man of Gothic origin, though his accent implied a life spent abroad. Theo would wager he had never set foot in Mater Spania.

"I doubt any of his people would claim him if he did," Silas had said, with contempt. "He is a man who has long lost his honour."

The slave master stood now with his chest bare, fat belly spilling over the rolled fabric of his trousers. He was barefoot, filthy, and carried the heavy stranded whip in one hand as if it conferred a kind of authority. Theo, who had a healthy dislike of whips after the weeks beneath Oppa's, did not like the way the man fingered the thick strands.

In the far corner of the market, the horses were penned. Theo's eyes roamed over a tall, dark horse. Something tugged at the back of his mind, but before he could think on it, Silas, noting the direction of his gaze, nodded at a platform close to the horses.

"That is where the slaves are sold," he said to Theo quietly. "The bidding will start close to sundown, when the merchants have made their trades and require labour to carry the goods to the ships. The slavers like to wait until throats are wet with wine before the bidding commences. Men are looser with their coin after they have been paid for their own goods and celebrated in the taverns."

Leofric spat into the dirt. "They wait, also, until imperial guard retreat to watchposts; traders do not like to chance losing their wares to the Greeks."

Theo looked between them. "You both know a great deal about the slave market."

Leofric and Silas wore uncharacteristically grim expressions.

"We have both," said Silas slowly, "had, shall we say, prior experience."

"I thought," said Leofric sourly, "I had been bought and sold for last time."

"You clearly do not appreciate your own value, *wenkai*." Silas grinned.

The corners of Leofric's mouth twitched. "Perhaps this time I will argue price myself. See if I can make go higher."

"Or perhaps," countered Silas, his smile widening, "I could put an apple in your mouth, and they might mistake you for a pig?"

"Excellent idea! And I could paint you up, sell you as exotic savage."

Silas was rocking with laughter. "How much do you think we could command, *wenkai*?"

"Ha! With apples and paint, the sky is limit, *ne*? We must for certain fetch big piles of coin!"

The two men were laughing so hard that they were gasping for breath, and Boric looked on at them in bemusement.

"You can laugh at this?" he said, shaking his head. "How?"

"How not?" Silas clapped Leofric on the shoulder with a rattle of chains. "If a man does not laugh, why does he live?"

Boric shook his head and turned to Theo. "And you? Do you find it so amusing to be sold like an animal?"

The slave master snorted derisively. "Marked as he is, none will pay good coin for the Spaniard, no matter the stories he tells." He glared at Theo. "You will be fortunate if they take you for the tin mines."

But Theo had ceased listening. He was watching a small girl approach. She tugged on the slave master's cloth. He bent down to listen to her, then turned in response to something she said. Theo, following the direction of his gaze, saw a buxom girl he took to be one of the dockside whores, smiling coquettishly in their direction.

The child pointed, and Theo saw another figure, face concealed by a cloak, nod briefly at the slave master, who licked his lips in anticipation. Two brawny men came to stand by the pen; the slave master himself took a last look at his charges, ordered them coarsely to obey their new guards, then eagerly followed the child through the crowd toward the buxom girl.

"Theudemir of Aurariola."

Startled, Theo turned to find the cloaked figure at the edge of the pen. He caught sight of the face beneath the cloak and realised it was a woman.

"We do not have much time," she said. "I am distracting your man, but it will not be for long, I fear."

She stepped aside to allow another figure to the edge of the pen. His face was veiled in the custom of the desert tribes, and he wore their long robes, layers of cloth over a lithe, sinewy build hardened by months in the deep sands. The eyes that met Theo's, though, were jarringly familiar.

"Theo?" whispered Yosef, shock making his voice hoarse. His eyes travelled over the raw, ravaged flesh of Theo's face, sympathy and horror warring in their depths.

Theo stared at Yosef, a strange, uncomfortable sensation rising in his chest. The market seemed to disappear, the noise of men and animals swallowed by a roaring somewhere deep within.

"How do you know his name?" he heard Leofric ask suspiciously.

"This is not your business," came the woman's voice; she was standing beside Yosef. "We thought you dead, Theudemir, until whispers came that people are searching for you." She glanced sideways. "Dangerous people, *aziz-am*."

Theo had not taken his eyes from Yosef's, but at these words the market snapped back into focus around him. As if from a great distance, he felt the odd sensation from before coalesce in his veins. He recognised it for what it was: rage.

"Dangerous people," said Theo tightly, "already found me."

Yosef swayed on his feet as if he had been hit.

"Oppa," Theo ground out, "knew all along we were working together. He attacked the fleet looking for you." He glared at Yosef. "Even now," he went on bitterly, "he will be in Spania, betrothing himself to Lælia. Whilst I am here" – he raised his chained wrists, his voice cracking with frustration – "unable to do anything to prevent it."

"I did not know," whispered Yosef. "I swear, Theo, I did not know."

"And what is it you want from me now?" Theo did not attempt to lower his voice, and people around them began to glance in their direction.

"*Aziz-am*," said Athanais warningly.

"Am I to return to the fleet?" Theo ignored Silas's restraining hand on his arm, his body taut with fury. "Continue in the service of a mission I do not even understand as if nothing had occurred?" He pulled the last tatter of silk from the cord at his neck, and it fluttered to the filth below to be trampled and forgotten. His throat closed over with emotion, and he finished the sentence in a hoarse whisper. "Oppa could already have attacked Illiberis, defeated Paulus, and have Lælia even now in his power, in his bed…"

The nightmare visions he had refused to contemplate in the long months of captivity rose like hot bile. Unable to finish through the blind pain in his throat, Theo shook his head, trying to draw breath.

"No!" Yosef's voice was low and urgent. "I will find a way to free you, Theo, I swear. Forget about me. Return to Spania, to Lælia. Save her. Save yourself."

"*Aziz-am*," the woman was saying, "there is no time for this. We must find a way to release him that will not arouse suspicion."

Silas snorted. "In a place such as this," he said, looking warily at Yosef, "coin is all that is needed."

"No." The woman shook her head. "Whore keepers do not pay for men; they are paid *by* men. If I pay, it will draw attention. If Yosef or any of the desert dwellers do, it will raise even more."

But Theo was no longer listening to either of them. A movement on the periphery of the market by the penned horses had caught his eye. In a flash of understanding, he saw two things at once: the horses in the pen bore the Illiberis brand, and the man who was bending close to study them was Giscila.

"You need to leave." Theo tersely cut across the conversation, addressing the woman. "The tall man by the horses," he said. "Do not look at him. If he finds Yosef, all is lost. You must leave, do you understand? And do not come back."

"But —" Despite Theo's warning, Yosef was openly staring at Giscila, his face creased in a puzzled frown. "He looks familiar," he said.

"No! Look away, before he recognises you. He is Oppa's man." Theo cut short Yosef's protests. He was watching the horses in the pen, frowning as he thought rapidly. "That tall, dark horse," he said.

"Find someone from the Karabisianoi and have them buy it. Bring it here, close to me, and I will do the rest."

"Theo," Yosef protested, his face pale.

Ignoring him, Theo addressed the woman. "You must get him out of here," he said roughly. "Now. And make certain that none in the fleet appear to search for us. It is better for all if I am thought insignificant and it seems that we are discovered by accident, rather than design."

The woman nodded. She gestured at two other figures clad in desert garb. They took Yosef between them and pulled him away from the pen, ignoring his hoarse protests, until their robes were swallowed by the crowd.

There was a strange expression on the woman's face as she looked at him. "We will meet again, Theudemir of Aurariola," she said.

The slave master was returning. Without waiting for a response, the woman was gone, melting into the crowd, her men with her as if they had never been. Theo, staring after her, felt the tangled emotion of a moment ago harden into icy resolve.

"*Wenkai.*" Silas leaned forward, speaking under cover of the market noise. "Do you understand this woman's words?"

"I am not trusting her," said Leofric suspiciously.

"Theo," said Boric, in a tone close to wonder. "You will be freed."

Theo reached for a sharp stone nearby and, holding up his open palm, dug the stone into it fiercely. "Do as I tell you," he said tightly, "and we shall *all* be freed."

* * *

The sun was an orange ball on the horizon, the air thick with dust and roasting meat. The market thronged with those who had come to buy. Theo sat as he had all that long afternoon, tense and hunched in his place in the line of slaves, oblivious to the heaving crowds.

Shame and anger warred in equal parts within him. When he had imagined, during his long months of captivity, meeting Yosef again, he had envisaged them as equals, sitting over a wine cup perhaps, regaling one another with tales of their adventures. In those visions, there had always been a vague, unconscious understanding that Lælia was somehow safe and they were both victorious, sure of the next step on their path and united in their successes. Never had he imagined being crouched in a slave pen, covered in his own filth, his skin raw and runnelled with scars.

He had for so long been intent upon simply surviving that he had given little thought to his changed appearance. The open horror and sympathy in Yosef's face had been a rude awakening, one bringing uncomfortable, hitherto unconscious fears, to the surface.

Is that how Lælia will look at me? he thought. *As a poor creature to be pitied?*

He was not entirely unaware of his wounds, had felt the thick, deep ridges that cut diagonally down his face from temple to chin. He knew the days of his mask were gone, that he was marked in ways that would forever tell men his story before ever he spoke. Somehow he knew that Oppa had meant for that to be his legacy, to have his handiwork and mastery over Theo indelibly etched upon the face with which he must meet the world, that all might know he had once been helpless and beaten.

Before today, if he had thought of that at all, it had been with defiance, the marks themselves seeming a symbol of his survival. Theo had always known his face to be a mask, but he had never before realised what the loss of that mask meant: that now, rather than an inscrutable shield, his face had become the means by which other men thought they knew him. Revulsion, Theo did not fear, for he had always known himself to be flawed. But pity – pity churned his gut and sparked a deep, burning rage.

He did not fear that Lælia would run from his face. She had always sensed the man beneath it, had said as much. But Theo had kept the entirety of that man well hidden. Had kept his vulnerabilities and flaws tucked away from sight, in a place where he hid his fallibility. He dealt with it in the depths of the night, when dreams choked him in fear and no man saw him wake sweating and cold.

He could not burden another with that man. Theo had been raised to know his duty, to meet responsibility without flinching. He was born to shoulder responsibility, not lay the burden of his soul upon another. He could not bear the thought of Lælia feeling that burden as her own, of coming to his arms not as his equal, but as she would to a wounded animal, as something to be healed and helped.

I do not fear her rejection, he thought savagely. *But her pity...* He swallowed hard. The thought of seeing the fierce bronze desire in her eyes clouded by concern made him sick in ways Oppa's whip never had.

He thought of Yosef, and his mouth tightened with self-loathing. The memory of his angry outburst made Theo's skin flush and his head hang in shame. It was not Yosef's fault that he was in chains, nor that Oppa had attacked the fleet and taken him captive. They were both helpless in the situation in which they found themselves, Yosef as much as Theo. Yet in the moment of meeting, when Yosef's horrified eyes had shown him the man he now was in the eyes of other men, he had felt powerless to contain the shame and rage warring within him.

The encounter had left him stony faced and silent throughout the afternoon, the heat of his fury keeping even his two closest companions at a wary distance after they had followed his initial terse instructions.

Now, though, Silas nudged him, and Theo looked up to see two men of the Karabisianoi approaching the horse pen at the far end of the market. The head of the tall, dark horse came up, and he saw rather than heard it snort aloud.

But would it stand in a fight? He heard Frogellus's voice, from a lifetime ago, on the Illiberis drill ground. *This animal is so calm I wonder if it will run at the first sign of battle...*

The big animal was Titus, the warhorse who had once savaged Oppa, the horse Lælia had been so loath to sell, the horse he thought he had heard on that long-ago night when he was lost in the sea. It reminded him of Lælia and the foals; an image of the black colt came to mind, bringing with it a surge of longing so fierce he felt it in his gut.

"Leofric," he said in a low voice. "Can you see the commanders of the Karabisianoi in the market?"

"Oh, yes," said Leofric, and there was something in his voice that made Theo look up. "But is not just any commander. That man is Apsimar – the greatest *strategos* of our time, and leader who took Thessalonica from my people. It is because of him I became Karabisianoi." He spat into the dirt.

"You hate him," said Boric, nodding.

Leofric turned his head and glared at the slave. "Hate the man who save me from starving and death, who give me new life, give me pride? No, fool, I do not hate him. Men live all their days without tasting even a mouthful of the banquet I ate from, every day, in his service. I would walk through fire to fight for such a man again. So would any who saw him in battle."

Silas grunted in agreement. "He is renowned, indeed. But not so much as the woman who walks with him now." He nodded at the tall figure beside Apsimar, smiling faintly.

"The woman?" Theo frowned, looking at her. She was tall – taller than most women he knew. Taking in the strong features and long strides, he thought she reminded him of Acantha. The similarity lay in the way she looked about her: a fearlessness, a sense of command that spoke of a woman beyond the bounds of normal custom, as Acantha, too, had seemed.

"That is not any woman." Silas watched the tall figure with something akin to awe. "That is Al Kahinat. She is a witch queen, a sorceress, whom even the Arabs fear. She walks with the old gods." He touched the earth reverently as he spoke, letting the grains of sand fall through his fingers. "Apsimar and Al Kahinat together," said Silas. "It can mean only one thing: war."

Theo watched as the pair drew closer to their pen, talking animatedly to each other. They were accompanied by two younger men, much the same age as Theo himself, who kept casting glances in Theo's direction. They seemed to be encouraging Apsimar to buy slaves; the older man was laughing with them. They were, Theo realised, the two young men who had earlier pulled Yosef from the marketplace.

"When I stand," Theo murmured to Silas, "stand with me."

Now the men in uniform were walking across the plaza, leading Titus and another animal. Well trained as they were, the horses moved through the cacophony of the market with no discernible fear, walking calmly on their ropes. Theo tensed as they neared his pen. As the men turned them toward Apsimar and Al Kahinat, Theo seized his chance. Holding a hand over his mouth, he made a noise, low in his throat – an angry buzz like a wasp.

For a moment nothing happened, and he paused, wondering if he had the signal wrong. Silas looked at him curiously. Raising his hand, Theo made the sound again, more loudly this time. Titus's head jerked up as if he had been stung by a bee; a moment later, chaos was unleashed.

Both horses began to rear and plunge, jerking the ropes from the hands holding them, looking around in startled confusion. Theo altered the sound subtly and saw Titus glance at him when he identified the source of the noise. The two animals began moving steadily and inexorably through the crowded plaza toward Theo's pen, squealing and lunging at any who tried to approach them.

Theo remained seated, his head bent, making the noise, until the horses were just beyond the pen. Then he stood abruptly, Silas and Leofric scrambling to their feet as he did so. From a distance, he heard the slave master shout at them to sit, but he paid no attention, focusing instead on the animals coming toward him. When they were close enough to touch, he reached out a manacled wrist, bringing Leofric's with him. He altered the noise to a low rumble, like water tumbling in a stream, and the horses came to a halt as abruptly as they had begun.

Stretching out his neck, still trembling, Titus tentatively plucked at Theo's hand, nuzzling his skin. Smelling his scent, he moved closer still. Inhaling deeply, he butted Theo, hard, then he raised his great head and settled it gently over Theo's shoulder, closed his eyes, and let out a heavy sigh.

"Friend of yours?" muttered Leofric, but his eyes, like all those in the pen, were on Apsimar, who had crossed the plaza in half a dozen long strides, Al Kahinat at his side, and paused in front of them.

"Take the horses," Apsimar ordered the young men with him, and they caught the ropes, casting Theo curious glances as they did so. Titus grunted as he stepped away, looking at Theo with a confused longing that hurt him somewhere deep inside; the horses, he realised, had thought they were going home. The knowledge made him feel both sad and guilty. He looked into Titus's face. *One day it will be so, my friend.*

"You." Apsimar moved close to the pen and studied Theo's face. "How did you do that?"

Theo could see why Leofric followed him. Apsimar was the most impressive man he had ever seen: tall, strong, and with a mane of flowing golden hair that glinted in the afternoon sun. He felt an answering pride in himself, a desire for the commander to see the man he had once been rather than the scarred slave he now appeared.

Beside him, Al Kahinat was like the night to his day, dark eyed and watchful.

Before he had the chance to answer, Apsimar lifted the coin and amulet about his neck and frowned. "From whom did you steal these?"

"I did not steal them," said Theo, and he was proud that his voice did not shake. "The amulet was a gift from my betrothed; she is heiress to the horse breeders of Illiberis. The coin is that of my grandfather, who was once a king."

Apsimar looked closely at him, studying his eyes. "Then you are kin to Laurentius Severianus," he said quietly.

Theo nodded. "He is my uncle. My mother's brother."

Apsimar nodded slowly. "We fought together in Greece, Laurentius and I. Many times. He spoke of Spania — of Geila, and Geila's brother, the king who united Spania." He looked keenly at Theo. "He was to send me recruits. You were aboard the fleet that left from Spania almost a year ago?"

Theo nodded. "We were attacked."

"Yes," said Apsimar slowly. "I heard of it."

"Wait." Al Kahinat reached out to touch the amulet. "She who made this one for you," she said, and Theo heard the strange lilt to her words, the odd construction of the sentence that said that Latin was not her maiden tongue. "She is of Illiberis?"

Startled, Theo nodded.

She searched his face with disquieting scrutiny. "You cannot remain a slave," she said abruptly. "Apsimar," she said imperiously. "You will buy him for the fleet. You there!" She gestured to the slave master. "Unchain him!"

"No," said Theo.

Al Kahinat frowned.

"No?" Apsimar raised his eyebrows, looking meaningfully at Theo. "You have grown so fond of chains?"

"I meant," said Theo quietly, "that I do not wish to be separated from the men I am chained to. We are all men of the fleet. The stigmas were cut from their hands" – he raised Silas's and Leofric's hands to show Apsimar the wounds. "I would not be alive were it not for them." He gestured behind him to include the entire crew. "If you would purchase my freedom for your service," he said, "then all of us equally deserve the honour to serve you, as we were intended."

Looking up from his hand to Leofric's face, Apsimar frowned.

"You," he said. "Don't I know you?"

Leofric grinned and bowed his head. "I was *prōtokarabos* under Kentarchos Lisius," he said.

Apsimar grunted once. "The Slav," he said. "You drank too much, I remember."

Leofric grinned happily, as if Apsimar had paid him the highest compliment.

"It is a crime to erase the fleet from a man's hand," Apsimar snarled, glaring at the man holding the whip.

The man cringed against the rear of the pen. "It wasn't I who did it, my lord," he whined.

"I am not your lord." Apsimar spat in contempt, dismissing him. Frowning, he looked over the ragged bones of the men who had been slaves long before Theo and his companions had joined them. Mouth twisting sceptically, he looked back at Theo. "All of them, you say."

Theo swallowed and nodded. He jerked his head to the crew, and as one they held up their hands. Every palm showed a fresh crescent wound in the place where the stigma of the fleet was normally found. They one and all still dripped blood.

"They are all my companions," Theo said, willing his voice steady. "And they are all brave men. Men who have endured more than most ever could." He drew a deep breath. "I will not leave them," he said quietly.

Apsimar's eyes scanned the pathetic crew, taking in the thin, pained faces barely daring to hope, the manner in which all seemed to lean slightly toward the scarred, fierce face at their centre. He tilted his head thoughtfully, looking keenly at Theo.

"What is your name, boy?"

"Theudemir," said Theo. "Son of Suinthila, Count of Aurariola, who is himself the son of Geila. My father is nephew to the king you speak of, and after whom he was named."

"Very well, Theudemir son of Count Suinthila," said Apsimar, nodding in wry acknowledgment. "Your little band of rogues may well live to curse you for your loyalty – but you have your wish. You!" Smile gone, he called to the slave master. "My men will give you the gold. Release these men at once – they belong in my service now."

Turning to the guards behind him, he said: "Feed them, and for God's sake find them clothes. Take them to the ships – they can join the recruits from Septem."

He nodded at Theo sternly, all trace of amiability gone.

"I said I knew your uncle," he said, "but in my service, no man finds favour he does not himself earn. Be sure to remember that. The men with you are here on your honour. Ensure they prove of value and do not besmirch it."

Nodding curtly at the small band, he turned his back. Together, he and Al Kahinat strode from the square. The tall woman glanced once over her shoulder, giving Theo a long, penetrating look of curiosity, and then they were gone.

Theo turned to find the men staring at him, mouths slack with shock. The slave master was unlocking their hands busily, eyes fixed on the bag of gold held by Apsimar's guard.

"You did it," said Boric, his voice not quite steady. "You said it, but I never believed it."

"You're the son of a count?" said another, looking at him with something akin to awe. "You never told us that."

Theo felt his face redden. "Doesn't make much difference when you're chained to an oar," he muttered, looking down.

Silas waited until the chains had fallen from his hands. Rubbing his wrists, he bared his teeth in the murderous gleam that passed for his smile and turned to Theo.

"We are in your debt, *wenkai*," he said. "But you are in the fleet now. And once again, it will not matter that you are a count."

"You will still be arsewipe to your commander," said Leofric cheerfully, glaring at the mate as he unlocked his manacles. "And now you must learn how to row *and* fight." He smiled gleefully at the rest of the men. "As for you," he said, grinning, "you heard Apsimar. You better pretend you know what you are doing, since this one lied his skinny arse off for you. We start training tonight, as soon as you have clothes. I will not be shamed by pack of coward slaves."

"Ho, coward slaves, is it?" Boric hooted at him, and the rest of the men catcalled good-naturedly. "Wait until I have my knife at your throat, Slav, and we will see who can wield steel better."

Leofric gave a mock bow. "I will enjoy the fight, peasant," he said.

Under cover of their banter, Silas turned to Theo, nodding at the coin and amulet. "Apsimar knew you by that coin," he said. "And he had come here to buy you back, anyway. But it was the amulet that caught the attention of the witch. Why is that?"

Theo touched the cord about his neck, feeling the memory of Lælia's touch like fire in his veins. "Perhaps," he said with a small smile, "it takes magic to catch a witch."

36

LÆLIA

SEPTEMBER AD 688

Toletum, Spania
Toledo, Spain

"Lælia!" Riccilo's voice was exasperated. "Take that animal outside!"

Lælia made a sullen gesture, and Jadis leaped down from the table upon which she had been basking atop a pile of fresh linen and prowled insolently past Riccilo's lowered brows.

"And do not forget we have guests tonight," Riccilo snapped as Lælia made for the stairs. "Did you hear me? Lælia!"

But the girl and cat were gone, down the stairs to the rear courtyard abutting the stables, leaving Riccilo red faced and annoyed
amidst the mess of linen.

The servants had become increasingly agitated at the presence
of an overlarge, still playful, feral mountain cat in the polished
order of the Toletum domus. Jadis, extremely unimpressed to be
excluded from her mistress's daily activities, had taken to
prowling the house in predatory silence, appearing unexpectedly
beneath piles of laundry or amidst fresh food supplies. In the
absence of trees, she found the elaborate wall hangings perfect
for climbing practice and didn't take kindly to being forcibly
detached from them. Perhaps most insulting to the servants, who
lacked the familiarity with wild animals of their rural counterparts, was that Jadis would not submit to a lead unless Lælia
herself held it. On the few occasions when the servants had
attempted to exercise her, Jadis had taken Lælia's scent and flown
like the wind in search of her mistress. The droppings deposited
in strategic locations about the townhouse had also tested the
practiced urbanity of Riccilo's manservant and provided Lælia
with an ironclad excuse to escape the confines of her aunt's
domus, which she contrived to do whenever her presence was
required at the interminable social engagements Riccilo seemed
determined to make her attend.

She entered the dim sanctuary of the stables now with relief
that immediately turned to wariness when Jadis growled a warning,
and she saw the strange horse in the stable, sweat still visible from
hard riding.

"Lælia."

She swung around, the knife she was never without already in
her hand. Jadis was crouched low, ready for attack. Both relaxed as
Alaric emerged from the stall, grinning and holding his hands up in
surrender.

"Please," he said, "inform that animal of yours that I come in
peace."

She gestured, and Jadis ceased growling, instead circling Alaric
warily, eyes alert as she took in the old, familiar scent.

Why do you hide in the stables?

"I knew you would come here eventually." Alaric's smile faded. "I did not wish to meet your aunt," he said shortly.

Why not?

As her eyes adjusted to the light, Lælia saw an unfamiliar expression enter Alaric's eyes. When he shifted uncomfortably, she realised it was embarrassment.

"Have they told you," he said, "that we are to be betrothed?"

Lælia nodded.

Alaric moved restlessly. "I do not wish to give offence…"

Lælia knocked hard on the wall, forcing him to look at her.

I do not wish to marry you either.

"Ah." Alaric wore such a profound expression of relief that Lælia almost laughed. "I thought you would not, but I did not know. I needed to know your mind before I confronted my father." He slumped down on an upturned bucket nearby, and Lælia settled on a blanket in the straw, leaning against the wooden stall, Jadis curled against her.

"He is very ill," he said quietly, "my father. The news of Theo's disappearance nearly killed him. They say he does not have long to live. His dying wish is to see Aurariola and Illiberis bound. He thinks betrothing us will keep them both safe." He looked grim. "I do not agree, but he is right in one thing: if you are not betrothed and Theo is believed dead, you – and Illiberis – are vulnerable."

Oppa is not here, Lælia gestured. *He has not been seen for many moons now.*

"The king can make you marry someone else."

She did not answer that. They both knew he was right.

Alaric broke the short silence. "Sunifred is using Rekiberga as a weapon to coerce me into doing his bidding."

At Lælia's raised eyebrows, he worked a piece of straw in his hands, evoking memories for Lælia of the last time they spoke in the stables at Illiberis.

"My father's lands in Emerita Augustus are held in his name only," he said. "In fact, they are mine, inherited from my mother. My father has nonetheless governed there for more than two decades, and for longer than that, he has headed the king's thiufae, who train in that city. I was raised amongst them, trained with them.

For some years now, I have acted as my father's agent there. The men are as much mine as his." He tore the straw in half and started on a new stalk. "Sunifred," he said grimly, "wants me to command those men – the *king's* men – to join his own in rebellion." He coloured. "It is the price of Rekiberga's hand in marriage."

He cast Lælia a faintly defiant look as he said this, as if waiting for her censure. When she did not immediately respond, Alaric's face darkened, and he began to rise.

Wait.

He settled back but crossed his arms in a defensive posture.

Your father would never agree to such a thing.

"Of course he would not," Alaric said bitterly. "My father believes that diplomacy will solve everything."

No. Lælia struggled for the right gestures. *I meant that your father would never use his own child as a tool for his own gain – as bait.*

Alaric stood and moved restlessly, gripping the edge of the stall beside Lælia.

"Do you think I don't know that?" he said fiercely. "Do you think I would even consider betraying my father in such a way if not for Rekiberga?"

If she loves you, Lælia gestured, *she will marry you without her father's permission.*

"I cannot ask it of her." Alaric shook his head. "She is Sunifred's only child, and her own mother is long dead. She will not leave him, especially now when he stands to lose everything." He glanced at her. "What would Theo do? If it were you?"

Her response came instantly. *Theo would never betray his father's trust, and I would not ask him to.* She met his eyes. *It is not honourable, Alaric.*

Alaric dropped his eyes first.

"Athanagild," he muttered, "said much the same thing."

Lælia, recalling Athanagild's cryptic comments the last time they met, gestured: *He worries for you.*

"Athanagild is changed," Alaric said. "I once knew all he did, could have told you every thought in his mind. Now he sometimes seems like a stranger. The Church seems to claim more of his soul each day."

He bent his head between the hands gripping the stall, kicking the straw with his boot. "He does not approve of Sunifred's talk of rebellion. There are times when I suspect he and the Church know more than he says, but it seems he no longer trusts me enough to confide in me. In the end" – he turned to look at Lælia from beneath his arms – "it seems you are the only person with whom I can speak openly."

He stood barely a foot from Lælia. She was suddenly aware of his nearness, the intimacy of the setting.

"Sometimes," he said slowly, "I think it would be so much easier if we loved one another, you and I."

Lælia did not shy away from the search in his eyes. Her own feelings, though, must for once have been open in her expression, for eventually Alaric smiled ruefully.

"You and Theo," he said, "are more alike than you know. You both seem to instinctively know what is right. I envy you that." He touched her with light affection on the arm, all trace of anything else gone from his face. "Perhaps that is why I sought you out," he said. "I needed Theo's counsel and sometimes, when I see your hands move, it is his voice I hear."

Lælia put her own hand over his, holding it quietly. She wanted to tell him how she longed for Theo's voice herself, how desperately lonely and lost she felt every moment in the city. Her hand rested on his lightly, but in it there was a silent plea for understanding and comfort. Alaric, though, was not his brother. He was lost in his own grief and had come himself for comfort, not to give it. He was not attuned to the silent whisper in her touch and Lælia, who had ever scorned the sympathy of others, did not now know how to ask for it.

"I must leave for Hispalis tonight," he said, oblivious to her tension. "To tell Sunifred that I cannot give him what he asks, even if it means I must give up Rekiberga." His jaw clenched in a hard line. "I wish," he said roughly, "that Theo were here still. Without him" – he shook his head, bending it to the stall once more so his face was hidden – "we are lost." His hand clutched hers convulsively. "My father, Athanagild, you." He gave a harsh cough that sounded something like laughter. "Even my infant sister Egilona asks when 'Teo' will come home."

He turned bloodshot eyes to Lælia, and she realised that perhaps he did see her loneliness, but he could not take it away for her. Alaric had his own burdens. They all did. Her battle was her own, and none could fight it for her – not even, she realised with a queer shock, Theo, if he were here. The inadequacy she felt every time she entered a mannered hall was something she alone must face and conquer. The realisation left her deeply shaken, as if she had crossed an unseen line within herself to a place where she was more alone than ever she had known herself to be.

"Until we were all cast adrift," he whispered, "I did not know he was the anchor that held us."

No. Her hand moved decisively. Alaric looked at her questioningly. *He never held us.* Lælia's hands fluttered, trying to find gestures for a complexity she barely understood herself. *He* saw *us,* she gestured finally. *And when he did not flinch, we felt ourselves to be safe. But now we are forced to see ourselves and somehow find the strength to live with what we see.*

In the dim light of the stables, the dust danced with the movement of her hands.

The only true safety now comes from within.

The gestures came from her but the voice she heard was Acantha's. The certainty she felt came from the caves and the women who had come before her. Even as her hands made the gestures, Lælia herself knew she did not yet stand in possession of the wisdom she espoused.

Alaric's eyes searched her face. "What is it you see, Lælia? When you look in the bronze?"

She hesitated before answering, and when she did, her gestures were halting and pained.

I see a lie.

Alaric nodded slowly. "*Ja,*" he said heavily. "*Ja.* I do too."

They remained by each other's side, untouching but in silent, mutual comfort, until the day faded and it was time for Alaric to ride.

37

YOSEF

SEPTEMBER AD 688

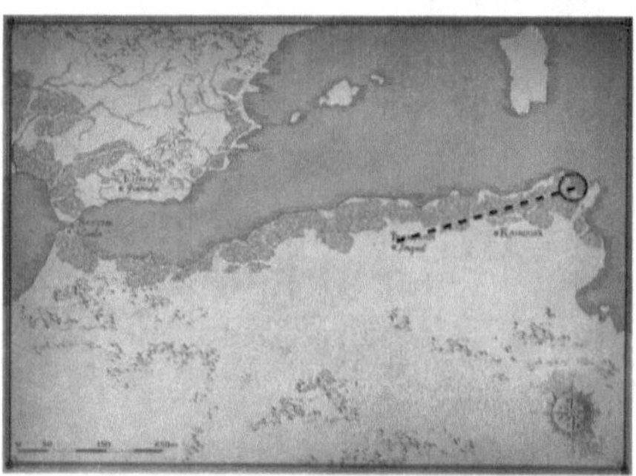

Carthage, Mauretania
Tunis, Tunisia

Apsimar had gone, the fleet taking an oily, early-morning tide. Yosef had watched the long, oval shapes slide onto the water and tried to pick out Theo amongst the rush of identically clad figures, but he could not. He had wanted to speak with him again, but Athanais had warned him to stay hidden, and Theo had not sought him out.

Yosef had not the heart to force another encounter.

Theo, he knew, was lost to him. Their friendship was gone. Yosef did not blame him. Nor did he wonder how he would succeed in his future endeavours without Theo to aid him. He found he no longer cared about those endeavours. Theo's bitter fury had entered Yosef's body like a poisoned arrow, striking at the heart of his resolve. He needed only to recall the vicious scars on his friend's face to remind him of all the reasons his mission did not matter and never could.

He had remained hidden in Apsimar's townhouse, tortured by shame and regret, waiting for his future to be revealed to him. Dahiya had not spoken to him since the encounter in the market. Now, though, he had received a message that she would see him that day.

Bagay and Khanchla sat with him in a lavish, tiled salon at the rear of the house, where they had been ordered to wait by one of Dahiya's men.

"It is not like our mother to drag out a punishment," muttered Bagay. "What is it you did that was so bad, Yosef?"

But even if Yosef had an answer to give him, there was no time. Footsteps approached, rapping out their stride with ominous efficiency. Bagay and Khanchla exchanged wary glances as the door was flung open and their mother stared at the trio, amber eyes flashing.

"Now the fleet is gone," she said tightly, "who will tell me the meaning of the little farce I witnessed in the market?"

"Well," began Bagay.

"You see," said his brother at the same time.

"Yosef?" Ignoring them both, Dahiya folded her arms and stared at him.

"Theudemir of Aurariola," said Yosef dully, "was the man I came to Carthage to meet. It is he who was meant to aid my journey at each port."

"I know this. How did he come to be enslaved in the market – and why such theatrics to free him?"

"The attack on the fleet." Yosef met her eyes. "It was done by Oppa, the king's bastard son. The same man who killed my father and who, even now, hunts for me. He enslaved Theo, and tortured him I suspect, in an effort to discover my whereabouts." He did not flinch beneath the intense scrutiny of her eyes. "It is no longer safe for you to harbour me," said Yosef quietly. "Oppa is dangerous, and he has agents here in Carthage. If he discovers I am in your company, neither you nor your men are safe."

"Oh?" A small smile played about Dahiya's mouth. "And do you think these 'agents' can follow the Jerawa once we melt back into the sands?"

"You do not know Oppa as I do." Yosef did not return her smile. "He will not give up. Athanais warned me that we must be exceedingly careful."

Dahiya, reading his face, nodded slowly. "Well, then," she said. "We will go the market, and you will point out these agents to me."

"Athanais said —"

Dahiya turned flashing eyes to Khanchla. "The whore keeper is not unknown to me," she said harshly. "She has her secrets. I have mine. Our ways are different. You are my sons; you will do as I bid." She turned to Yosef. "I know the whore keeper is a messenger for you," she said, in a slightly milder tone. "But regardless of her instructions, for a time at least, you must yet travel my way, and that means we must know who our enemies are. Do you understand?"

After the events at the market, Yosef derived a certain comfort from the news that he need not yet leave the security of the Riders.

"Will you know these men you speak of?" Dahiya asked as they slipped from Apsimar's townhouse into the bustling streets, which were lined with colourful lanterns and filled with men and women from every corner of the Circle of Lands.

"I will know one of them," said Yosef grimly.

It did not take long. At Dahiya's request, they went first to Athanais's tavern, where she told them a man had been seen drinking in a waterfront tavern frequented by merchants.

"He asks many questions, this man who seeks Yosef," Athanais told Dahiya. "He is not unknown to men here, but I do not yet know his name."

She turned to Yosef. "Do not return here," she said. "Soon you will leave Carthage. I will find you in the next place. For now, you travel as the Riders do. But from there, you will travel my way."

Nodding at Dahiya, she left them at the door, and Yosef had the sense that the moment his back was turned, the tavern, and Athanais herself, might well simply disappear.

They waited in the shadows beyond the waterfront bar until the man emerged, staggering slightly from drink. Yosef gripped Dahiya's arm and pointed.

"Him," he breathed.

Something passed over Dahiya's face, an expression Yosef could not read.

"I know this man," she said quietly. She looked at Yosef, as if weighing her words. "He was exiled from Spania many years ago when I was still young. He is a mercenary, paid to rob and attack. A man with dangerous friends and no honour. His name is Giscila."

"Theudemir told me he was one of Oppa's men." Yosef frowned. "But I think it is more than that. I think they are *faldenreis.*" Unthinkingly he had used the Gothic word, slipping back into the language of men such as Giscila. "Family," he explained, at Dahiya's confused look.

Although blunted a little by age and hard living, the long, hawkish features and deep-set black eyes were still unmistakably reminiscent of Oppa.

"Ah." Dahiya watched Giscila for a moment. Then she peeled back from the wall and began walking, Yosef at her side. They reached the turning for the townhouse and passed it.

"Where are we going?"

"There are things I must say," said Dahiya, "that should not be said in the walls of a city."

They slipped out of the gate and walked through the night to the Riders' camp. It lay over a rise behind which the lights of the city were no more than a dull glow, the scent of men and their business lost amongst the fresh breath of the desert.

Dahiya lit an oil lamp and placed it in the sand before them. It lit the rich material that lined the tent, casting a warm glow on the intricate patterns. She poured them both wine. Yosef realised she was struggling to find a way to begin.

"Long ago," she said finally, "before Bagay or Khanchla were born, a woman came to Septem with a shipment of Illiberis horseflesh. I recall it well, for it was the first time I had seen horses of their like, and the first time I had met a woman from Spania. I was curious about her, and she about me." Dahiya's eyes glowed in the candlelight. "We rode into the desert together," she said, "and talked of things women know and men cannot."

As she told her story, Dahiya turned the wine cup in her hands. The flickering light lit the ruby on her forehead the same blood crimson as the liquid they drank.

When she had finished speaking, the night was long still, and Yosef had walked into the past and returned. He sat immobile, face grey as death. Finally, he spoke. "I must tell Theo," he said abruptly.

Dahiya looked at him curiously. "Why?"

"Because he must know." Yosef stared at her. "He has a *right* to know."

"If he learns such a thing," said Dahiya, "it could risk all you plan together. I have known men like Theudemir before. He will not rest until he takes vengeance. His allegiance to you is already weak. This knowledge is like to break it completely."

Yosef was staring out of the tent to where a full moon lit the strange shapes of the desert earth. It was a water moon, that of the fish. A moon beneath which truth should be told but lies were easy.

"He is my friend," he said softly, as if to himself.

"The fleet has sailed," said Dahiya. "It will be many days before we can find it again, and dangerous for us to do so."

Yosef met her eyes. "Take me to him," he said.

38

THEO

SEPTEMBER AD 688

Mare Nostrum, Tripolitana
Mediterranean Sea, between Carthage and Libya

The harsh coastline of Tripolitana, Theo thought, did not favour attack by sea. But that had not deterred Apsimar from throwing his fleet at it daily in training.

He hunched over his oar, sweating heavily beneath the weight of the double leather and lamellar corselet. The iron lamellae were laced together with rawhide thongs, which, when soaked in salt water and sweat, gave off a rank, animal stench. His feet, accustomed to going unshod after the long months of slavery, had at first felt clumsy and heavy in laced sandals. But after racing daily over a hundred different rocky landings, Theo had learned to embrace their protection. Attempting to shoot arrows with accuracy and face a man with sword, spear, and shield was hard enough without sharp stones piercing his feet.

For the hundredth time, he touched his chest, reassuring himself that the leather baldric holding his sword was still buckled in place. He couldn't feel it beneath the weight of the armour, and on one particularly humiliating day he had reached for his sword to discover that the baldric had slipped off his shoulder and been left in the dromon. Now he followed Silas and Leofric's example and slipped the leather belt through the lamellar lacings at both shoulder and opposite hip. But it would take many more landings before he forgot the public humiliation Apsimar had subjected him to on that one occasion.

Despite Apsimar's caustic manner and harsh training, Theo felt a deep, almost worshipful admiration for his commander. A military upbringing had instilled in him a profound respect for the discipline and order of a well-trained force, and he had never seen anything to rival that of Apsimar's fleet. Every day of rigorous drill helped connect him to the life he had left and remind him of long-forgotten ambitions: dreams that felt almost treacherous to indulge, given his fears for Lælia's safety and the many dangers that Yosef and he still faced.

He found the rhythm of the fleet as natural as breathing and, despite his awareness of his own flaws, was yet honest enough to know that men were comfortable following him, and he was equally assured leading them. And yet with every day that bound him tighter to Apsimar and the core of the fleet, Theo felt guilty at his desire to stay and splintered by his concern for what Oppa's return would mean for Lælia and Illiberis if he were thought dead. His conflict, though, was internal and, in the face of their immediate threat, felt selfish to ponder.

He had not yet caught sight of the army that had defeated Aksil at Thamugadi but had heard the stories from the Riders who came with news of the army's movement: after the Imazighen cut off his retreat to Kairouan, Zuhair bin Qais had turned south and marched his entire army almost one thousand miles across the sands east, toward Barca.

Al Kahinat – the woman he knew now as Dahiya – had sent her men to watch the Arabs from afar. They circled Zuhair's encampment, and at night they stole horses, supplies, and his men's waning sanity.

It seemed at times incomprehensible to Theo that such a large force as Apsimar's fleet could travel the length of the coast, virtually parallel to the Arabic army, and yet remain undetected. But Zuhair's men, the Riders reported, were cowed by the long weeks of isolation in the sands and terrified of the ghosts that tormented them in the still desert nights.

"Do they truly believe the Riders are ghosts, do you think?" Theo asked Silas as they rowed.

The black man bared his teeth in his unsettling grin. "Strange things live in the sands," said Silas. "Entire armies have disappeared in them. It is not a place for a man to be afraid; when fear whispers on the desert sea, men are fast crazed. The sands sing at night. If a man is afraid, the song they hear is one of ghosts and torment. When a man believes the spirits of a place to be malevolent, then all about him becomes dangerous, the work of mysterious forces of evil beyond his control. It does not matter to the men of Zuhair's army if the Riders are men or ghosts. After so long in the sands, chased by devils they cannot see, they believe the desert an evil place possessed by darkness – and themselves the target of that darkness."

Theo shivered. It was hard to imagine the land the Arabs rode through. The coastline, though rugged, had water and grazing for the horses travelling in the wide supply dromons. In contrast, Dahiya's Riders had harried the enemy force south of the coastal mountains, pushing them relentlessly into the interior, where it was said men could march for a week without finding water.

Now the Riders were melting away, luring Zuhair toward the city of Barca, where the Arabic dromons waited, and with them

Zuhair's promise of escape. The Arab commander did not yet know that Apsimar's fleet crept along the coast even as he moved toward it, travelling toward Barca, fed information by Dahiya's Riders.

Like ants drawn to honey, Zuhair's army had taken the bait and was swarming toward the coast now, exhausted and terrified, wanting only to reach their dromons and sail away from the cursed shore.

War would come soon, and Apsimar spent every day preparing them for it, pitting them against one another in endless drills. Each drill had a different purpose, Theo learned as they went along, every landscape offering Apsimar another opportunity to challenge his men. At first, accustomed to the rigid drills of his father's training ground, he had found the constant shifts in tactics and technique confusing and unsettling – not to mention painful. There was barely an inch of his body not covered in bruises and scrapes. Had the skirmishes been real and the long *kontarion* been tipped with iron instead of blunt wood, he would have been speared a dozen times and cut through with sword even more than that. Unfortunately, he thought, wincing as he knocked an old bruise, little could blunt the strikes of stones from the slingshots many of the men carried. Leofric, in particular, had a certain way with them.

"We do not know where our opponents are," called Petros, the weather-beaten kentarchos of their dromon. He grinned at them, baring a mouthful of crooked teeth. "But then, we never do. What we know is that Apsimar is a wily bastard, so they won't be where we think they should be." He indicated the rugged spikes of rock that reared up directly behind the sandy cove they faced. "He will have put archers there," he said. "Possibly spear. But where will the foot soldiers come from? That is what we cannot know, and yet we must make a guess. Who will tell me their guess?"

Water lapped at the dromon with a wet slapping sound, and the oar rested in Theo's lap. This would be one of the longer days, then, if Petros was asking questions. A study in strategy.

"You!" Petros pointed at Theo. "From where will Apsimar's attackers come at us?"

Theo scanned the cliffs for a moment. "From the right, close to the water," he said.

Petros had particularly thick, bushy eyebrows. They shot up now as he regarded Theo with incredulity.

"The right is nothing but bare rock on a spit," he said, gesturing with his arm as the men chortled at Theo's expense. "Are you sure your baldric is strapped on today, Spaniard? It seems your head is not." He looked over the dromon. "Anyone else?"

"From the left, to the rear," called another voice.

"Why so?"

"The tops of trees show over the cliffs. The trees would provide cover."

"Good." Petros nodded. "I would guess the same." He gestured to shore. "So we will row in hard, as we would on any shore where we know an enemy awaits us. And how do we know they await us?"

"Gods, he likes his questions," grumbled Leofric from Theo's side. Theo grinned.

"Because there are watchtowers on every one of these cliffs," called one of the men.

"Damn right there are," called back Petros. "Never, ever forget that. In Tripolitana and Cyrenaica, there is no such thing as a surprise attack. Ever. Attack every coast assuming you will face a welcome party – or worse. The *skutatoi* first, with kontarioi and archers to cover, then the second ranks, with spear and sword." Petros grinned at the rear of the dromon where Theo, Silas, and Leofric sat with the others from the slaver. "Fight long and hard enough, and you may earn a place in the front ranks. Something to look forward to."

"I can barely wait," Boric muttered, to the low chuckles of his fellows.

Theo, however, noticed Leofric and Silas did not laugh. They had once been skutatoi themselves, standing at the stern armed with a kontarion, a twelve-foot-long spear tipped with a socketed eighteen-inch blade. Both had worked their way up from the ordinary rowers, the *elatai*, through the ranks of infantry before becoming *stratetai*, paid men of the Karabisianoi. Leofric's skill with a slingshot attested to his long years even before that in the *psiloi*, the lowest-ranking unit of foot soldiers in the land armies, fighting with only light armour and narrow hand shields.

"You are fortunate to begin in the fleet," Leofric had told Theo. "Even the *elatai* of Apsimar's forces are clad in armour and given bow, arrow, sword, and shield. In Armenia, we faced the field armed only with stones."

Petros's voice brought Theo back to the present. "Pull!" he roared, and they came forward in the half stroke, medium stroke, half stroke, full rhythm that brought the large dromon from a standstill to landing speed in moments. On the sixth stroke, the skutatoi at the bow pulled in oar and leaped to their feet, crouching so only the iron tops of their helmets showed over the spars, their kontarioi carefully positioned.

"Archers!"

Theo heard the ordered thud of ten oars drawn into the dromon in one movement and felt the sudden drag in speed as the men holding them ceased rowing, leaped to their feet, turned and drew arrow in one swift movement.

"Stroke!"

Theo gasped with the strain as he and the remaining rowers hauled hard, maintaining their rush at the shore. Then he heard it: the whistle of wood through the air as the waiting forces began to rain them with fire.

"Ease oar – shield!"

As one, the remaining rowers pulled in their oars, leaned forward, and raised their shields overhead. The arrows fired were only those used in training, blunt tipped and harmless, but the sound as they struck the leather and wood of his shield was real enough. The shields of the skutatoi were larger and more elaborate, with engraved iron studded into the centre, but the *elatai* bore lighter shields, and to Theo's mind, they offered little protection.

He felt the dull jolt of inertia as the dromon ground ashore. With a savage cry, the skutatoi raced forward. Theo leaped, turned, and drew his bowstring, the first arrow flying even as he bent his right knee to the rowing bench. It was a drill they had practised so many times, his knees were scraped raw. Theo had bashed his nose against the side of the dromon as often as his knee had hit it, much to the hilarity of Silas and Leofric, both of whom had learned the manoeuvre before. But after months of rowing and training, Theo knelt now with a steady aim as the arrows loosed, looking through the slit of his helmet for the direction of the incoming fire.

It came from the clump of trees to the left rear.

"You were wrong, *schnecke*," grunted Leofric as he loosed his own arrows.

Theo didn't answer. He took aim again, his eyes roaming high and right on the shoreline.

The skutatoi had leaped the bow, running under cover of arrow fire across the short spit of sand. They gained the shelter of the rock face and began to climb, long kontarion in hand, shields slung to their backs.

All the men aboard faced left, arrows singing into the air over the heads of the climbing men. Theo loosed his own and, as he reached for more, glanced briefly over his shoulder.

High on the far right of the small cove, a stream of men erupted from the rocks.

"Behind!" Theo yelled.

Close fighting aboard was different to anything Theo had learned in the windswept courtyard of the military drill ground in Emerita or fighting his brothers in Aurariola. He planted his feet solidly beneath the rowing bench, knowing everything depended on him keeping his stance strong. The dromon was not large enough to tolerate swordplay. Every encounter came down to a contest of strength and balance, and the seizing of opportunity.

Now the men of the dromon turned, struggling to regain their balance and aim away from where they had launched their attack, but their efforts were too late.

Their attackers came down from the right and over the sides in a torrent of iron and battle rage. Theo raised his short sword in time to counter a stroke and caught the man about the neck, forcing him close and into a contest of strength. As his combatant lunged forward, Theo ducked neatly aside, swivelled, and threw his weight behind the man's movement, pushing him into the side of the dromon so the breath grunted from his body as he fell. Theo put the sword at his neck.

"Dead," he said, and turned to face another.

His small victory could not stop the tide, though. The dromon was soon vanquished and the men climbing the cliff were captured, to the glee of their fellows playing enemy ashore.

The two forces met on the beachhead to have the drill reviewed by their commanders.

Apsimar stood with his hands on his hips, surveying them with a wide grin. He enjoyed these drills, Theo had learned. Where some commanders preferred to leave the training of their men to others, Apsimar liked to know each man as well as he could to oversee every aspect of his force. This had the dual effect of binding men to him in loyalty and having them curse him for his attentions, albeit affectionately.

"You." Petros beckoned Theo forward.

"This one," he said to Apsimar, "predicted your location." He turned to Theo. "How did you know they were in the rocks to the right?"

Reaching out, Theo touched a dark, round ball that was stuck on Apsimar's shield. "Bat droppings," he said. He nodded at the rocks behind them, which had concealed Apsimar's men. "They are found only outside caves where bats live, and deposits of such size as to be visible from the sea mean many bats. Which means caves big enough for many men." He lifted one shoulder. "It seemed a logical place to hide."

"Logical, hm?" Apsimar looked between Theo and the rocks, his eyebrows raised. A reluctant smile spread across his face. "Bat droppings," he repeated. "Did you hear that, Petros?"

"I did." Petros nodded. "It is possible these slaves are not entirely useless, *Droungarios*. Although it is also possible that they have a natural affinity with shit."

Apsimar snorted. "And how," he asked Theo, "did you recognise those piles as bat droppings?"

"I grew up on coastal lands," said Theo. "My brothers and I hunted in the caves by the sea."

"I grew up along the coast also," said Apsimar. "In Anatolia. And I have seen bat droppings a thousand times. But I did not see those. And even if I had..."

He tilted his head to one side in an ambiguous gesture and

glanced at Silas and Leofric, silent on either side of Theo. "You fight together," he said. A statement, not a question.

All three nodded.

Apsimar's eyes moved between them, taking in the scars and the lean, hard bodies, his eyes studying each of them carefully. He smiled again, this time meeting Theo's eyes.

"Good," he said. "Good."

* * *

They made camp in the late afternoon. Silas, Leofric, and Theo were mending ropes on the sand in the shadow cast by the dromon. They had made camp early in a cove with access to good feed, which meant Apsimar was expecting the Riders to come with news.

"When Apsimar sails from Africa, he will take us with him. Petros told me so." Silas was, as always, attempting to distract the others from the battle ahead. Barca was not far away, and tension was high.

"This is good," grunted Leofric in response. He glanced at Theo. "Is what you want, Theo, *ne?* To remain with fleet? Petros says after Barca, we sail east."

"*Ja.*" Theo threw the rope down and stood, brushing sand from his legs. "Our water supplies are low," he said. "I will take the *guerbas* to refill."

"They are full —" began Leofric. Catching sight of Theo's face as he bent to collect the goatskin flasks, he clearly thought better of finishing his sentence.

Theo left the beach and took the steep path up the cliff, emptying the *guerbas* as he walked. The men had dug a crude well half a mile inland. They had stocked up on water earlier, and now the path was deserted. Theo welcomed the solitude. Since the day in the slave market, he had found little time to ponder his encounter with Yosef. He had not so much as laid eyes on him again before the fleet sailed from Carthage. He had no idea where Yosef had gone, and he knew even less about what Yosef might expect of him now that he was part of the fleet once more.

321

The only thing he knew for certain was that Oppa had returned to Spania and that he, Theo, had not. Angrily, he kicked a stone in his path, almost welcoming the pain when it pierced his toe. Giscila would not have been in Carthage alone if Oppa were still here. After so long beneath Oppa's whip, Theo had come to know something of the mind that wielded it. Oppa would have left his uncle to continue the search whilst he returned to Spania. He could not risk Theo returning before him, standing up at court in Toletum and recounting the events that had taken place at sea. He would have returned to reassure himself that Theo was still thought dead. Once he did so, Theo knew, Oppa would take steps to betroth himself to Lælia and complete what he had hoped for when first he came south. It would not then matter if Oppa uncovered the alliance he suspected between Garnata and Illiberis; if he contrived to marry Lælia, he would control both regardless, and all Theo had done would be for nothing.

And he, Theo, would be far away, fighting with Apsimar in Anatolia, facing a fate more uncertain than any since he had left home. Leaving Africa meant leaving the last, fragile threads that held him to Lælia and his brothers. Yet he recalled Apsimar's approbation when he had correctly predicted his location during the drill and the pride he had felt at the older man's brusque approval. He knew a part of him desired more than anything to stay in the fleet and rise as he had once dreamed. Such ambition seemed so selfish that it brought colour to his face and made him glance about guiltily, ashamed that another man might see his eyes and know the self-serving nature of his thoughts.

Yosef's face passed before his mind. *Return to Spania,* he had said, *to Lælia. Forget about me. Save her. Save yourself.*

He wanted to return to Lælia – wanted it so much that when he thought of it, he felt the ache and longing inside as an open wound more painful even than those on his face. None would censure him for returning to Spania. They had all seen his face. They knew some, if not all, of what Oppa had done to him, the threat he posed to Lælia.

He walked on up the path, hitting the prickly coastal shrubs as he walked, wondering why, if it was so clear, he had not yet gone. He wondered why the prospect of leaving the fleet felt as much of a betrayal as his ambition. Most of all, he thought as he neared the cliff, he wondered why it felt as if he barely knew his own mind. Theo trusted neither his feelings nor his ability to decide on a rational course. Accustomed to clear and decisive action, to have his future undecided within his own soul was deeply uncomfortable and had, he knew, made him irascible company.

The well had a top bar made from one central acacia limb held atop two others planted in the ground. Two hemp ropes were tied either side of a wide goatskin joined at the top to a single rope, which in turn wrapped about the cross beam. The last person to have taken water had tangled the ropes, making it difficult to lower. In the fading light, he couldn't quite make out the knots. Theo got to work, welcoming any task that would distract him from the conflicting voices in his head.

"Theo."

At first, he thought it a figment of his mind. When he heard his name spoken a second time, however, Theo dropped the ropes and spun around, knife in hand.

"Yosef?" Recognising the robed figure, Theo lowered his knife. Neither moved forward in greeting. The last colours of dusk were behind Yosef, and his face was in shadow. Theo could not read his eyes. "You should not be here," Theo said, glancing about warily. "The woman – Athanais – said that people are searching for me."

Yosef nodded. "I know."

"Oppa knows there is a connection between us. He will have instructed his men to stay close to the fleet and report anything suspicious. By now, they must know I live."

"I know that too."

Theo stepped closer, trying to make out his face. "Then why are you here, Yosef?"

"There is something you should know." A darkness crossed Yosef's face. "Before you choose your path. Something important."

Theo frowned. "What can be so important that you risk your life to come here?" *When so much has been given to save it,* he thought, unable to entirely suppress a stab of resentment he knew was unfair. A shadow of his thoughts must have crossed his face because, for a moment, there was a sharp pain of awareness in the dark eyes, there and then gone, leaving Theo feeling deeply ashamed.

"The man you saw in the market." Yosef's voice was even and courteous, as if he had not noticed Theo's resentment, which did nothing to improve Theo's mind.

Theo nodded. "Giscila. He is Oppa's uncle."

"Yes." Yosef looked at him steadily. "He murdered your mother."

In the distance, the sea roared upon the rocks. Far above them night birds cried, and the first stars pricked the gloaming.

Theo heard the words as if they were calls from afar. He shook his head as if to clear it. "What —" he began, his arm making an angry gesture.

Yosef cut him off. "Listen," he said. "You must listen to me, Theo. We do not have much time." Glancing about, he drew Theo away from the well and into the lee of the rocks overlooking the cliff. They could see in all directions. Wind whipped across their faces, and Yosef put his mouth close to Theo's ear, so there was only the low sound of his words and the picture they painted.

"The summer after your mother died," he said, "Acantha came to Septem with a shipment of horses. She met with Dahiya; the two became friends.

"Acantha told Dahiya she had come in search of a man. A man who had committed unpardonable sins against her house. Dahiya remembers those words clearly: 'unpardonable sins'. She, too, had suffered at the hands of dishonourable men. When she met Acantha, Dahiya herself was engaged in a war against those who had murdered her father. She had suffered the loss of her own blood and understood Acantha's rage, her desire to seek revenge, as she herself was even then doing.

"But in Spania, Acantha told her, custom was different. Acantha had not been permitted to take her vengeance. Her daughter Callista, Callista's husband Beremund, and their entire household had been murdered in a brutal and unexpected attack. Murdered because a man who had once been rejected by Callista thought to kill her husband and take her, and Illiberis, for his own. The man was brother to the new king and thought himself beyond the law. His attack, though devastating, failed.

"Beremund helped his dying wife escape, though it cost him his life to do so, and she also later died. The tribes arrived in time to turn the tide against the attackers, who then fled. But the man who had led the attack and committed so many atrocities" – Yosef's voice was remorseless in Theo's ear – "that man escaped both justice and vengeance by fleeing into exile. He was the king's brother. Count Paulus and the other southern lords had sworn their allegiance to Wamba, who was already facing a rebellion. Such news would have turned the tide against the king. They stood down rather than placing the whole nation in conflict at a time when unity was needed."

Theo heard the wind roar in his ears. He stared at Yosef, as unable to look away as he was to process the words falling into the darkness.

"Count Paulus reluctantly agreed to keep the matter quiet. He ordered Acantha to accept the king's apology, and told her Giscila was gone," went on Yosef. "But she could not let such crimes go unpunished. She came to Septem under the guise of selling horse-flesh, determined to find her daughter's murderer and wreak her revenge."

When Theo spoke, his voice sounded hoarse in his own ears. "My mother died of the fever."

Yosef shook his head. "No. That is what they told you, Theo, what they told everyone. But she did not die of fever, any more than Lælia's parents did. Beremund's villa was attacked by Giscila and a party of his men because they thought that if they killed her husband, and Giscila took Callista to wife, Illiberis would be his." His eyes held Theo's. "Your mother was murdered for Giscila's ambition, Theo, as were all those in the household – all but two children, a boy and a newborn girl. You, Theo. And Lælia.

"It was Callista who carried you both away, in darkness amidst the slaughter, though she was wounded and dying herself. Days after the attack, tribesmen tracked her to the Valley of the Horse. They found her body deep inside the caves there."

Theo reared back from Yosef, examining his face fiercely. The eyes that met his were hollow, dark, and unmistakably honest.

"You and Lælia were found near death in a pool of Callista's blood," said Yosef quietly. "Another hour, they said, and you would both have been dead. You were two years old. Lælia was less than a month. You were barely old enough to speak, and yet you knew enough to drink the water Callista led you to, and make Lælia drink, too."

"They call it the Summer of Blood," whispered Theo.

"Yes." Yosef nodded. "A strange name," he said, "to call a time of fever, is it not? And Count Paulus would never allow that name in Illiberis."

"A man used it once in my father's presence." Theo felt the words scratch his throat like gravel. "It is the only time I saw him strike a servant."

"Theo." Yosef was watching him, dark eyed and serious. "When we met, you said you had met Lælia before, when you were very young. That you could not remember it clearly."

Theo thought of the dreams that had haunted him since childhood, how he had woken in the night, sweating and terrified.

"I dreamed," rasped Theo. "On the road to Illiberis. Strange things. Blood and horses." He stopped, unable to find the words. The dreams had been part of his secret world for so long that he had accepted them as his own, as a weakness he must never show another, something he fought in the early hours of lonely nights.

"Acantha and Count Paulus had only one daughter." Yosef's voice was relentless. "It is not possible Dahiya could be speaking of another."

Theo stared over the cliff, thinking of Acantha's tall, strong presence the night the foals were born, the fierce woman with flashing eyes who stalked the high mountains of Illiberis.

Yes, he thought with a sudden certainty, *Acantha would not have hesitated to seek the truth, against Count Paulus's permission and all advice.* "Acantha would have come," he said. "She would have come for vengeance, no matter who told her not to."

Yosef nodded. "Dahiya made enquiries," he said. "Ilyan, too. They knew the name of the man: Giscila. They even knew where he was. But before Acantha could take her revenge, Dahiya was called to battle herself. It was possible Septem itself might fall; Acantha had no choice but to leave and return to Spania. Dahiya told me that she never forgot the story Acantha told." He met Theo's eyes. "To the Imazighen, vengeance belongs only to the wronged. It cannot be taken on behalf of another. Dahiya let Giscila go." Yosef pointed to the amulet Theo wore. "Dahiya recognised this," he said. "She told me that the woman she had met back then wore an amulet the same as yours and commanded horses in the same manner you did in the market. It is the reason she allowed me to ride here to warn you."

Theo thought of the long days on the dromon with Giscila and Oppa and tasted metallic rage on his tongue. *I had him in my grasp,* he thought savagely. *I could have taken him, the man who murdered my mother and Lælia's. If I had only known.* He felt the fury deep in his veins, so hot he wanted to take his sword and run it through something.

"Giscila killed them." He said the words flatly. "And now his nephew, Egica, sits on the throne. Oppa" – he spat the name – "came to Illiberis. And Count Paulus entertained him. Ate at the same table as him."

"That was why they betrothed you and Lælia, to protect you –"

"*Protect* us?" Theo's voice shook with rage. "They have played with our lives. My father and Count Paulus did not seek justice. They did not so much as tell their own children how their mothers died."

He thought of the way his mother's name had hung unspoken in the shadows of their home, an uneasy presence at every meal, as if an empty chair had been left for her. Theo had long respected Suinthila's silence as his father's way of managing his grief. Now the memory of it infuriated him.

"He never spoke of her," he whispered. "Not ever."

He thought of his father's suspicion of, and hostility toward, Egica, long before the man ever came to the throne. Of Count Paulus's almost pathological fear that Lælia would be forced to marry Oppa and his grim determination to do whatever he must to prevent that from happening. Theo had thought it the act of a wily politician. Now it seemed to him to be the callous and cowardly act of a compromised man.

Did they know? Did they at least suspect?

Theo slumped to the ground. He could not order his thoughts. He remembered Oppa's unrelenting pursuit of Lælia, his seemingly irrational determination to see Illiberis destroyed, the unreasoning fury he had unleashed on Theo's face.

"We thought it was all for coin," whispered Theo. "That Oppa chased evidence to condemn the south. When all along it was blood that he wanted. He and his family, all this time, they have waited to finish what Giscila started."

"Oppa may not know the truth. But Dahiya believes Giscila could not have fled without the help of his family. Someone must know the truth. And given Egica's hatred of the south, I would imagine it is him." Yosef sat on the earth beside him, keeping a distance between them. "Which means that they seek both revenge and coin. But why?"

Theo shook his head. "Does it matter? Oppa seeks nothing less than the complete destruction of those who would oppose his family's legacy, as he sees it. He and his father are determined to make Spania irrevocably theirs. And Giscila is their tool." Theo frowned, remembering something. "When Oppa first took me from the sea," he said, "Giscila said something that stuck in my mind. Oppa said he had only one thing to ask, and Giscila replied: 'It's your father's gold, now, isn't it?' I thought then that Oppa must have been paying him for his services. Perhaps it is more than that. Perhaps Giscila has been in Egica's debt for years, ever since he fled Spania."

Theo turned to Yosef. "Giscila does not like being Oppa's tool," he said. "He does as he is bidden, but beneath it he is bitter. If he was exiled, as you say, he can bear little love for his now powerful relatives."

They were silent for a time. Thoughts warred in Theo's head, so many he could barely make sense of them. "Why did you ride here to tell me this?"

Darkness had fallen, and Theo heard rather than saw Yosef throw a stone down the path. "Because you should know," he said, "what they are capable of. Oppa and his father will reave Spania from north to south if they think it will return land and power to their family." He turned to Theo in the darkness. "You should return to Spania," he said. "Go back to Lælia and tell her what you know. Find a way to keep her safe. You could bring her to Septem; Ilyan would take you in. He has need of good warriors."

"And what of you?" Theo stared at him, trying to make out his features in the darkness. "What will become of you?"

Yosef made a hard noise. "None can know what will become of me, nor the outcome of my journey east. But I do know I will not have one more life lost on my account. Had I known what this journey would cost, I would never have allowed you to be part of it."

"You risked your life to tell me this."

Yosef made an impatient, angry sound. "And you have risked yours a thousand times for me." He stood abruptly, brushing the sand from his robes. "Zuhair's forces draw close to Barca," he said, his voice cold and remote. "It will be war, sooner than you might wish. I have seen Zuhair fight. You should leave Africa soon, Theo. Whilst you still can."

"Wait." Theo's voice was hoarse; the words hurt his throat. "I do not know what to do. I do not know what is right."

Yosef paused. "You are asking the wrong man," he said quietly, his face unreadable in the night. "I no longer have any notion of what is right, Theo."

His robed figure slipped silently into the night, leaving Theo alone with his indecision. He sat for a long time, thinking of Lælia, his brothers, and the lies that had led them all here to the cliff edge. He looked out over the sea toward Spania, the choices before him seeming as bleak as the rocks far below.

39

LÆLIA

OCTOBER AD 688

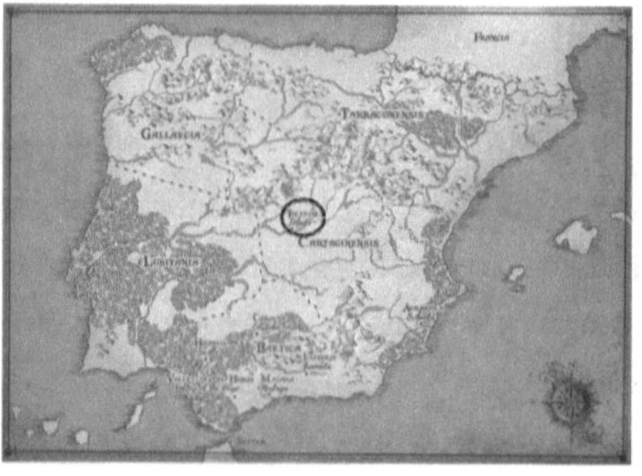

Toletum, Spania
Toledo, Spain

The old circus at Toletum had served many purposes in the two centuries since the Romans had fought their pagan games there. But Egica had a love of pageantry, whether in the great church with its jewelled votive crowns, or on a feast day when his nobles were gathered and he could demonstrate his power and authority. And so today there was to be a spectacle of sorts, though since all knew the old circus to be inhabited by pagan demons and all games to be the work of the devil himself, for once, Egica's horde of bishops was notably absent. Even Archbishop Julian himself, ever the politician "who seized any chance to stand in public beside the king", Riccilo sniffed, could not risk the impiety of appearing at such an event.

Lælia entered the circus with Riccilo, Jadis on a lead at her side. The forest-green gown she wore had roses embroidered on the neckline, and they prickled against her skin as if they bore the thorns of their natural counterparts.

"The king cannot call them games," Riccilo said, glancing at Lælia. "So he instead calls it a feast. In reality, it is the opening to a game of a different kind. Today marks the end of the harvest and the time when the forum moves from the military headquarters in Augustus Emerita to Toletum for the winter. All the nobles are gathered in the capital now, jostling for positions of favour with the king."

She nodded to where Count Paulus and Theodofred sat with Laurentius, not far removed from the king. "More is accomplished during such informal settings than when the forum meets to debate. To miss such occasions can be fatal to one's interests."

Lælia felt hot and uncomfortable. The heel of her boot caught on the crumbling stone, and she stumbled, reddening when titters arose from a group of girls standing nearby, with Amalfrida at the centre.

"Amalfrida's father is close to the king," Riccilo murmured beneath the pretence of adjusting her cloak. "She could be an important ally." She nodded toward the wooden platform, which had been built for the occasion and where the king sat amongst the men of his gardingi, surrounded by regal Christogram banners. "There are eyes upon you," Riccilo murmured warningly. "Be certain not to give them anything to comment upon."

Lælia glanced surreptitiously at Egica, taking in the sharp features, the long nose and dark, hooded eyes, so like his son's. She shivered despite the bright sunlight. Amalfrida's father was amongst those surrounding him. Lælia had never seen men so bejewelled and ornately dressed; every one of the nobles surrounding Egica wore precious stones woven into their braids and robes of intricate design. They glittered in the sun like the peacocks that roamed the palace grounds.

Lælia thought of her nightmares, of Theo somewhere upon a foreign sea suffering untold horrors. *Do you know?* she found herself wondering, examining the cruel cast to Egica's mouth. *Do you know what happened to him — and where your bastard son is now?*

As if drawn by her thoughts, Egica turned in their direction, and Lælia hastily averted her eyes, causing her to stumble once more. A strong arm caught her. "Don't turn," said Athanagild's voice in her ear. Riccilo was talking to a group some way distant, her back turned to them. "You need to follow me," Athanagild murmured. "Alaric is waiting for us just beyond the walls."

Moving to the edges of the crowd, they slipped through the archway at one end and headed for a clump of trees on the ground below.

Why the secrecy? she gestured to Athanagild. *What is so important it brings Alaric from Hispalis and forces us to meet beyond the city walls?*

"What Alaric knows could not be trusted to parchment," said Athanagild. His face was drawn and pale, hazel eyes glittering with an odd light that Lælia recognised was anger. "And Toletum has ears in every corner. Here there is no chance we will be overheard."

Alaric was on the low ground between the old Roman circus and the basilica, pacing beneath a large, scraggy holm oak. Even from a distance, Lælia could sense his agitation.

What is it? Lælia gestured as he looked up. *What has happened?*

"I did as you advised." Alaric began speaking before they reached him. "I told Sunifred I would not bring my father's men to his cause. I said I could not lie to my father nor go against his wishes." His eyes held an ugly gleam. Athanagild moved beside his brother. His face, too, was pale and set.

She gestured cautiously: *What did Sunifred say?*

The brothers exchanged a look.

"He asked," Alaric said tightly, "if my father had ever spoken to me of my mother's death."

Your mother died with mine. Of fever, during the Summer of Blood.

Alaric made a hard sound. "That was the answer I gave Sunifred. The lie I always thought was true."

Lælia stared at him. *The lie?*

"Sunifred thought I knew the truth. He thought that my knowing the truth was the reason I had allied myself with him. Then he began talking, and I was forced to admit I knew nothing of the tale he told." He stopped pacing and faced her. "Our parents did not die of fever." The rage in his face made Lælia take an involuntary step backward. "We have been lied to."

Jadis crouched silently at her feet, tail swinging slowly as she watched Alaric.

"They were murdered." Alaric's voice seemed to come from a distance.

Heat and cold chased each other through Lælia's veins. *Blood,* she thought wildly, through the roaring in her ears. *Blood, and running…*

"Cut down in a murderous, cowardly attack by a man called Giscila." Alaric paused, gripping her shoulders so tightly his fingers would leave marks on her skin. "Giscila was King Egica's uncle, Lælia. Brother to King Wamba." He stared at her. "Say something."

Lælia saw Egica's eyes in her mind, dark and cold. Her hand moved as if through mud: *What happened?*

"Giscila, with a handful of mercenaries, attacked the southern latifundium belonging to your father. Only a day before, they had all been there – your grandfather, visiting his daughter; my own mother Alys, Callista's closest friend; my father; Theodofred, who would one day marry Riccilo. They had meant, Sunifred said, to stay for some time, but a messenger had come in the night summoning them to the King's Council and so they left." He stared at Lælia, his eyes burning. "Sunifred knows this," he said slowly, "because he was part of the council they attended. He was there when they received news of what had taken place in their absence – and sworn to secrecy, just as they all were."

"Perhaps Giscila knew they would not be there," said Athanagild. "Or perhaps he meant to kill them all. We know only that Giscila and his men had murdered your father, his household guard, and nearly all within, when horse herders came from the mountains, drawn by who knows what instinct, and fought them off."

Lælia could see it of a sudden: the tribesmen, scenting blood upon the air, leaning to touch the ground, feeling the tremor of death in the earth, the sudden awareness that something was not right. She shuddered, closing her eyes and turning away from them, the scene in her mind so real she could smell the fear and blood.

"Your mother was badly wounded in the attack, but she must have fought, for they found men with her arrows through them. Your father and his men held them off long enough for your mother to escape." Alaric spoke from behind her and Lælia knew he had to continue, to take the story to its conclusion. "She rode her horse into the mountains. The tribes found it wandering in a valley. They followed it and found Callista's body, lying in mountain caves. You and Theo were with her. She had taken you both when she ran. You were still alive, just, but Callista was dead."

Grief and shock blocked her chest with a weight so painful that Lælia felt it might stop her heart from beating and her breath from coming.

What happened to him?

Her hands moved clumsily, and although she did not face them, Alaric must have understood, for he said in a harsh tone, "Nothing, Lælia. Nothing happened to him. They sat in that council – your grandfather, my father, and Theodofred – and they agreed not to seek revenge. They accepted Wamba's word that his brother had left Spania and would never again set foot on Spanish soil. They agreed to lie, to keep the peace."

Lælia thought of Acantha, who had never entered the villa at Illiberis, as long as Lælia could remember.

Acantha. Her hands moved. *Acantha knows all of this. It is why she walks with the herders rather than stand beside my grandfather. Do you think –* her hands moved slowly – *that Egica knows all of this? That Oppa does?*

"Of course they know!" Alaric was almost shouting. He shook her, not gently. "Lælia! Giscila is Egica's uncle. Is it just coincidence that Egica was welcomed to Wamba's court directly following Giscila's disappearance? Sunifred thinks Egica helped Giscila escape – and used his knowledge of the attack to force Wamba to welcome him back to court, even though Egica's own father, Ariberga, had been declared traitor and banished to Francia with his son. It was said that the son should not be judged by the actions of the father, but Egica was known to share his father's views. My father never trusted him – but now I think he had more reason than ever he spoke."

Shaking her once more, he stepped back, breathing heavily. "*Ja*," he continued bitterly, "and Sunifred says he has heard word of Giscila, that he lives still, that perhaps it was even he who made the attack upon the fleet."

He lives still?

Lælia stared between them.

"We do not know that," Athanagild began.

"And we do not know he does not." Alaric cut him off coldly.

Lælia's mind swirled with long-forgotten memories, things seen only in dreams.

Running in the night… blood, so much blood…

She had thought the dreams prophetic, a foretelling of the foals' birth, of the night the mare had died. But what if they had never been dreams at all? What if they were memories?

"There is more."

Lælia forced herself to turn and face Athanagild. "I am clerk to Bishop Sisebut," he said quietly, "whom all believe will be the archbishop in Toletum after Julian dies, and thus head of the Church. He has been corresponding with Sunifred. They have even met, more than once."

"Athanagild has read his letters," interrupted Alaric.

"Sisebut drinks." Athanagild smiled thinly. "When he does, he talks. I listen. Then, when he sleeps, I read his correspondence."

"Sisebut is encouraging Sunifred's rebellion," said Alaric. "He *wants* Sunifred to rebel. Once Archbishop Julian is dead, Sisebut will ally the Church to Sunifred's cause."

Why? Lælia looked between them in confusion. *What does the Church achieve by supporting Sunifred?*

Athanagild shook his head. "That," he said, "I do not yet know." His mouth hardened. "What I do know is that Sisebut is cunning, and he is ambitious. If he conspires with Sunifred, trust me when I say it does not bode well for Sunifred's cause. Sisebut would never willingly cede power to another, nor would he risk his own position.

If he conspires with Sunifred, he does so for his own reasons – and in the sure knowledge that Sunifred will fail."

Lælia's mind spun, seeing pieces connect in strange, ominous patterns.

Sisebut wants power for the Church.

Alaric nodded and gestured to his brother. "Athanagild believes he is using Sunifred to attain it." He shot Athanagild a half-guilty look of apology. "It is a secret of the Church, one he felt honour bound to keep, and one that has tortured him."

Lælia looked between them, the reason behind Athanagild's grim face of recent months suddenly much clearer.

Then Sunifred's rebellion is doomed to fail?

"Yes," said Alaric bitterly.

Yet still you support him?

Alaric pulled a twig from the tree with such force the entire branch cracked.

"How can I do anything *other* than support rebellion against those who have taken everything from us? Who attack us even now?" He ripped the branch from the tree and threw it to the ground. "What choice do I have?"

Lælia turned away from them both. Walking mindlessly into the shelter of the tree, Jadis prowling silently at her side, she tried to absorb all they had said, but could not. The sounds of the men above drifted down to them, odd shouts of hilarity that seemed startling in the deathly quiet beneath the tree.

They knew all of this, she gestured finally, turning to face the brothers. *Your father, my grandfather, Acantha. They knew, and still they would betroth us, Alaric. Order you to serve the king and me to appear at court as if I were Egica's most loyal subject. Control our decisions as if we were no more than pieces in a game, to be moved here and there on a whim. All because of their mistakes. They sent Theo and Yosef...* Unable to finish, she clenched her fists, shaking her head in frustration. *What will you do?* she gestured finally.

Alaric gave a harsh laugh. "I will return to Hispalis, to Sunifred's doomed cause. Perhaps I may yet find a way to make something of this mess of a rebellion."

And you? She turned to Athanagild.

His mouth hardened. "I will remain at Sisebut's side. I can be of most use there, as his confidant." There was a certain edge to the word "confidant".

Lælia nodded.

"What will *you* do?" Athanagild asked.

I know what I will not *do.* Jadis crouched low and growled, deep in her chest. Lælia met their eyes. *I will no longer be a piece in their game.*

* * *

SHE MOVED through the milling horses and men as if they were a river and she the barge. Her clumsiness was gone; her feet were smooth and sure over the ground. Jadis ran silently at her side, freed from the leash curled in Lælia's hand. She would not cage her cat anymore.

The men on the field competed on horseback with darts. The short lances were held at shoulder height and cast toward straw targets at high speed and from increasing distances. Each man had three darts, and he with the most accuracy won.

One of the horses bore the Illiberis mark. It was a dark bay she could remember as a colt that had left Illiberis not two years previously. The man astride it was outdoing his fellows. The horse was no small part of his victory, Lælia noted in an abstract manner, looking at his clumsy seat and the swift adjustments the horse made to assist his arm and throw.

"Lælia," said Riccilo. "We are not here to watch the riding."

Lælia turned, and Riccilo must have seen something in her face, for her eyes narrowed.

"I had intended you to join the other girls, but…" She bit her lip and glanced over to where a small coterie had gathered about the blonde head of Amalfrida, whose sharp laughter rang out over the ground like ice. She put a conciliatory hand on Lælia's arm. "I know it is difficult."

Lælia did not face her aunt. She was poised on a precipice. It would take little to push her over the edge.

"I was once as you are now," said Riccilo. "Trust me when I say that whatever darts the Toletum princesses may throw at you, I also have felt. But you cannot let them defeat you, Lælia. Do you understand me?"

She meant the words kindly, and at another time Lælia might have welcomed her sympathy.

They know nothing of anything important.

Riccilo looked worried. "Who they will marry is the most important decision that will be made on their behalf. And it must be yours, also, Lælia. Marriage is the one game in which a woman can wield her power."

Riccilo nodded at the men riding on the flat ground below. "Men may choose their battlegrounds, prove themselves a hundred different ways. Even the most impoverished peasant may rise if he chooses. But a woman, Lælia, has only her marriage as a weapon. She must choose the steel wisely and wield it with care. Do not judge the girls you meet. They all of them are simply seeking the best means to fight their own battle."

Lælia met her eyes. *Marriage did not save my mother when men killed her husband and tried to take her away.*

Riccilo froze.

This world will never matter to me. The battles you speak of – Lælia made a contemptuous gesture *– they are yours. Not mine.*

Riccilo's hand came up as if to protest, then fell again. "All women's battles," she whispered, "are the same, Lælia. Whether you believe that or not, it is true. In the end, we all must survive with what we are given. And no woman is given a sword."

Maybe not. Lælia's hand flashed like steel in the sun. *But that doesn't mean I can't learn how to use one.*

Her hand tightened on Jadis's empty leash as she moved into the crowd, away from Riccilo's worried scrutiny. She approached the group of girls. Amalfrida looked up, her eyes narrowing as she saw who it was. Then they dropped to Jadis, and her face stretched into a malicious smile.

"Well," she said, loud enough for the youths on horseback close by to hear her, "here comes the mute with her wildcat."

The girls about her tittered. Lælia felt her blood slow to a dull, angry pulse. The air around her seemed to shine with an odd incandescence.

"Is that a lion?" The man on the Illiberis horse turned, and the sun illuminated his face.

It was Ataulfo, Oppa's companion from the royal visit to Illiberis. The man whose poisoned arrow had nearly killed her. He held his arm at an odd angle. Their arrows, she remembered, had struck him twice in that arm, and the wound must have festered. He started as he recognised her, masking it by pointing an angry finger at Jadis.

"Is it a lion?" he asked again.

No. Lælia gestured abruptly, pointing to the lynx carved on a nearby pillar, her eyes remaining implacably upon his until he coloured.

"A lynx?" Ataulfo frowned. "But they are dangerous, are they not? It should be on a lead."

Lælia just stared at him. Jadis mewled low in her throat. Ataulfo's horse shifted nervously, catching the feral scent.

"It looks dangerous to me." Amalfrida cringed away from Jadis, eyeing her with suspicion. The cat's mewling turned to a low, warning growl. Lælia did not smile. Jadis could smell fear. Her growl grew stronger. The yellow eyes flickered between the boys on the horses and the cowering figure of the girl. Sensing danger, the cat tensed, coiled in defence.

Ataulfo had his hand on his sword. "Call off your animal," he said, frowning. Amalfrida looked at him admiringly but Lælia, who knew him, saw the flicker of fear in his eyes. Jadis was still growling, her tail swinging low.

"Why would you bring such an animal to a feast day?" Amalfrida tossed her hair and stepped closer, causing Jadis to growl even louder. "She has even less manners than you – though I thought that not possible."

The girls around her sniggered, and Amalfrida stepped closer still, pale blue eyes glinting maliciously.

Don't come any closer. Lælia turned hard eyes to her.

"Why not?" Amalfrida took another step, her eyes challenging. "I am not afraid. Surely if I come closer and she can smell me, that should calm her?"

She made the words "smell me" sound obscene.

"Amalfrida," said Ataulfo from his horse, sharply. "Get away from it. It is a wild animal."

"The cat?" said Amalfrida softly, taking another step, her eyes never leaving Lælia's face. "Or the thing standing next to it?"

Afterward, Lælia would wonder whether it was the sudden scent of her own fury that galvanised Jadis, or if the animal herself had simply had enough of Amalfrida's goading. One moment, the cat was hunched by her side, growling low in her belly. The next, she had leaped at Amalfrida, knocking the girl to the ground.

Amalfrida screamed.

The terror in her voice rose above the festival tumult, and the crowd stopped as one, turning to the source of the noise. Then, seeing blonde hair spread on the ground and a feral mountain cat spitting fire over the figure of a young girl, the first shout rose and the crowd began to converge on the scene in a tide of righteous anger.

Jadis looked back at her mistress, golden eyes wary. Ataulfo was leaping from his horse, seizing the sword from his side. The world moved around Lælia, and it seemed as if the rhythm of others was no longer the one to which her heart beat, that she was cutting through space as if she were drawing a knife through time itself.

One low sound and Ataulfo's Illiberis-bred horse was at her side, the long years of training instilled in its blood, and she was on its back in seconds. Ataulfo's bow was strapped to the side of the saddle. She had it raised and notched in less than the time it took for him to realise what she had done. Jadis had danced out of his way long before Ataulfo drew his sword and was crouching now beneath the belly of the horse, her tail straight out as she growled fiercely at the gathering crowd.

Ataulfo knelt beside Amalfrida, who was already sitting up, unmarked but for the mud on her gown. The fury and malice on her face, however, were more dangerous than the swords held by the men who approached.

"They attacked me!" Amalfrida cried, pointing at Jadis and then Lælia. "You all saw! She ordered the cat to attack me!"

The approaching men eyed Lælia cautiously.

"That's my horse," said Ataulfo, caught between astonishment and indignation. "She's got my horse. And my bow," he added unnecessarily, since it was trained directly on him.

"You need to move, girl," said one of the older men, coming forward with his arm out. "I need to get to that lion of yours. It's not safe." His eyes were on Jadis, knife raised.

She's not a lion. Lælia nodded at the pillar and drew the bowstring, staring him in the eye. *She's a lynx.*

She let the arrows fly.

One caught the man in his shoulder. From such close range, it was enough to knock him to the ground with a startled cry of pain. The other four caught his friends, each striking a non-lethal part of the body: legs, arms, another shoulder. With the horn edge of the bow, Lælia knocked Ataulfo out of the way as he came forward and, with another murmur to the horse, she was off, Jadis a golden streak at her side as they flew down the length of the old circus toward the arches at the end where the charioteers of old had once begun their races.

Perhaps, had she lowered the bow, the men on the ground might not have seen her as a threat. But she was running on instinct, and instead of lowering her bow, drew another five arrows as she had been trained to do on the Illiberis drill ground.

She heard Jadis yelp and saw an arrow falling away. Someone had taken a shot at her cat and, although Jadis ran still, her gait was unusually clumsy, and blood showed in a ruby line down her shoulder. Turning in the saddle, Lælia loosed another four arrows, taking down the archer who had hurt Jadis and another two who followed on horseback, ducking low so the return arrows sailed harmlessly overhead.

Above the noise of rage and confusion, she heard Count Paulus's voice roar over the crowd: "Draw on her again and you die!"

She saw his face, hard with fear as he watched her ride. Then she was through the arches and onto the plain, racing by the river, away from Toletum, Jadis panting in pain at her side.

She rode hard for the great bridge that crossed the Tagus. As she came closer, she saw the guards scrambling for their weapons, trying to identify who or what she was.

Move! She swept her arm as she came closer. *She is dangerous!* She gestured at Jadis. *Move so I can get her away from the city!*

Faces turning from shock to alarm, the men melted away from Jadis's sweating, foaming snarl. Nobody wanted to risk being touched by the fluids of a rabid animal.

Lælia clattered over the bridge and raced along the road. In the distance, she heard her pursuers shouting; the guards would realise their mistake in a moment. She barely had a lead. Turning into the olive groves on the side of the road, she put the horse's head south and rode toward the hilltops beyond the city.

She knew she could not ride for Illiberis alone and with a wounded cat at her side. But she had no intention of being caught and no intention of going back. Count Paulus would send someone to find her soon enough.

Riccilo was wrong, Lælia thought, leaning from the saddle and catching Jadis as she leaped into her arms, cradling her cat's trembling body as she rode. *All women's battles are not the same.*

I am Lælia of Illiberis, and I alone will choose my war.

40

OPPA

OCTOBER AD 688

Septem, Mauretania, Africa
Ceuta, Morocco, Africa

Oppa had heard much of Septem, and the reality did not disappoint.

"You are very welcome at my court."

Oppa thought that Ilyan, Count of Septem, was an odd figure, though nonetheless impressive. Taller even than Oppa himself, he was so thin he bordered on the emaciated. Piercing eyes sat deep in a face so hollow it seemed to have been carved out by the wind. A wild shock of hair stood out from his head in all directions, dark and streaked with silver. He seemed to have sprung from the very rock they stood upon, although he was not himself African or Amazigh. His features were carved with a fine, slightly exotic cast, and he had nothing of the burly, fair look of the Goths from Spania. His robes were of brilliant blue, embroidered in fine gold thread richer than any Oppa had seen.

In contrast to the bustling activity of the port, his palace was an oasis of serenity. Fountains bubbled amongst scented flowers, and tall walls surrounded beautifully tended gardens. The palace itself was opulent and airy, with a note of sensuality in every mosaic and sculpture. Not accustomed to feeling intimidated, Oppa was uncomfortably aware of being out of his depth, a sensation not alleviated by the faint air of amusement in Ilyan's features as he observed him now over the top of his wine cup.

"Your father's generous gift was most welcome." Ilyan waved his hand toward the stables. "We have allies amongst whom Illiberis horses are highly prized." A small smile flitted across his face as he spoke.

Oppa's eyes narrowed. "My father will be greatly pleased to hear that he has an ally in Septem. The security of Spania's border has been of great concern to him, particularly recently."

"Oh?" Ilyan, appearing not remotely concerned, raised an eyebrow. "Date?" he asked, pushing a dish toward Oppa. "They are very good – from a valley near the Draa River. I have them brought here specially."

Oppa shook his head impatiently. "Jews trade freely here in Septem," he began again.

"Oh, not freely, I can assure you." Ilyan idly popped a date into his mouth. "I am daily beset by delegations at my door complaining that the taxes levied upon them are positively iniquitous." Ilyan pointed to dishes on the table, which held olives, dates, honey, and bread. The silverwork was finely wrought, with superb detail. "My Jewish silversmiths do such excellent work, however, that I permit the tedium of their endless negotiations. One cannot, after all, argue with the coin their trade contributes. Their silverwork is prized from Constantinople to Carthage."

Taken aback, Oppa stared at him. "Many Jews who trade here are exiled from Spania," he said, endeavouring to maintain his cold hauteur. "They are traitors to our laws, to my father's rule."

"Unfortunate," said Ilyan lightly, frowning in distaste at an olive that appeared bruised. He put it to one side, wiping his fingers fastidiously with a white linen cloth. "I must confess, I am surprised that King Egica would so happily allow such a reliable stream of equity to flow out of Spania's grasp. Please thank him, however, on my behalf, for allowing it to flow to Septem. I believe the Jewish taxes are almost a greater gift than the horseflesh he sent."

Ilyan nodded his head so graciously that Oppa, uncharacteristically, found himself out of words. Ilyan pushed another dish toward him. "Camel cheese and honey? No? It's very good. So tell me, how does the fleet, which Laurentius Severianus promised me he would restore from the rotting hulls in the Baetis River at Hispalis? He was most excited at the prospect when he visited my court. And I sent quite a large amount of gold for the purpose, if I recall."

Seeing an opening, Oppa seized his chance, oblivious to the sharp observation beneath Ilyan's languid manner. "That is the very issue I have come to discuss." A slave approached with a silver wine jug, and Oppa frowned and waved him away impatiently.

Ilyan beckoned the slave closer, allowed a mere inch to be poured into his cup, and smiled warmly in thanks. "Then the restoration goes well?" He raised his cup, mildly inquisitive.

"I have not been in Spania now for many months." Oppa dismissed his question with a wave. "I cannot comment on matters there. But of the recruits chosen by Laurentius Severianus, I do have news."

He fixed Ilyan with a pointed stare calculated to intimidate. Ilyan, however, seemed entirely unbowed.

"Laurentius chose young men from amongst Spania's finest families to train abroad with the Karabisianoi. They were intended to return and take up command of our new fleet. However," Oppa went on coldly, "the dromons of new recruits were lost between Spania's coast and yours." He said the last in a pointed manner. "We believe they were attacked. It is possible that amongst the fleet were hidden goods of great worth, accompanied by the Jew who stole them. I have scoured the coast and every port in search of both, to no avail."

"Ah." Ilyan leaped up abruptly. Striding across the room, he spun on a slippered heel and retraced his steps, robes pinned behind his back with one hand. Startled, Oppa remained seated, feeling oddly at a disadvantage.

"And is it the goods you wish returned to you or the Jew?"

Ilyan's question was perfectly polite, but Oppa did not miss the slightly mocking edge to his tone.

"My father, the king, has no need to fret over some lost gold," Oppa said. He waved his hand carelessly in an effort to regain the ascendency. "And he cares even less for unrepentant Jews. However, aboard those dromons was a man we believe may have aided the Jew in his treachery. He may even have orchestrated the attack at sea, in an effort to disguise their escape."

Ilyan paused his restless pacing, arching one eyebrow at Oppa. "Laurentius assured me," he said, his tone mildly curious, "that the king himself would handpick men from Spania's most noble families to build the fleet for which I sent gold. It would be a great disappointment" – a faint frown creased his brow – "if your father's judgement was flawed."

It was a neat trap, and Oppa found himself momentarily at a disadvantage.

"Which is why," he said, searching for the right words, "we are so anxious to discover what has occurred. And why you find me here."

"Oh?" Ilyan cast him a look of faint bemusement. "I had understood you were searching for goods and a missing Jew?"

"And the man who may have helped him." Aware the conversation was rapidly deteriorating, Oppa hurriedly went on. "The man's name is Theudemir. He is the son of Count Suinthila of Aurariola. The Jew accompanying him, Yosef ben Arun Radhan, was from a family of merchants with a long history of trade beyond Spania's shores. We believe both Theudemir and Yosef may be hiding here in Septem amongst the Jewish merchants, aided in their schemes by those who harbour resentment toward my father."

Ilyan's eyebrows shot up so high they disappeared beneath the shock of hair, and for a moment the restless pacing stilled.

"Am I to understand," he said, with a tone of faint incredulity, "that you believe I condoned an attack close to my own shore, welcomed to Septem the man who orchestrated it, helped his accomplice to trade illegal goods, and now, having just sent a considerable fortune to Spania for the purpose of constructing a fleet to defend these very waters that lie between us, harbour those who would foster a rebellion against my ally? Even as I welcome you, the son of the Spanish king himself, to my court?"

His expression implied that Oppa had committed a grave diplomatic error.

Oppa's eyes flashed with anger. "What *I* understand," he said coldly, "is that you offer aid to those who are declared enemies of Spania. Those who have been exiled and disgraced. My father has thus far treated you as an ally. It would be unfortunate if I must inform him that this is no longer the case."

Ilyan idly spun his cup between long fingers.

"Exiled," he said softly. "Disgraced." He allowed the silence to stretch for a time, seemingly fascinated by the cup in his hand. "Many people," he said eventually, "have arrived on my shores, exiled and disgraced from Spania." The cup stopped turning. Oppa found the sharp eyes fixed upon his face. "One of them," said Ilyan, his smile quite gone, "was exiled for such murderous activities as to make decent men of all races shun him. And yet, I allowed him refuge. I even assisted him in buying men and vessels. All of this I did at the request of your family, Oppa sunau Egica. And for over a decade, the exile in question has worked within the very broad boundaries I place upon trade in my territory. Neither his depredations, nor his profits, have been overlarge."

Ilyan stood abruptly and walked to the latticed window, looking out over the bustle of the port below. "But recently, his adventures once again became so murderous that their aftermath washed up on my shores all summer long. Such events give a man pause. Cause him to question his previous leniency and his alliances. Since your arrival to my lands, I have found myself asking such questions, Oppa. Questions a man such as myself should have no reason ever to ask. The answers to those questions" – he turned back from the window – "surprised even me. I discovered, you see, that there are some things even my liberal parameters deem intolerable."

All trace of mockery had fled Ilyan's expression, replaced by a hard, remote glare as chilling as it was unyielding.

Stunned into silence, Oppa was able to do little more than watch him.

"I make it my business to know the activities of every vessel that passes Septem." Ilyan's voice was flat and cold. "I know of the attack on the fleet. I know who orchestrated it. I do not yet know if your father ordered Giscila to commit murder on his own country-men, or if that was a clumsy plot of yours. But I can assure you, I will discover the truth behind it."

His face showed cold contempt.

"Over a hundred men died in your attack. Their bodies washed ashore for months, and my waters are still black with waste from war fire. I was forced to compose a parchment to Emperor Justinian II, explaining how I allowed valuable men of his own fleet to die within sight of my shores. Now, after causing such chaos and horror, you have the temerity to accept my hospitality, whilst accusing me of not only harbouring fugitives but also aiding them in fomenting rebellion against King Egica, a man I once considered an ally."

Oppa sat very still. Ilyan leaned in more closely.

"If any man was fortunate enough to survive that hellish slaugh-ter," Ilyan said softly, "he is most certainly dead now. I know nothing of any such goods that you speak of. And I would suggest that should you arrive on my shores again, Oppa sunau Egica, implying that I betray the alliance between our countries, you do so with the full weight of your father's army behind you – for next time, I am unlikely to show you the same courtesy as I do today."

41

LÆLIA

NOVEMBER AD 688

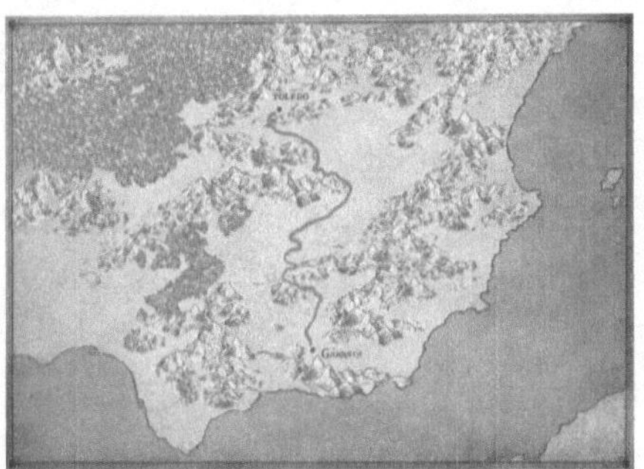

Illiberis, Bætica, Spania
Granada, Andalusia, Spain

Lælia raced across the drill ground. Jadis ran low and silent beside her, streaking in and out of the horse's legs. It had taken more than a month for the cat's wound to heal. It had taken just as long for Count Paulus to realise that Lælia would neither abandon her stubborn silence nor even pretend civility in Toletum. They had returned to Illiberis before the first snows fell.

Lælia leaned forward and drew five arrows from the quiver on her back. Raising her bow, she notched, then released them: five arrows, five targets, one after another, high and low, each striking home. Even as the last arrow hit, she reached behind and drew another handful from the quiver, holding the horse with her legs as one of the herdsmen rode hard toward her. As he drew close, she saw he held three round objects, which he threw in the air, one after another.

Three more arrows, and each target hit the ground.

Too late, she saw a second man wheeling in at the side. She cast her spear and it fell short. Their horses clashed. On her other side, the first tribesman leaped from his horse and drew shield and sword. Lælia spun the horse round and landed on her feet in the same movement, fumbling for her weapons.

"Too slow!" The tribesman grinned, cuffing her over the head with his shield, not gently. "You are dead now! Your only advantage is speed. You cannot hold a shield against a man, so you must be faster than him. Again!"

Turning, she trudged back to where the horse stood, head hanging, eyeing Lælia with what she could have sworn was shame. Jadis gambolled at her heels, nipping them playfully. The cat, too, was pleased to be home.

Lælia plucked the arrows from the target as she walked, leaping onto the horse in an easy motion. She was riding back to the start point when the herdsman behind her made a warning sound, and she turned to see men of the Illiberis thiufa riding up the long approach to the villa.

They weren't alone. Amongst them, jostled close in their midst, rode a small party of strangers, the chrismon-and-peacock standard of Toletum fluttering overhead.

Oppa.

Lælia knew it with a certainty deep in her soul. She rode toward the villa, leaping from the horse only moments before the party reached the portico. When she came to stand silently beside Count Paulus, her grandfather made no comment on her presence nor on that of Jadis, who was crouched at her feet, growling softly.

They waited where they stood. Oppa was mounted, Lælia noticed in disgust, on an Illiberis horse. He reined in barely feet from where they stood.

"I am recently returned from Septem." Oppa did not dismount or make them a formal greeting.

Count Paulus, his face as set as granite, did not offer one either.

"I was abroad on my father's business," Oppa went on, seemingly unperturbed by their lack of courtesy, "which included, you may recall, taking a shipment of your horses as a gift from my father to Count Ilyan of Septem." He stroked the horse's neck, eyeing Lælia with a cold, insidious calculation that made her skin crawl. She willed her face to show nothing of what she felt and faced him with blank indifference.

"We discussed many matters, amongst them the tragic loss of the new recruits who left Spania more than a year ago. Unfortunately" – Oppa's tone implied he found it quite to the contrary – "it appears there were no survivors from the attack at sea. Barely a handful were pulled from the water in the days following, none of whom were from Spania."

He made a careless gesture with one mailed hand, the metal and jewels gleaming in the sun. "I believe we must consider all aboard lost to us." He placed a delicate emphasis on the word "all", the meaning of which was lost on no one.

"You could have saved your horse the miles, Fráuja." Count Paulus's voice lacked any pretence at courtesy. "The south has been reconciled to the loss of its sons for the best part of a year."

"And yet," Oppa countered, "you claim, in your letters to my father, that your daughter remains betrothed to Theudemir of Aurariola, even whilst it is commonly known you try to betroth her anew to his brother."

Reaching into his tunic, he took out a rolled parchment and waved it in the air. Lælia did not need to look at her grandfather to know his face had paled. Nor did she need the parchment to be unrolled for her to recognise the broken seal upon it.

"It is unfortunate," said Oppa softly, "that you did not break the seal on the contract of betrothal yourself, Fráuja Paulus. Had you done so, you would perhaps have seen fit to teach your grand-daughter a little obedience."

He leaned forward, clearly enjoying Paulus's consternation. "She did not tell you then," he said, studying Count Paulus's expression and then sitting back, a slow smile of satisfaction spreading across his face. He shook the parchment so it opened, showing the blank space where her mark should have been. "Your whore of a granddaughter" – he said the words in the same smooth, untroubled tone he might use at court – "did not affix her name to this document. No woman may be married without her consent."

Oppa smiled silkily. "You, of all people, Count Paulus, who were once counsellor to kings, know the laws by which we abide. Your granddaughter was never betrothed at all, least of all to the dead man named on this parchment."

Count Paulus's mouth twisted in contempt. "The betrothal was done before God, witnesses, and me. It stands, as any scholar will assure you." Turning, he began walking away. "Come, Lælia," he said over his shoulder.

Glaring at Oppa, fingering the bow at her hip, Lælia turned to follow.

"Theudemir of Aurariola is dead."

The cold certainty in Oppa's tone struck Lælia like a physical blow. She met her grandfather's eyes for the first time since riding from the circus in Toletum, seeing in them a shadow of her own fears.

"You seem very certain of that fact, Fráuja," said Paulus, slowly.

An unpleasant smile passed across Oppa's face. "I am as certain," he said softly, watching Lælia, "as if I had seen his death myself."

Her hand dropped to the sword at her side, drawing it halfway before she caught herself. With an effort, she unclenched her fingers and thrust the blade home again, forcing her customary mask back in place. She was too late. The gleam of satisfaction in his eye told her Oppa had seen beyond it, to the fear and uncertainty she fought so hard to conceal.

Oppa wheeled his horse round, leading his men away down the

approach. "My father, the *king*, summons you to court in Toletum in order to discuss this and other matters."

He paused, turning back to meet Lælia's eyes. "I suggest you hurry." His gaze travelled over her body with a slow, lascivious assessment that made her skin crawl. "We are to be married, *dulcissima*, and I have waited quite long enough."

42

THEO

NOVEMBER AD 688

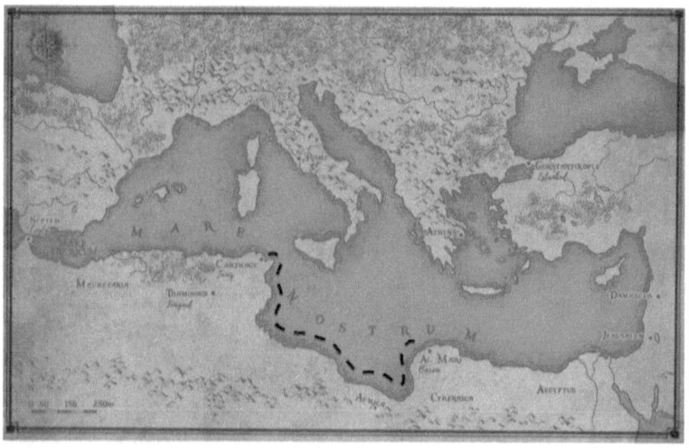

Mare Nostrum, Tripolitana
Mediterranean Sea, near Benghazi, Libya

"Aurariola!"

Theo looked up from coiling rope and straightened as Apsimar's tall figure strode toward him.

"You will walk with me," said his commander.

They moved away from the men working on the shore and around a narrow cove to a quiet beach.

"Battle is coming." Apsimar walked with his hands clasped behind his back, staring directly ahead. Theo nodded, unsure how he was supposed to respond.

"I have watched you. You have been trained well."

Theo coloured, but didn't answer.

"That face doesn't hurt, either." Apsimar gave him a half smile. "It gives the appearance of ferocity, even if I know you for the same soft-hearted bastard your uncle was."

His wry expression took the sting from his words. "Laurentius Severianus was one of my best," he said. This time, when he looked at Theo, his face was serious. "If you remain in my service, you might also rise as he did."

Feeling something was expected of him, Theo said, "Thank you."

Apsimar snorted. "I did not come to make the sun's rays shine from between your arse cheeks, Aurariola. Soon we will meet Zuhair." He cracked his knuckles, his eyes keen. "After we beat him, you will have decisions to make."

Theo looked away. He did not wish Apsimar to see his eyes.

"Men of the fleet put the Karabisianoi first. They have no room for doubt. In war, doubt is death. If you are to lead men I have trained, I will know your loyalty or send you back to Spania on the next merchant dromon we pass."

"My loyalty is not in doubt," Theo began hotly.

"Yes, it is." Apsimar cut him off so brutally that Theo was startled into silence. "Do not think me stupid, Aurariola. Dahiya herself asks after you. The whore keeper from Carthage follows my fleet. The horses in the market did not find you of their own accord."

"None of that affects my loyalty."

"It does if you use my fleet for your own ends. You will serve it, or you will leave it. What you do in your own time is your concern, just as it was for your uncle." Apsimar turned hard eyes to him. "Men follow you. They respect you. I have wars to fight far from here, wars that need men others can follow, for I will not always lead the fleet. I, too, have plans beyond those at the helm of a stinking dromon. My plans can help a man such as you rise in ways your Spanish brethren can only dream of. But you will not be returning home to your woman, and you will go where I send you, regardless of what other promises you have made."

Theo opened his mouth to respond, but Apsimar held up a hand.

"I did not come for your answer. You will think on what I have said. Days from now you will swing your sword against the Arabs. After we have killed them, you will know your decision."

He did not wait for Theo's answer, merely turned on his heel and strode away.

* * *

THEY HAD DONE landing drills all day, and Theo was not the only member of his crew who was exhausted.

"Zuhair's forces are close," said Silas as they ate fish blackened from the coals. "I heard the Riders speaking of it today."

It was dusk, and the hollow desert wind had died with the sun. They sat in the lee of the dromon in a small cove, sand churned from the day's exercises.

Leofric snorted. "I will not be sad to draw my sword for good purpose. I am tired of swinging it at your ugly face," he said, stabbing the fire with more force than necessary and shooting Theo a wry look. "I begin to think you like the drills as much as Apsimar, by God."

The flames lit the scars on Theo's face, throwing his unsmiling countenance into relief. "I like them better than being chained to an oar," he said curtly.

Silas and Leofric exchanged a worried glance. "That is not much of a comparison, *wenkai*."

A sound behind them had the men on their feet, swords drawn and crouching low, then the slender figure of a woman stepped from the shadows and they all moved back, startled into silence.

"Theudemir of Aurariola." Athanais smiled a greeting at them all. "May we speak, *aziz-am*?"

356

Leofric spat in the dirt and glared at her. "Battle could come tomorrow," he said. "Theo has no time for woman."

Silas nudged him.

"What?" Leofric said, indignantly.

"Be quiet," said Silas genially.

"But –"

"Be. Quiet."

Theo, ignoring them, rose and brushed the sand from his legs.

"I will eat your fish," called Leofric after him, as Theo and Athanais moved away from the fire.

"Your friends worry for you," said Athanais.

Theo inclined his head but made no answer.

"It is understandable. Men bent upon battle do not expect to find a woman in their midst. They wonder what it is I want from you."

"And what is it that you want from me?" Theo did not look at her when he spoke.

"There is a merchant dromon drawn up on the shore not four miles from here. It is bound for Spania."

"Spania," Theo breathed. It seemed a lifetime ago.

Athanais nodded. "I am wondering," she said, watching Theo carefully, "if you wish to board it – or if not, what message you would send home."

Home.

The moon was rising full, and it lit the pools of still water on the beach. Glancing down at one, Theo caught the strange, silvery reflection of his own face, and he felt his pulse slow and thicken as light caught the savage scars.

It seemed I saw your face…

He wondered, as he had many times since Oppa's whip first touched his skin, if this was the face she had seen. He did not think Lælia would shrink from his scars. In some strange way they seemed to belong to him, part of his soul in a way his old, clear mask had never been. He was yet to become accustomed to the way men regarded him, as if they were both afraid and awed, but he was beginning to understand that the scars, too, were a mask, but of a different kind. He was no longer the perfect son and soldier, the man other men looked upon in envy and admiration. Now men stared in fear and awe, and they whispered as he passed, scared of the pain they themselves could not imagine. He was learning to accept that the scars were part of him, a living expression of the pain that had existed in his soul for as long as he could recall, from the moment, perhaps, when his mother had died beneath Giscila's blade.

The thought tightened his body, reminding him of Lælia and Yosef, the promises he had made, and the decisions he now faced.

"I promised Lælia I would return."

"Eventually you will."

"I will not leave her at the mercy of Oppa and his father."

"Did you not make other promises?"

"None so important as that."

Athanais tilted her head to one side, looking out over the water. "And is it you who decides which promise is important and which is not?"

"There is nothing more important than Lælia."

"No," said Athanais softly. "Not, perhaps, to you."

"How could anything else possibly matter now?" Theo's voice was harsh. "Now that I know what they are capable of? Oppa will go to Illiberis. He may already be there. He will take Lælia."

"You seem very certain of that, *aziz-am.*"

"I know Oppa." Theo gripped the sword at his side, his hand working convulsively.

"But you are knowing Lælia, also."

"What can she do against Oppa?"

"Who knows what she can do?" Athanais met his eyes. "For months now," she said, "you have watched Dahiya lead the Riders whilst Apsimar leads the fleet. She has risen from the leader of her tribe to amgar of all the Imazighen; you have heard of her battle against an entire Arabic army. Do you think Apsimar liked standing by whilst his woman – the mother of his children – fought a battle to the death?"

"Lælia is not Dahiya," said Theo fiercely. "She is a girl who has never seen war. And she does not know what Oppa's family have done, the evil they are."

"You do not know what she does and doesn't know. And Dahiya, too, was once a girl. A girl who saw her own father murdered and was then forced to marry the murderer. A girl who took her father's sword – the sword no woman was ever supposed to touch – and used it to take the life of her conqueror, then raised an entire tribe in rebellion. Her men now call that girl amgar, men who swore no woman would ever lead them. Her enemies call her the Sorceress, enemies who never believed a woman capable of meeting them in battle, let alone defeating them."

Athanais's eyes gleamed in the moonlight.

"Lælia," she said, "is unlike any girl you have known, yes?"

Theo nodded, swallowing hard and turning so she would not see the longing in his eyes.

"Do you not think," she went on, "that she would trust you to do what was right?"

"Returning to her is right."

"And what of her right to find her own path?"

Theo's head jerked back in surprise. Athanais met his eyes steadily. "You assume," she said, "that Lælia waits, helpless, for your return. For your rescue."

Images flashed through Theo's mind: Lælia facing down the boys from Illiberis long ago on a high mountaintop, her commanding Titus to attack Frogellus, her turning to Oppa, arrow notched and drawn.

"Ah." Athanais nodded as she watched the shifting expressions move over his face. "And now you begin to remember the girl you know."

Theo leaned forward and gripped the rock before him, staring unseeing across the night sea.

"Yosef is alive. His journey – it continues. You, too, are alive and in the fleet as planned. I am thinking that your promises and your presence, *aziz-am*, are still being required, no?"

"Oppa has not been seen," Theo said, his voice cracking. "He could have been back in Spania for months. Even as we speak, already he could have made Lælia his wife. And I am here." Guilt and frustration made his gesture savage. "Serving my own ambition and a mission I barely understand."

"Ah." Athanais smiled. "So it is your ambition you fear."

Theo frowned at her. "Ambition is selfish."

"Ambition is necessary. It guides us to where our talents lie, asks us to pursue them."

"What use is it if my talent lies in swinging a sword?"

"But you know war is far more than swinging a sword. It is leading men. Diplomacy. A gift for languages." She looked at him. "The ability to see bat droppings outside a cave."

"Those things cannot help Spania."

"Of course they can. In the years that come, perhaps they are the *only* things that can help Spania."

Theo looked away and did not answer.

"And again, I ask you," she said softly. "Who are you to be deciding who matters and who does not, which promise matters and which does not? In a moment in time, you made a promise to help Yosef on his journey. This is your promise, your word, made because you felt it must be done. In another moment, you made another promise, to Lælia, because you knew this, also, to be true. Serving the fleet was never a promise. It was your destiny – the rock upon which those other promises were built.

"If those promises, made in different moments, were not in conflict when you were making them, then why must you be choosing to make them a conflict now?"

Theo shook his head in despair. "If I stay, I can tell myself it is to do my duty by Yosef, but in reality is it serving only my own desires? To stay is to abandon my duty to Lælia, leaving her to an unknown fate – but would returning, also, serve my desires?"

"You ask the wrong questions, *aziz-am*."

Theo looked at her. She clasped his hands. He did not pull them away.

"My religion – of which you are not knowing, but it does not matter – and my master, Zoroaster, teaches only three things: good words, good thoughts, good deeds." Her eyes glistened in the moonlight. "Every man must choose himself what he knows to be good words, thoughts, and deeds. For every man, he is knowing, in every moment, if he chooses the good or that which is not good within him. Every man must live with that choice. You have made promises that, I am believing, came from the place of good inside you. But only you, *aziz-am*, can choose what thoughts and deeds will follow those words. Choose. And live with your decisions."

Theo looked strangely at her. "Someone else said that to me once," he said. "Long ago, on the road to Illiberis. As I rode to meet Lælia. It was Shukra; we spoke together, of duty."

"Ah." Athanais nodded. "Duty," she said, a light smile on her lips.

Theo looked at her. "Duty matters," he said curtly.

"Duty is nothing. It is smoke." Athanais clicked her fingers in the air, a gesture so reminiscent of Shukra and his mercurial humour it momentarily silenced Theo. "We give our allegiance to what is in our heart. What comes from within." She touched her own heart, then Theo's. Her pale fingers gleamed ivory in the moonlight and felt cool and strong on his chest.

"Shukra said that, also."

"Shukra and I drink from the same cup." Athanais tilted her head to the side, dismissing Shukra. "In your heart," she said, "if you believe that Lælia wishes you at her side out of this duty, then yes, *aziz-am*, you must go. In your heart, if you believe that your place is here, then you must stay. Either choice leads to an unknown future. Only your heart can tell you which unknown path is truly yours. And your only duty is to heed the wisdom of your heart. All else" – she clicked her fingers again – "smoke, *aziz-am*."

"How will I know?" said Theo hoarsely. "How will I know what it is that I must do?"

"Are you thinking life is coming with a map and strategy?" Athanais stepped away, the shadows falling over her face. When she spoke again, her words came through the darkness, disembodied, floating on the night.

"It is simple, *aziz-am*. Follow your heart."

Theo, staring at the place where a moment ago she had stood, thought that nothing in the world had ever seemed less simple.

43

LÆLIA

NOVEMBER AD 688

Illiberis, Bætica, Spania
Granada, Andalusia, Spain

L ælia followed Paulus into his study. Her legs were strong and steady, and despite the recent encounter with Oppa she felt not a moment of failing. Her course seemed set, as if by something greater than herself. All she needed to do was follow it. Her feet moved of their own accord, and when her grandfather turned a frowning countenance to her, Laelia's hands, also, began to move, smoothly and without hesitation.

I will not marry Oppa.

Paulus waved her away wearily. "You have made your opposition more than clear, Laelia. We will travel to Toletum tomorrow, and I will find a way out of this."

No.

Her movement was calm and sure. She held his eyes, seeing them narrow fractionally.

"No?" Paulus leaned back in his chair, folding his arms.

I leave today. I am riding to the caves where they found my mother's body.

The grim lines in her grandfather's face deepened, his eyes seeming to recede into dark hollows. "You are not," he said flatly.

Lælia shrugged and began to walk from the room.

"Laelia!" he barked from behind her.

She stopped and turned.

"I do not know who told you how your mother died. But Callista *is* dead, Laelia, and nothing will change that. I will not indulge your tantrums. You are a woman grown, not a child."

You are right. I am no longer a child. She lifted a shoulder and let it fall, a gesture as simple and eloquent as any words could be. *I can no longer follow the path you set, Grandfather.*

She felt the hard ball of emotion within her rise to the surface, saw his eyes flare with something like fear at the raw power of it. He physically recoiled, as if stunned by the mingled fury, grief, and longing she had kept within for so long. She held his eyes, forcing him to feel it, and slowly shook her head.

I cannot.

This time when she turned, he did not try to stop her.

* * *

LÆLIA RODE to the abbey in the mountains with her horse already packed for the ride ahead. For once, her grandmother did not await her in the yard. The door to the abbey was open. When Lælia entered, the tapestry on the far wall had been pushed aside, and the entrance to the caves below yawned open.

She stepped within and followed the earthen passageway downward until she reached the place where water tumbled into the pool.

Acantha was there waiting, her face as flat and unyielding as the stone upon which she sat. Lælia breathed in the scent of cold water, stone, mineral, and grass. She sat opposite her grandmother and raised her hands.

I need your help.

She smiled at Acantha's surprise.

Sometimes, she gestured slowly, *when I sit in the church in Toletum, I think of this place. Amidst the king's nobles, clad in their finest robes and jewellery, whilst the priest speaks his words in Latin, I close my eyes and smell the cut plants and water coming from rock. I hear the words spoken in the old tongue, the one you and the horse herders speak here. The language Grandfather speaks when he curses, and the gods he prays to when he thinks I am not listening. Gods not so different from those the Goths themselves once worshipped. I think of every tongue and god other than the one I am supposed to when I sit in church. But most of all, I think of here — and I think of you.*

She found herself oddly shy for she had never tried to express such things, but the gestures came nonetheless.

You and Riccilo both speak to me of women and their sacrifices. The reality is that churches and Latin are the way men understand divinity. They take prayer and make of it a government and an army, give it rules and punishments so that they may pretend control over forces of which they are innately terrified. But women — we understand the immensity of the divine, the complexity and thousand faces it owns. We feel what they call God working in our own bodies with the cycle of the moon, and thus we know truths no man ever can.

She looked at Acantha, gestures tumbling from her as water from the rock above. *You taught me how to understand the One within myself. How to see it at work within all of us. You taught me not meaningless ritual, but the joy of celebration and harmony. I learned at your side, beneath the moon and stars and down here, in the water.* She held the older woman's eyes. *You taught me to heed the knowledge within. Now I hear it call, and I must follow it. I would like you to come with me, but I will go alone if I must.*

Seeing the unspoken question, Lælia gestured: *You know where I am going. To the Valley of the Horse. The caves where they found my mother.*

Acantha made a soft noise. Pain wrinkled across her face at the mention of the valley, and the echo of blood and violence passed across the cavern like a red shadow, but Lælia did not look away.

You told me once that I must face the challenges life has already given me. I am tired of being afraid, of feeling inadequate.

The stern lines of Acantha's face softened.

I must find my voice. I know it lives in the place my mother died. I have seen it, in dreams. Felt it. She struck her chest with one arm, fiercely. *I cannot allow others to fight battles that are mine. I cannot run from them anymore. And I will no longer suffer them in silence.*

When she answered, Acantha's voice was uncharacteristically thin, rasping in her throat. "To open such doors," she said, "is to reach into places you have not begun to understand."

Lælia dashed angrily at the tears that threatened to fall. *Please.*

"You do not know what you ask."

Lælia's mouth twisted. Her next gestures were fast and bitter. *You and the priests are not so different.*

Acantha frowned.

You both live with God in your own ways, but neither of you are able, truly, to live with yourselves. Lælia glanced above through the hole in the rock to where the sky had darkened, late afternoon creeping in whilst they had been speaking. *I have no time for this.*

She stood, stiff and cold, inhaling the scent of her childhood. *I must go.*

"Lælia." Acantha stood in a fluid movement, her eyes glowing with a dark, fierce light. "I will take you."

44

LÆLIA

NOVEMBER AD 688

The Valley of the Horse
Near Ronda, Andalusia, Spain

They left in the still hours when men die and spirits walk. Stars glittered high above, finding a reflection on the white mountains to the east. Lælia was wrapped in a thick cloak, Jadis running silently at her side. They had supplies enough to last for days, and many miles to ride.

An entire *decania* of Grandfather's thiufa, clad in full armour with sword, bow, and spear, rode escort. They were led by Gratimo, the Illiberis thiufadis Lælia had known all her life. He had one eye and one arm, his face gnarled and twisted with scars. He barked constant orders to the men who rode about Acantha and her grand-daughter in a phalanx, scouts riding well ahead in every direction. Never had Lælia gone anywhere so fiercely protected. Their presence, she knew, was the bargain Acantha had struck so Count Paulus would allow this journey. Lælia had thought it wise not to voice any objection to their presence.

The days passed quickly, although little was said as they rode. The caves lay past the old Roman ruins of Acinipo. The party skirted the new town. The caves were a secret known to the tribes alone and closely guarded. High, bare peaks unfamiliar to Lælia swooped to broad valleys below.

The day was growing late when they rounded the mountains along a narrow path, surrounded by oddly shaped conifers with glaucous leaves arranged around long, greenish-pink cones. The trees themselves grew four times the height of a man. They appeared still and strange to Lælia, not rustling as trees are wont to do but rather sitting in hibernation, present but no longer watchful, as if they belonged to another age. She found their thick growths alien and vaguely sinister.

They came to a halt on a barren piece of hillside with no discernible shelter and a valley rolling open far beneath. Acantha dismounted and bade Lælia do the same.

"You know where to wait for us," she told the herdsman at her side. His name was Tosius and, like Gratimo, Lælia had known him since infancy.

Gratimo came forward. "You will take a guard into the caves," he said. His lone eye looked about grimly. Lælia could smell his tension, read it in the tight grip on his reins, the slight uneasiness of his horse. Gratimo was afraid, she realised. The thought sent a thrill through her veins. She could not see the caves he referred to.

"No." Acantha spoke quietly, but the resolution in her tone made Gratimo frown. "You may post guards at a distance in every direction. But only Tosius will stand sentinel at the opening. It is sacred ground, not to be walked by those who do not know its secrets, nor approached with disrespect. Not on a night such as this."

She nodded to the eastern horizon, where the sky was indigo and gold and the full moon was due to rise.

"It is the full moon of the Bull," she said to Gratimo. "A woman's moon, one of the earth and power. I have obeyed Count Paulus's orders to here. But now the journey belongs to Lælia and me, and your role is only to keep us safe from any who would approach the caves — not to enter them with us. Do you understand?"

Gratimo's face darkened. "I would at least check within, to ensure it is safe," he said.

Tosius made a noise. "None are within." He spoke with certainty. "There is only one way to reach the caves and none have passed here since I did so." He indicated a boulder and some low bushes nearby. "I know this place," he said.

Gratimo nodded. He did not ask how he knew. The tracking abilities of the tribes were well enough known in Illiberis. To most, the boulder and bushes were simply that. To Tosius, they told a story, each leaf and crack in the boulder speaking of the creatures small and large that had touched them, no matter how briefly or how long ago. If Tosius said none had passed, then none had.

Lælia, seeing a shadow pass his face, realised it must have been he who had first tracked her mother to this place. Glancing sideways at Gratimo, she wondered if his scars, too, had been inflicted during those dark days.

"It was Tosius who found Callista." Acantha spoke abruptly, answering her unspoken questions. "Gratimo arrived with him at the villa. They led the tribesmen who fought off your mother's murderer."

They followed a narrow path around to a small plateau.

"It is time," said Tosius, casting his eyes skyward.

Acantha nodded. They were facing out over the valley, a yawning expanse rapidly turning dark. Lælia heard the faint sound of water in the distance.

"The Valley of the Horse," murmured Acantha. She made a sign in the air with her right hand — it came across from the left, then down in a long stroke, spiralling into a finish immediately in front of them. She pushed faintly outward at the last point. Lælia had known her to use the symbol before when she was working with horses or healing the sick, but she had never truly seen it. Now she found she felt sealed in behind it, as if the air beyond Acantha's hand was a world apart.

"When we enter," said Acantha, "you will follow me closely. Do what I tell you. And do not question me. Do you understand?"

Lælia nodded. She knew better by now than to question Acantha, no matter how strange the situation or her actions.

Acantha lit a small fire and then a torch from that, one built to burn for a long time.

"It will be dark," she said. "Very dark. Follow me closely."

They left Jadis lying on her belly beside Tosius, watching the valley below, and entered a low opening, a shallow depression in the rock wall. It looked nondescript indeed, no more than a few paces wide in each direction, the sort of unremarkable space men would use to store grain or vegetables for the winter at home. Acantha moved behind the rock face, and another opening yawned before them. Taking a last look at the dusk-filled valley, Lælia followed her.

At first, it seemed much like the many caves near Illiberis used for storage: smooth rock walls, hard earthen floor. But only a few paces in, the way turned and darkness fell, sealing them off from the outside world.

The air was still and temperate. The earth itself seemed warm and alive; the cutting cold of the night was gone. Long protrusions grew from both ground and cave roof. They were opaque, made of an odd subterranean material from which water dripped in slow, measured drops. Some grew in long, cone-like formations, others in oddly shaped clumps like twisted root vegetables. They seemed to have a life of their own, like a peculiar type of soft rock, growing at an ancient, unhurried pace. They were almost watchful. Some were so great they had grown to join roof and floor in a series of straight columns. Acantha paused at these, touching them lightly. Reaching behind a stone, she withdrew a long animal bone. She tapped a column and it made a low, melodic sound that resonated through the chamber. One after another, she played them, creating a swell of music that vibrated through Lælia's body and seemed to wake the air itself. When at last the sounds died away, she paused, listening to the air. She nodded in satisfaction. "Now we are truly here," she said.

She turned the torch to the wall. There were pictures, crude markings done by ancient hands: fish and animals. She moved the torch slowly across them until she came to one and stopped.

Lælia gasped in wonder.

It was a horse, drawn in ochre, a fine spray of colour so delicate Lælia could not imagine how the artist had wrought it. The horse was in flight, at the point mid-stride when all four feet are from the earth and the horse seems to glide through the air. But it was not simply an outline, a suggestion of the figure of a horse as most pictures are, those she had seen made on tile or in the books in Count Paulus's study. This was something else: an explosion of colour and animation, which seemed to move in the flickering light of the torch. It was so vivid, she felt it as a living thing, an animal of life and breath that existed, the spirit of it contained here on the rock.

She reached out to touch it, compelled to become part of it, wanting to fall into the moment and never come out.

Acantha caught her hand before she reached it.

"We do not touch them," she murmured. "Only once, when we are infants. Follow me."

Lælia followed, feeling the animal on the wall watch as she went.

They walked deeper into the earth. The blackness was absolute. Lælia had never known stillness such as this. It seemed to press about her, but not heavily; rather it simply held her, as if the very air itself were a structure, warm and supple. The walls were blackened. After a time, she realised the discolouration was staining from soot and smoke, evidence of a thousand fires from those who had lived within. Lælia felt the echo of those distant lives, the spirit of the fires, alive in the air and earth about her. It was comforting, as if they lived still.

They climbed through a narrow fissure and came down past more of the opaque growths, sprouting from the walls in weird shapes like gigantic cauliflowers. They came to a pool. The water was brilliant aqua and completely clear, fed by an underground spring. Acantha paused and placed the torch between the rocks.

"Come," she said.

Lælia stood like a child whilst Acantha stripped her naked in the dim light, then led her to the pool. Lælia gasped as the water from Acantha's cupped hands poured over her head. The air in the caves may have been mild, but the water was ice cold and made her skin tingle. It had a strange mineral flavour, rich and heavy. It felt provocative on her flesh. When she stepped from the pool, her body felt different, alive, attuned to the air of the cave.

Acantha had carried a bundle down the cliffs. Now she unbound it and withdrew a small corked flask and a simple linen shift, which she drew over Lælia's head. She lit another torch from her own, handing it to Lælia and bidding her follow along another pathway away from the pool. They were so deep inside the cliff now that Lælia doubted she could find her way out alone.

They came to a low chamber with rounded walls. Acantha laid a woven mat on the floor, bade Lælia sit, and wedged her torch between the rocks again so it cast light upward, leaving Lælia in shadow.

"The torch will burn down soon," said Acantha. "When it does, you will be alone in the darkness." She handed Lælia the flask. "Drink."

Lælia drank. It tasted bitter and strong, hitting her body in a rush of warmth, stealing through her veins like a thief, taking with it the cave and Acantha's face, so they began to recede from her vision.

"When the light leaves you," said Acantha, her voice seeming far away now, "and the moon outside rises, you will see things. Things that can be safely seen only here. Visions meant only for you. I will leave you, but I will remain in the caves, and my music will protect you. You are safe here. None can harm you. Do not be afraid, no matter what you see or hear; in the caves, time moves differently. The tribes believe all past and future lingers here in the earth. In the darkness, we become one with both."

Her voice was already fading, falling over Lælia like a wave and receding again. She breathed in, drawing air through her nose, feeling it fill her body and pour into every crevice of her being. She held it full inside for a long time before letting it go. Never had she noticed how it felt to be full of breath. It seemed as if the air were made of a million tiny fragments that exploded upon entering her body, racing around it in an effervescent, complex draught. Each breath seemed filled with infinite possibility. She became fascinated by the feel of it travelling beneath her skin and within; every breath came slower as she followed it through her body and she, in turn, fell inward, further into the darkness of her own being, the somnolent warmth of the cave seeming to dissolve the barrier between herself and the air she breathed.

"May what you see," Acantha's voice echoed in the darkness, "bring what you need."

Lælia was vaguely aware that somewhere in the distance Acantha had begun to play the columns, a strong, rhythmic melody that vibrated the walls and floor of the caves. The water in which she had bathed trembled on her skin; the particles she breathed danced in her soul. The torch in the rocks flickered and went out, and Lælia was alone in the blackness.

Her eyes fluttered closed.

45

THEO

THE MOON OF THE BULL

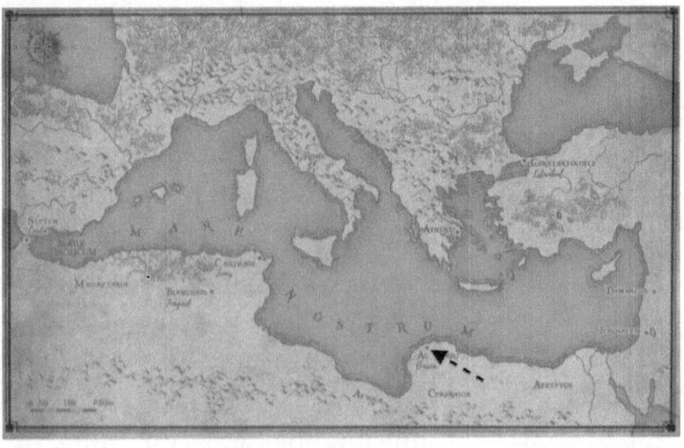

The Battle of Barca

The night felt thick, the full moon of the Bull beaming down upon the black sea, and Theo's heart thudded in sick anticipation as the rocky cliff came closer.

Apsimar's fleet would attack Barca from the sea, as Theo had spent months training to do. The Arab forces had finally marched to the port the day before, and now victory for Apsimar and Dahiya's combined forces depended on speed and secrecy. Apsimar needed to take the city whilst Zuhair's men were still weak from their long desert march and before their position became unassailable.

The sea was silent and slick in the lee of the rocks. Moonlight shone on the harbour beyond, showing every shadow.

"Look," grunted Silas as they pulled, and Theo glanced over his shoulder. They were rounding the cliffs, and Barca had come into sight.

"Pull!" roared the kentarchos, standing tall at the prow with kontarion ready. "They can see us coming! They know they face death! Give them something to fear!"

The men roared, and Theo glanced again over his shoulder. The tall, elegant pillars of the forum gleamed in the moonlight. Men scurried to defensive positions on the shoreline, shields glinting as they mounted the curved steps built into the hillside. There were virtually no fortifications on the seaward face of the city, just as Dahiya's spies had told them.

"You die tonight!" Apsimar, bare headed with crimson cloak streaming behind him, stood proudly at the helm of his dromon, roaring his challenge to the men onshore racing for cover. His men screamed their battle rage, and Theo felt a thrill run through his body.

"Karabisianoi!" roared Apsimar, turning to his fleet. "Today you are men! Today you will not die!"

Silas and Leofric were howling for blood on either side of him and Theo felt it, the moment when his body knew that battle was coming and he became one with the men of his fleet, a part of the brilliant force that followed Apsimar's gleaming blond head and the corded muscle standing out from leather vambraces.

"Pull, you bastards! Hit them hard! Pull!" Petros roared from the helm.

Theo grunted with the force of his stroke, feeling the power surge beneath him and the dromon leap through the water. There was a fractional pause at the height of their stroke, a point where oars lifted and the dromon shot ahead. With an odd, heightened sense, which seemed to make every moment a glittering point of clarity, Theo felt the call coming before the first word left Apsimar's mouth, and he was already hauling in his oar when it came:

"Archers!"

He leaped with Silas and, notching his arrows, waited for the second call:

"Stroke!"

Until only days ago, Theo was the one who pulled that final stroke; he knew the pulse of the dromon as well as his own heartbeat. He waited for the moment when the oars raced through the water and the vessel ceased jerking and glided across the surface instead. When it was in that silent moment of ease, he let fly and his arrows soared through the air and hit home just as their dromon rammed a fulk at anchor in the harbour.

"Skutatoi!"

Feeling blood bubble in his veins like oil on a fire, Theo roared as he leaped from the dromon, his kontarion taking an Arab soldier in the neck as he landed in the flat bottom of the fulk, screaming for death and wrenching his spear from the man's neck as he wielded his spatha against another.

He was screaming words he did not know, guttural sounds from inside him of fury and rage, and beside him the blood was rich and dark in the moonlight on Silas's black arms, and the big man was twirling with spear and sword, ducking and lunging as men fell about him into the sea and onto the planks of the fulk.

Theo did not remember leaping from the fulk to shore, but suddenly he was there and a wall of Arabs stood before him, their pointed helmets strange and provocative, their screams bloodcurdling and odd to the ear. Leaping into the air, Theo thrust forward with his kontarion, taking the first soldier in the shoulder and ramming the point home, wrenching it out as the man fell, twisting to escape the spear of another.

"Shield!" screamed Silas next to him, and Theo held the round disc above his head as arrows rained down from the archers on the steps, the Arabs before him retreating under the onslaught of spear and regrouping behind the archers' fire.

Charging forward again, Theo threw his kontarion and saw it

strike home in the neck of another before it was too late for spear, and he was amongst the fight with sword in hand. And then it was blood and heat and rage, and Theo knew not how he moved or whom he struck, was barely aware even of the earth beneath his feet. Everything he was flowed into the steel in his hand, so his body became poetry, a lithe song of pure exhilaration that blocked all but the next turn, the next thrust, from his mind; he had an almost eerie precognition of the blades coming his way. He spun and flew through the air and found himself laughing out loud, an odd guttural cry of exultation as he felt his steel cut through flesh and bone and as men fell away from him like fruit from a tree.

He could not have said how long it went on for, nor if they were winning, but the air about him began to move differently, and when he cut the next body down, there were horses coming over the ridge led by a raging barbarian god with a great horned head, shrieking unintelligible curses in a fearsome wail, scattering men like ants to the dust and wreaking death with every stride and cut.

It seemed that the battle paused, like a long indrawn breath. A man fell beneath his sword, and Theo downed another with an almost distracted blow as he watched the horned figure plough through the mass of men and steel. As the terrifying apparition drew closer, Theo realised the horns were welded to a battle helmet and the great sword was wielded by human hand. But it was only as he saw a man's head cleaved from his shoulders in one stroke from the great war sword and heard the fierce, savage scream of triumph that he realised the hand wielding it belonged to a woman.

In a daze, Theo spun beneath a blade and kicked his attacker beneath the jaw, knocking him senseless. He then disarmed another whilst his eyes never left the wild, magnificent figure of Al Kahinat as she plunged her men into the destruction, facing the enemy with a fury beyond courage, screaming defiance at death itself.

It did not take long after that.

Theo found himself, sword in hand, screaming his rage as he spun to meet the next blow only to find the air empty and nothing but prone bodies crying in anguish on the ground. Leofric, face dripping with gore and a crazed grin on his face, was gripping his arms and saying over and over, "*Ja! Ja, schnecke, ja!*"

And it was then that he realised it was done, and Barca was theirs.

46

LÆLIA

THE MOON OF THE BULL

Place beyond Time

It is dark, and we are running. My mother's breath rasps in her chest. She stumbles, her arms tightening about me. I can feel her fear and I begin to cry, a thin, high sound that cuts through the night.

"Hush," she whispers, her hand about my head. She is carrying the boy on her back and he is clinging to her, wide eyed and silent, his white hair gleaming in the moonlight. The sound of men and steel rings out across the night ground and I hiccup, staring at the boy with the big green eyes.

My mother trembles beneath our combined weight. She is searching for something, running through the olive grove, slipping between rock and tree like a shadow. One of her feet dislodges a stone, and it tumbles down the hill toward the rising smoke and the men with swords and death in their hands.

I cry out, a high-pitched scream of terror, which carries clearly across the ground. I feel rather than hear the sob of terror in my mother's throat. She sinks to the ground behind a boulder and lays us down beside her. I scream louder at the loss of her warmth, and the boy beside me picks me up, cradling me against him, muffling my cries. He smells like smoke and horses, familiar scents, and I am comforted.

My mother raises the bow and takes careful aim. The boy holds me up, and I see the men fall, one after the other. My mother slumps over the bow, breathing hoarsely and clutching her side. There is a dark stain spreading through her clothes. I can smell it on my own body. It is metallic and wet and frightening.

My mother takes me up and holds me in front of her.

"You must be like the wind," she whispers hoarsely. "The wind screams, but nobody says where it lives."

Her eyes are the colour of the setting sun and usually they glow with love when she looks at me. Tonight, they are shadowed with pain and fear and something else, something that causes my screams to choke painfully in my throat. I know I must make no sound. My voice is strangled in my throat, choked to silence with fear.

She whistles low on the night, and moments later a mare steps silently through the trees. I know Hera. She is my mother's mare. In the first days of my life, she was allowed to nuzzle my body with her velvet nose, and I gurgled at her touch. My mother places the boy on the mare and clambers on after him, holding me close to her chest.

"Now," she whispers, turning the mare with her body. "Now we are the wind."

I swallow my cries painfully into my chest, and I become the wind.

We ride through the silent forest, staying in the shadows as the moon rises huge and silver in the sky. My mother sways on the mare, and her life spills onto my body so I am slick and slippery with it, the taste of metal death all around me, dripping onto the boy in front of me who holds Hera's mane and urges her onward when my mother ceases to speak.

In the early hours, we take a steep path upward from the valley to a flat plateau and my mother tumbles from Hera, barely conscious. She mutters an order and Hera squeals indignantly, stamping her hooves and shaking her head, snorting in anger and alarm. My mother snaps at her, louder this time. Hera tosses her head in confusion and backs away, head down, eyes exhausted and wounded.

"Go," my mother whispers hoarsely. "You must go."

The mare snorts a final time, then turns. I watch her stumble down the path, head down, legs trembling beneath her. My mother moans low in her throat. She turns to the entrance of the caves and makes a sign with her hand, shutting off the world outside.

The caves are silent and warm, blacker than any night could ever be. But my mother knows every step, and somewhere within I know we are safe here, that nothing can harm us amidst the uneven rock and strange sculptures falling from ceiling to floor. She lights a taper and stumbles through chambers blackened by soot from a million fires to one that opens up, high and tall. She falls to her knees in front of the pictures – bison, fish, wolf, all drawn in dramatic relief on the limestone by hands far older than any in living memory.

"The wall of stories." She sobs the words, her hands clutching me. "The tribes bring their children here when they are born. They touch the paintings once, that they may know to whom they belong and allow the spirits of the ancestors to enter them. May they watch over you now."

She takes us further, to a cavern with a still, clear pool of water. Falling to her knees, she cups her hand and holds it first to my mouth, then to the boy's. She draws icy water across my forehead.

"Now," she rasps, her voice barely there, "the ancestors know of you. They know you live." When she lowers her hand, a drop of blood falls into the pool, sending ripples all the way to the edge, taking the message.

"You must watch," she says in a low, urgent voice to the boy. "This is how you drink. Do you understand? You must drink to stay alive."

He stares at her and nods slowly, eyes wide and frightened, and she moans.

"You must remember to drink." I can feel her weakness now, her fingers barely able to hold me.

I open my mouth, the scream of terror and abandonment rising in my heart as I see the life begin to fade from her eyes. Her hands close over my mouth, and I taste the metal death upon them.

She shakes her head feebly. "No," she breathes in a thready voice. "You cannot cry out. They must not find you. You have no voice now, Lælia. You are the wind, remember, *liefs*? The wind screams, but none can say where it lives…"

Long after she becomes cold and still, I stay in her arms, turning this way and that, emptiness clawing painfully in my chest where once my cries had been. Finally, the boy takes me in his own and carries me to the wall of stories, crooning his own childish song to my silence. The ochre lines of the horse are drawn so simply, and yet with such vivid life, the horse seems poised to leap from the rock and into being.

The boy hums his song as I reach out and touch it, singing to the spirit of the horse and the soul of the child as one melds with the other. I can feel his song vibrating in my body, but I am silent.

The wind screams, but none can say where it lives. And I – I have become the wind.

47

THEO

THE MOON OF THE BULL

The Battle of Barca

The air was thick with blood and dust and the sounds of men crying their death to uncaring gods. Theo lowered his sword as Leofric and Silas roared their victory beside him, the fury of battle racing still through his veins. He was barely aware of the steel in his hands. A distant memory tugged at his gut, drawing an invisible line between himself and the horned figure still cutting a swath through those last few who dared face her. He watched the horse surge and fly beneath Al Kahinat, and in the sick red glow of war fire, the brand on its shoulder seemed to writhe like a living thing. Theo's hand went up and involuntarily grasped the amulet at his throat. It seemed to pulse in his hand, hot and feral, as if it screamed a wild war cry of its own. He felt a rush of lust rip through his body like nothing he had felt before, a tidal wave of savagery that had him look about blindly, ready to grab the nearest woman and reave her into the earth, to commit the atrocities he had heard of men in war and never once considered himself capable of.

Lælia, he thought fiercely.

His body afire, he crouched with muscles taut and hard as Al Kahinat matched his wildness with her own, and it seemed to him that the Sorceress had become Lælia, flying across the high mountains of Illiberis, hair streaking behind her as she became one with her horse, her slender body flowing into it like a sensual river as she screamed her own lust and loneliness out to him, crying his name. He knew, with a horrible certainty, that it would one day be Lælia herself leading men into battle, that the same spirit wielding Al Kahinat's sword lived, too, within the girl he loved. He knew it with the hard clarity that comes from beyond. He felt it. The realisation cut through his months of indecision with the clean precision of a razor's edge and the same lightning agony. He knew what would be and at the same time felt everything within him reject the knowledge. He stared at the woman shrieking war into the night with agony and exhilaration warring in his veins, driving him to the point of insanity.

Theo threw his head back beneath the blazing moon and roared his fury and longing into the night, vision and memory rippling through his body in a tide of blood and lust until he could not distinguish the two and saw only Lælia's face and the strange, shimmering figure of a horse leaping from rock. It was then that he felt the blood on his own face and tasted the gore dripping into his mouth.

Around him, men had already been taken by the same impulse, tearing women from behind walls and taking them where they stood. Theo watched, heart thudding and mouth dry, as a young girl no older than Lælia screamed as her gown was torn from her body, her face turned to the wall.

And that was what brought him out of it. He sank to his knees, retching into the dust, shame and sickness sweeping over him along with a sudden deep, flattening exhaustion.

Silas reached for the man violating the young girl and tore him roughly away, pushing him against a rock. Gently covering the girl, he gestured her away up the hill to safety, holding her attacker easily with one great hand.

All about Theo, chaos reigned, and women fled in fear before men crazed with blood and lust. The horned god rode amongst them, sword raised and then brought down upon another man who held a woman to the ground. The woman pushed the man's body from her own in revulsion and stared fearfully at her savage rescuer as she scrambled away, casting terrified looks behind her.

Then Apsimar was there amongst them, calling for order and sending his men in to enforce it. Theo watched his commander stride through the morass, Apsimar's eyes glittering with fierce elation, his body burned and scarred with war as he cut a path directly through the fallen toward the mounted figure of Al Kahinat. As Theo watched, Apsimar wrenched the god from its mount and tore the horned mask away, revealing the glorious woman beneath it, her amber eyes glowing with rage and passion. Apsimar pulled her into his arms and crushed his mouth to hers, kissing her on and on, amidst the carnage and blood on the shore.

Al Kahinat was gone. Dahiya remained. Theo watched them both, feeling bittersweet understanding shear his soul in two.

48

LÆLIA

THE MOON OF THE BULL

Place beyond Time

The torch had long since guttered out, and Lælia could no longer tell whether her eyes were open or closed. Time ceased to move, and there was only the steady drip of water from the growths on the wall and the velvet black stillness. Somewhere in the distance, the muffled throb of Acantha's music thudded dully in the air, and somewhere in the recesses of Lælia's mind, the boy's voice crooned his song.

The horse danced still beneath her fingers, and again she fell deeper, away from the caves. Away from her physical life. Further into the past, beyond blood and savagery and the cold, dead memory of her mother. Further back in time, until the world and all she knew of it was gone and there was only wind, rippling through a valley of long grass.

* * *

I AM LYING in the grass, the sun warm on my back. The horses are

385

grazing only a short distance away. One moves closer than the others. She shows no alarm at my presence. She is drawn to me, whether she knows it or not. I have watched her for many moons now. We are already one. I have only to make it so.

I lie still, the long stems flattened beneath me. The filly comes closer, muzzle rummaging in the grass for sweet blades still moist at the root after the long, hot months. Soon the cold will come, and my people will move into the caves. I must make her mine before that, so she knows to return here when the snows are gone.

She moves close enough to nuzzle my back. I lie still and feel the velvet tickle of her lips on my skin, the warm snort of her breath. She inhales my scent and moves along my back until her nose rests on my neck. She nips me lightly.

I roll over slowly. Our eyes meet. I see myself in hers and allow her to see inside me, to find her own reflection. Her nostrils flare; she comes down on her knees, and I flow onto her back.

And then we are running, fleet and smooth across the valley floor, my body liquid with hers. My fingers are twined in her mane and my legs lock about her; I am no longer Girl and she is no longer Horse but rather we are become something else, a new being that we can only be together, linked by an invisible force that flows through us both. I feel her wild strength in my veins as she allows me to guide her. We move as one, mounting the ridge where I know the men will be.

The cattle are running toward me, great horns aimed directly at where we stand, and I feel a rush of fear and danger pass through us both. The people of my tribe run behind, urging them forward into the valley, and the herd thunder away from their advance, running blindly.

I feel the moment when he joins me. His horse halts on the far edge of the ridge. I do not need to look to know he is there. I can feel him. I know he has found his horse, as I have. The filly trembles beneath me with the same awareness. She snorts at the oncoming cattle but does not move as I draw my bow; she, too, knows we must eat.

He draws as I do, and together we release the long arrows high into the air. The animal in the lead, a great, strong bull, falls beneath the dual piercing, stumbling into the grass.

The herd parts around the body and continues, the people following them, taking, one after another, meat for the winter.

We ride to the bull. It lies on the ground, snorting in pain and fear, and we slip from the horses to its side. It looks at me as we draw our knives. As one, we plunge them into the heart and warm blood pulses over our hands as life drains from the animal. We hold it, murmuring the words as light fades from its eyes, singing its spirit into earth and sky as it returns to become part of the One.

The horses behind us make a soft noise as they feel it pass through them, and I feel the heaviness in my limbs as blood settles into the ground. Then I feel something else, a dull throb deep within. I look at him, and deep green eyes stare back at me. He feels it too. He touches me, blood on his hand, and my skin feels a thrill.

Dusk is falling. Tonight is the full moon, and we will eat meat. Already the people are coming over the ridge to take the bull. He cuts out the heart and holds it up, and the women of our tribe cackle in delight, their laughter echoing across the valley. He eats of the heart and passes it to me, and I feel the warm blood and flesh enter my veins in a surge of power.

The horses nuzzle each other and then nudge us. They turn toward the indigo line on the horizon where the moon will rise and glance back. I nod dismissal, feeling the connection break; then my filly is gone, the black colt at her side. They race toward the rising moon, shadows in the gloaming.

I can still feel the grass beneath my hooves and the exhilaration of the hunt. I feel a throbbing within, a rich pulsing that sets my skin aflame, and liquid heat run through my veins. I shiver with it. I turn to find him staring at me with dark intent, and the old women of our tribe, they who hold the wisdom of the earth, see it and began to sing, a low, crooning song like wind through rock.

We walk toward the caves, held by their song, carried by a rhythm that pulses between my legs until it is all there is, swollen and full and aching. We turn to face the horizon at the mouth of the cave. Inside, they have begun to play, melodic and thick, the sound calling us within.

The women sing still. We feel the song within us as the disc of the moon rises, silver and bright, climbing over the ridge to bathe us in her blessing. Below us on the plain, the men butcher the meat and begin to prepare it, washed by starlight and dew, blood staining the silver grass. One of the old women comes to us with the skull of the great bull, blood dripping from it still, horns long and curved. She places it on his head.

I feel it, the moment the bull takes him. I know it is time to take him within the caves, deep into the place where we will perform the ritual that ensures the bull's life force is taken into the earth to nourish it over winter. I feel urgency in my blood, need racing through me. The moon of the Bull is full in the sky, and it is time. I draw him within, past the first chamber where the people sing the song of winter, past the player who makes the columns sing with his bones. I feel the song pass through me and close my eyes, breathless with the pulse of it.

We come to the pool and I step into it, turning to face him, naked and hot with longing. The feeling of the water over my skin makes me cry out. He makes a low noise and pulls me from the pool. I feel him raw and urgent against me and I have never wanted anything as I do him in this moment. My legs part, my head goes back, and he catches me, laying me down on the stone. He tears through me in a moment of exquisite pain and ecstasy, and then we are one, the great horned bull moving over and in me and my blood spilling onto the stone as he plunges within.

The world around me convulses. Wind roars in my ears, and I scream aloud.

* * *

LÆLIA'S EYES FLEW OPEN. The cave was silent, though the echoes of the player's bones, of Theo's song, quivered still. One hand went tentatively to her throat. Her mouth felt dry and unused, and her heart fluttered as she parted her lips, staring up into the silence.

"I know where my voice lives," she whispered to the darkness. "And I know what I must do."

49

THEO

DECEMBER AD 688

Barca, Tripolitana
Mediterranean Sea, near Benghazi, Libya

It was a dark night, and the man pissing against the rocks did not hear footsteps approaching.

"Yosef," Theo murmured. The figure spun around, knife

in hand. Theo held up his own to show he had no weapon. "It's me. Theo."

Yosef stared at his scars, still covered in blood from the battle. Theo smiled grimly. "They are a sight, are they not?" He glanced around warily. "Where can we talk?"

"This way." Yosef nodded to a narrow track barely visible in the night, leading away from the Riders' camp.

Theo waited until they were beyond earshot.

"I have never thanked you," he said. Seeing the confusion on Yosef's face, he went on: "For Carthage, and your help there. If not for you, I would still be chained to an oar."

Yosef's face twisted. "If not for me," he said harshly, "you would never have been chained to an oar in the first place. Those scars are my fault."

Theo realised it was not revulsion he had seen on Yosef's face a moment ago. It was self-loathing at the thought that he himself had been the cause of Theo's wounds.

"No." Taken aback, Theo stared at him. "These scars are not your fault, Yosef. The only person to blame for any of this is Oppa."

Yosef shook his head. "If it were not for this journey," he said, "we would both be in Spania still. I would be arguing with my parents about marrying Sarah. And you and Lælia —" Yosef choked on the words.

The thought of what could have been was bittersweet on Theo's tongue. He pushed it away. "Neither of those things would have come to pass." Emotion made his tone curt. "Oppa determined that the day he raped Sarah and killed your parents." He looked steadily at Yosef. "Illiberis has always been Oppa's goal. Perhaps it wasn't so important before the day he saw Lælia in the woods; perhaps he always intended to destroy it. I don't know what drives him, but I do know that none of it – what happened that day in Garnata, the attack on the fleet, Oppa's whip on my face – none of it was your fault."

He gripped Yosef's shoulders. "And we do not have time for self-recrimination, Yosef. Not anymore. Do you understand?"

Yosef nodded, frowning. "What do you need from me?"

"I need to know what you will do," said Theo. "What you plan next."

"What I will do?" Yosef stared at him. "What do you mean?"

Theo stared back, equally confused.

"Where are you going from here?" he asked. "What is your plan? And what am I supposed to do to help you?"

Yosef's eyes were hollow in the darkness. "I can't answer that," he said slowly. "I don't know how I will get to where I am going, nor what the plan is that will take me there. And I don't know when, or how, I will need you."

"Tyr!" In a rush of unaccustomed frustration, Theo's fist drove into the cliff, crumbling rock to the ground below. Yosef, standing close by, didn't flinch. Theo turned away, his chest heaving, confusion and pain blinding him.

There was a long silence.

When Theo spoke again, he could hear the catch in his own voice. "Athanais asked me what message I wanted to send to Lælia." He glanced sideways at Yosef. "There is a dromon nearby, bound for our country. But what could I say?" He gestured angrily at his face, his back. "How can I send messages of love, as if I were unchanged, as if none of this had happened, as if I were the same man who kissed her goodbye and promised to return? But I cannot bear" – he turned away again, struggling to find the words – "I cannot bear for her to think I have forsaken her, broken our vow. Not when it is the only thing that has kept me alive."

"If you return now," said Yosef quietly, "you can tell her yourself. The dromon will leave in a matter of days. Sail with it."

"My promise to Lælia is not the only one I made." Theo laughed harshly. "As Athanais reminded me."

Yosef's mouth tightened. "I do not need Athanais to beg on my behalf. Any promise you made to me is long discharged. I do not hold you to it, and nor do I expect any other to suffer, or die, for this journey. If you wish to return to Spania, Theo, do so with my blessing." He looked closely at Theo. "Is that why you came here tonight? To gain my permission to leave?"

"I don't know why I came here tonight."

Theo stared out over the port below, still teeming with the aftermath of their victory. He looked at Yosef, searching for the words to explain. "During the battle, I felt her. Lælia. As if she were there beside me." Involuntarily, his hand went to the coin and amulet at his neck. "Ever since I left Spania, she has been with me. In my dreams when I slept. Beside me as I rowed. Even when I was in the sea, when I thought I was lost." He stopped, unable to explain what he meant.

"But now we are leaving these shores," he went on eventually. "Sailing to the other end of the Circle of Lands, to places where none know of Spania, or care. Where no word will reach her for months, if not years. To battles I may not survive. How can I send her word that I live, when I do not know for how long? What right do I have to hold her to our promise?"

"I told you." Yosef's tone was harsh. "You can return to her. On the dromon. You will be in Spania within a month."

"And what then?" Theo braced his hands against the cliff, leaning out against it, his head down. "Do I wait for Egica to over-turn our betrothal and insist that Lælia marry his son? Do I murder Oppa in the night? For to accuse him of what I know will cause civil war and the destruction of both our families."

He stared up at Yosef. "Your father and Count Paulus, Lauren-tius and Shukra, despite all they knew of the past, all the secrets they kept, they planned this mission you undertake for a reason. They know that to survive Egica's reign, we must find ways to thrive that are not dependent on the Crown. Now that I have truly seen what Oppa is capable of, what he and his family will do to hold on to power, I know that we must succeed, Yosef. That *you* must succeed. But if we are to do so, we must become smarter than our enemies."

"How do we do that?"

Theo shook his head. "I don't know," he said wearily, and the weight of the unknown seemed to press in upon him with the night. "Athanais told me the fleet was my destiny," he said eventually.

"Do you believe her?"

"Lælia is my destiny."

"Perhaps they both are."

"There is your journey too." Staring into the darkness, Theo shook his head. "I used to think duty was simple. Now it seems impossible."

Yosef's eyes searched Theo's face. "I promised that I would make this journey," he said quietly. "And I swear that I will, Theo. I will make it, and I will return to Spania." He reached out as if he would touch Theo, then let his hand fall away. "But I will not ask any more of you," he said softly. "I won't ask anything of anyone. Not ever again."

Theo reached out his arm, gripping Yosef's tight at the elbow. "I promised you once I would not be the reason your journey failed," he said roughly. "I meant it."

"I do not expect –"

"I know." Theo gave him a twisted smile. "But my promise stands nonetheless."

Yosef gripped his arm tightly. "Go well, Theo."

Theo nodded. "You too, Yosef."

Theo watched him walk away. There was more, perhaps, he could have said, but he knew within himself there was no point.

Good thoughts, good words, good deeds.

Lælia's face swam before his eyes, and he felt his gut twist with longing. He gripped the stone so that it crumbled beneath his fingers. *How do I tell her?* he asked silently. *And how do I live with it?*

A night owl called, and in the distance, the whispers of broken dreams wandered amongst the sands.

50

LÆLIA

DECEMBER AD 688

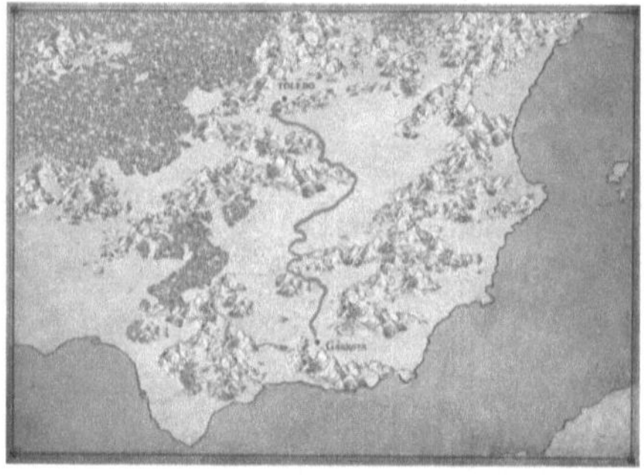

Toletum, Spania
Toledo, Spain

Lælia could feel the presence of the parchment as if it had a life of its own.

The Toletum night was frigid and cold, mist winding up from the river. Beyond the palace men gathered around fires in the taverns, the sound of their wine cups and song muffled by the city stone. Here in the dark and deserted corridors of the royal chambers, the air was cold and still as death, and Lælia shrank against the wall for fear of being seen.

She had shadowed Oppa for days, had searched his horse, and had paid tavern wenches to search his cloak. She had followed him to the brothel by the river, discovered the woman who had birthed him, and in the early hours of the morning when the whores finally slept, had searched every crevice of the property.

What she sought, though, was not there.

Lælia had known it would not be. Oppa would not make such a thing so easy. He would hide his treasures, horde them. But this did not disconcert her. Oppa might be a predator; Lælia was a hunter. He preyed upon the weak; she chose her target and ruthlessly stalked it.

Now she pushed open the heavy wooden door and noiselessly slipped inside. The figure on the wide bed moved restlessly. She became utterly still, part of the shadows cast by the faded city moon through the crack between the shutters. Gradually the figure stilled, the breathing once again becoming deep and regular.

The chest was at the rear wall. After watching for days, she knew where Oppa hid his treasures. The parchment was at the bottom, wrapped in linen and stowed inside a long-forgotten tunic. She slipped it from its wrappings, replaced it with another of similar size, and neatly refolded the tunic. A shaft of moonlight fell across the bed where Oppa lay face up, his face cold and still as stone.

I could kill him. The thought was as savage and immediate as it was unexpected. Lælia's hand went unthinkingly to the knife at her waist. *None would know. He could never marry me. He could never harm any of us ever again.*

She stood over the long, lean form, her hand caressing the blade at her side. In the odd shadows of the night, Oppa's face seemed to flicker and alter: one moment the sharp evil of the man who had held her in the woods, the next an oddly vulnerable boy barely older than herself, dark hair uncharacteristically dishevelled.

Kill him, she told herself fiercely. She had not come here to do so, but now that she was here, his helpless form beneath her, she wondered why she should not. It would end so much. Avenge so much. *Kill him.* She imagined her steel sliding into his heart and knew she was not afraid of it.

He stirred on the bed, his mouth twisting faintly. She felt again the weight of his eyes raking her up and down in Illiberis, remembered that he thought her already his.

No, she thought, stepping back from the bed. *Death is too easy for you.*

She slid through the window like a shadow and landed by Jadis, who lay on her belly on the dark stone below, long tail swishing slowly behind her. At the sight of her mistress, she growled deep in her chest and stretched, front legs out first, then arched her back, her eyes glowing in the dark with a silent question.

Lælia bent in a fluid movement, scratching the cat beneath the chin. "I have it," she said softly, the thrill of spoken word still strange in her throat.

She did not return straight to her aunt's domus. Instead, she flowed through the silent streets to the villa of Laurentius Severianus, who, after his father's death, was custodian of the greatest private library in Toletum. Once there, she went to the large volumes she sought and read until dawn touched the sky, carefully committing the passages to memory. As the light grew, Lælia took quill and ink and carefully, in the blank space beneath her name on the contract of betrothal, wrote: *Lælia Bæticus, Illiberis.*

Then she made her way back to the domus and waited for the day to begin.

51

YOSEF

DECEMBER AD 688

Barca, Tripolitana
Near Benghazi, Libya

Yosef knew it was time to leave. He had known it before the Battle of Barca and certainly afterward. He had known it the night Theo found him in the Riders' camp.

He sat now in the close, steamy atmosphere of the makeshift

desert bathhouse, staring out of the narrow slit between the two camel blankets to the fine points made by stars in the desert sky. The bathhouse was, in reality, no more than camel blankets draped over a wooden frame, surrounding a hole in the ground full of hot rocks. Water cast on these created steam in which the nomads scrubbed themselves down and washed. It was a luxury they had only when a good water source was nearby and they planned to remain in the same camp for more than a night or two.

Yosef tugged the blankets aside and stepped naked into the desert night. The fresh air felt like a benediction on his skin, and he stood with his head back, allowing the night breeze to dry him. It was the new moon, the time when all those of his faith would make Mikvah. Bathing made a connection, no matter how thin, to a past that often seemed utterly insubstantial to Yosef.

He was pulling robes over his head when he heard a noise behind him. He spun around and crouched low, knife in his hand. The new moon had long fallen behind the western horizon and the night was black, lit only by starlight. He frowned at the cloaked figure until the hood was put back and the familiar form of Athanais emerged, grey and indistinct in the night.

"An odd place to seek a man out," grunted Yosef, tightening his belt and sliding his knife back into the scabbard.

"I will sail tomorrow," Athanais said. "We may not meet again, Yosef, not for some time."

"Where do you go?"

"Where I must." The lilt in her voice was for once sombre. "It is time for you to leave the Riders, Yosef. You know this."

He was silent. He knew.

"It is better that you go now. It is dangerous for you to be so close to the fleet for so long. Men seek you. They come closer. You should be gone when they arrive."

Yosef turned his back on her, unwilling to show his face. "I know this."

"Then you know what you must do." She put her hand on his shoulder, gently turning him toward her. "Come, Yosef. We will tell her together."

Yosef allowed himself to be led to Dahiya's tent. It was placed at a distance from the main Riders' camp, not least, he knew, because Dahiya shared it with Apsimar. The commander, too, seemed reluctant to leave Barca. Yosef suspected his decisions were little to do with military matters and everything to do with the woman he so clearly loved.

He paused at a respectable distance before calling a greeting. In the desert, the thin walls of a tent were respected as city walls would be. None would approach without first announcing their presence from a distance.

"Come," said her low voice, and he stepped inside.

Yosef was always impressed by the luxury within Dahiya's tent. Even when travelling light, the embroidered cushions were not sacrificed, nor was the delicately patterned material that lined the roof and walls. Dahiya herself sat cross-legged on neatly arranged camel blankets, her sons on either side. Yosef sat with Athanais on blankets opposite, aware that the tableau was unusually formal and the expressions on the brothers' faces uncharacteristically solemn.

They drank honey and cinnamon flavoured goat's milk from carved cups and ate dates served on an intricately patterned platter. There was in Dahiya's tent the unmistakable sheen of royalty, even here amidst desert, rocks, and war.

"My army must ride on." Dahiya spoke without preamble, looking at Yosef. "However, it is time you continued on your journey."

Yosef bowed his head but did not speak. Though he had known it must come, the thought of leaving Bagay and Khanchla, and the security of Dahiya and her men, seemed lonely and daunting.

Dahiya nodded at Athanais. "Give him what you must."

"I should have been gone long before now." Athanais reached into her cloak. "But I was waiting for these." She withdrew several scrolls. The first was a heavy, rich parchment, marked with unfamiliar characters.

"This," she said, handing it to Yosef, "is a letter of introduction. You must be guarding it with your life, *aziz-am*; the man who issued it is no longer alive, and I will not be having such a chance again. It is addressed to the caliph in Damascus, Abd al Malik bin Marwan, and it will be guaranteeing you reception at his court."

Yosef's eyes widened. "I am to go to Damascus? To the heart of the Arabic court?"

Athanais nodded briskly. "If you are to reach Ērān and Serica, first you must go through the Arabs. Is not being possible to go around. This is the mistake your other people are making before and why they do not pass. For you, Yosef ben Arun, it is time you make alliances with our Arab friends. The future of your people depends upon it."

"Friends?" Bagay and Khanchla reared back, looking between their mother and Yosef, shock and alarm spreading on their faces. "After all these months, even as we engage in battle against Zuhair and his forces, you would befriend those we call our enemy?" Khanchla lowered his head in disgust. "I do not like this business of yours, Yosef."

Again, Yosef thought bitterly, shrinking into himself and dropping his eyes in shame. Must this journey always take from him what mattered the most – Sarah, his home, even the friends he found in foreign lands? Must he always find himself impossibly torn between the task he had been given, those whom he loved, and causes he believed right?

"It is not only Yosef who will be befriending the enemy. You, my sons, will both accompany him to the court in Damascus."

Yosef was so immediately flooded with passionate relief that it took a moment for him to notice the outrage and hurt on his companions' faces.

"You would send us away?" Khanchla looked at his mother in blank incomprehension. "Now, when we have the Arab invaders on the run?"

"Fighters I have," said Dahiya, returning his anger with a level stare. "I do not need to sacrifice my two sons, also, to Altava. No." She held up a warning hand as her sons began to protest. Yosef, seeing the grim set of her mouth, the heat in her eyes, knew that what she said now was far harder than any battle she had fought.

"Your father knows these Arabs." It was so uncharacteristic of her to mention her relationship with Apsimar that Yosef and her sons were shocked into silence. "He knows Abd al Malik. Apsimar says he is smart and determined. He has fought a war with his own people and won. Now it is Africa he desires, and Africa he will take, no matter how many men must be lost to do it."

"Then why fight?" Khanchla flung at her, not trying to hide the hurt in his voice. "Why even bother fighting Zuhair if our cause is lost already?"

"I will fight for Altava until the ground is scorched and there is no kingdom left to fight over." Dahiya struck her chest, her eyes flashing, and even her sons subsided at the fire in her tone. "I will spill my own blood, and you, my sons, I have raised to do the same. But I would ask something else of you now, something of far greater importance than wielding steel in battle.

"We know nothing of this enemy who comes at us with greater and greater strength. The Arabs are not the Greeks or the Romans before them. They follow a different prophet and have different customs and laws, a history and beliefs strange to us. If we are to defeat them – and if we are to find a way through their defences – we must also understand them. And this can happen only by living amongst them, by learning their language and culture."

She looked between Bagay and Khanchla and held out her hands to them in a gesture that both pushed them away and asked for forgiveness. "You are my own blood," she said softly. "The two I trust most in this world. Never must I question your loyalty nor your allegiance. And, far more importantly" – she smiled at them both – "you have inherited my intelligence, so I need never question your understanding of what you see, and I know that you will see what must be known."

The two boys looked at her, their faces changing from hurt and anger to grudging attention and, finally, to reluctant acceptance.

"But how long?" Bagay asked. "For how long must we leave our homeland and live amongst the enemy?"

"The Arabs are coming," Dahiya said quietly. "It is no longer just a question of one force, of one battle. Zuhair is dead, but after him there will be another. And another."

She looked at Yosef. "Those who sent you on this journey believe that with the right wealth, the right connections, you might build a better world. They believe it for your country; perhaps it is true, also, for mine. What I do know is that this" – she gestured beyond the tent to where the remains of the battle still smouldered far below – "does not build a new world. It only destroys the old."

She gave Yosef a hard, strained smile. "When Apsimar first spoke to me of this," she said quietly, "I would not hear him. He asked to take his sons with him when he sails; I could not consent. My sons, I said, belonged here by my side."

"Altava!" said Bagay and Khanchla as one, striking their chests as they would in a war council, looking at their mother with the same unquestioning loyalty that led men in their thousands to follow her.

"But then I thought of you."

Yosef stared at her in confusion. "Me?"

Dahiya nodded. "You, Yosef. You and your scarred friend."

Yosef shook his head. "Why?" he muttered.

"I have ridden far in my life," Dahiya said. "I have met many men and seen acts of bravery and desperation I could not have imagined. But never have I known any who have sacrificed as you and he have done. And yet still you remain. Still you continue. Though you do not know the destination toward which you travel, nor what it will bring when you arrive, you continue because you believe. You believe in it just as I do in Altava."

"But I do not," Yosef whispered, the words hurting his chest as he said them. "I do not know that I believe in anything anymore. Not even my own faith."

Until he said it aloud, he had not known it was true, and the thought itself shook him profoundly.

"And yet still you walk unthinkingly into the future." Dahiya looked at him solemnly. "Do you know why you do so, Yosef?"

Yosef stared at the ground, at the small tracks made by a beetle in the sand in front of his blanket. They wound in intricate patterns this way and that as if completely without reason.

"I know only my allegiance to Theo," he said thickly. "To him and to Lælia, the girl he left behind." He felt his face grimace in a smile. "She is my oldest friend."

As he spoke, he saw Lælia's flashing yellow eyes, her complete absence of fear as she stared down Oppa in the woods, raising her bow with no thought of her own life.

"I know," he said, the words rasping painfully in his throat, "that Lælia would no sooner surrender to fear or an enemy than she would lose her life. And Theo – so many times, Theo could have left this journey, taken a different course. He has left Lælia behind to face enemies worse even than those we faced here at Barca. Men who are ruthless, and merciless in their ambition. And yet still he trusts her." He met Dahiya's eyes. "As Apsimar trusts you.

"Theo, too, has had to learn that faith. If he can find it in himself, if I know that back in Illiberis Lælia will fight whatever comes to our home with that same faith, then who am I to falter and doubt? What kind of man would I be?"

Dahiya nodded, sitting back, a small smile of satisfaction on her face.

"So," she said. "You believe. As must I. As must we all. And if I will not send my sons into the heart of our enemies and believe that they will one day return better men for the experience, men able to lead Altava into the future for which it is destined, then in what do I truly believe?"

Athanais had been silent whilst they spoke. She leaned forward now, looking between Yosef and the brothers. "If you are to do this, *aziz-am*, you must cease to talk of enemies – all of you." At Bagay's sceptical look, she waved a hand in impatient dismissal. "The Arabs burned my homeland," she said. "They destroyed the fire temples of my faith, tore down cities that were built by divine hand centuries beyond memory. They conquered my people and drove my faith into hiding. Do you hear me speak of enemies? No! You are not ever hearing this from my lips, for all enemies are existing only within the soul, never in another person."

Yosef saw even Dahiya look up at that and frown.

Athanais, seeing the incomprehension in their faces, clicked her tongue with impatience. Handing Yosef the other two scrolls, her tone changed and became businesslike. "This one bears the mark of Ahura Mazda, of the Zoroastrian faith. It will be trusted by the Sogdian merchants, who control the passes through the mountains they call the Rooftop of the World, and which lead to the East."

Yosef peered closely at the symbol stamped in the black wax

seal. It looked like the wings of an eagle, with the sun rising from the centre.

"And this" – she held Yosef's eyes – "I believe you know what this signifies." On the second scroll, small but perfectly depicted, was painted the symbol of the silk tree. "You are having no need to search for the person to whom you will be giving this one," she said. "When you reach Chang'an, they will find you. All you must do is gain entry through the gates."

Yosef nodded, swallowing, his heart thudding with a sudden excitement.

"With your permission" – Athanais looked at Dahiya, who nodded – "a word of advice before you travel into what you are seeing as enemy lands?"

Bagay and Khanchla scowled, but under the watchful eye of their mother, turned their attention grudgingly to her.

"Do not be looking at the Arabs as your enemies," said Athanais, addressing all three of them. "Notice instead where their fear is, for there also is their weakness, as it is with all men. See where their love is, and there you will find their strength. Like this, you can work with this force you call your enemy. All that you are exists also in these men. But if you fight their love with your fear, you will always lose, just as if you meet their fear with your love, you will win them. To notice the light and dark in men, you yourselves must be becoming like the wind – no colour at all. Can you do that?"

For a moment, Yosef imagined himself as the wind, free to dance amongst the world of men without being touched by it. "Yes," he breathed. "Yes. I can do that."

"Good." Athanais smiled, her deep brown eyes dancing with secrets that, it seemed to Yosef, only she understood. "When we meet again, Yosef of Spania," she said, "you will know the words of Ahura Mazda – and the way of your own soul."

"You are sons of both Africa and Greece," Dahiya addressed her sons. "Carry the strength of both within you. You will return to me carrying the spirit of yet another world. It is perhaps the greatest gift I can give you, though it is one for which I pay the highest price of all."

The boys bowed in submission, emotion clear on their faces. They moved forward and knelt before her, allowing her to place her hand on their heads in blessing.

"Yosef." She turned to him and bestowed one of her rare smiles. "I wish you good fortune."

Yosef murmured his thanks, his mind already on the road ahead.

The night was clear and cold after the closeness of the tent.

"Well, Jew." Khanchla nudged him roughly. "It seems our pathways run together for more time yet, does it not?"

Bagay slung a friendly arm over his shoulder. "You know what this means, brother, don't you?"

"What?" Yosef felt a warmth steal through his soul at their open willingness to embrace the journey ahead.

"Women," said Khanchla, with round satisfaction. "They say that the palace in Damascus has an entire wing dedicated to housing the caliph's beauties."

"No," said Yosef. "Truly?"

Bagay nodded, rubbing his hands together and grinning. "Pack your belongings, Yosef. We have many miles to ride and a letter that says we will be treated to the caliph's hospitality. Arab or not, I intend to partake of it."

As they walked across the hard ground, bantering together, Yosef felt the darkness recede temporarily. An odd memory crossed his mind, of the piece of silk his father had once shown him, long ago in the cave in Garnata.

It was a gift from a dear friend… if her gods and ours will it, one day you will meet her.

I may yet meet your friend, and see your journey completed, Father, Yosef thought.

In the hem of his cloak, the scrolls felt warm against his body, as if they had a life of their own.

52

LÆLIA

DECEMBER AD 688

Toletum, Spania
Toledo, Spain

Lælia dressed for the King's Council with great care. She sent Riccilo's servant away, latching the door behind her. For this she must ready herself in ways no maidservant could understand.

Tosius had been given his instructions. The horses would be packed and ready in the stable by the palace. If it came to it, Lælia would fight, and she would ride. Either way, she would leave Toletum as Lælia of Illiberis, betrothed to Theudemir of Aurariola, or she would allow her blood to leach into the city stone and her body to grow cold upon it.

She strapped her long hunting knife to her leg and another, shorter, dagger to her arm. She drew on a gown of soft wool dyed midnight blue. It was cut low at the breast, edged in silver, and clung to her form in long, elegant folds. Beneath it she wore tall leather boots in which she could ride if she must. She brushed her hair until it shone and wound it into long, intricate coils piled high upon her head. Amongst the coils she threaded a silver chain that Acantha had gifted her on their return from the caves. A single teardrop sapphire hung from it, a deep piercing blue against the black mass. It had come from Africa, a gift, Acantha said, from a woman who wielded a sword of her own and led men to war.

On the wooden table lay the serpent torc that had once belonged to Lælia's mother. Lælia closed her eyes. The torc felt warm and alive as she slipped it about her neck. The serpent's head snaked down to the cleft between her breasts, and it lay against her skin as if it had been carved to fit her. When she looked at her reflection, the serpent's sapphire eyes stared boldly back.

Lælia barely recognised the tall, regal woman in the warped bronze. She was strong, with a face burnished by the southern sun, and her eyes glittered with a dangerous fire.

A knock came at the door behind her. Lælia stood and swept across the room to open it.

Riccilo stared at her. "Lælia," she breathed.

Lælia remained still for a long moment, then she tilted her chin toward the street and the sounds of men and business.

"You cannot attend," said Riccilo. "The King's Council is a place for men."

Lælia raised her eyebrows but did not answer, just looked at her aunt steadily.

It was Riccilo who looked away first. "If you go," she muttered, "then I must accompany you."

Lælia shrugged. *Come,* she gestured.

When they left, it was Lælia who led the way.

* * *

SCENTING BLOOD, the Toletum nobles had come from near and far. The airy council chamber in the palace was a crush of humanity, all vying for the best position from which to observe the carnage to come. It was a secular council, and there were only two places set on the dais: one for the archbishop, over which hung the rich crown Egica had gifted Julian, and Egica's own throne below the archbishop's, as God had decreed. The regal votive crown hung above the throne, the jewels on it gleaming in the midday sun, casting rainbows across the waiting faces.

The guards at the external entrance moved forward as they approached; then they recognised Riccilo, wife of Theodofred, Duke of Corduba. Their eyes ran curiously over Lælia, but as she was clad in rich gown and jewels and accompanied by Riccilo, the guards stood aside, and they crossed the marble atrium to the council chamber.

They were not the only women there, but they were the only two who entered the chamber alone, and conversation fell silent as they stood at the open doors together. Lælia paused for long enough to stare at the curious faces turned her way. She saw Amalfrida, eyes pale and filled with malice, and stared at her baldly until the blonde girl turned away. She let her gaze sweep over the chamber, meeting all who dared look her way, until she found her grandfather's face, lined and stern as granite, flanked by the tall, blond figure of Theodofred and another man with an oddly familiar face who looked grey and wan. With a shock of surprise, Lælia realised it was Suinthila, Theo and Alaric's father, come to stand before the king.

She swept into the chamber, looking neither left nor right. People fell away as she crossed the wide floor, murmuring to one another as she passed. Lælia ignored them. They mattered as little to her as ever they had.

Count Paulus did not speak, nor did she offer a greeting of any kind. He stepped aside to make room, and she stood between her grandfather and Suinthila as Riccilo came to stand by her husband.

There was a noise at the rear of the hall as Sunifred entered, surrounded by a large party of his thiufa.

Beside her, Suinthila tensed. "Xristus," he muttered. "I told the fool to stay away."

"We all did." Count Paulus's mouth was grim set. "Sunifred has never listened to any but his own counsel."

"You knew he would come?"

"I hoped he wouldn't."

"Alaric is with him." Suinthila paled.

Alaric met his father's eyes and then Lælia's, an odd mix of defiance and guilt in his own. Lælia nodded in acknowledgment. She had known he would be here. Alaric had come because of Theo. In a way, Lælia knew, they had all come because of Theo. Surreptitiously, she touched the knife beneath her gown. She would not marry Oppa even if her refusal meant war. She could not, no matter Alaric's choice, nor who asked it of her.

Sunifred was tall and burly. He had thick, wild, red hair worn in beaded braids and an ugly scar that twisted down his neck and chest. He was a man who had wielded iron and looked ready to do it again. He had the florid colour of a heavy drinker, and his blue eyes were hard and attentive. One large hand gripped Alaric's shoulder possessively, and when he moved through the crowd, he bore the younger man before him as if he held a prize. His eyes were on Bishop Sisebut, who stood on the dais waiting to announce the king.

Lælia recalled Alaric's words the day they had met beneath the tree outside the circus: *Sisebut is encouraging Sunifred's rebellion... once Archbishop Julian is dead, Sisebut will ally the Church to Sunifred's cause.*

Yes, she thought now, watching the bishop's plump hands clutched excitedly before him as he looked out over the congregation. *Sisebut is a man who craves power, whilst Sunifred is a man who foolishly believes he already has it.* Studying their faces, Lælia found herself feeling the weakness that underpinned that alliance. *They are doomed to fail,* she realised. She knew it in the same way she knew that when she rode from Toletum today, she would be changed, set upon a new, different course.

Athanagild, on the dais, was pale faced but composed. His eyes flickered to Suinthila. Lælia remembered Theo telling her once that whilst Suinthila was not Athanagild's father by blood, he had raised him as his own. That relationship, Lælia thought, seemed clear when Athanagild looked to Suinthila, as if he sought his reassurance – or his approval.

Athanagild nodded at an instruction from Sisebut and moved to hold the throne ready. The king's gardingi moved into place before the dais. The rear door opened, and Julian entered before the king.

The archbishop's face was pale, his body thin as paper, but the hollow eyes seemed to blaze with the last of his energy, scorching the crowd before him with an intensity bordering on contempt.

King Egica entered with head bowed, prostrating himself before Julian with every appearance of humility. When he took his throne, however, the jewels above cast a dazzling light upon him, conferring a sense of divinity Lælia knew had been carefully calculated.

Oppa entered after them both. He stood behind and slightly to the side of his father's throne. Their eyes, Lælia thought, had the same hooded, predatory cast. Both father and son were still and dangerous as they surveyed the crowd.

For a moment, Oppa's eyes rested on her. She forced herself to meet them. His upper lip moved in a faint sneer, and she felt resolve coil in her belly. As Egica began to speak, she tore her eyes away but felt the weight of Oppa's remain for some moments before he shifted his attention to his father.

"We have before us," said Egica, forgoing the formalities required by a council of his bishops, "several matters of grave importance." He looked down at a parchment in his hand and would have continued, but a loud voice interrupted him.

"There is only one matter of importance." Sunifred swaggered to the centre of the hall. He did not kneel. "There has been a claim on my land and title before this court for nigh on two years. I rode here to learn the outcome."

Egica regarded Sunifred with contempt. "If you have ridden here – in strength, I note – to force a conclusion, you have made a wasted journey. The matter remains under the consideration of the council and will not be addressed here today."

"It is a simple enough matter," Sunifred went on as if Egica had not spoken. "I am Duke of Hispalis, with rights to all the lands asso-ciated with that title. Frogellus claims he has the right to both. With whom do you believe the right lies, *reiks*? With my family, which is your own wife's family, the descendants of kings, of the very man who united Spania itself? Or with your friend Frogellus, a man who has a weak claim at best?"

"I will not be coerced here, in my own court!" Egica's voice rose and he stood, glaring down at Sunifred, who did not flinch. "You will leave my court, Fráuja, and you will await the judgement of my bishops – and of God – just as we all must."

"God! Tyr!" Sunifred spat.

Those around him recoiled, and on the dais Julian rose, eyes flaming. "You dare invoke that pagan name in this place! Do you consider yourself above the judgement of God, Fráuja?"

"It is not upon God that Egica waits." Sunifred returned Julian's anger, raising one hand to point directly at the archbishop. "It is for your death."

The crowd gasped, and Julian paled.

"Do not think," Sunifred went on, glaring at Egica, "that I do not know you delay this decision until there are none to stand against it." He turned, addressing the crowd, which was hanging avidly on his every word. "But I will wait no longer. Nor will I acknowledge this court's authority over the decision. Hispalis is mine, and I will kill any man who states otherwise."

A roar of unrest swept through the hall, and Sunifred, a mocking smile on his face, stared at Frogellus, who stood close to the dais. "If you wish to take my lands, Fráuja," he said softly, "then you had best gather your thiufae and prepare them for a long fight." He gave Egica a hard look. Then, without waiting for dismissal, he turned and strode from the hall. "Come," he barked at Alaric as he passed.

Alaric hesitated, looking between his father and Sunifred, his face an agony of indecision. Suinthila met his son's eyes but made no move to speak.

"Will you stand there?" Alaric said, his voice low and pained. "My mother is dead. Theo is gone. Oppa plots to take Lælia, and

Illiberis with her." He searched his father's face. "Will you do nothing?" His voice rose. "Even now?"

Suinthila stood with Paulus and Theodofred, all three of them grim faced and silent despite the anger in Alaric's voice.

"If you walk with Sunifred from my hall, Alaric sunau Suinthila," said Egica, his mouth curled in a knowing smile, "you forgo every claim to land or title you may have. I will not permit a known traitor to inherit property or title given by this crown in good faith."

Suinthila stared at his son, hollow eyed.

"Rekiberga," said Alaric, his voice catching on the word. His eyes searched his father's, seeking some kind of sign, but Suinthila remained stony faced. "I love her. She will be my wife, Abba."

Alaric glanced at his brother on the dais, whose face was as stark white as the marble behind him. Athanagild nodded once, a tiny, painful movement of farewell.

At that, Suinthila finally spoke. "What kind of man," he said contemptuously, staring hard at Sunifred, "trades his daughter as bait?"

Sunifred's eyes flashed. He clapped a broad hand on Alaric's shoulder. "Come, Alaric," he said, loudly enough for the entire court to hear. "There is nothing left for you here."

Alaric's eyes hardened as he stared at his father. Then, turning on his heel, he followed Sunifred from the hall.

Lælia could hear the heavy, painful beat of her own heart. From beyond Paulus she heard Riccilo make a low sound of pain and regret.

"It seems" – Egica's voice rang out over the hall before pandemonium could erupt – "that your son, Fráuja Suinthila, has allegiances other than to his family of origin." His eyes slid sideways to Lælia. "And wishes for a wife," he said softly, "other than the one you chose for him."

A rumble swept through the court. Suinthila, grim faced, opened his mouth to speak. Oppa stepped forward. "Twice," he said smoothly, "you have tried to claim Illiberis for your sons, Fráuja Suinthila. First it was claimed its heiress was betrothed to your younger son, Theudemir, then to Alaric, the elder." He stared at

Lælia. "But Theudemir is dead. And Alaric, as we have seen, is gone."

He reached into his tunic and withdrew a roll of parchment sealed in leather.

A deathly stillness fell through Lælia's body, and the chamber slid away. She felt the knife at her leg and the slow pulse of lifeblood. This was it. This was the moment.

"Lælia of Illiberis," he said, "was never truly betrothed to any of your sons, Suinthila of Aurariola." He tore the seal and unrolled the parchment, holding it up to the light. Upon it, Theo's name was marked. In the space where Lælia's should have been, there was nothing.

Count Paulus strode forward, his eyes flashing. "It matters not what lies upon that document, Oppa Egicason. The betrothal was done in my own presence and that of witnesses." He glanced up at the dais, and Athanagild stepped forward.

"I witnessed the betrothal," he said.

Shukra came to stand beside Count Paulus. "I, too, witnessed the betrothal and the signing of the contract."

At Shukra's words, Count Frogellus stepped forward, his teeth bared in an unpleasant smile. "This man," he said, pointing at Shukra, "may wear the uniform of the emperor, but he is no friend of Spania and has no respect for our laws. I do not accept him as witness."

Lælia thought of the long-ago day on her father's drill ground when Shukra held a knife to Frogellus's throat. Looking at Frogellus's sneering smile, it was clear that the count, too, had not forgotten – nor forgiven – that insult.

Oppa wore a faint smile. "And these, Count Paulus, are your witnesses," he said sardonically. "You offer a foreigner who has no knowledge of our laws, nor allegiance to our soil, and a man who has as much to lose as his brother. Neither can be deemed reliable."

He turned away in dismissal and then went on: "To quote our own book of law: *No woman may be married without her consent.* As you can see, Count Paulus, your daughter did not sign the contract." He looked around at the chamber, his smile becoming wide and unpleasant. "And as we are all aware, she cannot give her consent verbally. My father, the *king*," he said with pointed emphasis, "has granted me permission to marry Lælia of Illiberis, not once, but twice now. I come before you today, Your Grace" – he bowed deferentially to Archbishop Julian – "to ask respectfully that you bless our marriage and formalise it here before all the nobles of our country."

Lælia felt her grandfather surge forward angrily. She put a restraining hand on his arm and shook her head: *No.* Stepping forward, she drew a deep breath and stared up at the dais.

"You are wrong," she said.

The words felt hot and uncomfortable in her throat, and for a moment Lælia had thought they would not come at all, but when she saw the sea of faces turn to her and the shock in Oppa's eyes, she knew it was done. "I am more than able to verbalise my consent."

The words in her mouth tasted like freedom.

"I gave my consent to the marriage to Theudemir of Aurariola then, as I give it now."

Reaching inside her own tunic, she withdrew the parchment she had removed from Oppa's chamber the previous night and held it up in full view of the chamber.

"As you see," she said, "the contract of betrothal is here, with me, where I have held it since the day I gave my word I would marry Theo, and I will carry it until the day I die. I give it to you, Your Grace" – she handed the parchment to Archbishop Julian – "to attest to the signatures you find there."

"She is lying!" Oppa stared at her, high points of colour on his cheeks, dark eyes flashing dangerously. "That must be a forgery –"

"No." Lælia's voice was low and sure, and it stilled his protests with the finality of water on flame. "The contract you hold is the forgery, Oppa Egicason. I do not know by what means you contrived it, but I assure you" – she turned to face the assembled nobles – "it will stand no scrutiny."

At the archbishop's gesture, Oppa stepped forward, staring at the contract as he handed it over. Lælia saw his face slowly pale as he looked more closely at the writing upon it, and she felt a savage stab of triumph.

Archbishop Julian frowned as he scrutinised the two documents side by side. "The name is made ill on this," he said, looking closely at Oppa's. "It is indistinct, the characters blurred so as to render it unreadable, and the writing itself done in one hand only." He held up the other document. "It is plain that this is the original; it bears three separate hands. Child" – he beckoned Lælia forward – "will you write your name, so all may see what is your hand?"

Taking the quill from his scribe, Lælia leaned forward and signed her name with the same simple, long strokes that covered the contract of betrothal that she had stolen back from Oppa and signed last night.

Julian held up the contract next to the example she had just given for all the chamber to see. "They are quite the same," he said unnecessarily.

Julian turned to Athanagild. "You," he said, "are clerk to Bishop Sisebut himself, are you not?"

Athanagild nodded. "Yes, Your Grace."

"Will you swear here, in this place, under fear of God himself, that you witnessed this betrothal?"

Athanagild nodded. "I will."

"And you." Julian turned to Shukra. "You wear the emperor's uniform and served in his highest office. Will you likewise swear, as a man of the Empire who fights under the sign of God himself, to this betrothal?"

Shukra nodded. "I will."

"It matters not." Oppa's eyes glittered dark and hard. "Theudemir of Aurariola is dead; I saw the wreckage of the fleet with my own eyes."

Lælia gave a contemptuous laugh. "That you saw the wreckage," she said, "I have no doubt. But will you stand here, Oppa son of Egica the king, before God, your father, and all others and swear that you saw Theudemir of Aurariola's dead body?"

In the charged silence that met her words, Oppa became still, his eyes twin points of anger that bored into her.

"*No woman,*" Lælia quoted softly, "*in the absence of her husband, shall have liberty to marry another man.*"

"You would dare," said Egica in a cold voice, leaning forward, "quote the *Lex Visigothorum* here, amongst the very men who wrote it?"

"Allow me." Oppa cut across the conversation, ignoring Julian's darkening expression. "I had thought it might come to this, though I had expected it from you, Fráuja Paulus, not the child in your care."

Lælia's grandfather, arms folded, stared flatly back at him.

"Shall I read you the relevant passage from the *Lex Visigothorum*? You will find it in Book Three, I believe." Without waiting for permission, Oppa began to quote: "*No woman, in the absence of her husband, shall have liberty to marry another man*" – he raised a finger to emphasise the next line – "*until she has learned, by certain evidence, that her husband is dead, and he, also, who wishes to marry her, must make diligent enquiry for that purpose.*

"I can assure you, Fráuja," said Oppa, smiling coldly at Paulus, "that I have made the most diligent of enquiries. From Septem to Carthage, in fact."

His eyes roamed her form with a slow, sickening intimacy that would once have crushed her chest with impotent frustration. Lælia inhaled deeply into the part of herself where the wind dwelled. When she spoke, the words fell with ice-cold clarity.

"Your diligence notwithstanding, Fráuja," she said, "you have neglected a second – and most pertinent – part of that passage." She turned to Archbishop Julian. "With your permission, Your Grace, of course?"

A faint smile passed across the archbishop's stern features. He made a slight gesture of assent.

"*But if they should neglect to do this,*" Lælia quoted, "*and should be unlawfully married, and afterward the former husband should return, they shall both be delivered up into his power to be disposed of at his will, and he shall have the right to sell them or do whatever he pleases with them.*" She quoted the passage directly, needing no paper for reference, as she held Oppa's eye.

"I would return to your studies," she said coldly, "and research previous occasions on which the law has been applied. You will find, I believe, that it is customary to not only wait the full twelvemonth before declaring a man dead but to also have witnesses who will verify his death."

"A twelvemonth has passed." Oppa spat the words without any pretence of civility.

"Perhaps." Lælia's mouth twisted in a hard smile. "But more than one soldier has left Spania to fight abroad and been given up for dead only to return years later, as men here in this chamber can attest. The seas are dangerous, as you yourself said. And aside from you, Fráuja Oppa" – she raised her eyebrows and looked about the chamber – "are there any here who can claim to be witness to the death of Theudemir of Aurariola?"

In the silence that fell, Oppa's eyes turned to Nicalo, who stood at one side of the chamber, his dull, heavy face partly in shadow; he met Oppa's eyes and his own slid away.

Lælia felt a surge of fierce exultation. *He will not do it*, she thought. *He is afraid that one day he will stand before this same council, this time with Theo's sword at his throat.*

"Your Grace." She turned to the archbishop, who was watching her now with open amusement. "Will you give the Church's ruling on this matter?"

Egica leaned forward. "Your Grace," he began.

"Respectfully." Archbishop Julian held up his hand without looking in Egica's direction. The king fell silent, but the eyes that watched Lælia were brittle with rage.

"I once met your grandmother," the archbishop said, looking at Lælia. "She stood before me in this chamber and demanded justice for a wrong done against her family." His eyes bored into Lælia's. "Against you, child," he said softly.

Lælia swallowed hard.

"I could not give her what she asked." The deep caverns of his eyes dismissed Oppa, then rested upon the king himself. "But this I can. This is law, argued as any woman of Mater Spania has the right to argue before a council of her peers, using laws designed, as you yourself said, *reiks*" – he turned to Egica – "by men in this very chamber."

He turned then to Paulus. "Your granddaughter," he said, "remains entrusted to your care until such time as her intended husband should return or we should determine his death."

Amidst the clamour of excited conversation and the twin stares of rage emanating from the king and his son, Lælia turned to her grandfather. "My horse is outside," she said quietly. "And Tosius waits with a *decania* of men. I will ride from Toletum now, today, for home."

Count Paulus stared at her for a long moment, then the craggy old face broke into a smile. "I will ride with you, child," he said.

53

THEO

DECEMBER AD 688

Barca, Tripolitana
Near Benghazi, Libya

"Why we stay here?" grumbled Leofric as they gathered wood from the sparse scrub near Barca. "Surely the emperor has other battles to fight. We are no more than nursemaids for a city already won."

"He stays to hold on to the memory of his woman," said Silas, white teeth flashing in the dusk. "None of us sail willingly from the shores of those we love." He glanced at Theo, who did not meet his eye.

Leofric made a dismissive noise. "Al Kahinat is gone," he said. "It helps no one to hold on to what is already lost."

He, too, cast his eyes to Theo, his gruff manner unable to mask his concern.

Theo moved away from his companions and onto the higher ground. He had been avoiding their eyes, and their questions, for days now. If Apsimar lingered in Barca, Theo, too, welcomed the delay. Every moment they stayed on these shores was another day he avoided the betrayal he could not bear to think of.

The dromon to Spania would sail that evening. He wanted it gone, and he longed to run to it.

Yosef had left. One day during training, Theo had looked up at the tall cliffs above the cove to see three figures silhouetted on the ridge, robed and veiled as the men of the desert rode. They were mounted on camels, watching the activity below, unnoticed by any but Theo. For a long moment, he had stared at them with the oddest sensation that they, too, were searching for him. Then one of the figures, slowly and clearly, raised his arm. Perhaps it was the nature of the gesture, so uncharacteristic for the impassive nomads of the desert, that told Theo instantly it was Yosef. Standing on the prow of the dromon, Theo had raised his own arm, returning the salute, and held it. His heart was constricted with a bittersweet pain, for even as he longed to throw down his tools and race for the clifftop, he knew the gesture for what it was – one of farewell.

Finally, the robed figure nodded, then all three turned and rode away. Yosef's journey, then, continued. Athanais, too, had sailed.

Who are you to be deciding who matters and who does not, which promise matters and which does not?

Her words echoed in his mind long after she had sailed, and Theo felt no closer to reconciling them than he had the night they were spoken. The thought of Oppa riding to Illiberis made every muscle in his body taut with rage and lent a fury to his sword arm, which had moved Leofric on more than one occasion to remind him, mildly, that it was not necessary to slay his own companions in the effort to improve his skill.

Yet he and Yosef were tied by more than just words. They were joined, now, by the savagery they had witnessed and the life they had shared, albeit separately, so far from home. There had been a poignant courage in the farewell gesture from the cliff. Theo, no matter how he tossed and turned at night, could not forget the measure used by both Shukra and Athanais: good thoughts, good words, good deeds.

To leave, Theo knew, could never, for him, be a good deed. Nor could he forget the Battle of Barca, the manner in which Dahiya had ridden into the midst of men and war, shrieking her defiance, or Athanais's words: *You assume that Lælia waits, helpless, for your return. For your rescue.*

Theo knew he must trust Lælia to find her path, no matter how it screamed against his every instinct. Knowing it did not make composing a message to her feel any less than a betrayal. If he chose the fleet only because of Yosef, Theo thought, he could at least say it was duty.

But he was an honest enough man to know the fleet was more than that. Following Apsimar was more than that. Theo wanted the seas and shores ahead just as much as he wanted Lælia beside him, and it was this that made his message hard to write, for whilst he could forgive himself for abandoning Lælia for duty, he did not know how to tell her he left to follow his heart – and he loved her too much, he knew, to lie.

Theo realised he was gripping the wood so hard it had cut into his palm.

"*Wenkai!*" Silas's hiss in his ear made Theo drop the wood and spin, spatha in hand, looking around warily.

What is it? he gestured. Leofric had already disappeared inside the sparse camouflage of a thin desert bush, and Silas was low to the ground, a dark, motionless shadow. The big man nodded imperceptibly to the ridge on their right. Riding down it, mounted on Illiberis's finest horses, were Giscila and three of his crew. They were obviously looking for someone.

"Do not move," murmured Silas beneath his breath, then made

a low noise of frustration as Theo stood and walked out of the shallow cover to stand in plain sight.

"What are you doing?" hissed Leofric furiously. "Get down!"

But an odd recklessness had overtaken Theo. Destiny called, and Giscila's presence here seemed in some way a part of that, another thread in the odd tapestry of events that had brought him to here. He touched the woven cord about his neck and stepped forward.

"Fráuja," he said formally, the Gothic word clumsy and unfamiliar on his tongue after so long in the Greek-speaking fleet.

Giscila eyed Theo suspiciously. His face bore livid red welts that, although nowhere near as bad as the ravages wrought upon Theo's own, were unmistakably Oppa's handiwork.

"No man should have survived that," Giscila muttered by way of greeting, staring at the hard ridges cutting across Theo's face. He hawked and spat uncomfortably.

"And yet," Theo said curtly, "here we both are."

He stared at Giscila until the other lowered his eyes.

You killed my mother. The words hovered on Theo's lips. He could taste them on his tongue. To speak them would mean steel and death, justice for his family, and revenge for the years of lonely silence where a mother should have been. Theo caressed the sword at his side. Something of what he felt must have shown in his eyes, for Giscila looked about nervously and said, "Oppa bade me find you."

"Did he send you to kill me?" Theo asked calmly. "Because I assure you, Oppa's handiwork will seem like child's play next to Apsimar's fury, should our *droungarios* discover the man who was responsible for the loss of his recruits."

Giscila's eyes narrowed and darted to either side before he reassured himself that they were alone.

"But Apsimar is not here," he said eventually. "And I have a dozen men behind me. You would not have time to scream before I cut your throat – and theirs, too," he said, nodding to Silas and Leofric, who had taken up position behind Theo, swords in hand, eyeing the landscape warily.

"You did not come here to kill me." Theo looked at Giscila without fear.

"You hope," muttered Leofric behind him.

"Why don't you tell me what you came for?"

"You know why I'm here." Giscila's eyes cut over Theo to the city below. "I want the Jew. Tell me where he is, and we will let you play at war with your friends."

"And if I do not?"

"What do you care?" Giscila's face hardened, and he spat to one side. "If you wanted Spania, and your little whore, you would have returned there by now. You are a man without honour, just as I am. A man who fights for coin and is willing to kill for it too, although I promise you, I pay better than the fleet."

Silas hissed behind him. Theo made a low gesture of warning with one hand, unseen by Giscila.

"And if I tell you what you wish to know," said Theo, his voice dangerously low, "you will pay me a share of this treasure you believe you will find?"

Giscila, clearly wary of a trap, nodded slowly.

"*Ja.* Ask any of my men. I pay what I say I will."

"Then I have a condition," said Theo, ignoring the mutinous rumblings from Leofric behind him.

"I am listening," said Giscila, his eyes glinting with avarice.

"Oppa."

Giscila's eyes narrowed.

"You will send word to him that I live. You will ensure he finds the fleet. Finds me."

Giscila stared at him for a moment.

"After what my nephew did to you," he said slowly, his eyes once again landing pointedly on Theo's face, "you would wish for more?"

"My back is much worse than my face," said Theo conversationally. "I wash in private, so men do not ask and women do not cry. In the streets, children run from me, believing I am a demon sent to torture them. Would not you, in my place, wish for a chance at revenge?"

Giscila considered him. "Oppa wants you dead," he said finally. "He is a dangerous man. And we did not part on good terms."

"Then perhaps I will earn more from you than just coin when

he finds me," said Theo. "It will benefit you, will it not, to see him dead?"

"If Oppa finds you," said Giscila with certainty, "you will die."

"You will allow me to disagree." Theo gave him a thin smile. "Oppa has tried to kill me many times. Thus far he has not succeeded. Nor has he discovered the whereabouts of the other he seeks."

Giscila nodded, but he was staring at Theo in a way that implied he wasn't listening.

"Your name," he said. "It is Aurariola."

Theo raised his eyebrows. "You know of it?" It took all his restraint to keep his voice steady.

Giscila gave him a searching look. "Perhaps," he muttered, lowering his eyes and spitting to one side. "Long ago."

You murdered my mother.

Theo forced himself to meet Giscila's eyes, keeping all trace of his thoughts carefully buried. "If you do as I say," he said softly, "I can ensure you discover riches beyond anything Oppa may have promised. And I assure you, Oppa will not live to punish you for taking them."

Giscila's expression turned from cynicism to one of grudging admiration. "You're a hard bastard," he said, nodding. "But I think I understand you. And I believe we are now speaking the same language, *ne?*" Giscila glanced over Theo's shoulder. "Your companions, though, may not agree."

"They will do as I command," said Theo flatly. "I've saved their lives more than once."

He felt Leofric's indignation behind him and stifled a smile. It would take more than a jug of wine to soften that particular blow.

Giscila chewed his lip for a moment, considering him. Then he nodded. "*Ja.* So. I will send for my nephew." He looked at Theo. "Where do I tell him to go?"

"Tell him to follow the fleet," said Theo.

Giscila smiled unpleasantly. "We have already followed the fleet; I went to Carthage, and now here I am in Barca, with the fleet once more. But not a trace of your Jew have I found. You will need something better, for I know he does not travel with you."

Theo tilted his head to one side. "Not a trace?"

Uncertainty showed briefly on Giscila's face.

Theo nodded. "You heard rumours, did you not? In the market at Carthage? And again, other rumours that led you here?"

"Rumours are not enough." Giscila's tone was harsh. "None can tell me on which dromon he sailed, with whom, or to where. I have paid good coin in every port from Septem to here, for nothing more than whispers. He has been seen, yes. But he is like a ghost – seen and then gone again."

"If you cannot find him," said Theo, "then neither can those who would stop his journey. Whispers mean Yosef succeeds and prospers, which we need him to do if we are to profit from his endeavours. Eventually, however, he will need to return home. And when he does, he will need the fleet." Theo held Giscila's eyes. "He will need me."

"Then the Jew follows you?"

Theo shrugged. "Let us say only that our fortunes were once tied and that Yosef believes them still to be. But now, as you say, I am a man with no country." He touched his face. "A man with nothing to return to. This" – his gesture incorporated the sea before them – "is my home now. And I intend to make my fortune upon it."

He stared at Giscila with hard eyes. "I did not say I would tell you when you would find him. Even I do not know that. Yosef is a Jew, and his people hold their secrets close. But if he lives, eventually he must find the fleet – and me – if he wishes to return home. And when he does, the riches he holds will be far greater than any in his possession now. Follow the fleet, follow me, and eventually you will discover him."

Giscila returned his stare. "And what do you suggest I tell Oppa? He wants you dead, told me to send word when I found you."

Theo's mouth twisted. "Oppa does not want you to kill me. He wants to enjoy that himself, and he wants what I know. Do as he asked. Send word. Tell him I live. Tell him you know where to find Yosef. Tell him you have the evidence he needs to condemn Count Paulus of Illiberis. Oppa will come, faster than you can sail."

Theo took a step closer to Giscila, who watched him warily.

"Make certain that Oppa finds me," he said softly. He touched the hard, rigid scars on his face. "And remember this: his life belongs to me."

Theo watched Giscila ride away, fist clenched hard on the hilt of his sword.

I could have killed him. He thought of his brothers, imagined Alaric's blind fury if it had been him with their mother's killer in sword length. He imagined Lælia, and what she might do if she found herself standing before the man who had left her an orphan. Then he thought of Yosef's face, shuttered and wary, facing an unknown future with nothing but faith.

Forgive me, he thought despairingly. *I know of no other way to do what I must.* He looked down at the Spanish dromon in the harbour. *I know what message I will send.*

* * *

THEY SAILED EARLY the next morning.

"So, you are coming with us after all."

Theo watched Barca's shoreline recede before him and touched the cord at his neck. "*Ja*," he said. "I am coming with you."

"And will you be taking that whoreson's gold at the other end of our journey?" Leofric's tone was conversational, but there was no denying the steel beneath it.

Theo grinned. "What do you think? Do you think I like the feel of Giscila's gold in my hand?"

Beside him, Silas gave a grunt of laughter.

"You sounded very convincing, *schnecke*," said Leofric, though the steel was gone from his tone.

"I hope so." Theo leaned back into his stroke.

"And this is all you say to us?" Leofric yanked his oar, earning a frown from the kentarchos. "For weeks you are silent, making life very difficult, I might say. You face a man who tried very hard to kill us and tell him that you will betray your friend in return for his gold. Then you ask that the man who tortured you for months should come to find you. I am not certain, *schnecke*, that travelling in your company is something a wise man would choose."

"You should be happy," Theo said. "I hear we are bound for ports in the East that are home to enough whores that even you should find one to tolerate your ugly face."

The men guffawed, and Leofric clouted him over the head without missing a stroke.

They bantered as they rowed, and only when a lively discussion erupted over the various merits of whores did Silas address Theo under cover of the men's laughter.

"What if Oppa does not take your bait?"

Theo's face grew grim. "I must trust that he will."

"It is a big gamble, *wenkai*."

"But one that is taken now," said Theo, putting an end to it. Silas glanced at him, but seeing his face, he did not argue.

"This journey," said Silas, changing tack, "that your friend makes. You resent it, then?"

"No." Theo looked at him in surprise. "I don't resent the journey, or Yosef for making it; I admire him."

"Then what angers you?"

Theo was quiet, pulling the oar whilst the men about him laughed amongst themselves. Silas was right; anger had sat like a silent companion on his shoulder for weeks now. He had meant it when he said he did not resent Yosef. The anger was something else, something sad and painful that no amount of training or rowing could seem to undo.

He considered telling Silas that Giscila was the man who had murdered his mother. But the secret seemed too big, and too painful, to place in the dromon amongst the men who had become his companions. To explain why he had not killed the man when the chance presented was even more complicated.

Theo wondered sometimes if even he truly understood why he had let Giscila live. He could not entirely explain it. He knew only that he was caught in a great game, one in which the pieces seemed to move slowly, yet with a certain precision even he must obey. Giscila was destined to die at the hands of those he had wronged. This much Theo knew.

But not yet.

"You sent Lælia a message, did you not? With the dromon?"

He nodded, his hand rising instinctively to his throat to touch the cord, then falling away again. Silas's eyes widened.

"You sent her the coin," he said.

"I sent the coin as proof I live."

They rowed in silence for a time.

"With what message?" Silas said eventually.

Theo frowned at him.

"*Wenkai*," said Silas, undaunted. "A woman waits. For more than a year, she waits. Surely you send her more than a coin."

Theo smiled grimly. "I told her," he said, "what she would trust."

Silas shook his head. "They say Goths have not a romantic bone in their bodies. I begin to believe this is true."

"Ah," came an amused voice from the dromon beside them, "but they also say Goths can swing a sword better than any man in the Circle of Lands."

Theo looked up to find Apsimar astride the prow of his dromon, grinning at him. The commander raised a metal cup from which he was clearly drinking wine despite the early hour. "I see you made your choice, Spaniard."

Theo hauled his oar through the water. "I did."

"Good." Apsimar toasted him. "I have plans for you, Aurariola."

"Xristus," muttered Leofric under his breath. "That is all we need – for Apsimar to make you his hero."

"I heard that, Slav." Apsimar threw a *guerba* through the air, and Leofric caught it squarely. "Wine, to keep you happy. It is your job to ensure he does not die."

"Ha," Leofric growled, but his face was pink with pleasure. "No man has enough hours in the day for such a task."

"Where do we go?" Silas called, white teeth grinning at Apsimar.

Apsimar laughed into the wind, holding his cup high. "To war, my friend," he said. "To whatever war needs us."

His men roared their approval, and the dromon surged ahead, Apsimar grinning as he passed them.

Theo realised he had not given Silas an answer to his earlier question. "I do know one thing," Theo said to Silas as he watched Apsimar pass. "When we fought at Barca, my anger was gone."

"Ha!" Leofric leaned forward and clapped him on the shoulder. "Then this is good. We are sailing to Apsimar's wars, and Apsimar loves to fight. You will have much time ahead to use your anger in service of the emperor, *ne?*"

Theo grinned. "Are you sure you trust me after I offered to take Giscila's gold?"

"Pah!" Leofric swiped the air, making his oar jump. "But still, how will you deal with Giscila, when day comes for you to deliver what you promised?"

Theo tilted his head as he rowed. "That is something we will have time to work out."

"Oh," said Leofric, nodding knowingly. "So, it is 'we', now, *schnecke*, is it?"

Theo looked between them: Silas with his shiny bald head and slightly crazed smile, Leofric scarred and hairy with a glare that sent many packing before he had so much as spoken. "It has always been 'we'," Theo said quietly. "It always will be."

The noise about them faded, and the three men looked at one another, the sea stretching before them in a glittering expanse. Then Silas laid his large hand on Theo's shoulder, and Leofric clouted him over the head. They fell into rhythm, and the dromon moved away from the shore, into the unknown.

54

OPPA

JANUARY AD 689

Toletum, Spania
Toledo, Spain

When the summons to his mother's brothel arrived, Oppa was surprised. He dressed carefully, swallowing the dread in his throat. His father was not a man to forgive mistakes.

He arrived by the back entrance, as he always had, and made his way along the darkened corridors. Nobody came this way. It was his secret. Oppa found himself wondering if perhaps it might be time to take his secrets and run. He touched the knife beneath his cloak, but he knew it was a senseless gesture. If his father wanted him dead, no knife would save him. He knocked, and when his father's voice bid him enter, he did.

"You told me Theudemir of Aurariola was dead."

Oppa felt a faint chill down his spine. His father's tone was calm, conversational almost. Egica was standing in front of the fire, staring into the flames. His hair was slicked back from his face, and light flickered over the predatory features.

Oppa cleared his throat. "He was all but dead when I last saw him. And there has been no trace since. Not in Carthage nor Septem."

"Septem." Egica repeated the word in the same bland tone. "The port ruled by Ilyan, a man who conspires with our enemies."

Egica's voice was as smooth as the fine wool of his tunic, which fell in neat folds to polished boots. The gold cuffs on his wrists glowed, and the eagle fibula at his sword belt was so richly decorated that the stones shone a rainbow on the wall.

Oppa lowered his head, hiding his resentment.

"And where did Giscila go after leaving you?"

"I ordered him to Carthage. He said he would await your orders."

"He said." Egica tapped a parchment against the mantelpiece. "Just as you said my enemies were dead. And yet it appears you both lie.

"He writes to tell you he has met Theudemir son of Suinthila." Egica held up the parchment. "That Theudemir does, indeed, live – thrives, even, in the service of the fleet. And not only does he live, but the Jew, Yosef ben Arun Radhan, does too." He tapped the parchment menacingly, glaring at his son. "The Jew you assumed lost."

Oppa swallowed heavily.

"I sent you to the south," Egica said. "I gave you gold and the resources of our family. You had only two tasks: to discover evidence of the alliance between Illiberis, Garnata, and Septem; and to kill those who would bear witness against us." He stared directly into his son's eyes. "You failed in both tasks."

The colour had fled Oppa's face. He tried not to watch his father's hand, still resting on the whip at his side. He knew from personal experience how quickly that hand could draw blood.

"No, I am not going to kill you." Egica's mouth curled in contempt. "You do not deserve a quick death, and you can be of no further use to me dead. Come."

Abruptly, he turned from the fire and strode to the chest Laurentius had brought from Ilyan long ago to fund the restoration of the fleet.

"I have already said that I have no intention," he said coldly, "of wasting good coin on a fleet to protect us from a threat that does not exist. Particularly when that fleet is created and manned by my enemies."

Oppa frowned. "The Arabs are a real threat. I have seen their armies, Father. I –"

"The Arabs are godless savages, as are the barbarians of Africa." Egica's flat dismissal halted Oppa. "They will never launch an attack on Mater Spania – they know they could never prevail."

His father's unequivocal rebuttal stunned Oppa into silence. He thought of Zuhair and the army that had marched across Africa as he left those shores. Could his father truly be so blind as to believe Spania immune from that might? Behind the bland mask of respect that he showed his father, Oppa's mind was racing. *If my father does not see the Arabic threat,* he thought, *what else does he not see?*

Egica, however, gave him no time to ponder the question.

"You will take this chest," he said, nudging it with his foot. "You will use part of it to buy horses – as many as you can – from Illiberis. After Sunifred's performance today, Paulus will not dare refuse you." His mouth tightened briefly, then he went on. "Armies always need horses. You will bypass Ilyan's court. It is better if he does not know our plans. You will go to the fleet and ingratiate yourself with this Apsimar, or whoever it is who leads the fleet. Make him a gift of Illiberis horse and assure him that he has an ally in Spania's king. Do whatever you must to create a place for yourself in his company and with anyone else who holds power. The Karabisianoi will become your home. You will know every piece of terrain upon which it fights and every man who fights for it."

The careful illusion of sophistication fled as Egica came closer. Oppa could smell the wine and rage on his sour breath, feel the heat of his wrath.

"You will wait, and watch, and plan, and when the Jew returns to find his Illiberis friend, you will murder them both. But not before you have discovered with whom they conspire across the water, and every detail of their business – and turned the remainder of that chest to a profit that will benefit this family and our hold on power."

Egica put both hands about his son's neck, tightly enough that Oppa flinched.

"You will murder them yourself," he said softly. "With your own hands. You will tear their bodies to pieces and watch them die. For if either of them ever returns to these shores" – he fixed his eyes upon his son, and Oppa shrank from the rage he saw in them – "they will come with knowledge that will destroy all we have built here. That cannot happen. If you dare return to me with this undone" – his hands tightened – "then it will be your body that is torn to pieces. I will see to it myself."

He stared at Oppa for a long moment, then shook him hard and released him.

Oppa's hand went up to his neck. He stood still, heart thudding, watching Egica's back. Eventually he spoke. "Giscila is not always biddable." Oppa chose his words carefully. "The more I know about him, the easier it may be to work with him."

Egica raised a silent eyebrow.

"Why, exactly, was he exiled?" Oppa asked bluntly. "You have never told me the details."

"Giscila," said Egica flatly, "made mistakes. He was sent to enact a plan. Instead he acted from passion and jealousy. When one allows emotion to rule, mistakes result." He eyed his son. "I would advise you not to make the same mistakes. Not unless you, too, wish to spend the remainder of your days picking scraps from shipwrecks."

"What mistakes?"

Oppa saw his father's eyes narrow, but he stood his ground. Something flickered in Egica's eyes.

"My uncle," said Egica eventually, "was supposed to ensure Callista of Illiberis's husband died in such a way none would suspect foul play. He would then take Callista to Tuy, to our family's lands. Once there, reaved and ravaged, none could have gainsaid their marriage. Illiberis would have been ours. There might have been some talk, for a while, perhaps; but it would have died down soon enough." His mouth hardened. "Instead, the fool murdered the entire household. In doing so, he destroyed all I had worked to achieve."

His eyes gleamed, and Oppa stared at him. "You planned it," he said, unable to hide his surprise.

"Of course I planned it." His father made an impatient gesture. "Giscila loved her. From the moment he first laid eyes on the pagan bitch, he loved her. And the fool would have done anything to win Wamba's respect." His face grew ugly. "Giscila was my father's brother, but he had none of his intelligence. He did not understand, as my father did, that Wamba would never accept either of them. Nor did he understand that power must be taken, not begged for. Wamba had long turned his back on his family and given his allegiance to the south. He would never have accepted Giscila, just as he never forgave my father, even though my father fought only to restore what had been taken from our family. Wamba had long become Chindasuinth's creature, feeding from the same hand that took the crown from Tulga, my grandfather." His eyes were dark with old bitterness. "But if Giscila had at least succeeded in marrying Callista, none, not even Wamba, could have denied him the right to take Illiberis by law."

He shook his head, as if dismissing the past. "As it was, I used his failure twofold. By ensuring Giscila fled into exile, I saved my uncle Wamba from facing the trial of a second traitorous brother, so soon after my own father's disgrace. I earned his gratitude, and my place at court. I also made Giscila into a loyal servant, completely dependent on my goodwill, and ready for when the time came to use him." He looked at his son. "I gave you enough knowledge to manipulate him. Perhaps I should have trusted you with the whole."

"If she died," Oppa said, still intent on understanding the story of Callista's death, "why does her daughter live still?"

"Because Callista got away," Egica said flatly. "And took her whelp with her – along with that bastard Aurariola. Illiberis has kept that secret ever since, waiting to use it against us."

When Egica turned to face him, the rage of earlier was gone. In its place was a cold, ancient hatred that chilled his son far more than the hands on his neck had done.

"Knowledge in the wrong hands is a weapon. If we do not break those who hold it, eventually they will break us."

He gripped Oppa tightly. "I am close to breaking the south. You are the only person I trust to represent our family abroad, to do what must be done to ensure our hold on power is never again threatened. Can I rely upon you, this time, to do what I ask?"

Oppa nodded. "I will not fail you again," he said, holding his father's eyes.

"I know you will not." Egica released him. "And this time, when you return, the south will be broken."

"And Lælia will be mine."

Egica smiled grimly. "If you still want her – then, yes. I will see you wed to Illiberis."

They gripped arms tightly.

"Remember," said Egica. "Return with our enemies dead, and what I ask for accomplished, or do not return to Spania at all."

EPILOGUE

LÆLIA

April AD 690
One year later

The messenger arrived as the first figs grew and winter blazed into spring. Lælia had returned from taking the herd high to graze when she saw the unfamiliar horse in the stables.

Not all messages spell doom, she told herself. Taking her time, she unsaddled the horse, trying to ignore the rapid pace of her heart.

"Your grandfather asks that you come," said the servant who came to fetch her. "Your grandmother is with him."

In the aftermath of the Council, Paulus had questioned how Lælia had contrived her ruse. He had chuckled outright more than once but had also been unable to restrain himself from criticising various aspects of her plan's execution.

"You were damned lucky," he had said grimly. "Luck doesn't always hold, Lælia."

But he had ceased to talk of marriage, and Lælia had thought that was a victory at least.

Not long after her return a request had come from their agent in Carthage for a large shipment of Illiberis horses. Filling the order and training the upcoming herd had occupied much of the ensuing months. The activity had left little time for introspection or discussion, for which Lælia had been grateful. She had silently accepted the permanent company of Paulus's guards whenever she rode from the villa grounds. War was in the wind, and nobody knew when the storm would come.

Lælia was wary now as she entered Paulus's study. Both of her grandparents in the same room rarely foretold good tidings.

"Lælia." Her grandfather's smile was so unusual as to be startling. "We have a visitor from Septem."

The messenger was nothing like the merchants who usually came to Illiberis. It was a woman, for one thing – a beautiful woman.

"You are Lælia." The woman looked at her with frank curiosity as she held out her hands. Her skin was cool to the touch when Lælia took them. "I was sent by a woman named Athanais," she said, "a name you will not know; but she is as a sister to one you do: Shukra."

There was a lilt to her speech that made it plain Latin was not her first tongue, and she wore a gown of such daring cut and rich fabric that Lælia found it almost shocking.

"Ah," said the woman, smiling, "you must not be fooled by my dress. Sometimes the best guise for a woman is the one men most expect. I am young, beautiful, and alone. Clearly, I am a whore." She smiled, shrugging one shoulder carelessly, as if the label both-ered her not at all. "So," she said, "a whore I have been, and thus I am able to come to you unremarked, for no man cares what a whore does after he has had her."

Her eyes roamed Lælia's face and form, seemingly not at all perturbed by the blank silence with which she was met. Lælia did not intend to be rude. But the discovery of her voice felt new yet, and there was a comfort in her silence she was not entirely ready to relinquish.

"Athanais sent me to Ilyan with a message bound for you," the woman went on. "But Ilyan had a request to add to her message, and so he sent me here rather than one of his own men."

"And you will return to Septem?" It was Acantha who spoke. There was an odd tension in her voice.

"Yes. She will not be alone there."

Lælia frowned at that. "Who will not be alone?" she asked bluntly.

"Ah." The woman was still smiling, but the levity was gone. "First, Lælia of Illiberis, the message I was sent to give you."

She reached into her cloak and withdrew something. When she opened her hand, Lælia turned cold, then blazing hot, rooted to the spot. She reached out and touched the object in the woman's palm tentatively, as if it might burn.

"He gave it to Athanais as a message to you," said the woman softly, watching her. "He said you would know what it meant."

Lælia's fingers closed around the coin of Geila, and she heard Theo's voice in her head: *It reminds me of my duty, of the honour all men must find within. If I listen to it, I know what I must do, no matter how hard the path.*

"He sent something else."

Lælia, unable to speak, stared at her.

The woman raised one hand and put it over her heart. "He said you would understand what this meant."

Lælia found, suddenly, that her legs could not hold her. She staggered and fell to the ground, crumpling in an odd pile of limbs on the floor, legs folding awkwardly beneath her as the room swirled.

"Promise," she whispered, seeing Theo's face as it had been in the stables.

Nobody spoke for a long time.

"He lives," she said finally.

"Yes." The woman nodded. "He lives."

"Child." Her grandfather's voice was unusually gentle. "There is more."

Lælia turned to him dumbly.

"Ilyan believes it might be – safer – if you went for a time to Septem."

"Septem?"

"We are due to send another shipment of horses," Acantha cut in. "You will travel with them, Lælia. None will remark when you leave Illiberis with the herd, for you have accompanied many shipments to the port this year. The only difference is that this time you will not ride back."

There was something so harsh in her voice that it jolted Lælia out of her stupor.

"Why?" she said, looking between her grandparents. "Why would you agree to this?"

"Oppa came to Ilyan's court," said Paulus. "Ilyan knows what he is and what he seeks. He will keep you safe, and in Septem you will be well out of Oppa's sight. Ilyan also knows the mission upon which Yosef and Theo are set. He will share any news with you."

"That isn't all," said Lælia.

"No." Acantha's face wore a strange smile. "We have another ally in Africa, one you have not yet met. A woman. Yosef travelled with her and we are told" – she nodded at the messenger – "that she, too, met with Theo, spoke with him. She returns to Ilyan's court even now. You will meet with her, learn what she knows."

"Do you know this woman?" Lælia asked.

Acantha's smile deepened, as unexpected as it was mysterious. "Oh, yes," she said. "I know her. And she will know you. Her name is Dahiya, and I suspect there is much you might learn from her."

"You will permit me to do this," Lælia said flatly, staring at Paulus.

He cleared his throat. "I could say it is because you are not safe here," he said gruffly. "And that would be true." He caught Acantha's eye and went on, "But you have proven yourself resourceful,

Lælia. And she is right." He nodded at the messenger. "Men see what they expect. If you go dressed as you seem to prefer" – he looked pointedly at her hide trousers and boots – "all they will see is another horse herder of the tribes."

Lælia's heart fluttered in her chest and began to beat in a new rhythm, one free from choking and quite without fear. "When do I leave?" she said, trying to keep her voice steady.

"As soon as you are packed." Her grandfather stood, his smile incongruous amongst the grim lines. "But you will come back, Lælia."

Lælia stared at him, and her face broke into a smile, so wide it hurt. "Of course I will come back," she said. "I am the heiress of Illiberis."

END OF BOOK ONE

AFTERWORD

The story of Visigothic Spania continues in The King's Coin. To receive updates on new releases, please go to www. paulaconstant.com.

The Saharan Queen, Dahiya's story of origin, is available as a free prequel novella on my website, www.paulaconstant.com, or on any online bookstore.

To understand more of the background, and for character lists, maps and further detail, please see the following pages.

* * *

The Votive Crown was born long ago, during a three year expedition I made on foot, walking over 12000km through eight countries, including over 7000km with my own camel train in the Sahara. You can follow the links to my website if you wish to read my books about that journey, both published by Random House.

During my walk I became fascinated by the Arab conquest of North Africa and medieval Spain.

Whilst all Spanish schoolchildren learn the names of the Visigothic Kings who ruled their country for nearly three centuries, to the average reader the world of the Visigoths is largely unknown. I come from Australia, a country that was colonised less than three centuries ago. I became fascinated by the idea that a nation which stood for longer, at the time of writing, than mine has been colonised, could crumble in less than one generation. The question I asked myself was: *how would it feel to live through the fall of one civilisation and the rise of another?* A generation of extraordinary people did exactly that, having to adapt to a completely different language, culture, religion and rule of law, virtually overnight. I wanted to explore that concept.

I moved to Granada, Spain, where I lived for several years, immersed in the extraordinary period that followed the collapse of the Roman Empire and the rise of Visigothic Spain. The Visigoths had a sophisticated code of law that would go on to influence legal structure centuries into the future. Their church was so influential that had it not been for the Arab conquest, it may well have split with that of Rome to become a seperate entity.

On a global level, the 7th century in many ways saw the birth of what would ultimately become 'western civilisation'. It is during this period that the Abrahamic traditions of Islam, Judaism, and Christianity collide for the first time, and ancient pagan beliefs fade from the pages of history. In China, a female empress sat the throne, whilst in Constantinople the Eastern Empire sowed the seeds of its future dominance. Often forgotten in modern history, the Imazighen people of North Africa fought a bitter war against Arabic conquest of their desert land. To this day the indigenous people of the Sahara distinguish themselves from the Arabs who live on their land. The Amazigh are a proud, independent people with a rich literary and cultural tradition that only now is beginning to be heard. Any liberties I have taken with Dahiya's story are my own interpretation. For a true understanding I strongly encourage you to discover the incredible treasures of Amazigh culture for yourself by visiting countries such as Algeria and Morocco and taking a local tour.

The Gothic gods to the best of my knowledge and based on my research mirror those of the Norse pantheon, with some minor additions and variations. There is another layer of myth and legend by the 7th century, though, taken from the experience of exile and displacement the Goths suffered at the hands of Attila the Hun. Terms such as 'heliarun' stem from this experience.

Whilst the exact origins of the Goths are not known for certain, it is largely accepted that they were an agricultural people based on lands east of the Danube River. With the arrival of the Hunnish tribes across the steppes in the early 5th century, the Goths fled into Western Europe, where they gradually became absorbed into the Roman Empire. The name 'Visigoth' was not one Goths would have given themselves. It merely means 'West Goths', just as 'Ostrogoths' means 'East Goths', and is a later label referring to where the tribes themselves settled. For a better understanding of the Visigoths in Spain I recommend The Goths in Spain, by E.A Thompson, and Visigothic Spain 409-711 by Roger Collins.

Mixing fact and fiction is always a delicate balance. My passion for world history is profound, but I am an amateur, and The Votive Crown is a work of fiction. Any errors are mine alone and I welcome reader feedback.

LIST OF PRIMARY CHARACTERS

FICTIONAL, NON-FICTIONAL, RELATIONSHIPS AND DETAILS.

For the most part character names have been anglicised. There are some exceptions, notably Count Ilyan of Septem. Rightly his name should be rendered as Julian. However, as there was already a Julian of Toledo, I kept the Spanish pronunciation for ease of reference.

A note regarding fictionalisation of characters

All kings are verified by church records of the time. Unless stated below as fictional, all those mentioned as 'count' or 'duke' are equally attested, usually as signatories to the well documented Councils of Toledo. That said, I have in many cases created the family relationships between characters, based upon my understanding of geographical, political, and genealogical associations. My characterisations are not meant to be definitive but are rather my own perceptions. The Votive Crown is a work of my own imagination, interweaving fictional characters and events with what is known from primary sources of the time.

Lælia of Illiberis
Fictional
The township of Illiberis is attested in numerous church records

(please see 'Place Names' following this page), as is a Count of that place. Evidence of horse worship in the area is plentiful, and horses from the region are mentioned from Roman times, both in Spain and on foreign shores. Lælia herself is a fictional character.

Count Paulus of Illiberis
Actual
Count Paulus is attested as one of King Reccesuinth's *seniores*, or senior advisers, in the Councils of Toledo records, but not associated with a particular place. His association with Illiberis is fictional as are his personal relationships.

Acantha of Illiberis (Baeticus)
Fictional
The name 'Baeticus' is found on early Roman graves in the Illiberis area, denoting the local chiefs/power holders found when Romans first arrived in the region. Acantha is a generic Gothic name. The tradition of female inheritance was both Gothic law and associated with tribes indigenous to the area.

Yosef ben Radhan
Fictional
The Rhadanite merchants are famous, though largely associated with southern France. The Jews of Garnata are well attested, however, and a man named Yosef from Garnata became well known in Moorish Spain. Yosef is a fictional amalgamation of those elements.

Arun ben Radhan
Fictional
Arun is entirely fictional.

Theudemir of Aurariola
Actual
Count Theudemir is well attested in numerous documents as the Count of Aurariola, later Orihuela, on Spain's west coast. I have created a fictional backstory for him, as there remain no truly reli-

able records of his lineage. His relationship to rebel king Geila is my creation.

Alaric
Fictional
I created Alaric to represent the military expertise of the time.

Athanagild
Fictional
Athanagild was created to represent the Church culture of the time.

Count Suinthila of Aurariola
Fictional
Since Geila's descendents are unknown, I made him the patriarch of Theudemir's family, and Suinthila's father (Geila's brother was the great king Suintila). The circle of nobility was small and highly interconnected during the period, meaning most noble families were familiar with one another if not directly linked by blood or marriage.

Geila (Iudila)
Actual
Geila (Iudila) is described as 'one of the greatest generals' of Visigothic Spain. His brother, Suintila, was also described as great military strategist, who oversaw the unification of Spain and expulsion of Greek Imperial forces. Coins minted in Illiberis and Emerita named Geila as king in opposition to Sisenand, suggesting his support was found in the south of Spain.

Duke Theodofred of Corduba
Actual
Theodofred was a son of King Chindasuinth, and Duke of Corduba during the reign of Egica. He is widely attested in documents of the period as the husband of Riccilo and father of Roderic.

Riccilo

Actual

Attested as wife of Theodofred and mother of Roderic. Her relationship to Illiberis is fictional.

King Erwig

Actual

Attested as son of Ardabast (a Greek), husband of Liuvgoto, and father of Cixilo.

Liuvgoto

Actual

A formidable figure, Liuvgoto is well attested as the daughter of King Sisebut; wife of King Erwig; and mother of Cixilo. Her relationships to Sunifred and Suinthila are fictional, however her very interesting backstory allows fertile ground for speculation.

Cixilo

Actual

Liuvgoto and Erwig's daughter, wife of King Egica, and mother of Wittiza.

King Egica

Actual

Well attested as the son of Ariberga (son of King Tulga), husband of Cixilo, and father of Wittiza, Egica is also strongly regarded as fathering the illegitimate Oppa.

Oppa

Actual

One of the most shadowy figures of the era, Oppa is nonetheless well attested in varying roles throughout history, including as a Bishop of Hispalis. His parentage was murky, though it is generally accepted he was a royal son.

Wittiza

Actual

Wittiza was Egica and Cixilo's legitimate son and co-ruled with his father for several years.

Giscila
Actual character, gender unknown

Giscila is often considered as having been female, however in Gothic nomenclature the name is a masculine one, and evidence is nebulous at best. I have heavily fictionalised this character so whilst a 'Giscila' certainly existed as Egica's offspring, the rest is my invention.

Ariberga
Actual

Ariberga is attested as Tulga's son and Egica's father. His treason is my invention based upon the disappearance of Tulga's infant sons following Tulga's forced tonsuring by Chindasuinth and the brutal coup surrounding his fall from power.

Wamba
Actual

Archbishop Julian of Toletum wrote 'The Book of Wamba' on this king's rule, one of the few intact documents of the time.

Dahiya (or Diya, Dihiya, Kahina, Al Kahinat)
Actual

Dahiya (or Diya, Dihiya) was an Amazigh leader, or amgar, in the Sahara attested by multiple sources.

Count Ilyan
Actual

(Anglicised, 'Julian') was an actual Governor, or Count (known as both) of Septem.

Archbishop Julian of Toletum
Actual

Attested in Church records.

Bishop Sisebut
Actual

Sisebut's role in the church and in Sunifred's rebellion is attested, however his proclivities are my creation - based on decisions made in the 16th council of Toledo.

Laurentius Severianus
Name attested, character fictional

A scholar by the name of Laurentius is mentioned as possessing 'one of the best libraries in Toletum' in writing of the period. A Count Severianus appears repeatedly as a signatory to the Councils of Toledo. I have associated Laurentius with this name, as it is a Roman one, and the name itself with the lineage of Isidore of Seville, as this house was well known as one of Roman aristocracy and scholarship. The connection is of my making and used as an example of the old Roman ruling class that still held (symbolic) power two centuries after Gothic conquest.

Shukra
Fictional

Entirely fictional but based on Zoroastrian warriors attested in Imperial forces of the time who escaped the Arab conquest of Persia or were simply conscripted. In Shukra's lifetime there was widespread destruction and burning of Zoroastrian fire temples under the Arabic conquest.

Apsimar
Actual

Apsimar is known to history as the Greek Emperor Tiberius III.

Sunifred
Actual

Sunifred is attested in coins minted in his name and records of the time as a rebel King during Egica's rule. I have made him a son of Ricimer, which would make him Liuvgoto's cousin, and give him the perceived right to make a bid for the throne. Given the small circle of nobility and his lofty position, he must have been related or connected in some way to the ruling families of the time.

Frogellus
Actual

Attested in church documents during the rebellion against Egica.

Egilona
Actual

Egilona is an extraordinary character who plays a larger role in later books in this series. She is attested in multiple records. However her origin story as Theo's sister is one of my creation.

Rekiberga
Fictional

Alaric's betrothed is a fictional creation. I named her for King Chindasuinth's wife.

PLACE NAMES

Place names in Spain have been used as they are noted in the Council of Toledo records, or in the works of scholars of the time such as Isidore of Seville. If not found in those records, the names used are Roman, as the Visigoths were in essence a continuation of the Roman Empire. However, there are some areas of confusion. I explain my reasoning on these below.

Illiberis

In AD 324, a church council was held in the area now known as Granada, in southern Spain. This council is variously known as the Synod of Elvira; the Council of Illiberis; and the Council of Eliberri. 'Elvira' is the Arabic rendering of the Greek Illiberis, which in turn is a rendering of the earlier Roman Eliberri. This is not to be confused with another town, also called Illiberis, now known as Elne, on the border of Spain and France.

The actual location of the original Illiberis is not known for certain, though the mountain named Sierra Elvira is often thought to be home to the church in which the synod was held. There is a Visigothic era bridge over the river at Pinos Puente, and this I have used as delineating the north eastern border of Count Paulus's latifundium, and Pinos Puente itself as the location of the township of

Illiberis. Please note this is my own decision and one I understand may be debated.

There was also an important township on the hillside of what is now the Albaicin in Granada, and I have seen this characterised as Illiberis; however it seems more likely that this area was the Jewish settlement that Arab conquerors called Garnata, especially since the gate at the eastern end of the Albaicin is named 'Puerta Elvira' - the gate to, or from, Elvira (Illiberis). In probability, the main Jewish town was on the other side of the valley, where the Alhambra now stands, and the Albaicin was the home of a Christian community that had fallen into poverty after having been sacked by the Goths.

The villa of Illiberis is fictional and placed roughly between modern Pinos Puente and Atarfe. Though fictional, the villa itself is loosely based upon the Roman ruins found at nearby Salar, one of Spain's most important Roman archeological sites. The fortress Theo rides through is the one on the top of the Alhambra hill, whereas that Oppa passes is the fort at Moclin, truly one of the most impressive hilltop fortresses in the area.

Garnata

Garnata in my books refers to the area of both the Albaicin and Realejo barrios of modern Granada, and the location of the Alhambra.

Sexi

Sexi was the Roman name for the modern port town of Almuñécar, which was a major Roman city complete with garum, or fish oil factory, the remains of which are still visible today.

River Baetis

This is the modern Guadalquivir river in Seville (Hispalis). However, its actual course during the Visigothic period is somewhat debated. Currently it is navigable from Cadiz to Seville, but in Roman times it ran all the way to Corduba, posing a significant security threat from coastal attack.

Serica

Taken directly from Wikipedia: "Serica was one of the eastern-most countries of Asia known to the Ancient Greek and Roman geographers. It is generally taken as referring to North China during its Zhou, Qin, and Han dynasties, as it was reached via the overland Silk Road in contrast to the Sinae, who were reached via the maritime routes."

Africa

The name 'Africa' in this context denotes the North African coast and Saharan Africa in entirety. Whilst the Exarchate of Africa changed shape multiple times, during the period I write of there was so much movement in governance that I have used the term loosely to cover the entire region, to save the reader confusion. Sometimes I have used the names of provinces such as Tripolitana, Mauretania, and Cyrenaica, but it is important to note that borders and governance were fluid. Whilst Africa is sometimes termed Ifriquiya in documents of the period, this is an Arabic rendering. I chose to stay with the Roman for simplicity.

Toletum

Toledo was the Visigothic capital.

Emerita Augustus

In an earlier version of this book, I had centred the plot around the modern city of Merida (Emerita Augustus), as it played such a vital part in Visigothic Spain, and the ruins there are the best reminders we have of the period. I strongly suggest visiting the Visigothic museum there. It is fascinating.

In relation to other names, such as those of the sea, the modern names are placed beneath them on chapter headings.

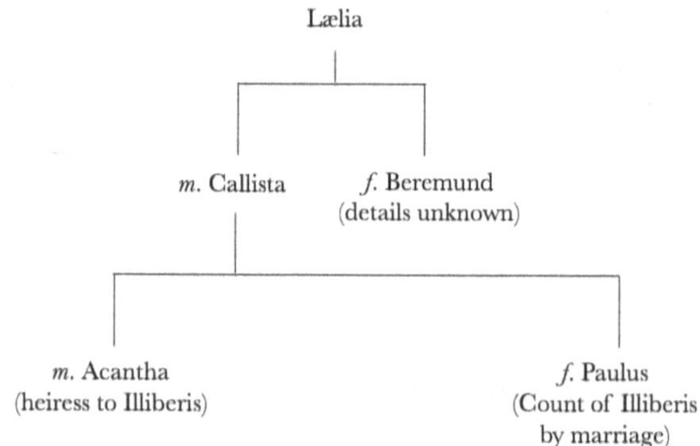

Lælia
m. Callista
f. Beremund
(details unknown)
m. Acantha
(heiress to Illiberis)
f. Paulus
(Count of Illiberis
by marriage)

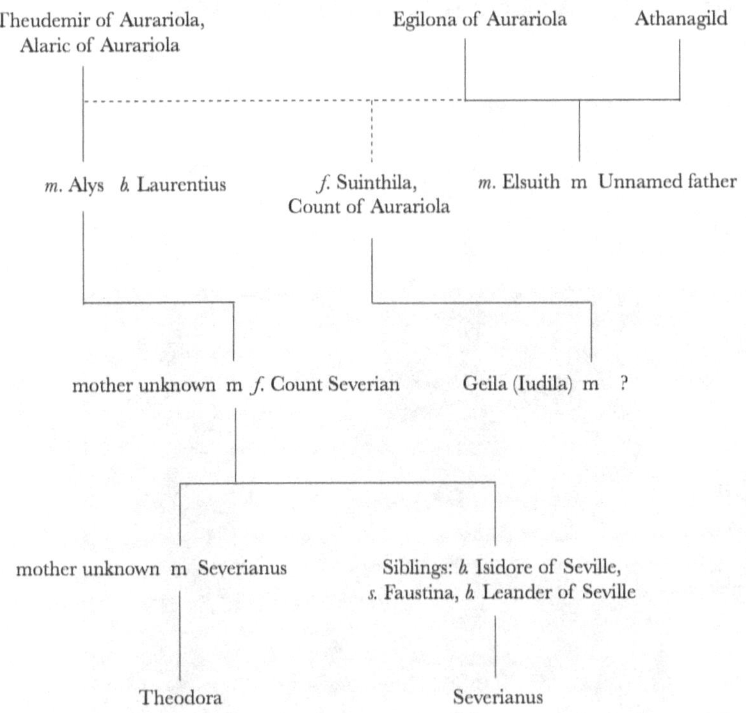

7TH CENTURY AMAZIGH KINGDOMS

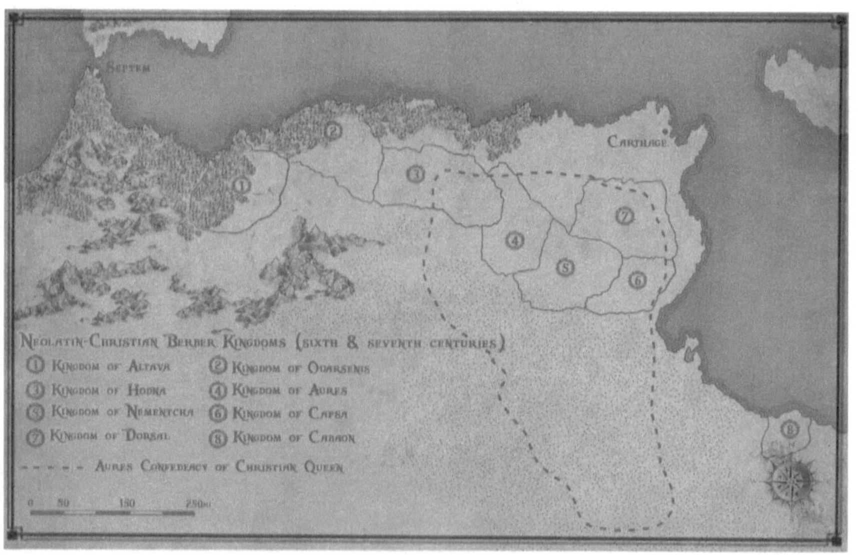

YOSEF'S PLANNED JOURNEY TO SERICA (CHINA)

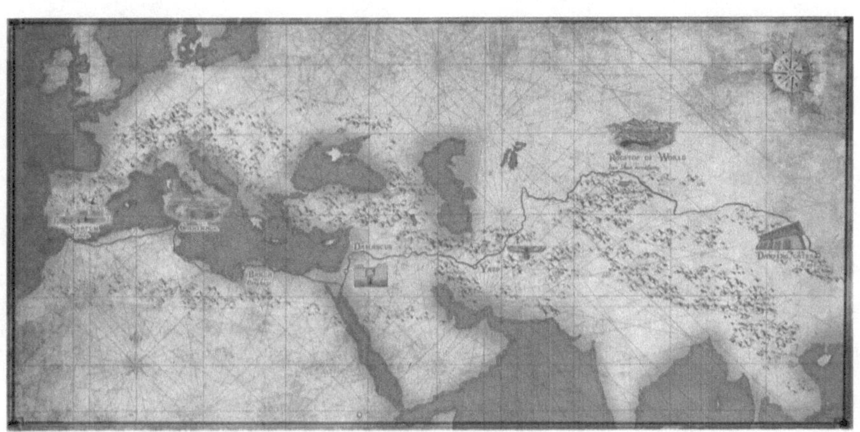

ACKNOWLEDGMENTS

Whilst my book began life as a story of Spain, it rapidly became obvious to me that I could not limit it to that country if I hoped to give an accurate picture of the people and mentality of the time. What ensued was over a decade of dedicated research in universities and museums from Europe to the US. I am forever indebted to the University of Texas at Austin Linguistics Research Centre for their work in keeping dead languages alive. I hope they will forgive my efforts at ancient Gothic. The University of Granada was incredibly generous in allowing me access to the library there. I spent hours in Granada's extraordinary School of Arabic Studies, asking questions that were always met with patience and kindness. Various students took me on walks around Granada, explaining the ancient architecture, and to all of them, I am indebted. Dr Jamie Wood of the University of Lincoln very patiently answered many of my questions and reassured me that placing Theo in the Karabisianoi was not crazy. I have met with other lecturers and academics too numerous to mention. To all those who offered help, from the anecdotal tales told in mountain villages and around Saharan fires, to academic responses, I am truly grateful. For any mistakes made, however, I take full responsibility.

Likewise, the Arabic I have used, and any mistakes, are entirely my own. I learned (very) limited Arabic in the Sahara - the Hassaniya dialect. In writing this I consulted numerous sources to gain an idea of what informal, uneducated Arabic may have sounded like in the 7th century. Again, please accept my apologies for any inaccuracies.

My editors at The History Quill are exceptional. Kahina Necaise is a magician. She, Andrew Noakes, and the entire team are quite the nicest people I've had the privilege of working with. Thankyou all, and I'm looking forward to working further with you.

Thanks to Nick Castle for the magical covers, patience, and wonderful professionalism. Incredible job.

Finally, on a personal note, I want to thank:

Dr Som Ling Leung: my mentor, inspiration, and dearest friend, who has shared every step of this book and been on the end of the phone when I feared I would not finish it. I simply could not have done it without you.

My FIFO mates: all those I have been privileged to work beside in mining for the past four years, who have had input on characters, plot lines, and style, and listened to me simply rant about my book whilst knee deep in Pilbara dirt, flies, and heat. You are all legends.

And to you, the reader, thanks most of all, for allowing my world to be part of yours.

Paula Constant
Broome, North Western Australia
2020